DEAD MAN'S HAND

Dead Man's Hand

A PIKE LOGAN NOVEL

Brad Taylor

WM

WILLIAM MORROW

An Imprint of HarperCollinsPublishers

DEAD MAN'S HAND. Copyright © 2024 by Brad Taylor. All rights reserved. Printed in the United States of America. No part of this book may be used or reproduced in any manner whatsoever without written permission except in the case of brief quotations embodied in critical articles and reviews. For information, address HarperCollins Publishers, 195 Broadway, New York, NY 10007.

HarperCollins books may be purchased for educational, business, or sales promotional use. For information, please email the Special Markets Department at SPsales@harpercollins.com.

FIRST EDITION

Designed by Michele Cameron

Library of Congress Cataloging-in-Publication Data has been applied for.

ISBN 978-0-06-322205-2

23 24 25 26 27 LBC 5 4 3 2 1

For my newlywed sister, Mary Beirne, and her husband, David. May you have the same amount of joy together as I found with Elaine.

I do not understand what I do . . . For I have the desire to do what is good, but I cannot carry it out. For I do not do the good I want to do, but the evil I do not want to do—this I keep on doing.

—Paul the Apostle in Romans 7:15–19

DEAD MAN'S HAND

November 2022
Kherson, Ukraine

The old man looked tired. Not like he'd worked at an auto factory all day, sitting-in-a-La-Z-Boy-after-work tired, but bone-chillingly weary. Tired enough for his skin to begin to tighten on his frame from the lack of nutrition, like he was a POW in the Pacific campaign of World War II. Tired enough that the old coat that he used to fill was now draping loosely around his shoulders, like a child who'd been given an adult garment from a Goodwill store, the bones holding it up as if he were a human coat hanger.

Hovering his hands over a small fire buried in the earth of the hut, he said, "How many made it back?"

His deputy, Dishka, broke into a smile and said, "All. All made it back."

Dishka wasn't his real name. Nobody used real names in this war—even the ones who had worked together for months. To do otherwise would put their families at risk from the Russian machine. Everyone used a pseudonym. Dishka chose his for the antiaircraft gun that protected the people of Ukraine.

The old man was known as Perun, the God of War in Slavic mythology. He had penetrated the Russian lines over one hundred times, leading to significant attacks—including the destruction of an airfield deep in enemy-held terrain and the main bridge crossing the strait from Crimea to Ukraine proper. He was held in high esteem by all the resistance fighters, but anyone could see the war was wearing him down.

He wasn't even old by conventional standards, but continual combat had not been kind to his body, his hair thinning and limp, his beard unkempt. His eyes were still crystal blue, but the sockets were perpetually darkened, the wrinkles emanating from them now deep set as if he'd aged two years for every one that passed.

At the ripe age of forty, he had been a store clerk in a small town selling trinkets to the Russians who visited on tourist trips from the Crimean Peninsula, coming across after the original invasion of 2014. He didn't mind selling to them—he had to make a living, after all—and then the Russians had hammered through the door for real, shattering everything he knew. No "green men," no hybrid warfare, it was a full-scale invasion with tanks, artillery, and aircraft. They had been repelled in Kyiv, but had come in hard in his part of the world, slaughtering everyone in their path. He'd lost his parents, wife, and children in the onslaught, and become ensconced behind enemy lines.

He could have done like others, choosing to flee into the woods, but he did not. He'd heard President Zelensky say, "I don't need evacuation. I need ammunition," and thought, *That's right. That's what I need*, and chose to stay.

He'd ingratiated himself with the new Russian occupation, acting if he was just too cowardly to run and supportive of their efforts. Helping them when they'd asked, but watching when they weren't. Waiting on the day to come when he could get retribution. Waiting to start the death count. He didn't know when that day would come, or how, but he knew it would.

It had, when he was walking with a friend and they had seen a Russian soldier drunk, the man staggering around in the streets of their small town. The friend said, "Let's kill that fuck."

Perun had been shocked at the utterance, because any sign of disloyalty would bring instant repercussions if it were known, and nobody trusted anyone anymore in the lockdown they lived within. Sympathizers were insidious and everywhere.

He'd said, "You want to fight them?"

The man, now fearful at what he'd uttered, hesitantly said, "Yes. Yes I do. You?"

Perun gave a wolf grin and said, "Oh yeah. How many others think like us?"

"I don't know. Let's go kill that fuck while we have the chance."

And Perun knew he had a new path in life. One that would help his country. He said, "No. We don't kill him. We find others like us. But slowly. Find them quietly."

In two months, he had a network. In four, he had connections to NATO's Special Forces, who'd trained them in the dark arts. In five, he was killing Russians. Now, almost a year after he'd begun to kill, he wasn't sure it ever even mattered.

Regardless of what they did, the Russians continued on. His small band would make the news, giving some morale boosts to the citizens of Ukraine, but they never accomplished what he wanted: the ejection of the Russians from Ukrainian soil.

He thought about his family often. The death of everything he loved coming to naught despite one raid after another. He'd come to believe that nothing they did mattered. He was losing kids half his age on raids that did little more than poke a pinprick in the Russian bear. Yeah, they'd assassinated some important Russian officers and officials, and had made some spectacular attacks against the Russian military machine, but the hunt to find them had caused many, many innocent people to be slaughtered.

He'd had a growing conviction that anything he did would only bring more sorrow to the people he was trying to protect, and that there was only one man who could decide their fate. One person he could eliminate like the generals he'd killed that would cause the success he wanted. But that wish was impossible. And then he'd met a man who thought the same way.

Only he was a Russian.

Dishka said, "What's wrong? I told you they all made it back. It was a good hit. Three Russian officers, and all of our men made it out. They made the mistake of driving down the same road again. Good intelligence."

Perun gave a weary smile and said, "No, no. It's good. Sorry. I'm just tired of these little strikes."

"What? You want to do another airfield hit? I'm game, but they've upped their security since the last one. It will be hard. What's the Ukrainian command think of that idea?"

Perun rubbed his hands, thinking if he should tell Dishka what he'd been working on. Wondering if it was something he would believe.

He said, "No. Nothing like that. Bring in the others. Only the leaders. I have to discuss something in a war council. We need a decision."

Dishka nodded, unsure of what was being asked, but went to get the others in their band.

They called themselves the Wolves. They had no formal chain of command with the Ukrainian Army, and were just one cell of many killing the Russians, but they had proven to be better than most. In fact, the best cell of partisans in the entire theater. They would listen to the Ukrainian high command, taking their intelligence and their training, but would only attack what they wanted to attack. And now Perun had a mission he wanted to execute, regardless of what the Ukrainians or the West thought.

The men filed into the small stone hut, the windows draped with blankets to hide the light, the candles making their faces flicker in a macabre glow. They all squatted next to the small fire in the center of the hut, holding their hands out to warm them up.

Dishka said, "So, what's up? You said you had a mission?"

Perun looked each of them in the eye and said, "Yes. I have a mission, but this one is purely voluntary. No orders—all volunteers. I need people who are committed. People who are prepared to die."

Dishka scoffed and said, "We're all prepared to die. What's that mean? You want to go kill Putin or something?"

Perun looked at him, a grin splitting the taut skin of his face, turning his visage into a skull in the flickering light.

"Yes. Yes, that's exactly what I mean."

CHAPTER 2

The head of the Russian state gazed out the window of his mansion, watching the falling snow dance in the glare of the outside klieg lights. It gave him comfort. The coming of winter always buried the mistakes of the past, and it would do the same here, even if he had to engineer it.

Located on Lake Valdai halfway between St. Petersburg and Moscow, the mansion was originally built in 1934 for Joseph Stalin. Back then, it was a simple construct, but it has been expanded much since the fall of the Soviet Union, most of it funded by oligarchs who wanted the president's favor. Now a massive compound, it sprawled across the shores of the lake, including an indoor spa spanning an entire floor, a helicopter pad, and a separate building encompassing everything from a bowling alley to an indoor cinema.

Hidden deep in the woods, with nothing of the Moscow cityscape to bother him, every noise muffled by the falling snow, the dacha gave him a sense of calm and was where he always came to relax when he was under pressure. A place where he could come to collect his thoughts without the chattering class of the Kremlin and outside oligarchs rattling in his ears. Only now, the chattering classes were becoming overpowering, even here.

Everyone was talking about the errant missile strike in Poland, as if he'd planned it. As if he wanted to cause a wider war. One missile was now being used to cause fear of his whole endeavor in Ukraine, and *it wasn't even his missile.* Those idiots in Ukraine had let one of their Russian S300s go astray and land in Poland. It wasn't *his* missile. It was theirs, but all anyone wanted to look at was the country of manufacture.

The entire expedition into Ukraine had foiled him at every turn, but he had lived a ruthless life, and understood that victory could be leveraged by the very fear he instilled in people, both in Russia and abroad.

It was exactly why he'd damaged the Nord Stream pipelines. *That* had been a controlled attack, precisely because it would send a signal without any actual damage. Neither Nord Stream pipeline was pumping gas, so it was just a shot across the bow. A little bit of a brush against the powers facing him, showing his ability to affect the conversation on the world stage, but this was something different. A missile strike into Poland—a NATO member—would cause significant repercussions, not the least to his own base of power.

Only he hadn't launched that damn missile. Even the United States was now saying that the strike had come from Ukraine, but it didn't stop the chattering classes. They didn't care who'd fired the missile; they wanted to know what he would do to prevent another accidental attack. Could he control the outcome of the next strike? Could he prevent NATO forces from engaging full force in his ill-gotten attempt at conquest?

If he wasn't careful, the vagaries of war were going to drag him further into its embrace, leaving him vulnerable. Even now, the hidden power base of Russia—the oligarchs and competing government structures—were starting to whisper the unthinkable: his removal. And that just wouldn't do.

He had decided to protect himself, as only he could.

There was a knock on the door, then Victor Petrov entered the room. The commander of the new Russian National Guard, he had previously been the commander of Putin's personal security service. The man who'd been entrusted with ensuring Putin's survival, which was to say he was a devoted loyalist. A tall man with broad shoulders, he looked the part, with the only thing out of place a birthmark that started on his forehead and burrowed into his right eyebrow, like someone had thrown chocolate pudding at him, catching the right side of his face.

The National Guard was a fairly recent creation. Established in 2016 by presidential decree, it was responsible for all aspects of internal security, and as such had consolidated a host of different security organs dedicated to that purpose. It was one of the few elements of the defense establishment that Putin directly controlled, and one of the most powerful.

Victor approached Putin's desk hesitantly, unsure of why he'd been summoned. He said, "Sir? You wanted to see me?" As if he'd just come across from a different building instead of traveling from Moscow for the meeting.

Putin waved to a seat in front of his desk, Victor thinking the chair looked like something from the era of the tsars, full of gold leaf fabric and tall wings. Victor sat down and said, "Is this about the missile strike? Because that has only hardened your support with the people. There is no need to do anything internally. There are a few protests, but if we repress anyone, it will only inflame the masses."

Putin said, "Did you see the news reports yesterday in the Western press?"

"Yes, but that missile wasn't us. They can talk all day, but that wasn't us, and they know it."

Putin put his dead, shark eyes on Victor, and Victor felt the danger they represented. Something was coming. He'd been the head of Putin's primary security for years, since he had become prime minister in the early 1990s, and then after he had risen to the presidency for the first time. He'd seen what Putin was capable of—had in fact helped Putin on his rise—doing whatever it took to protect him both physically, in the form of direct threats, and more artfully, in the form of removing threats that weren't of a physical nature. Which is to say, he had blood on his hands in the service to the presidency. Something Putin knew and rewarded.

It was precisely why he'd been given the command of the new National Guard, and the responsibility for the internal security of the entire country—the largest by landmass in the world, spanning eleven different times zones.

Putin said, "We have two distinct threats occurring right now. The West, and those inside my country who wish to see me gone."

"Sir, I'm telling you, the people don't care about that Polish strike. In fact, some are hoping it *did* come from us. There is no fear there."

"I'm not talking about the people. I'm talking about the ones I've allowed to make enormous money based on my favor. The ones who now think they're so important they can actually dictate what Russia does. As if they're more important than my security council. They're making problems, and it's growing."

Victor smiled and said, "But you've handled most of those problems, haven't you? I think you sent the signal very clearly."

Since Putin's invasion of Ukraine, multiple oligarchs who had made disparaging comments about the war had ended up dead, most by either "tripping" down a staircase, or "falling" out a window. So many had died that the world press now laughed every time it occurred. While the majority found their demise outside the borders of Russia, some had met their end inside the country—which had been Victor's work.

"Yes, that's true, but apparently that signal isn't being taken to heart.

I'm hearing things that concern me, and I've come up with a way to deter them."

Unsure where the conversation was heading, Victor said, "Sir?"

"You remember the Perimeter system? For our nuclear forces?"

"Yes, sir. The Dead Hand."

"And you know about the Sarmat 28 missile system, yes?"

"Of course. The largest nuclear missile in the world." Victor forced a chuckle and said, "The West calls it Satan Two."

"Yes, they do, and for good reason. They're afraid of it, as they should be. We have a total of five in silos right now, and I've tied them into a new Dead Hand, separate from the old Perimeter system."

He opened a drawer and pulled out what looked like a smartphone. He slid it across the desk and said, "I'm giving you an incredible responsibility. I'm giving you the ability to destroy the world."

"Sir?"

"You are to become my fourth Horseman. There are three others like you, loyalists to the Russian state. I obviously won't reveal their identities. Each of you controls one of these devices. It works on anything available—the cell network, Wi-Fi, or direct with Bluetooth, but I doubt you'll be close enough for that one."

Feeling a little queasy, Victor said, "I don't understand."

Putin turned up the corners of his mouth in what Victor presumed was an attempt at a smile, but it did nothing to show any warmth. He said, "Those devices are tethered to a communications relay missile. Should you initiate—from anywhere on the earth—it will launch, and will send the override launch codes for the RS-28 missiles. From there, Western Europe and the United States will be struck."

Still confused, Victor said, "But that's what the Dead Hand does. You mean this is a backup? If NATO or anyone else conducts a first strike on our country, I'm the backup to retaliate?"

"No. This isn't against a first strike from the West. It's against the very people who want to take me down."

Victor shook his head and said, "I still don't understand."

Putin leaned forward and said, "You initiate the response if I'm removed from power. If I have a 'heart attack' or 'fall down the stairs' or even if there is a full-on military coup. If I'm dead, you launch."

"Why? Why would I do that?"

Putin leaned back and said, "You won't have to, and that's precisely the point. I'm protecting our ability to succeed. Too many people are questioning me, and they need to know there is a price to be paid for disloyalty. In this case, if I'm removed from power, so is the state of Russia. If they try to kill me, they'll engender their own demise. I'm calling this system the Dead Man's Hand to distinguish from the old Perimeter system. The old Dead Hand."

And in that instant, Victor realized how paranoid President Putin had become. He was willing to cause a nuclear holocaust over his vain attempt at reestablishing the Soviet Union sphere of influence in Ukraine.

He said, "But how will this work? Your internal enemies have to know that the Dead Man's Hand exists. If they don't, there is no deterrence."

"They know. I've spread the word. They know."

"The West? The United States?"

"No, no, of course not. To let them know would be to show I have a weakness. The only ones who will be told are the idiots talking about a regime change here, in the Motherland."

Victor hesitated, then blurted out his final thought. "What if they were to attack? What if NATO were to attack?"

Putin snarled, "Then you initiate. They reap what they sow."

"But they don't know the repercussions."

Putin stood up, glaring, and Victor knew he'd overstepped. He'd seen it many times before when he was but a security man at the back of the room. Putin said, "Do you not want to be a Horseman? I have three others who didn't question my quest for Russian dominance. For Russian rejuvenation."

Victor jumped out of the chair himself, assuming the position of attention. He said, "No, sir, of course not. It is a great honor. Thank you for your trust."

Putin nodded, then said, "We have served together for a long time. We have seen the worst of the beast, and we both know the price for victory. I trust you implicitly, just like the other three. But there is another problem set in motion that only you can take care of."

Victor remained at attention, his head pivoting wherever Putin moved. Putin said, "Sit, sit."

He did so, and Putin said, "I created the National Guard and put you in charge for a reason. I don't have to go through the security council to employ you, and I have a mission for you."

His head spinning over the revelations of the Dead Man's Hand, Victor had trouble assimilating the words. There was more?

CHAPTER 3

Victor said, "Yes, sir. Of course. Is there a problem I can solve?"

"Yes. Sweden and Finland are about to gain their bid for inclusion into NATO. I cannot let that happen. I can't do much about Finland, but Sweden has upset our friends in Turkey. They have placed several requirements on Sweden for the extradition of Turkish citizens believed to be involved in machinations against the president of Turkey. Sweden has denied that request up until now."

Completely outside of his depth now, Victor said, "Yes? So?"

"I believe they're going to agree to the demands and extradite a Turkish citizen currently held in a Swedish prison. A rabble-rouser that Turkey wants. If that happens, it will pave the way for Sweden to join NATO. I need you to stop that. Finland will be bad enough, but both together is a disaster."

Incredulous, Victor said, "How? Is there someone here in Russia that I can leverage?"

"No. There is a man who works in the Swedish Ministry of Foreign Affairs. In the Security Policy department. He's the man who's negotiating with the Turks. I want him removed from the playing field."

"What?"

"If he is killed, it will throw the negotiations into turmoil. Turkey will back off, and Finland will have to go it alone. It will create a seed of disruption that we need right now."

"You want me to kill him? Sir—"

Putin interrupted and said, "Yes. I want you to kill him. I have plenty of 'useful idiots' burning Qurans and causing trouble in Stockholm, but Sweden has forged ahead. Get rid of this man, and it will set them back for months, if not a year. In that time, Ukraine will be ours."

Putin slid across a folder, and Victor picked it up, seeing the picture of a forty-something diplomat, along with all the requisite targeting information. He didn't fault the logic, and had no compunction about the action, but he didn't understand why he was being tasked with the mission. It wasn't his skill set. He did internal control for the Russian state. He didn't do extrajudicial executions in foreign countries.

He said, "Sir, I agree, this will help, but I'm not the tool here. The GRU has Unit 29155. That's what they do. They've done this very thing all over the world. They've killed more people than I can count. I do internal security. We aren't trained to operate outside of Russia."

Putin laced his hands together and said, "Remember when I said we had two threats? One external, in the form of NATO, and one internal?"

Now starting to sweat, Victor said, "Yes, sir. It's why I'm a Horseman. I get it. I accept the responsibility. But this isn't that. Sweden isn't coming for you. . . . are they?"

Putin put on his Halloween mask smile and said, "No, it isn't Sweden. It's the GRU, which is your second mission."

Dumbfounded, Victor said, "What?"

"I've learned that the GRU Unit 29155—the one, as you've said, has been used all over the world to eliminate threats to the Russian state—now has an inkling to eliminate *me*. They've formed a little cell called Valkyrie, and they aim to kill me. Which means I can't trust them for this mission. I can't even trust them to root out the problem. I have no idea who is involved and who is not."

The revelation hammered one more nail into Victor's world, but it wouldn't be the last. He stuttered, "Sir . . . sir . . . are you sure about this? They're your most loyal unit."

Putin said, "No, they aren't. They don't answer to me. They answer to the security council and the military high command. They have lost their way. *You* are my most loyal unit. You are the one who protects me. And you will protect me again, like you have in the past."

"How do you know this? What is Valkyrie?"

"How I know is irrelevant. As for Valkyrie, it's named after the mission to assassinate Hitler by the Nazi high command during the Great Patriotic War. Can you believe that? They're using a code name for the assassination of our enemy in World War Two." Putin's hands balled into fists so hard Victor could see the whites of his knuckles. He said, "This, after I invaded Ukraine to get rid of Nazis. It is infuriating."

"Are you sure? Maybe this is Western disinformation."

"I thought so, too, at first, but it's not. There are disloyal members of the GRU who want me dead. They're working with the Ukrainians for this very thing, thinking it will end the war, but it won't, because I have you."

Becoming incensed himself, Victor said, "I cannot believe they would do that. Not from the heart of our intelligence. Russian soldiers?"

Putin relaxed and said, "That's the same thing America said when Snowden showed up at our door with his treasure, begging for Russian asylum. They couldn't believe something like that, either, but it happened. Trust me, it's real. They are out there, but unlike that shitweasel Snowden, they have the ability to kill."

"How can I help? I don't have any inroads into the GRU."

"I want you to find out who this Valkyrie unit is and eliminate them."

Victor nodded, his mind adrift, thinking of the other mission he'd been given. He fervently wanted to support his president, but the taskings were a little overwhelming for the resources he had at hand.

Putin said, "Do you understand?"

Victor focused and said, "You want me to kill a diplomat from Sweden, and also hunt down members of the GRU for attempting to assassinate you?"

"Yes, that's it."

Victor hesitated for a moment, then laid it out. "Sir, I don't mean any disrespect, but I can't do that. I don't have the men. I don't have the skill. I'll be hunting the very men who excel at this work. I will fail."

"You have always supported me, through our worst times. Remember the FSB fiasco with the apartments? When it was discovered that it was the state who'd killed our own people? You solved that problem. You have the skill."

"Sir, that was an internal Russian problem. I could control the men, and I could control the press. I can't do that for this one, inside Sweden. The GRU is formidable, as you well know. They don't hold the National Guard in high esteem. They'll be on to us from the minute we start to hunt. How will I do this?"

"The Valkyrie unit is outside of Russia, and outside of the GRU command. It's a small cell, and the GRU itself is hunting them. They haven't told me this, of course, because it would cause me to start lopping off heads, but they know they're out there, and are hunting. We don't know who they are, but we know they exist. I will give you what I can, but you'll have to find them."

Exasperated, feeling impending failure, Victor stood up and blurted out, "How? How am I going to do that? The National Guard does internal security work, where we own the monopoly of power. We don't do external work. How the fuck am I going to do this?"

Putin glared at him, and Victor immediately calmed down, resuming his seat and saying, "I'm sorry, sir, but it just seems too much for my element."

Putin said, "You have the SOBR, right?"

The Special Rapid Response Units—or SOBR—were the special operations teams embedded within each National Guard division, spread throughout the Russian state. Half military/half police, they were formed after the creation of the new National Guard, and were comparable to United States SWAT teams.

"Yes, I do."

"Well, use them. They have the skill. They just haven't used what they know with your mandate for internal security. But they have the skill."

"They do organized crime and internal security. They don't do external assassinations. They can't work outside of the Russian state."

"The ones in Kaliningrad do. They're all ex-Spetsnaz. Every single one. In fact, several of them served in the GRU Unit 29155. Their whole point was to conduct unconventional warfare against Poland. You will use them. They may be rusty, but they have the skill."

Kaliningrad was a Russian spit of land separated from the Russian state. Sandwiched between Poland and Lithuania on the Baltic Sea, with Belarus between it and the Russian Federation, it was an outpost that Putin had used for years to project power.

Victor took that in, his head spinning with the revelations of the last thirty minutes, but he saw the possibilities. He said, "Yes, you're right. I've always put the best in the Kaliningrad SOBR because of the external threat, and they're separated from Russia, so no one will see them coming. They're perfect for the Swedish mission, but . . ."

"But what?"

"But I don't think they can ferret out this Valkyrie thing. The GRU will know before we even launch. They are everywhere, and if *you* don't even control them, how can I attack them?"

Putin leaned forward and said, "It may be hard, but it is imperative. Go to the signals intelligence room when you leave here. Tell them I sent you and ask for the Roadrunner team. It's an air-gapped intelligence cell that's following the Valkyrie, completely impenetrable from their side. They will give you everything we know, which, honestly, isn't a lot, but it's enough to start the hunt. We think there are eight traitors. If you find one, you'll find the others. I want the head of this Valkyrie cell on my desk within a week."

Victor let out a thin chuckle, thinking he was kidding. He said, "I'll do everything in my power to support you, sir." He then gave out a joke of his own: "Should I tell my men to pack garbage bags for the heads?"

He saw the dead, shark eyes staring right at him. "Yes, they should. I want their heads on my desk. I want to see the heads."

Victor's smile left his face almost as fast as he left the room.

CHAPTER 4

Daniel Sokolov shut off the four-by-four truck, the world becoming quiet, with nothing but the ticking of the engine reaching the cab. The falling snow danced between the branches of the trees in the glow of the headlights, making it hard to see down the rutted, muddy lane.

The man to his right, Stepan, said, "Might want to kill the lights as well."

"Not yet. I want them to know we're here. And that we're alone."

Stepan chuckled and said, "Well, we might find out from a quad-copter bomb smashing into us from someone who doesn't know what we're doing."

Daniel considered, then turned off the lights, the cold from Ukraine starting to seep into the cab of the vehicle. He said, "There are more than likely three different observation posts watching us right now. Probably five different reticles on our heads. I hope these guys don't do anything stupid, because I'm sure they believe we have the same."

Stepan said, "Too bad we don't."

He said it flippantly, like he was as cool as the snow falling outside, but Daniel heard the strain in his voice. And he honestly felt the same way. They were taking a huge risk meeting the Ukrainian resistance cell called the Wolves, but Daniel was resolute, even as it meant going against the very state he'd sworn to protect.

A tall, rawboned man with a narrow nose and a pinched mouth, he rarely smiled, hiding the lack of dental work he'd experienced as a child, his teeth jagged, growing out of his skull as if each one was hell-bent on a different path, ignoring the DNA from his parents.

Stepan was his opposite in every way. A short, portly guy with a beard that grew in patches on his face like weeds in a neglected yard, he had a good sense of humor, seeing the irony in everything that was Ukraine. Together, they had made a formidable team for the GRU, executing targeted operations throughout Europe, back when they believed in what the Federation was trying to achieve.

Now they weren't so sure. They still believed in the Russian state, just not the man running it.

Daniel looked at Stepan and said, "We might have some of our own reticles out there, but if they're here, they're on our skulls as well."

"You think they're already on to us?"

"I *know* they're on to us. I would be by now. They just don't know the method of delivery, which is why I chose this path. They might get our team, but they won't get the Wolves."

Stepan said, "Well, maybe the Wolves will get us first. Killing a couple of GRU officers would be a great coup for them."

"It would, but they're putting in the risk here. Kill us, and they get two unknown intelligence officers. On the other hand, if we kill them, we wipe out one of the most effective resistance organizations in the entire theater. If they show, it's them taking the bigger risk."

Stepan started to reply when they both saw a flickering in the woods. Headlights coming through the snow, strobing against the tree trunks. A vehicle approached down the rutted road, then stopped fifty meters away. It did nothing for a moment, then the headlights died.

Daniel reached for his own headlight switch, saying, "Well, here we go."

Stepan said, "This place is a perfect ambush zone."

Daniel flicked the headlights once, twice, three times, saying, "Well, they were a little hesitant to meet at their headquarters. And I couldn't get them to come to ours."

Stepan gave a nervous chuckle, then said, "Too late now anyway."

They saw the SUV ahead flash three times, the final one staying on. Daniel said, "Show your hands."

He opened the door, his hands raised, and they slowly walked into the light. Daniel saw the rear doors of the SUV open and two men exit, both holding AK-47s with collapsible stocks. They wore ski masks and said not a word, gesturing with their weapons. In short order, both he and Stepan were lying facedown on the ground, their bodies being searched for weapons and electronics. When none were found, the men yanked the two to their feet, pointing to the open doors in the back of the SUV.

Daniel took the left and Stepan the right, taking a seat in the back of the vehicle. Daniel felt a barrel push into the back of his skull from the rear compartment. He glanced at Stepan and saw the same. The man in the front passenger seat said, in Russian, "Do you wish to die tonight?"

His hands on his knees, keeping them in plain view, Daniel said, "No. Of course not. That's not why I'm here."

The man turned around, and Daniel was shocked to see he wasn't wearing a mask. Or maybe he was, because his skin was stretched taut across his cheeks like a movie villain, so strained it looked fake.

He said, "Why are you here?"

Daniel said, "I have information for you. Information that you may use to end this war, but I need to know who I'm talking with."

The man smiled, his face split into something between mirth and pain. He said, "My name is Perun, and I'm the one you contacted on Telegram. I'm here at your request, at great risk to myself and my team.

You are within a breath of being killed and left here in the woods, so speak up before I lose my patience."

Daniel drew a breath and said, "I want to end this war, and I believe there's only one way to do that. Remove Putin."

He expected shock, or at least a draw of a breath. Instead he got, "Yeah, sure. Remove Putin. Why didn't I think of that?"

Daniel leaned forward, then felt a hand at his neck. He sagged back again and said, "Nobody in my country wants this war. Most simply ignore it, but others are fighting the slaughter. The sanctions from the West and the threat of the total destruction of Russia are growing. I can't stand by and let that happen. I don't want my family to live in a pariah state."

Perun looked out the windshield, seeing the snow fall in the glow of the headlights. He said, "Why should I believe you? What can you offer as proof of what you say?"

"Honestly, nothing. Except for the fact that I met you here, in Ukraine, on a logging road, without any weapons or help."

Perun nodded, saying, "There is that. But why should I believe you have the ability? Maybe you're infatuated with your own skill, and yet you can't really do anything. We have many, many people who show up like that on our side, here in Ukraine. People who promise they're the next Rambo or James Bond, and they end up as just another corpse, only it's alongside my men."

Daniel took a breath, then said, "They aren't like me. I'm not pretend. I'm the same man who's been slaughtering your men like clockwork."

Perun returned to him and said, "If what you say is true, I should just kill you and leave you on the side of the road."

"You do that, and you lose what you really want: the end of this war. I have the infrastructure and intelligence, and I have the skill."

"Once again, why should I believe you? I hear bragging like that all the damn time, mostly from my own side."

Daniel looked at Stepan, then back at Perun. He said, "You're due to leave here in four days to Denmark for a NATO roundtable on unconventional warfare in Ukraine. It's a who's who of NATO special operations, and you've been selected to attend as the only indigenous partisan fighter group out of the entire theater. You have seven slots, and you're supposed to forge relationships that will help you coordinate with more official commands in the fight against Russia. In the fight against me."

Daniel saw Perun's eyes turn to slits. Daniel said, "Is that proof enough for you? If I'd wanted, I could have just blown your team up on the way to the train station. I didn't. I reached out instead."

"Why? Why did you reach out? How do I know this isn't just a trick to get more intelligence you can use? A larger target set?"

"Look, I'll be honest here. I have no love for Ukraine, but I do for the Motherland. Putin is going to destroy Russia with this cesspool he's created. You won't win outright, and neither will he. He'll bring all of us down with him and his ego. You get rid of Putin, and it all ends. The regular army is looking for a reason to leave. The Wagner mercenaries will cheer wildly, because they've all been let out of prison to fight. They have a pardon whether we win or lose. They know they're all dead if they stay here."

"And what do you propose?"

CHAPTER 5

Laurinburg Airfield, North Carolina

The smell always gets to me. It didn't matter if I was boarding a commercial airliner or walking up the ramp of a military aircraft, when I smelled the exhaust from the jet fuel, my adrenaline rose because my body equates that odor with leaving an aircraft in flight. Like Pavlov's dogs, I start "salivating" underneath my arms, my body instinctively thinking about leaping from an aircraft with nothing but a piece of nylon to stop the effects of gravity.

In this case, I was in fact leaving an aircraft while in flight, so it fit. I stood with my arms out, letting Knuckles check my parachute harness, my eyes on Jennifer across the way, like we were two convicts being searched before being let into the penitentiary.

Her eyes were wide, the only indication she didn't like this. Which was odd to me. Jennifer had no fear of heights, at least when she was touching what made the height. I'd seen her scale walls that would scare the most seasoned climber, and that under pressure from someone right behind her attempting to kill her the old-fashioned way—with a gun. She could climb up a ninety-foot piece of plate glass with only spit on her hands for contact, never worrying about the fall, but jumping out of an airplane for some reason scared the hell out of her.

She gave me a smile, trying to show confidence, but I knew she didn't have it. That was okay, though, because my team did. We could carry her to the opening.

Knuckles finished with my rig, then held his own arms out for me to return the favor. I started working my way down the jumpmaster checklist, making sure his life-support was good, and he said, "She really hates this shit."

I laughed and said, "Yeah, I don't get it. But I'll say this: someone who hates a thing and keeps doing it because it's a part of the job is worth more than some asshole who loves it."

Veep finished with her rig, and then turned to me, because she wasn't a jumpmaster. I checked his harness out, and he said, "She really doesn't want to do this next evolution."

I looked at him and said, "As in you think she'll flake out?"

"No. No way. She's just not comfortable like you and me."

I looked at Jennifer and saw her eyes open, as if she were in a car crash in slow motion. I nodded at her, giving her a little confidence. What we were doing wasn't that big of a deal, and I wanted her to rely on herself. I knew she had what it took, deep inside.

Knuckles saw the nod and said, "That's it? You're not going to give her any support?"

"She doesn't need it."

He shook his head and said, "And I thought you were some sort of leader."

Before I could stop him, he started walking to Jennifer. I hustled to catch up. He reached her and said, "Hey, you okay?"

She looked at me, afraid to say anything that smacked of fear, and said, "Of course I'm okay. Just another jump."

But it wasn't just another jump. This was the big one, prior to the BIG one. Combat equipment, O_2, at 30,000 feet. Well, literally 29,999 feet, because the pilots had some sort of bullshit about breaking the 30,000-foot limit.

She'd been trained on HALO—High Altitude, Low Opening—parachute jumps, as she was a member of my cell, but she'd never liked it. And she loathed these rebluing sessions.

The military standard for jump proficiency was a free fall every three months. Because we were a far cry from the military, we couldn't do that. We'd settled on once every six months, with a concentrated four days of jump after jump. It wasn't optimal, as I used to jump at least twice a month with full combat gear, but, given what we did, it was the best I could manage.

We all notionally belonged to my company, Grolier Recovery Services, which was dedicated to helping universities or governments unearth archeological finds around the world. Since most of those places that hadn't been explored were in lands that had a little bit of an authority or terrorism problem, we were often retained to help out with the job.

It was a good cover, as Jennifer really knew the world of old shit, and I really knew the world of guns. And, like I said, most of those places were in ungoverned lands. Which meant that terrorists used it just as much as I did, and my company gave the United States access to start hunting them, but in order to do that, we had to maintain proficiency in infiltration techniques, which was why we were here.

Twice a year, we came to the airport in Laurinburg, North Carolina, to do a "company event," where everyone from the company got a few days of free jumping, as if it were a perk we provided to our "employees."

Roughly thirty minutes outside of Fort Bragg—now known as Fort Liberty, but it'll always be Bragg to me—and about three hours away from Charleston, South Carolina, where my company was based, it was the perfect place. Home to the United States Army's Golden Knights and two different drop zones, with a boneyard of aircraft and a world-wide security contracting company on-site, it was the best place to do what we needed, although it had its limitations.

Because of our cover, we couldn't let them see us in full combat gear, with oxygen masks. We were supposed to be just regular free-fall people, and so that caused a little bit of an issue when we did our full mission profiles. There was always someone watching, be it official military people from the Golden Knights, or just other jumpers filming themselves next to their aircraft.

We didn't officially do true HALO stuff, as we were supposed to be just a company doing a free-fall weekend. Which was accurate the first couple of days, but now, we were going to, which meant we had to conduct the jumpmaster checks outside of the aircraft, in full view of anyone watching before we loaded, then, once inside the aircraft and out of prying eyes, snapping on the equipment that would prove deadly if not handled correctly.

Knuckles pretended to check out Jennifer's harness, and said, "You good?"

She said, "I'm always good."

He said, "That last jump didn't work out like we wanted. This one will."

Our last jump had been a Hollywood one, with nothing strapped to us. We'd exited in a circle, all of us holding hands, and then had buffeted, breaking up the formation. We weren't the Golden Knights, that was for sure.

The breakup had caused her concern, because, unlike a stone wall she could climb in her sleep, she didn't own her own fate. The other flyers did, and Veep had been the reason for the breakup. He knew it, and honestly didn't care, because he was like a fish in water with a parachute, which is to say, he could have remade the linkup in five seconds if she hadn't just broken off completely and decided to go her own way.

And she knew that.

She looked at me and said, "I'm good. Let's do it."

Knuckles glanced my way and said, "Maybe we should repeat the last evolution, without the combat gear."

As the jumpmaster for the mission, he was within his rights, but I knew he wasn't going to cancel the jump. He was checking her.

She became incensed and said, "What? Why would we do that? This is the final jump before tonight. We can't do the night jump without this one." She looked at him, then me, and said, "You assholes don't trust me? Is that it? You think I can't do this?"

Now I knew where Knuckles was going. Jennifer had a problem with self-doubt, but only until you called her on it. She would doubt her ability on anything you asked her to do, right up until she got sick of you underestimating her. Then she became what she was.

She glared at me and said, "Get in the aircraft."

I nodded, glad I hadn't been the one to confront her, and we went to the rear of the Shorts aircraft. A twin-engine plane with a ramp at the back, it had been designed by the military to do cargo hauling on unimproved runways, but was now routinely used by skydivers as an aircraft of choice for free-fall operations. This one was covered in about twenty-two different shell companies, but on call for leasing with my company, and was the one we now used to get jump proficiency for a unit called Project Prometheus.

Built out of the experiences after 9/11, Project Prometheus was designed to defuse the inherent fight between the intelligence agencies and the direct-action units that fought the war on terrorism at the tip of the spear. Fully created to exist outside the boundaries of the U.S.

Constitution, it was a little bit sensitive, to say the least, which was why we spent so much time faking things on this airfield.

We boarded the aircraft from the rear ramp, took a seat, and watched it close. I wasn't averse to jumping, but I'll tell you, when that sight happens, it always got my adrenaline pumping. The only way I was leaving that aircraft was out the back, in the air. And the only way I would survive was with some piece of cloth strapped to my back. In that sense, I was with Jennifer.

Now closed from prying eyes, the plane began taxiing, and we began strapping on the combat equipment, starting with putting O_2 bottles in the sleeves on our harness and cinching a mask to our faces. Ordinarily, the military would require you to pre-breathe for thirty minutes prior to a jump greater than 20,000 feet, but we didn't have that time. I figured a few minutes here or there wouldn't matter.

CHAPTER 6

The plane lifted off with us still strapping on our gear, circling the sky to get up high enough. I went to the cockpit, seeing the pilots on oxygen as well. I clicked my radio and said, "Same track. Just a higher profile."

The lead pilot said, "Same thing tonight?"

I said, "Exactly. Same thing tonight."

The culmination exercise after four days was a night combat equipment, O_2 jump above 30,000 feet. After that, we'd be certified for another six months. But honestly, we were cheating. It's one thing to do ten jumps on the same airfield, culminating in a night jump. It's another to jump blind into a hostile environment, but we could only do what we could do.

He kept spiraling into the air, and I went back to the team, seeing them snaplink rucksacks to their harnesses. We didn't prepare any weapons because they would have to be threaded through the parachute harness itself, and weapons just made everything more complicated in today's world. I didn't want any questions on the airfield, and their absence didn't really matter. We weren't going to do any shooting on the ground, and the weapon wasn't the enemy on a jump—it was the mask on your face and the rucksack between your legs.

Jennifer completed her attachment and then stood up, arching her back to make sure she could get stable. I went to her and said, "Hey, this is just like the jump before. No issues."

She said, "The jump before, we scissored like a damn wave and then broke apart."

I laughed and said, "You can fly. I've seen you fly. Don't worry about the group. If it breaks up, do what you know."

Her eyes were wide, and I could see she was scared. She *really* didn't like this. I said, "I'll catch you if you fall."

And she finally smiled, saying, "You'd better, because this isn't what I signed up for."

Knuckles came to me and said, "Check it."

I did a jumpmaster check on his kit, then turned to Brett, doing the same. When I finished with Brett, he turned to Jennifer and did the same, while Knuckles checked out Veep.

I heard Brett say, "This thing is not good. I wouldn't jump it."

I turned to him, saw his smile, and then saw Jennifer's eyes yet again. She said, "What's he talking about?"

Brett said, "I think her breasts are going to cause it to slide with the airflow. She can't jump it."

I heard the words, but they had no meaning to me. He was a Marine Force Recon jumpmaster. *Breasts? What the hell is he talking about?*

Jennifer screwed her eyes up, wondering what he meant as well, and then she realized he was ribbing her. She slapped him on the head, causing him to laugh, and I saw he'd broken through her fear.

Brett and Jennifer had formed a bond after our last mission, one that I didn't completely understand, but she trusted him like she trusted me, and his words caused her to relax. Which was exactly what one needed to be upon exiting an aircraft while in flight.

It was counterintuitive, but when the ramp of an aircraft opens, and your body tenses up, with every nerve and sinew begging you not to go forward, you need to tell those same muscles to relax. It was hard to do, but Brett had just managed it with Jennifer.

We spiraled up into the sky until we reached 25,000 feet, with the pilot shouting through the intercom, "Six minutes!"

The loadmaster gave us the hand signal for six minutes, and the ramp lowered, the sky looking huge, the earth far below. The wind raced into the back of the aircraft and we all got ready. I don't care how many jumps you've done as a civilian, doing one at 30,000 feet with fifty pounds of dead weight between your legs while wearing an oxygen mask will cause a rise of adrenaline.

Knuckles, as the jumpmaster, went to the edge of the ramp and began looking for his indicators. The wind blasting through the cargo hold, the men around me, the earth so far away, I felt at home. In my world. I looked at Jennifer and saw the same wide eyes that were there before. I winked at her, and she seemed to calm down.

Knuckles bounced his hand on the floor with a thumbs-up, and that was it. We were going to exit the aircraft at 30,000 feet. Well, if we jumped up a foot on exit, that is.

He stood as stoic as a statue, his mask hiding his face, the gear making him look like some image from a *Call of Duty* poster, and then pointed his hand into the wind.

We went out of the back of the aircraft like lemmings, all of us falling forward. I hit the air, stabilized, and immediately began looking for my teammates, the ruck between my legs fighting me for control. I saw Jennifer and began moving toward her, working my arms and legs like little stabilizers.

I reached her at the same time Brett did, both of us trying to get an arm. She remained flat and stable, understanding what we were doing. I got her left arm and Brett got her right, and we circled together, falling at 120 miles an hour to the earth. I saw something over Brett's shoulder and recognized Veep flying in like a torpedo.

I thought he was going to hit us, but just before that happened, he pulled up short, jerking his arms up and cocking his feet until he was floating right beside us. Jennifer released her hand from Brett, and he floated in.

We had four. Where was Knuckles?

I checked my altimeter, saw we had at least another thirty seconds, then saw Brett's eyes go wild. I looked up and saw Knuckles right above us, desperately trying to slip away. He came right through the formation in slow motion, breaking us apart, his rucksack actually hitting me in the head.

We spun apart and I was facing him. I moved forward, touching his hands, and we fell together for about a second. I moved my head left and right and broke off, looking for Jennifer. I saw her below me and tucked my arms, turning into a missile.

I reached her level, cupped air, and floated to her. She was flying flat and stable, wanting no more of the theatrics. I got to her, took her hands, and got eye contact. I smiled, but she could only see the crinkles of my eyes with the mask. It was enough.

I saw her eyes crinkle in return, and we floated the rest of the way down. At 4,000 feet I nodded. She returned it. At 3,000 feet I let go and spun away. At 2,500 feet I pulled my chute, feeling the satisfying scrunch in my groin from the pull of gravity against the canopy.

I gained control, cleared my airspace, and circled around, seeing Knuckles' canopy as the low man and the others behind me. I got in the stack as his number two and watched everyone else follow my lead above me. I watched Knuckles land and I released my rucksack on its lowering line, hearing it hit the ground. I flared my chute, touching lightly and rotating, the canopy falling to earth. I immediately began hiding my oxygen mask and bottles, not wanting anyone to see them, and then ran up to Knuckles, saying, "What the hell was that? You SEALs always brag about your ability to jump and you pull that shit?"

He was embarrassed and said, "I miscalculated. Sorry."

I saw he was really upset about the mistake, even though it was not that big of a deal. I massively wanted to give him a going-over about it, but realized it was no longer funny. I said, "Well, you're going to hear about it from Jennifer."

He said, "Yeah, I guess I deserve it."

We waited on the rest to coalesce around us, with each man giving him a ration of shit on his skill. He took it in stride. Jennifer finally arrived and didn't say a word, other than "One more done. One more to go."

Knuckles looked at her and said, "That's it? That's all I get?"

She said, "I'm pretty sure you know you screwed up. No reason for me to hammer that home."

We stood for a moment in silence, then broke out laughing at his expense. Knuckles smiled, looked at me, and said, "I now know why you get to stay with her. As many fuckups as you do on a daily basis, I always wondered how she tolerated it. Turns out, she just tolerates fuckups."

We told jokes and swapped lies, getting ready for the final jump of a combat equipment, O_2 night release above 30,000 feet. We acted like we didn't care, but we did, because that sort of thing is just downright scary.

We sat on the airfield until the Shorts landed again, and I went to talk to the pilot. Surprisingly, he came out of the cockpit to meet me. I said, "Hey, we're going to get some chow and wait for the sun to set. We'll be back here in a couple of hours."

He said, "Uh . . . no you won't. I got a call from Blaisdell. They need you in DC. Right now."

CHAPTER 7

Kherson, Ukraine

Daniel waited on Perun to start talking again, but he didn't. He just sat in the front of the SUV like he was waiting on some inspiration to find him. The air in the car began to grow cold, the barrel at the back of his neck becoming constricting. Finally, Perun said, "Do you know how many people have talked about taking out Putin? Do you think you're the first?"

Daniel said, "No, I understand that, but I'm the only one who isn't blustering. I can get it done."

"Then why don't you just do it?"

Daniel shifted uncomfortably, then said, "There is no way that I can do it alone. It's why I sought you out. My men are tracked. My men are known. I can't do it without you."

Perun took that in, then said, "Okay, I can see that, but I'll ask again, what do you propose?"

"You go on your trip to Denmark, and you meet my people there, while you're at the conference. They will give you passports and further instructions. We'll set you up to eliminate Putin."

Perun scoffed and said, "How? You make it sound like you're simply asking me to take out the trash. How is it that easy?"

Daniel said, "Look, I don't know the how yet. I have some ideas.

What I do know is the intelligence necessary to take him out. I have that. I just haven't determined the method of attack."

The honesty seemed to placate Perun. He said, "Okay, given what you know, what are you thinking? What are your options?"

Daniel said, "Can you take the gun off the back of my head, so we can talk like professionals?"

Perun waved his hand, and Daniel felt the barrel leave. Perun said, "Okay, so now we're professionals. What do you propose?"

"Do you remember that Iranian nuclear scientist who was killed by remote control a few years ago?"

Perun laughed and said, "No. A few years ago I was selling tourist trinkets."

Daniel shook his head and said, "Okay, okay. Point taken. In 2020 the head of the Iranian nuclear program was killed inside Iran. The method of the killing was a remote-controlled machine gun utilizing artificial intelligence. Israel literally built a robot machine gun that they could control from satellites outside of the country. They emplaced it and then hosed down his car on a hairpin turn of a road. Killed him and only him."

"And you have this gun?"

"No, we don't. Not yet. We have multiple inroads into Israel—you wouldn't believe how many Russian Jews are there—but we don't have the weapon yet. We're working on it."

"And so? You want me to start this journey without an endstate?"

"No. We also have some Iranian Shahed 136 drones. The same ones that are being used against your country. We have to get them in place, but they are also worthy of consideration."

"Once again, it sounds like you're pulling at straws for this. Why would I risk the existence of my entire organization?"

"Look, the method of death isn't that big of a deal. The intelligence to engender the death is the key. For Israel they knew exactly where the scientist would be to get the kill, and spent months building up the infrastructure, infiltrating the weapon into Iran piece by piece. That's what I offer. I know where Putin will be."

"You and everyone else knows where he will be. I mean, if I wanted to kill the president of the United States, I'd just say, 'Hit the White House.' Sounds simple, but executing is very, very hard."

"Yes, you're correct, except we aren't going to hit him in Moscow. We'll use his dacha in the country. He always flees there, and it's perfect for a kill either with the remote machine gun or the drone. It's isolated. All by itself. It's not the White House."

Perun nodded, thinking. After a moment he said, "So what's the next step? We just leap off a cliff waiting on you to tell us how to kill the man?"

"Unfortunately, yes. I'm still trying to work out the specifics. Honestly, it doesn't really matter either way. You're going to Copenhagen anyway. Just meet with my people there and then make a decision."

"And if I decide it's not worth it?"

"Then you decide it's not worth it—but I think you'll continue. It's the only way to stop this slaughter. If you remain here, you'll eventually all be dead."

Perun nodded, knowing what Daniel said was true. "Okay, if I do decide to continue, how will we meet in Copenhagen?"

Daniel said, "Your man that searched me took a cell phone. I'll use that to contact you with further instructions."

"You want me to take a smartphone provided by the Russian GRU? That is insane."

"You have a better idea?"

Perun smiled and said, "We think alike." He nodded at the men in the rear of the vehicle, and a hand reached out over Daniel's shoulder, holding an old-school flip phone. Daniel took it and Perun said, "There is a single number in the contacts list. You can use that."

"You now want *me* to carry a phone from the Wolves? I have the same problem you do. I can't take this back to my headquarters. I'll end up getting nuked wherever it stops."

Perun laughed and said, "You came to me, not the other way around. I'm not taking your phone, and if you want to continue, you'll take that one."

Daniel considered, then said, "Okay. We must build trust somehow, and if it's to be me, I guess that's the risk I take."

"Good. That's a good first step."

Daniel pulled up the phone and turned it off. He looked at Perun and said, "Of course, it doesn't mean I need it broadcasting 24/7."

Perun smiled and said, "Agreed. We leave in a couple of days. So I should just stand by and wait for a call?"

"Yes, but one thing, you need to make sure you're talking to me. I don't think my organization is on to me—but believing that is asking for failure. I have a healthy appreciation of what my unit is capable of, and I have no doubt there are whispers right now. Do you know what a Valkyrie is?"

"The old Norse myth? The ones that take the fallen to Valhalla? Yes, why?"

"Whenever you're contacted, be it through me or someone I've delegated to, make sure they mention Valkyrie in one form or another. If they do not, they aren't with me."

Perun slowly nodded, and Daniel could see he was coming to grips with the fact that what Daniel proposed was real, and that Daniel himself was a professional putting his own life on the line.

He said, "Wasn't Valkyrie also the mission to assassinate Hitler in the Great War?"

Daniel smiled and said, "It was indeed. I thought it appropriate."

CHAPTER 8

Jennifer came up behind me, saw my face, and said, "What's up?"

I heard what the pilot said, but it didn't make any sense. "What do you mean, Blaisdell needs us in DC?"

"Don't know any more than I told you. While I was circling and you were punching holes in the sky, I got a call on the SATCOM, straight from the boss. He wants you in DC, and I'm supposed to take you."

"Like right now?"

"Yes. Like yesterday."

Jennifer said, "What? We're supposed to fly to DC immediately? What about our cars? Our hotel rooms? My damn luggage? What's the crisis here?"

I said, "She's got a point. We can't show up to Blaisdell Consulting in jump overalls."

He said, "I'm just the pilot here. SATCOM's in the front."

I boarded the plane, sat in the pilot's seat, put on his headset, then looked at the copilot and said, "What the fuck is going on?"

He said, "I have no idea," then fiddled with the SATCOM radio, saying, "Prometheus base, Prometheus base, this is Lancer, you there?"

"This is Prometheus base, I have you five by five."

"Stand by for Pike."

I looked at him and said, "This is in the green, right?"

He nodded, meaning it was encrypted. I said, "This is Pike, who is this?"

"Prometheus base. What's your status?"

I heard the words and wanted to throttle the guy. I literally hated talking to commo guys, because when they transmitted a message, they had the ability to alter world events. I said, "My status is I'm trying to figure out my status. Can I speak to whoever told the pilots here to fly me up to DC?"

"Lancer, stand by for Blaine Alexander."

Which was not good news. I'd sort of hoped there were some crossed wires and the pilots—coupled with the commo guys—had made some mistake, but Blaine Alexander was the deputy commander of Project Prometheus, and not someone who would call us up on a whim or a mistake.

He came on the net saying, "This is Beast. Who is this?"

I thought, *Yeah, Beast. Because you threw up at a party I held after eating a bunch of raw meat.* But I couldn't make fun of his callsign out loud. He was a good man, and someone I trusted. I said, "This is Pike, and why are you breaking up my full mission profile?"

I heard nothing for a moment, then the click on the SATCOM. He said, "Hey, we need your team up here riki-tick. Like now. We have a problem, and you can solve it."

"What's the problem?"

"It would be better to do this up here. It's serious."

"I can't get on this plane with my team wearing jump gear. We can't show up to 'Blaisdell Consulting' like a bunch of rodeo clowns."

"Nobody wants that. It's not *that* urgent. Who said that?"

I laughed and said, "The pilots. We'll go to our hotel and change out, but you're paying the hotel costs and the rental car agreements. We'll have to leave them here, and keep the rooms."

"I got it. No issue. Don't let the hotel know you're leaving. We'll brief you, then you'll come back, check out, and get a clean break."

"Wait, what? What do you mean a clean break?"

"Pike, you've got a mission, and it's pretty important. Get your ass up here."

If anyone else had said that, I would have laughed, but when Blaine said it, I knew it was real. I said, "Roger all, sir. See you in a few hours."

I gave the team what I knew, we went back to the hotel, changed out of our jump gear into civilian clothes, and returned to the airfield. Knuckles and Brett, living in the greater DC area, brought their suitcases. Veep, Jennifer, and I, living in Charleston, just brought ourselves. We loaded the Shorts, and in a couple of hours we landed at the Dulles International Airport FBO, next to a bunch of Gulfstream and Learjet aircraft from power brokers coming to DC to make sure their stock values didn't dip. Our twin-engine propeller-driven beast didn't exactly fit in, but it wasn't that odd.

We thanked the pilots, told them we'd be back in a few hours, and went into the corporate lounge, where we were met by Bartholomew Creedwater sitting in a chair and eating free Cheetos like someone had forgotten their child.

I shook my head and said, "Creed, they sent you to get us? We were going to Uber."

He stood up and said, "I volunteered. Anything to get out of the office."

Creed was the head of our network operations cell, which in real-world terms simply meant he oversaw our computer hacking unit. He was always fantasizing about "getting out on the street" and "doing Operator stuff," but truthfully, he'd have trouble running to the bathroom even if he had explosive diarrhea. But he was good at his job, and his skill had saved my ass on more than one occasion, so I let his little groupie stuff slide.

Knuckles said, "Where's the ride?"

"Outside. Black SUV."

He led us to the front of the FBO, away from the flight line, and sure enough, there was a giant black SUV, like we were in the government with hired protection. I said, "Wow. Really inconspicuous. Can't wait to ride up to our secret headquarters inside that thing."

He said, "Needed room for seven, and it's covered as a Blaisdell Consulting vehicle."

"But we don't work for Blaisdell Consulting. That's the whole point. We can't be tying my company—Grolier Recovery Services—with Blaisdell Consulting. Do you know how many cameras are on us right now? Filming my men getting into *your* company's vehicle?"

He spluttered for a second, Brett stifled a laugh, and I said, "Just get in. Try not to turn on any sirens or lights on the way to the building."

Once on the highway to Arlington, I said, "Okay, Creed, the only good thing about you picking us up is I can get some skinny on what the hell is going on. Why was our jump profile canceled?"

He said, "Beats the hell out of me. Blaine said you were inbound, I said I'd pick you up, and that's about it."

Blaine Alexander was one of the few who had run operations from the ground since the formation of the organization. He'd been promoted up the ranks to deputy commander of the whole shooting match, but really didn't like the headquarters work. Which made him the perfect guy to do the headquarters work.

Anybody that preferred sitting behind a desk was the last guy I wanted telling me how to run an op.

I said, "He told you to come get us? And that was it?"

Creed shuffled in his seat a bit, then said, "No, it wasn't like that. I heard you were coming up and just took a vehicle. He doesn't know I'm here. I just thought I was helping."

Which is about what I expected. No way would Blaine tell him to pick us up in an SUV that looked like Beyoncé would be in the back. I let that go and said, "Okay, so what did Wolffe say?"

George Wolffe was the commander, and the one who would have called this little meeting—but only after the National Command Authority had told him to. Our operations were slow-burn, long-term activities, where we built up targets—sometimes for a year—before executing. We didn't do the "ticking time bomb in a subway" scenario. Others in the national security establishment were good at that, and we didn't duplicate efforts. We had our niche, and they had theirs.

Creed became a little bit surly, saying, "Sorry, but I'm not privy to Taskforce mission planning. I just execute network stuff when told."

I smiled at that, because he was correct—except for this little pickup at the airport. He was like me, willing to bend the rules when asked.

He used the nickname we all used for Project Prometheus. Since we couldn't actually utter the name without breaking some sacrosanct code of omertà, we just called Prometheus the Taskforce.

I said, "Come on, Creed. I know you. You're like the secretary in a boiler-room bond-trading scam. You always have the dirt."

"Not this time. All I can say is that Kerry Bostwick and Easton Beau Clute were in the office for an hour, walking around waving their arms. Then you got the call."

Kerry Bostwick was the director of the CIA. Easton Beau Clute was the chairman of the House Intelligence Committee. Both had real jobs in the world of the United States government, but they also held a secret position known to a very few: they were members of the Oversight Council that provided supervision for Taskforce activities.

Composed of thirteen people from the U.S. government and private citizens, it was a who's who of the elite at the tip of power. They risked a lot to be on the council, since what we did was decidedly illegal, and I understood the threat they were under, because if we were ever exposed, they'd all be going to jail in the biggest political television showcase of a feeding frenzy since Watergate, full of bloviating politicians who'd never heard a shot fired in anger thundering in hearings that held no meaning to the people whose lives we'd saved.

Among the whispers of the ones we couldn't.

I honestly *did* appreciate their service, but too often the very fear of discovery made them hesitant to protect the lives of innocents. It was a constant question: *How far do we go to protect the nation, when the protection could engender our destruction?* It wasn't a trivial question, because every operation held inherent risks—and I'd busted just about all of them at one time or another—but at the end of the day, the council had to determine if going to jail was worth saving a single life, especially given the fallout of discovery could possibly guarantee the death of many more.

Trade-offs, trade-offs, trade-offs. Save the one, go to jail, causing the loss of many more in the future. Or, let the one die in order to protect the organization, never knowing if the risk of saving him or her would have mattered one way or the other.

I said, "You're sure it was Bostwick and Clute?"

"Yeah, it was them. And they stayed a long time, almost like Wolffe was fighting them."

Which meant the intelligence I'd been called up to see hadn't come from internal Taskforce assets. It had come from the outside intelligence community, meaning they were asking us to do something they couldn't do, using intelligence we hadn't developed.

From what Creed told me, due to the length of the meeting and the hand waving, Wolffe didn't like it.

Which meant I probably wouldn't either.

CHAPTER 9

My team entered the Blaisdell Consulting conference room, still wondering why we'd been called forward. The room was something out of a Hollywood movie, a stereotype of what you'd expect from a boutique lobbying firm that Blaisdell Consulting pretended to be. Lined in oak, it looked not unlike the club in *Trading Places*, with books and artifacts along the walls, as if the room had a history that predated the Constitution. The centerpiece was a long cherry table that ended facing a wall of gigantic flat-screen monitors. It was almost a parody of what one would expect in a secret government world, and honestly, outside of Blaisdell Consulting, I'd never seen such a thing. But I was sitting in one now.

It oozed power, but I'd long since been disabused of the notion. I no longer cowered under the awe it was supposed to instill. It only took one bullet next to your head before you realized that oak bookcases and money meant nothing. There were people in power who enjoyed such rooms, and they could order you to hunt, but at the end of the day, *you* were the hunter. And they might end up the prey.

Blaine Alexander entered the room, saw us sitting around the table, and said, "Glad you guys could get here on such short notice."

Blaine was a little bit of a bulldog. Short and squatty, but full of muscle, he was someone I'd done many, many operations with. If you wanted to be in a bar fight, he was the guy you'd pick, not least because he'd start throwing fists regardless of the insult, based solely on the fact that he was backing you up. I loved the man, but this was a little bit much.

Knuckles snorted, and I stood up, saying, "What the hell is this all about?"

He held his hands up and said, "Okay, slow the roll there, commando. No reason to go ballistic right off the bat."

Jennifer touched my thigh, and I looked at Knuckles. He shook his head, telling me to back down.

Blaine was once one of us, out in the muck. Now he was the guy who would *always* piss me off, because he was in charge of my operations. He didn't deserve my anger.

I sat down again, saying, "Okay, so what's the fire?"

Blaine said, "It's a little bit of a weird one. You get the slot because you decided to be an archeological cover company."

"What's that mean?"

The commander of the Taskforce, George Wolffe, entered the room and said, "Keep your seats," which caused a laugh, breaking the tension, because there was no way my team would jump to attention for any man, and he knew it.

Wolffe was an old-school paramilitary officer from the CIA. A wiry guy with a full-on handlebar mustache, he was the exact opposite of Blaine. One was a linebacker, designed to plow through problems with brute force. The other was a Ninja master, used to manipulating the momentum of his opponent to succeed, without exerting his own force, but they worked well together.

Wolffe had seen the worst of the evil in the world, and the worst of our own bureaucracy. He was a good man now elevated to the position of leading an organization of knuckle draggers like me, when he only wanted to be an Operator again. He didn't want to be the guy controlling things. He wanted to be the guy *doing* things.

Which, whether he knew it or not, meant a great deal to people like me. People *doing* things.

Wolffe said, "So, are you good on parachute infiltration? You guys can execute what I want when I ask?"

I said, "No, because you jerks cut it short. Jennifer still hates the drop, and Veep can't seem to control himself in the air. I needed the jump tonight, but we aren't getting it. So why are we here?"

Veep bristled at the words, and Jennifer looked embarrassed, but the one thing the Taskforce had was pure honesty. Which is why I said it. I wanted Wolffe to know that I was baring my team's soul, and so should he.

Wolffe said, "Okay, I got it. But we have a problem that you—and you alone—can solve."

I looked at my team, then said, "What is it?"

Wolffe said, "You know about Sweden's and Finland's bids to join NATO, correct?"

"Yeah, breaking their stance of neutrality because Putin's rampaging in Ukraine. What's that got to do with us?"

"Turkey and Hungary are the big sticks in the wheel here. In order to join NATO, it has to be unanimous. We think Hungary is going to drop any reservations in the next few months, but Turkey is something else. They'll possibly back Finland, but Sweden is another story. Some right-wing wackos burned a Quran outside of the Swedish parliament, and then literally burned an effigy of Erdogan, which has caused Turkey to go nuts. We can't prove it, but we believe the right-wing guys are paid by Putin. He's trying to stop the joining, and he's splitting off the members to do so."

I waited, and when he said nothing else, I said, "Okay, got that. Once again, what's that have to do with us? We deal in substate terrorist threats. We don't do state system stuff. Why are we getting involved? This is a State Department issue."

Wolffe clicked a screen and the giant monitors came to life. He said, "You ever heard of the Kurdistan Workers' Party?"

"Yeah. Of course. The PKK. They're on the Foreign Terrorist Organization list. They're a target. You want me to hunt them? Is that it?"

"No, unfortunately, that's not it. Sweden has some PKK members under arrest, and as an agreement to allow Sweden to join NATO, Turkey wants those bodies extradited to Istanbul. Sweden won't allow that to happen, because it will be basically saying their judicial system is crap. Just because Turkey screams doesn't mean Sweden is going to relent. It's a huge sticking point on the NATO thread."

"I am still at a loss here. I'm hearing nothing but State Department echoes. What does that have to do with the Taskforce?"

"The Swedes have begun thinking about extraditing one of the men in their prisons. Sending him back to Turkey. It will be a great show of good faith, and a breakthrough in the ongoing NATO negotiations."

Dumbly, I nodded, then said, "Once again? Why do I, as a Taskforce team leader, care? Is he going to try to blow something up once he's free?"

Blaine stepped in, saying, "No, nothing like that. We have a threat against this transfer. We don't know the target, but we do know it's coming from Putin. He's going to try to kill someone inside Sweden to muck up the works there. He wants to stop the two countries from joining NATO, and antagonizing Turkey is his method of choice. Your job is to prevent that."

Incredulous, I said, "Prevent what?"

"Prevent them from interfering in the negotiations."

"Where did this intelligence come from?"

"Kerry Bostwick. It's CIA."

Now feeling the squeeze, and not liking it, I said, "And why are they not doing anything? I mean, it sounds like the guys who know this problem are all running away from it."

Wolffe glanced at Blaine, then said, "Look, I don't like this any more than you do, but apparently, there are some issues with the CIA working inside Sweden. Trust issues. They can't operate, but you can."

"Trust issues? Seriously? They can't operate in the country, but you want me to? What's my backstop? If they get screwed over, they flee the country on a diplomatic passport. What am I going to do? Or my team?"

"I understand, Pike. I get it. You'll have the backing of the National Command Authority. We know this is outside the charter, and outside your mission set."

"Outside my mission set? That's putting it mildly. You want me to interdict an assassination attempt in a supposedly neutral country, all the while evading the very intelligence agencies that are supposedly on our side? Is that what you're asking?"

"Yeah, it is. Like I said, I don't like it any more than you do, but it is what it is. The CIA can't operate—but you can."

"How can I operate? I'm a damn niche archeological firm."

"Ever heard of Runriket?"

Of course I hadn't. I looked at Jennifer. She said, "The old Viking kingdom. Viking runestones are constantly being found all over that country. It's sort of right up our alley."

CHAPTER 10

I looked at Jennifer, not liking her acquiescence, and said, "So we're going to scrape a couple of runestones as Grolier Recovery Services, and that'll get us close to the killers? Who's thinking this through?"

"We don't know who the killers are or who their target is, but we do know the first meeting site. It's a place called Arkils Tingstad. It's on a lake, and it's where Viking elders apparently adjudicated justice. We have a cover for you in place already. You'll have to endure some research work on other rune sites, but you'll be at this one when the meeting is supposed to occur."

I could see Jennifer's eyes brighten at the thought of actual research, but I ignored it, saying, "And then what? You want me to smoke them or what? What's the mission?"

"Track them to the target. We don't know what they're planning."

"Why not just let me break it up? Hammer them right there? Or do you not believe they're worthy of the hammer just yet? What are you bringing my team into here?"

Wolffe sighed, and that told me everything. He said, "We need to know who they are and why they're hunting. We don't have the fidelity to simply smoke them. Yes, we don't know they're bad just yet."

"You mean they might actually be what they say they are? Some other archeological firm?"

Blaine cleared his throat and said, "Yes. That's about it."

I said, "You know this is way, way outside our charter. You're talking about me taking on a state system. Who is it? GRU? Wagner? I've had a little bit of experience with both of them. They play for keeps. We miss the shot here, and they'll come back full force."

"It's not them. We know it's not Wagner, and it's not the GRU, but it *is* the Russians."

"So you know it's not the GRU, and it's not Wagner, but you *don't* know who it is? Are you just fucking with me now?"

Wolffe said, "Pike, we have a well-placed source inside the Russian establishment. That's all I can tell you. The intelligence is accurate."

I could tell he was getting borderline aggravated, and so I backed off. I'd spent many an operation working with "sources" like he was describing. Nine times out of ten, they panned out. One time out of ten, I was left cleaning up the pieces of a debacle. And he knew that.

I said, "So, let's just short-circuit the entire problem set. I'll just set up an ambush and take them out. How about that?"

Blaine said, "Can't do it. Sorry."

Which I knew would be the answer, so I went to the next stage. "Then why not just give the Swedes this information? Let them deal with it?"

"We've tried. There is some friction between U.S. intel and the Swedes right now. It's too long to go into, but they don't believe us, and we have used some extremely sensitive sources and methods for this information. The call from the National Command Authority is to execute unilaterally. If the Swedes don't believe us, we'll just help them ourselves."

I took that in, then said, "NATO means that much? Even if Russians do the killing, stopping the near-term joining of the membership, so what? They'll join eventually. You want to put our entire organization at risk for this?"

Wolffe said, "Honestly, I fought it. I agree with you, it's not a good use of our skills. It's way outside of our charter and sets a dangerous precedent."

"Yeah, basically, the National Command Authority is holding me out to dry. They can't get it done, but they have me, so let's burn me."

Blaine said, "Except the president himself approved it. Look, it's against our charter, I got that, but at the end of the day, it's just trade-craft. The CIA can't do it because all of their members in-country are declared to the Swedes, and they're risk averse right now. They don't want to upset the applecart. You are not. You won't be tied to them, and thus won't be tied to the United States. But it's just a mission."

I stood up and said, "Do you hear yourself? This is exactly what Kurt Hale wanted to prevent. Our organization exceeding its charter because someone sees the weapon and decides to use it, even when it doesn't fit. Something outside our charter—because we're easy. I'm not going to *become* easy. If you want this shit to happen, you do it the right way. You don't throw my team into the breach and then hope for forgiveness."

Blaine looked at Wolffe, who looked at me. Blaine said, "So you're disobeying a direct order for a mission? That's what you're saying? The NCA has asked for your help, and you've said no. You know, that cover organization you run is still a *government* organization."

I never would have expected that out of him. I stood up, locked eyes with him, and said, "I don't know where your head went after I served with you in the mud, but if you want to solve this problem downstairs, in the parking garage, I'm available."

I unlinked my watch from my wrist and slid it into a pocket, telling him I was about to beat his ass into submission. Jennifer realized that we were on the verge of being locked in combat, and stood up, saying, "Wait, wait. Why are we doing this?"

It was a double entendre, meaning why was I about to beat the shit out of the DCO of the Taskforce, but also why were we even in the mission.

I kept my eyes on Blaine, and we went to a staredown for a split second. He could feel the violence coming out of my face, and I said, "You alone should know that I don't take our security as a joke. You alone know what happened when I walked off the reservation to save a life. You cannot, in good conscience, tell me I don't believe in the mission."

The heat in the room grew until it was about to self-combust. Knuckles defused it, standing up with his hands in the air at chest level. "Okay, just say it. Up front. You've told us over and over on missions that we couldn't do the right thing because it's 'against the charter,' and now you're telling us you guys don't think our charter is worth a shit, and I'm a hired gun to do whatever you want. At least be honest on this."

Blaine said, "Would that help here?"

I snarled, "Really? You think we're that cheap? No, it fucking wouldn't! We don't do that!"

He looked at me, rolled his eyes, and then said, "Honestly, Pike, I was torn with bringing you up here. On the one hand, you have an overinflated sense of your self-worth, but on the other, you always succeed."

I took a deep breath and said, "Meaning you wanted someone who would just roll over, and I wouldn't, but you needed what I bring to the table. Hear what you're saying. Blaine, please tell me you are the same man as before. That dealing in the new political world hasn't altered your ability to see right from wrong. That you want to fight for the right reasons."

He looked at me strangely, then said, "I'm not fighting about this. It's from the National Command Authority."

I smiled and said, "You're not the one hanging his ass out on the line. I am. And my team."

Geoge Wolffe said, "Stop that shit. We're not going to the mats to decide this. We aren't a bunch of savages. You'll do the mission because I said you'll do the mission. Is that clear?"

I looked at Knuckles and he shook his head, telling me to let it go. If he thought it was okay, then it probably was. I said, "Okay, so what's the next step? I still have hotel rooms in Laurinburg."

"We'll solve that problem. You need to go do your runestone stuff. When you find the guys, you track them."

"And then what?"

"I'm not sure at this point. Just find out what they're doing, and we'll take it from there."

I shook my head and said, "Bullshit, sir. You know what that means, right?"

He sighed, then said, "Yeah, I know what that means. Trust me, I was not the man saying let's bring in a wrecking crew."

I looked at Knuckles, then Jennifer, then said, "But that's what you're getting. You want me to solve this problem and I will. But it's going to be ugly at the end. You know I'm not going to just follow these guys. They have a target, and I'll have to prevent them from eliminating that target. It's going to go kinetic."

"Not until we give you authority. Best case, we simply pass it to the Swedes at that point."

"You know that's not going to happen. If I find the intelligence, it'll probably be because I'm about to see them kill someone. I'm not going to stumble on some nefarious plan for the Swedes to disrupt. I'm going to do the disruption. You get that, right?"

Wolffe said, "I get it. I get it."

"And if we get arrested after the fact? How's that going to play out?"

"We'll have to take that one step at a time."

"Seriously? You're literally making me the equivalent of the Russian Wagner Group here. You're going to hang us out to dry?"

Blaine said, "Nobody is going to be hung out to dry. Look, we have the skill here, and we should use it."

Knuckles said, "That's easy to say when you won't be hearing the gunfire. Easy to do when you're back here reading a SITREP after we've sent it, then bitching about how my grammar isn't correct."

He smiled and said, "Yeah, except this mission is so sensitive, I'll be on the ground with you. You won't be sending the SITREP. I will."

And that gave all of us a pause. I said, "You're coming with us? On the ground?"

He said, "Yeah, Pike, I am. Is that an issue?"

It wasn't an issue at all, to be honest. It showed me how much they worried about the mission.

I said, "Only if you think you're going to be in charge."

CHAPTER 11

Lars Karlsson adjusted his tie in the mirror, turned away, and bumped his skull on the dormer of the roof. He grabbed his scalp and cursed, hearing his wife below asking what was wrong.

He shouted, "Nothing. Just banged my head."

He glanced at the tiny spiral staircase leading down from his cramped little bedroom and wondered again if the location was worth the sacrifice. A tall man with a trimmed beard and round glasses, he radiated authority for no other reason than his looks, and he'd used them to great effect. He'd worked most of his adult life for the furniture manufacturer Ikea, now one of the world's most profitable companies, and he'd been very successful.

He glanced around their minuscule space, seeing the Ikea furniture of the college student he'd once been and wanting to wince. A short time ago his family had been living an extravagant lifestyle in a mansion on the Swedish archipelago next to the Baltic Sea, a world away from Stockholm. Then he'd been contacted by an old university friend asking about his networks in Turkey.

He knew his friend now worked as a civil servant in the government of Sweden, specifically in the Ministry of Foreign Affairs, and hadn't thought much of it. Yes, he had plenty of contacts in Turkey, all the way up to the top of the government. It was his area of expertise in Ikea's relentless quest for dominance. When the pandemic had hit, and the supply chains from Asia had become bottlenecked, Ikea had wanted to start manufacturing in Turkey to make up for the shortfalls, and the many Turkish government roadblocks to the creation of the factories were obliterated in no small part thanks to Lars's efforts.

He was a salesman at heart, his entire life based on the ledger sheet of profit and loss, and now he was working in a world he didn't quite understand, solely because he had relationships within the opposition.

In the past, he could live wherever he wanted because his work was international. His actual home location didn't matter. Now? It most certainly did. For the first time in a long time, he was tied to a place.

He snaked his way down the spiral staircase, finding Ingrid, his wife, making breakfast for their son. She gave a smile, but he could see it was forced. She was growing tired of the cramped space as well.

She said, "Is today the day?"

He knew what she meant: *Can we move back home soon?* He poured a cup of coffee and said, "Hopefully."

She saw his eyes and said, "That's not true. It's not today, is it?"

"No. It won't be today. The Turks are being assholes, which is why I'm here. To leverage them with our economic power. But it'll be soon."

She laughed and said, "Economic power? Do you think Erdogan gives a damn about Ikea? Is that what this is about?"

He sagged against a counter and said, "No, Erdogan doesn't, but I've made some friends in the Turkish government. Powerful people. They trust me." He took a sip, looked out the window, and said, "And now I have to use that trust."

"Well, that sounded great when you were offered the job, but now . . . I'm not so sure. We had a good life before." She waved her hand toward their small living room and said, "We now live in this cramped flat without even a dishwasher. Erik is sleeping in a corner with a pullout couch like we're camping. It seemed to be a little adventure at first, but the fun's worn off."

He knew exactly what she meant, because he felt the same way, but he couldn't let her know that. When he'd been asked to broker Turkey's increasingly bitter demands for allowing Sweden to join NATO he'd been flattered. Very few people were called upon by their nation to serve, and it was supposed to only take a couple of weeks.

Given a title of deputy assistant minister within a subcommittee of the Directorate-General for Euro-Atlantic Affairs and Security Policy, he'd felt important and needed. But it was turning out to be a chore. His entire skill set was his Rolodex of people he knew from his time in Turkey, and he didn't have a relationship with any of the people Turkey had sent. It was like a second link on the social media site LinkedIn, where he knew somebody they knew, but they didn't know each other.

As their true home was hours away from the foreign services offices, he'd rented a flat in Gamla Stan, a little spit of land surrounded by water that was the historical origins of Stockholm, complete with the ancestral Royal Palace of Sweden and the current parliament building bumping hips with the pubs and restaurants that dotted the area. It was a short walk across the bridge spanning Lake Malaren to the foreign ministry's offices, and Lars thought it the perfect place to bring his family.

Two months later, the quaint apartment was starting to wear on the both of them.

He said, "Honey, I get it, but I can't back out now. I should have said no at the beginning, but it's too late. I'm committed. It'll be over soon. The Turks are starting to waffle."

"Waffle? There are idiots burning the Quran outside of the Turkish embassy. If anything, they're becoming more entrenched."

Lars was convinced it was Russian subversives who were protesting and burning the sacred Muslim text, but what she said was true; it most definitely was making things harder.

Their son, Erik, entered the room, saying, "Are you guys fighting again?"

Lars said, "No, not at all. Just talking."

Only eight years old, but precocious beyond his years, Erik, Lars knew, could sense when things weren't what they seemed. Like a cadaver dog sniffing a crime scene, he could find the thread and then would want to unravel it. He took a seat at their small island table and began eating his breakfast, saying, "I don't mind it here. If that's what you're fighting about."

Ingrid patted him on his head and said, "It won't be much longer, I promise."

"I really don't mind. Papa is doing something important. I can sleep on a pullout couch."

Ingrid looked at Lars with a question on her face, saying to Erik, "How do you know that?"

"Because Papa told me last night."

Lars said, "Wait . . . but . . . I didn't say that. Well, not exactly that. I was just explaining why we moved."

Ingrid grinned, saying, "Hard to compete with the salesman in my own house." He started to protest again, and she put a finger to his lips, saying, "Stop. I get it's important. Just don't make 'important' our entire life."

Lars said, "I won't. I promise. It's not like I'm enjoying the work."

She said, "I know. I know. Honestly, maybe it's for the best. Makes us appreciate what we had."

Lars smiled and said, "Always the optimist. That's what I love about you." He leaned in to kiss her, and she theatrically turned away, saying, "Not good enough. Solve the problem and then I'll kiss you."

He laughed and grabbed his leather satchel, saying, "I have to go.

Tomorrow's the showboat excursion where I take them all over like a damn tour guide."

She came to him and kissed him on the lips, saying, "See you tonight," and he exited the flat, going down four flights of stairs to the ground level, once again regretting his choice of living arrangements.

The building was as old as the town, which is to say it had most definitely been constructed before the invention of the elevator. The first time he'd walked up, it had been quaint, with the history radiating off the railings of the staircase. Now it was just a pain in the ass.

He exited into a small alley and went to Skeppsbrokajen, the street that paralleled the water. He broke free of the alley and felt the wind off the sea, a brisk blast of November air. Refreshing and not unduly cold. The tourist season over, there were few people on the street at this hour, and he enjoyed his time alone. He cinched his jacket against the chill, passing by the Royal Palace before reaching the Norrbro bridge, thinking about his path in life and his role in the current negotiations.

Sweden had been habitually neutral for two hundred years, including the last two wars that defined the European continent. It was their calling card—they were neutral when world affairs turned to combat. Come to them for trade or diplomacy, but don't ask them to fight. That all changed with the Russian Federation's barbaric invasion of Ukraine in 2022.

Now fearful of the Russian bear, they—along with Finland—finally left the land of neutrality, asking to join the North Atlantic Treaty Organization, the granddaddy of defensive pacts designed to counter the Soviet Union in the Cold War. Putin had intended for his little "special military operation" to split NATO apart at the seams, and instead it had only hardened the determination of the members to the point that both Finland and Sweden now wanted to join. It was the worst endstate

Putin could have ever envisioned, and Lars knew he was determined to ensure it never came to pass—which is why he believed the Quran burning was staged.

In order to join the pact, all other members had to vote yes, like some fraternity deciding whether a new pledge could enter the hallowed halls. To that end, Putin had an ally in Turkey. A member of NATO, Turkey had already been a thorn in the sides of the other members for years—even buying Russian air defense systems that could be used to give Russia intelligence on cutting-edge fifth-generation NATO aircraft.

That purchase had caused the United States to block sales of the F-35 fighter, and had created a rift in the NATO alliance. Who buys a weapon system from the very enemy the organization was designed to thwart?

Now Turkey was the final blocking vote for Sweden from joining the alliance. Turkey's reticence was that Sweden was ostensibly harboring members of an organization whom they considered terrorists. Kurdish separatists that Turkey said were destabilizing their country. They wanted the offenders extradited to Turkey before they would agree to vote for admission.

Sweden's position was that wasn't going to happen, as the men had done nothing to break Swedish laws, only had vague allegations by the Turkish government, and such an extradition was against their own constitution. No proof of complicity in terrorism had been given, and thus no extradition was forthcoming.

And that was what Lars had walked into, now using his Rolodex of contacts in Turkey through Ikea to broker a breakthrough. He didn't know if he could do it or not, but he had hope. One of the supposed terrorists was actually in a Swedish jail for breaking Swedish laws, and he thought he could get that guy extradited to Turkey. Maybe that would be enough.

Truthfully, in his heart he liked being the linchpin of one of the most consequential actions in his country's history. If he made this happen, he would have done something monumental in the service to his nation. Not many men could say the same. In his mind, there were only two entities involved: Sweden and Turkey. He gave not a thought to the one nation being most affected by the action. Having not served in the high-stakes world he had now entered, it never crossed his mind that Russia might have a vote beyond burning Qurans.

Because of that, he failed to notice the men who were tracking him, all dressed for the cold as he was, with scarves hiding their faces against the chill.

CHAPTER 12

From a park bench next to the water, Dmitri Nikitan kept his eyes on the receding back of Lars Karlsson, seeing him walking along the same path he'd used the day before. He made a single radio call: "He's moving, and on the projected route."

His team was a little short right now, as he had two going north to get their weapons, but he still had three, and they were enough to confirm the pattern of life of Lars for a follow-on attack. It was something he had once been good at.

He was a team leader in the Viking SOBR of the Kaliningrad Oblast, but before that time, he'd actually served in a GRU Spetsnaz unit created to sow sabotage during the Cold War. As such, he knew a thing or two about operating behind enemy lines, because he'd done it once before. Well, almost done it. The Cold War was long over before he'd entered the world of espionage, but the new Russian Federation still held to the old school of threats. He'd done plenty of operations inside the Baltic States, working to obstruct their governments' slide to the West, and had actually conducted real combat time in the 2008 invasion of Georgia, executing selected assassination missions of pro-West government officials in South Ossetia.

He'd learned what it took to swim within a civilian population while completing operations that were definitely not civilian endeavors. With blond hair and blue eyes, he appeared Nordic, even as he was pure Russian.

He received a call back on the radio, "I have him. Same trajectory. Same pace."

The trickiest thing about surveillance was precisely following the subject when he or she was on the move. That's when one would be found out, if the subject had any situational awareness at all. Which, luckily, Lars did not. After that first follow, when one developed a feel for where the target would be at certain times—when one developed what was known as a "pattern of life"—it became easier. All one had to do was position along the same route and simply confirm.

Static surveillance was almost impossible to detect, because the target was walking *into* the surveillance box, not being trailed by the following team. The only way to defeat it was to vary routes and times, forcing a mobile surveillance effort to continually shadow, and thereby expose themselves.

Fortunately for Dmitri, Lars had no such skills, and following him had become almost routine. He had no idea he was being hunted and blundered about as if the civil society around him alone would provide protection. He didn't understand that the wolf never showed its hand until it went for the jugular. By then it was too late.

Dmitri had no specific instructions about killing Lars. Unlike the GRU, he wasn't going to use some elaborate plutonium poisoning or Novichok nerve agent. It would be a simple killing, and then they'd flee exactly as they'd come—traveling as Belarusian businessmen on a commercial airliner to Poland before switching to Russian passports and crossing back into the Kaliningrad Oblast.

The key thing that had been driven home to him was that the death had to occur before any agreements had been made with Turkey. Killing Lars after that happened would be irrelevant. It needed to happen before a decision was made.

He wasn't too worried about it. Time was on his side. All he needed was the weapons to make it happen, and his men would be getting those tonight through contacts his boss, Victor, had arranged. It was almost too easy, making him wish there was a little bit of drama he had to overcome for the mission.

He didn't *really* wish for that, but even if he did, it wouldn't occur here, he was sure. The Swedes' neutrality over the past two centuries had made them soft.

Nobody was hunting his team here.

The tour guide began her monologue of the historic nature ascribed to the scene in front of me, but I wasn't buying it. I took a look at the ring of stones and thought, *Come on. This is* not *a Viking tribal council setting. It's a bunch of rocks put in a circle for tourists like me to come see.*

Because that was literally what was in front of me: a mown field with a circle of flat stones high enough to sit on. Nothing else. Outside of a couple of runestones that supposedly described the place, there were no other archeological detritus, no pottery shards, no nothing. Just a ring of stones. Maybe it *was* an ancient tribal meeting place—called a Ting—but then again, maybe it was a campfire built in 1910 for the Swedish version of the Girl Scouts, and now everyone thought it was some ancient court.

Jennifer could see I was getting a little tired of the tour and bumped my hip, reminding me that I needed to drag this out to let the team explore, because this was the targeted linkup point we'd been given.

After being given the entire mission profile in DC, to include our cover mechanism, we'd split up, returning home to pack. Knuckles and Brett just went to their places in DC, while Jennifer, Veep, and I returned to Laurinburg, scrubbed the hotel, returned the rental cars, and packed up in Charleston.

In truth, the intel was weak and the cover was ridiculous, but at least they let us take the Rock Star bird. A Gulfstream G650, it was an aircraft just like the rock stars used, but it had a little bit of something extra in the cabin; instead of a spinning king bed with rubber sheets, it held a multitude of different surveillance capabilities and weapons, all built within the frame to escape notice from customs officials.

It was "leased" to my company through a maze of cutouts, but was actually owned by the U.S. government. Getting permission to use it on this mission was a give-and-take that required a little bit of debate, but the fact that they'd ordered me to exceed our own charter, operating within an allied country without their knowledge no less, gave me the upper hand. Well, that and the fact that they'd detailed my cover without my involvement—and it was about as weak as I'd ever used before.

Usually my company was hired by a university or some other establishment of repute, such as the United Nations Educational, Scientific and Cultural Organization—UNESCO—to help with the excavation of an archeological site located in an area that was less than hospitable for the average doctoral student. I had the security expertise both on the ground and with various government agencies, and Jennifer, with her anthropology degree, could work her magic with the customer on-site, but in this case there was no establishment of repute we were facilitating, and the host country most definitely wasn't hostile.

Which is how I and the team found ourselves traipsing behind a tour guide who could barely speak English, going to one runestone stop after another. It was ridiculous, as if the idiot on the Oversight Council who'd set it up had no idea how a cover actually worked—something I was now sure was the case.

Cover is nothing more than camouflage for operational acts—much like a ghillie suit is for a sniper—and has two basic levels: cover for status—why you're in the area you're in; and cover for action—why you're doing something specific.

Say you were stopped by hostile secret police: *Sir, what are you doing in my country?* Cover for status: *Why, I'm a software engineer invited to attend the computer conference at the convention center. See? Here's my entrance badge and invitation.*

Hostile secret police: *Okay, why are you walking next to our supersecret military headquarters? The convention center is behind you.* Cover for action: *Military headquarters? I had no idea. I'm going to that computer store two blocks from here. My laptop power charger died.*

The cover didn't have to be perfect. It just had to be plausible, and the one we were using here in Sweden was not that. We were lucky we were inside an allied country instead of operating against a paranoid intelligence service. It reminded me of a cardinal rule I had—never let someone who *facilitates* an operation *design* an operation—but I was in it now.

After landing in Stockholm, we'd immediately met our guide and started out on the tour of the runestones—known as Runriket—stopping in one farm field after another, wandering through the grass until we found a flat stone placed upright with cryptic messages and intertwined snakes like something out of the movie *Conan the Barbarian.* Jennifer found it incredibly interesting, and I did my best to act like I cared, but we honestly could have just driven to the meet site by ourselves for all the good this cover was doing.

Called Arkils Tingstad, it was supposedly a thousand-year-old meeting spot from an important family of a Viking clan, and, to give it its due, it did have a couple of runestones detailing the family—although the tour guide could have been making up half of what she said and we'd have never known. Lord knows that happens in my hometown of Charleston on just about every single tour.

The circle of stones was near a neighborhood, but set off in the woods adjacent to a large lake, with several hiking paths threaded through the trees around it. I could see why it had been picked as a linkup point, because it was a known location easily found between two units who hadn't worked together, and it was far enough away from any structures to remain secret—especially if the meeting was held at night.

As soon as we'd arrived, Veep, Knuckles, and Brett had set off exploring the area while Jennifer and I suffered the trials of listening to the tour guide. She seemed a little miffed that the rest of my team didn't want to hear her spiel, but Jennifer told her they loved the outdoors and not to get upset. In this case, the shitty cover worked, because the guide was making her money no matter what and had no idea we were supposed to be some niche archeological company. If we'd been truly working our cover, it would have been harder to let them loose.

The tour guide finished her talk and asked if we had any questions. I, of course, wanted to ask how in the hell they knew this ring of stones was from the thirteenth century, but I did not. Jennifer asked about the clan, giving our men more time.

Eventually, they came out of the woods, and the tour guide said, "Great of you to join us. I'm sorry you missed the presentation."

Knuckles said, "Sorry, but this country is so beautiful I just wanted to walk around for a bit. You didn't tell us this place was on a lake. That thing is huge."

She smiled and said, "Yes, we have many lakes like this. But they have nothing to do with the Runriket."

Knuckles looked at me and gave a slight nod and I theatrically looked at my watch, saying, "Thank you so much for the tour. It's getting late, and we have other engagements."

With a sour look, the tour guide said, "Okay. If you wanted to just see the woods, you didn't need me."

Jennifer said, "No, no. I really appreciated the tour. We just have other things to do." She held out a couple of bills, saying, "Thank you so much."

The tour guide looked insulted, saying, "Please. I don't take tips. My pay is your enjoyment."

She looked at me and said, "I assume you can make your way back?"

I nodded and she stormed off, going to her beat-up Volvo and driving away, gravel flying.

Brett said, "Well, if we wanted to prove our cover, we failed. She'll remember us forever as the assholes who didn't care about the runestones."

I said, "Yeah, but we can blame the Taskforce for that. It was *their* ridiculous cover. What do you have?"

"Two OP sites, three beacons. We're ready to go."

CHAPTER 13

Now back on the same park bench he'd used in the morning, Dmitri received a call from his surveillance box, "He's headed back. Same pace, same schedule, but this time he's got a trailer."

Dmitri sat up and said, "What's that? A trailer?"

"Yeah, he's got a little entourage with him. Looks like he's bringing the Turk home with him, and that guy's got a little bit of security."

"Security how?"

"Two other goons. I've got the target in a suit walking next to another guy in a suit—who I presume is the Turk—and two guys trailing along in casual gear, looking left and right at anyone who approaches. They're security, but I can't tell if they're armed or not."

Dmitri took that in and said, "Let them go. I'll pick them up and decide what we're doing."

Twenty minutes later, he saw the group on the street next to the water, Lars and another man in the lead, and two others following. They entered the small alley where Lars's apartment was located and Dmitri watched them go inside. One of the security men stayed in the alley, lighting a cigarette.

One of his outside surveillance men, Konstantin, reached him and took a seat on the bench, saying, "He didn't deviate from his route at all. We get the weapons tonight, and we can take him on the way to work tomorrow morning."

Dmitri nodded, thinking about the options. Konstantin said,

"We closing down the box for today? I need to prep for exfil after the hit."

Dmitri said, "No. It's the first time we've seen him with the Turkish envoy. They're obviously going to dinner or somewhere else tonight. I want to get Control a picture for positive ID."

"The Turk isn't the target. We have our hands full as it is."

Dmitri heard the words and felt a twinge of anger. The team he'd been given had none of the experience he had in the outside world of the Russian Federation. He knew what Victor wanted with Lars, but he also knew Victor didn't understand what had been presented to them.

Victor wanted the stoppage of any advancement for Sweden into NATO, and the Turkish envoy provided another thread to exploit, possibly shutting the effort down for good.

He turned to Konstantin and said, "We're not taking him tonight, which means you still have some work on the clock. Set up a box on the apartment and let's track him for a couple of hours. Get the photos of the Turkish envoy and send those back."

Konstantin started to rebut the words and Dmitri held up a finger to him and said, "We're not taking him tonight, so it's no threat. Set up the box on the apartment."

"We've only got three guys. That's not optimal, and we already have our mission. We don't need to do this."

Dmitri glared at him and said, "Do as I say. I'll trigger from here."

Konstantin slowly nodded, and Dmitri returned his eyes to the alley. Konstantin stood up, and Dmitri touched his arm. Konstantin looked at him, and, in a whisper, Dmitri said, "If you question me again, I'll see you disappear. Do you understand?"

Dmitri saw the requisite fear in Konstantin's face, his head nodding rapidly, and Dmitri said, "Go. Get Yuri and set up a box at the other end of the alley."

"What if he heads back into the city? On his usual route?"

"He won't be coming this way again. If I were to guess, they'll eat deeper in Gamla Stan, not in the city proper. If that were the plan, they'd have just stayed on that side of the river instead of coming home."

Konstantin nodded again, and Dimitri said, "Go, before he comes out. I'll trigger when he leaves."

Forty minutes later, the setting sun losing its warmth in the fight with the chill of the wind coming from the water at his back, Dmitri considered calling it a night, believing the dinner was happening inside the apartment. He started to key his radio when he saw the outside security man stand up and move to the door. He waited, then saw the door open, Lars and his Turkish companion appearing with the final security man. They took a right, heading deeper into the old town.

He radioed, "They're on the move, coming your way."

Yuri came back, "Headed south, next to the George statue, passing our hotel. I didn't get a photo of the Turk. No time."

Konstantin said, "I got 'em, I got 'em. They're just strolling. No issues. Street is crowded."

Dmitri stood up, moving rapidly south on the road next to the water, intent on getting ahead of his quarry. After three blocks he cut into the narrow streets of the old town, running into a boisterous group of football fans all singing in unison and blocking the road.

He threaded through them trying to reach a cross street to interdict his quarry when Konstantin came on, saying, "I've lost them in a crowd. A bunch of drunk football fans."

He started to press faster, bumping into the men singing and drawing their ire. One slammed him against a wall, saying, "Watch where you're going."

He pushed back, ready to fight, and realized he was compromising the entire mission. He held up his hands, said he was sorry, and the crowd swirled forward, flags snapping, beer bottles dropping, and the man who'd shoved him slapping him on the shoulder like it was nothing and moving on. Within seconds, he was alone on the street again.

He looked up the alley to the north and saw Konstantin, who shrugged, meaning they'd lost them. Yuri came on, saying, "Got eyes on the target. I don't know the street. No signs, but they're in a square passing an American Burger King."

Dmitri googled on his phone and saw the fast-food chain only fifty meters away, in a small open area with the intersection of five different avenues. He said, "I'm close. I'll follow up. Stay on them."

He reached the Burger King and said, "Which way? Which road?"

"They're headed northwest on a shopping promenade called Vaster-something-or-other. Moving slow and talking, stopping every few steps to stare into a window."

Dmitri looked at his phone, saw the street named Vasterlanggatan, and called Konstantin, saying, "Get ahead of them. I'll back up Yuri."

He threaded through the pedestrians at a rapid pace, and then saw Yuri looking in a window, Lars and the rest just a few feet ahead. He slowed and let them continue. Eventually they took a left turn on a side street, and he heard Konstantin say, "I've got them. Pull back."

He reached Yuri and they held up at the corner, waiting. Konstantin said, "They just entered a pub. Liffeys or something. Do you want me to penetrate with them?"

"No. I'll go in with Yuri. You stay outside."

Yuri said, "You want to go in? What's the point? The longer we stay on him, the greater the chance he'll spot us. It's not like he's going to repeat this track in the future. It serves no purpose."

"I want a picture of the Turk for higher. This is as much about him as it is Lars."

Yuri started to protest, then simply nodded, resigned. Dmitri said, "I'll go in first, to the far side of the establishment. You come in a minute after, posting on the near side. First one to get a picture calls it and we're out of here."

Dmitri didn't wait for a response, turning and threading through the pedestrians on the street until he reached the outside of the pub, now surrounded by football fans cheering and shouting. He saw Konstantin and went to him, asking, "Did they get a table? Is it dinner?"

Konstantin said, "I lost them. I don't know, but I can't see eating in that place right now. It's insane."

Dmitri looked at the crowds and nodded, saying, "Stage out here. Wait for my call. Yuri will be in shortly. We get a picture of the Turk, and we're gone."

Dmitri went inside the pub, pushing through the cheering fans, moving deeper into the establishment. It was open, paneled in dark wood with high-top tables, a long bar, and couches threaded throughout, packed with drinkers taking up space wherever available. A giant ninety-inch wide-screen television was on the far side, with standing room only watching the football match.

He threaded through the patrons, looking for his prey, and located them at a table against the front window, the two men deep in conversation, the security personnel sitting on either side, looking uncomfortable. He saw Yuri come in and nodded, getting his attention on the target, then continued forward, wading into the crowd in front of the television.

He pretended to watch the game, thinking about how he could get a picture. He turned, saw the men standing up, and pulled out his phone. He focused on the Turk and attempted a photo, getting jostled just as he pressed the shutter. The picture came out unusable. He raised it again and saw one of the security men staring, looking right at him. He rotated the phone and pretended to take a selfie of himself in the crowd.

They circled around the tables until they reached a stairwell Dmitri hadn't noticed before, then disappeared below, the security man staring at him the entire time. Dmitri tapped a man on the shoulder and, in English, said, "Where's that go?"

"Cellar bar. But they don't show the game down there."

"Why are people going down then?"

"Karaoke. Stupid-ass karaoke." The man turned away to focus on the game again.

CHAPTER 14

Early November in Charleston meant I'd be still wearing shorts and driving with the top down. Not quite the same in Sweden. Once the sun went below the horizon, the cold started creeping in no matter how many layers I put on, the ground sapping the heat from my body like I was sitting on a bag of crushed ice. I stuffed my hands in the pockets of my down puffy and said, "You guys couldn't find an OP with a stump or something to sit on?"

Hunkered down next to me, Knuckles said, "You're getting soft with this GRS stuff. It's always good to get back to the roots. Back in the woods."

I grumbled, "Like *you* ever spent any time in the woods. Six months at BUD/S doesn't make you a forest warrior."

Knuckles was a Navy SEAL, which meant he thought he was God's gift to humanity, but at the end of the day, while he was most definitely skilled, after my time in the Army, I'd spent a hell of a lot more time in the woods than he had.

He laughed and said, "That's not what you said in Bosnia."

Which was a little true. He'd saved my life there once, but it was from the back of a helicopter, and he'd never let me live it down ever since.

I said, "What the hell does you flying in to save the day, after waking up in a hotel, have to do with an OP in the woods?"

He said, "You're breathing, aren't you? Although at this point, my judgment might be a little debatable."

I chuckled and said, "Well, I saved your ass on a boat once, so there's that, Navy man. You don't see me bragging about my seamanship because of it. And *you* set the observation point manning. You'd rather be sitting here with Veep?"

"I'd rather be sitting with anyone who didn't cry about the sticks and grass like you do."

Which we both knew was a lie. Knuckles was my 2IC—second-in-command—and he'd picked our OP locations. He wanted me here because he knew what I'd do in a gunfight. Nothing more. We were closer than brothers, and he wanted his brother next to him.

Not that Brett or Veep would be any slouch if push came to shove. Brett Thorpe—callsign Blood for a comment he'd made a long time ago about putting the old mother's cure mercurochrome on the stump of my lost finger, calling it Monkey's Blood—was a former Force Recon Marine, back before MARSOC was even a thing, and now a CIA paramilitary officer. Nicholas Seacrest—callsign Veep because when he'd joined the Taskforce he was the son of the vice president of the United States, who now happened to be the president—was a special operations Airforce Combat Controller. Both of them were handy in a gunfight, but Knuckles wanted me next to him. Most probably because of my witty disposition instead of my gunfighting skills.

He ignored my last comment, keying his mic and saying, "Blood, Blood, you okay?

Brett hated his callsign. Mainly because he was African American and thought it made him look like a gangbanger. Which is exactly why it stuck. Shouldn't have made that joke about Monkey's Blood when I was missing a finger.

He came back, saying, "This is Blood. Full view. No activity."

Knuckles said, "Roger. Koko, Koko, you good?"

Jennifer also hated her callsign, mainly because it came from a gorilla that could use sign language to talk. Nobody earned a callsign for doing something heroic, but some embraced them while others did not.

She came back, "In position. No change."

I'm sure Blaine was pissed that I hadn't called him. He was in the car with Koko, but I'd be damned if I was going to give him the satisfaction of a radio call. It was my team, and my rules. Not to mention the only reason we were freezing our ass off out here was because he'd ordered me to be here.

We had no idea what was about to happen. The only clue we had that anything was going on against an unknown Swedish diplomat was this meeting location, on this date. We didn't even know the time, just that it would be after sundown. So now we were stationed in two different OPs watching two different avenues of approach.

Knuckles and I were near the lake, overlooking a little picnic area. Brett and Veep were on the Ting itself, about fifty meters away, tucked into the wood line from the ring of stones. Blaine and Jennifer were in a car parked along a dirt road next to the small gravel lot for the entire area. The plan was simple: the OPs would see the meeting and determine if anything nefarious was afoot, and at the same time, Jennifer would beacon whatever car that showed up for follow-on operations.

If the meeting was benign—although that would be a stretch for anyone meeting out here after sundown—then we'd call it a wash. If we saw something that indicated future trouble, we'd track the vehicle to a bed-down location and continue from there.

We sat for about six hours, picking the grass and freezing our ass off, and I'd had about enough. I decided to call clamshell, meaning we were done.

I keyed my mic, gritting my teeth, because I'd have to talk to Blaine as the overarching commander, and said, "Beast, Beast, I think this is a dry hole."

He said, "Sun hasn't come out yet. Let it ride."

I knew the pressure he was under, working a covert operation inside an ally of the United States, and I wasn't going to increase it from my side. I actually pitied him a little bit. If they'd left it up to me, I'd be the one to blame, but now it was on him.

I said, "Roger all, sir. Standing by."

Right after I gave that report, Knuckles said, "I got something."

I said, "What?"

Jennifer came on, saying, "I've got an SUV coming in. Lights out, parking lights only. Driving slow."

I said, "Roger all," then to Knuckles, "What do you have?"

"A boat. Coming this way."

A boat?

I keyed my mic and said, "Koko, Koko, what do you have?"

"Vehicle went by us. Lost sight."

Jennifer and Blaine's vehicle was outside the parking area, about a hundred meters away, and no use. The nearest OP was Brett and Veep. I said, "Blood, Blood, what do you have?"

"I see them. I see them. SUV is parked. Two men, looking skittish."

I felt the adrenaline rise and fought to control it like I had a thousand times before.

I said, "Okay, this is it. Keep eyes on them. Koko, you ready?"

Jennifer came back, saying, "I'm ready. Just let me know they're at the meet. I need one minute."

Knuckles said, "That boat is coming in. Right here."

I looked out at the water, thinking, *Some drunk teenagers are going to break up our operation?* I had no idea how wrong I was.

Brett said, "I got them. Two men, walking through our area. They're coming to you."

Knuckles said, "The boat is coming in. Right here."

Brett said, "They have long guns. Two men with long guns. They're bad guys."

I watched through my NODs and saw them coming to the picnic area. I said, "Koko, Koko, I have them. Put on the beacon."

She said, "Moving."

Knuckles said, "Two men on the boat. One has a long gun . . ."

He paused and I looked at the lake, seeing the boat coming in. I said, "What?"

He said, "That gun's got a thermal."

I focused on the bow of the boat and saw a man with a rifle and what looked like an incredibly long scope. A thermal imaging device, meaning it wouldn't matter what camouflage we had, our body heat would show.

I said, "Have they seen us?"

"Not yet, but they will."

Knuckles had the only long gun in our little OP, because we really had no reason to think of a threat, but I trusted him to keep me safe. Now with a little bit of urgency, I keyed my mic, pulled out my Glock, and said, "Koko, Koko, you got the beacon? We have to exfil."

She said, "Roger. Beacon in place. What's up?"

And I heard the first snap of a round, right by my head. Then the world erupted in gunfire. The two men from the SUV began shooting all over the place, without any target, and I really wanted to shoot back, but doing so would have given away our position. The men in the boat weren't as wild with their firing.

I heard three more rounds punch by my head and said, "That fucker with the thermal has us. Get his ass."

Knuckles tucked into the butt of his weapon, got a sight picture, and squeezed the trigger. His voice as cold as the ground below us, he said, "Thermal guy is down. Fight or flee?"

I said, "Fucking fight."

I rolled to the right, brought up my Glock, drew a bead, and punched one of the SUV guys in the leg. The other began firing my way and I rolled back around the cover. Another round from the boat snapped by us and I said, "I thought you got the thermal guy?"

"Driver's got the weapon. Stand by."

He cracked a round, said, "He's down, too, but the SUV guys are running."

I rolled around my cover again and saw the two guys from the SUV sprint to the boat, diving in. The boat backed up, the two men shouting in a foreign language, and then it raced away. The world grew silent again.

I said, "What the fuck just happened?"

Knuckles laughed and said, "Well, if I were to guess, that intel was real."

"No doubt about that." I keyed the mic and said, "Beast, Beast, we're exfilling. Coming your way. Blood, Veep, break down the OP, meet back at the vehicle."

To Knuckles, I said, "Go get our equipment from the landing. I'll police this site up for brass. I want to be gone before there's any reaction from the locals. And by 'gone,' I mean out of this country."

He looked at me and smiled, saying, "I don't think that's going to happen now. We're in it on this one."

"I don't want to be in it. This isn't our mission set."

"Well, you've got Blaine here. For the first time ever, you don't need to make the decisions. Let him do it."

I grinned and said, "True. I hated this mission from the get-go. Let him figure it out."

CHAPTER 15

Yuri reached Dmitri by the television at the Irish bar, the crowd still shouting at the screen. He said, "We done?"

"No. I missed my picture, and I think the security guys are wary of me now. You go down to the cellar. Find them, get a snap, and get back up."

Yuri nodded and disappeared down the stairwell. Dmitri settled in to wait, thinking about actually buying a drink and enjoying the game with the rowdy patrons, but decided against it. One never knew what would come.

After twenty minutes he was growing tired of the crowd, the men all jostling back and forth, yelling and spilling their beer. He broke out of the group, looking for a table, but there wasn't one vacant. He thought about leaving and joining Konstantin outside when his radio earpiece came alive. He heard nothing but shouting. He ducked his head and clicked in, "Say again? Who is this?"

He heard more garbled words, overridden by the shouting, but caught "Yuri."

He said, "What's happening?"

He got garbled words back, and said, "Konstantin, Konstantin, did you get that?"

"No. I couldn't make it out."

Dmitri swore, making his decision. He didn't want to enter the cellar because of the interest the security man had shown him, but something was going on down there.

He went to the stairwell, seeing a black maw disappearing into a stone basement with a feeble overhead bulb at the end. He entered it, skipping down the stairs. He reached the bottom, the ceiling low, making him want to duck his head even as it was high enough to walk normally.

He turned right, saw a bar swarming with people a little different from the crowd upstairs. There were no football fans, just a rowdy group ranging in age from thirty to seventy. Echoing through the brick was a caterwauling of a voice singing—butchering—a song. He went past the bar, turning it to a narrow tunnel leading to another room that looked like it had been created for pirates to store their treasure, the stone of the pillars giving no confidence it could hold the floor of the bar above.

He entered and was immediately met by the target group headed the other way. The tunnel was so narrow he had to brush past them, ducking his head. He saw the security man from above follow him with his eyes and kept going, cursing himself. *Yuri was calling to say they were on the move. That's all.*

As soon as he entered the karaoke room, he recognized why he hadn't understood Yuri. The noise was deafening in the small enclosure. He looked around the dark room, lit with neon and spinning disco balls, and a forty-ish man on the stage singing an ABBA song.

He didn't see Yuri and knew his radio was useless in the din. He went to the bathroom, a cave with a cow-trough urinal against the wall and a smaller room much too large for the single toilet. He went inside the toilet room, closing the door. He keyed his radio, saying, "Yuri, Yuri, are you on?"

Behind him, he heard, "Speaking Russian. That's strange."

He turned and saw the security man from the upper level, his body half in the stall. Shocked, he immediately slacked his face to hide his surprise, but he knew the man had seen. In English, he said, "What? What was that?"

The security man said, "I said you're speaking Russian."

"No, I don't speak Russian. Who are you?"

The man smiled and said, "Look, we're just going to stay inside here for a few minutes. That's all."

"Why?"

"Because I don't trust you and I don't want you following my people."

"What are you talking about? I'm here for the football match. And I'm leaving to go back upstairs."

The man said, "Really? Who's playing?"

Dmitri stammered for a second and the security man pulled out a pistol, saying, "You're going to stay right here until my principal is home safe. And you're going to give me your radio."

Dmitri backed up, raising his hands, saying, "Whoa, whoa, what is this?"

The man fully entered the stall and Dmitri saw Yuri appear behind, lunging forward, a knife in his hand. The security man's eyes sprang open in pain and Dmitri launched himself at the man, trapping the pistol while slapping a hand over his mouth. Yuri raised the body off the ground, twisting the blade, and the man bucked for a few seconds, then grew still. Yuri lowered him to the floor, pulling out a dagger from the back.

Dmitri hissed, "What the fuck did you just do? I could have talked my way out of this."

Yuri checked for a pulse, wiped his blade, and said, "Bullshit. He was on to you. Best case, you would have talked your way out, but he would have become extra vigilant because of this. Worst case, he would have had you arrested tonight."

Incensed, Dimitri said, "*This* is the worst case. The fucker is dead! How is that going to look for tomorrow?"

"At least he didn't tell anyone what he feared tonight. You wanted a picture of the Turk." Yuri dug through the man's pockets, pulling out a cell phone. He pointed it at Dmitri and said, "I'll bet he has one of you too. I just prevented him from using it to figure out who you are."

Dmitri grimaced and said, "At least tell me you got one of the Turk."

"I did," Yuri said. "Come on. Let's get him on the toilet."

Dmitri grabbed the dead man's arms, saying, "They're going to wonder where he is." He flicked his head to the pool of blood under the body, saying, "It's not like we can hide this. When he's found, it's going to be a shit storm."

Yuri grabbed his legs and said, "Couldn't be helped. We'd be fucked either way. All we need now is to get out of here. It will look like a mugging."

They shoved him on the toilet, Yuri pushed his head back against the wall, and Dmitri closed the door, hiding the body from view. They threaded through the karaoke singers at a rapid pace, taking the stairs two at a time. They reached the top, saw the same football crowd from before, but no sign of Lars or his Turkish friend. They exited, with Dmitri saying, "Get that picture to Control. Tell them the opportunity."

"Opportunity? We kill Lars tomorrow morning and we're done. Let's not make this more complicated."

Dmitri called Konstantin and got a fix for his location, then turned to Yuri and said, "The Motherland is the mission. Send the picture and ask for further guidance."

Yuri did so, and they linked up with Konstantin at the same cross street where they'd split, with Dmitri saying, "Did you see the target leave?"

"Yeah, they left minus the last security guy. Just went about their way. I followed them for a couple of blocks and quit when you called. What's up?"

They started walking back to their hotel, Dmitri telling him what happened. Konstantin heard the story and was amazed. He said, "We can't continue now. How can we continue?"

Yuri said, "They don't know it was us. It's just a dead body."

"Yeah, but they'll be on edge now. Looking for us. We need to reassess."

Dmitri said, "We need to succeed in the mission. That's all. We kill that guy tomorrow and we'll fly home. We take him in the morning on the way to work, before he meets the Turks and their security force."

They reached the hotel and entered the lobby, seeing the bartender wave at them. Dmitri's phone rang and he pulled it out, saying, "Man, that guy loves us. Go get us some drinks."

Yuri and Konstantin walked away, Yuri letting Konstantin order while he kept an eye on Dmitri. Yuri watched him speak, seeing him become agitated. Eventually, Dmitri joined them at the bar, grabbing his drink and taking a long pull. They took a seat at a table in the rear of the lobby and Yuri said, "So? What's up?"

"We can't take him in the morning, when he's by himself. We have to do it the hard way."

Konstantin said, "What's that mean?"

"They want the Turk as well. We kill them both, when they're out tomorrow."

Yuri slapped the table with his hand, saying, "How are we going to do that? A gangland hit? We'll never get out of here without getting arrested. We don't even have weapons."

"We'll get the weapons. That's the only thing that's going right in this mission."

And then his phone rang again.

CHAPTER 16

Sitting in an ornate chair in the anteroom of Vladimir Putin's cavernous study, Victor's left knee ripped up and down like a jackhammer, the adrenaline something he couldn't control unless he tensed the quad muscles of his leg. He'd done so, then began thinking of the problem, losing focus on the leg, and it began again, unbidden.

From his meeting yesterday afternoon, he knew Putin was less than pleased, both at what he'd told him and because of the latest news coming from Ukraine. Putin had put his faith in Victor, and Victor had let him down. The killing in Gamla Stan was reminiscent of the mistakes the GRU had made in their recent operations around the world, and now he had something worse to tell the leader who held his fate.

Yesterday's meeting had not gone well. Putin was under enormous pressure, with Finland saying for the first time that they would accept NATO membership without Sweden being admitted simultaneously, and the battle for cities in eastern Ukraine becoming a debacle. The killing in Gamla Stan was not welcome news, but the picture of the Turkish diplomat had been a little silver lining in the storm.

Victor had said that they could take the Swede the following morning, and, almost apoplectic, Putin had ordered that the Turkish man die as well. Victor knew that would be exponentially harder, but he was too fearful to say anything, truthfully glad that there was somebody else to redirect Putin's anger. He'd agreed, then received the situation report from the weapons transfer.

And now he had to report that as well.

The door opened and a man he hadn't seen before waved him in. He entered, and the man stood respectfully by the door. Wearing a three-piece suit that was too small for his body, a hitch on his hip from a gun, he was clearly security.

Behind the desk was Putin, pretending to be studying some papers. Putin looked up and waved him to the same wingbacked chair he'd sat in before, saying, "I thought we were done yesterday. Is there some other news? Good, I hope?"

"No, sir. It's bad. The weapons transfer was hit by someone. Someone unknown."

Victor saw Putin's face go red and waited for the explosion. It didn't come. He said, "What does that mean?"

"We used the criminal contacts I told you about to get the weapons, and the linkup plan was secure, but someone was there, waiting. There was a gunfight. The two men with the weapons were killed."

"So what's that mean? You cannot do the hit?"

"No, sir, we can do the hit. My men got out and have the weapons, but someone was there. They were waiting on us. I'm not sure we should continue, because I believe we've been compromised by Western intelligence somehow."

Putin thumped his fist on the desk and said, "It's not Western intelligence. It's the GRU. It's Operation Valkyrie. They're trying to stop you. Stop *me*."

Victor was startled, saying, "Sir? Why would they do anything in Sweden? It would only expose them."

"They know about my plans. I don't know how, but they know. You can still do the hit?"

"Yes, sir."

"Then do it. Take out both the Swede and the Turkish envoy. We can't show weakness by fleeing."

Victor nodded, afraid to reiterate his concerns.

Putin said, "Where do we stand in Copenhagen? What are the chances they're compromised as well due to your incompetence?"

Victor stiffened and said, "Sir, there was no incompetence on my part. Whatever means they used to learn about that linkup came from somewhere else, most likely with the criminals we were buying the weapons from. You know they work with everyone, including the GRU. Someone must have talked, and that sloppiness cost them with their lives."

Mollified, Putin said, "Okay. So, where do we stand? Is there risk like in Sweden? Did you deal with leaky criminal elements?"

Victor relaxed and said, "No. We infiltrated the team into a lawless village called Christiana, a little area that's literally its own enclave in Copenhagen. It's a little bit of a live-and-let-live type of thing, with the authorities looking the other way while the village sells drugs and other things. The team is secure and isolated from any other elements, but we still only have that one tenuous link to exploit. It's not like Sweden, where we have a known target. I can't promise we'll get anything from it, unless you have more intelligence to increase our fidelity for targeting."

Putin said, "I don't, but that link will work. It's solid." He smiled, saying, "It came from the GRU. Use it to track these Valkyrie bastards, and then destroy them."

George Wolffe followed the national security advisor Alexander Palmer into the Oval Office, expecting to see the principals of the Oversight Council. While the council held thirteen seats, sometimes, due to the speed of events, the five most important members would convene, called the principals. In this case, he only saw President Hannister and the director of central intelligence, Kerry Bostwick, which was a little bit odd.

The second odd event came when Palmer exited the room, leaving them alone. That had never happened before. Palmer was a bit of an information hog, constantly trying to weasel Taskforce inside information well outside of his authority, and his leaving the room caused Wolffe no small amount of angst.

The door to the Oval Office closed and Wolffe said, "Sir? Where's everyone else? The rest of the principals?"

"We don't need them for this. The circle here has gotten quite small due to the sensitivities in play." He held up a situation report that Wolffe had sent about the activities the previous night in Sweden—the reason for Wolffe's presence at the White House—saying, "No more formal SITREPs. From now on, this is all verbal, and just between you, me, and Kerry here."

Which was saying something, since the activities of the Taskforce were the highest classification the United States had in its arsenal. They were already illegal, so if the president of the United States was now saying that the usual protocols for Taskforce reporting were too great a risk, they were entering uncharted waters.

Wolffe said, "Okay, sir. Got it, but why?"

"This is extraordinarily sensitive. So much so I want it compartmented even from the Oversight Council. We're operating in an allied country that's currently working very hard to support our efforts in Ukraine. If it's exposed in any way, it will be explosive, and the reverberations will be felt far beyond the simple operation itself. This won't just be a diplomatic spat, like I bugged the German chancellor's phone."

Taken aback again, Wolffe said, "Sir? We're going to compartment this from the entire council?"

"Well, just you, me, and Kerry here."

Then the implications sank in. "Wait, do you mean you want me to continue? You want the team to continue after the gunfight? It's exactly the potential explosive results you just described. It's my recommendation that we exfiltrate the country immediately. Actually, it's not my recommendation. It's the team's recommendation. Like I said in the SITREP, they don't feel like they can continue without compromise."

Kerry finally spoke. "George, I understand where you're coming from, but this isn't a lone-wolf terrorist out to blow up a car. This is much bigger. We're in great-power competition here, with repercussions to the national security of the United States extending from Europe to the Taiwan Strait. If we fail here, we're looking at a long, dark time against peer competitors beyond the fight in Ukraine."

Wolffe rolled his eyes and said, "Okay, Kerry, save that speech for the next time you're in front of the Intelligence Committee trying to increase your budget. I don't need it. The bottom line is we had a gunfight, the men escaped on a boat, and we don't have a thread to follow even if we want to. How about you vaunted CIA guys start doing something for a change? This is *not* our mission set."

Usually compatriots, with the D/CIA being Wolffe's ally in every argument involving the Oversight Council, Kerry's face colored, shocked at the attack.

Wolffe backed off, saying, "Sorry, Kerry. That was uncalled for, but you know this isn't what we do."

"It *is* what you do. It's manhunting. What we're talking about is *exactly* what you do, but the repercussions just happen to be much greater."

President Hannister held up his hand, stopping the discussion. He pointed to the situation report Wolffe had provided, saying, "What's this about a vehicle that you beaconed? Can't you follow that?"

"No, sir. We believe that the men at the linkup spot were planning on returning to the vehicle, which is why we placed the beacon. After the gunfight, they escaped in a boat. The vehicle is still there. They more than likely aren't going back to it. Wherever they are now, it's probably not going to involve that vehicle again."

Wolffe started to say something else, then thought better of it. President Hannister saw the hesitance and said, "What?"

Really wanting to get Pike's team off the continent, but feeling the responsibility of his command—of reporting exactly what he had—Wolffe sighed, saying, "Pike broke into the vehicle. There was nothing inside that would help identify who the men were or where they may be going, but it has a system attached to it that Pike thinks functions like OnStar here in the United States, so the rental company can protect its investment."

"What's that mean?"

"It means if we hack it, we can determine wherever that vehicle has been. We can see where it came from, which might—I stress, *might*—be where they're going back to."

President Hannister smiled and said, "Well, there you go. Get to work on it."

"Sir, I really think we should be leaving the continent. Pike is extremely skittish of this mission, and he's *never* skittish."

Hannister said, "Well, tell Pike it's not his call. He continues. We'll reassess if this thread doesn't work out, but he continues."

"Sir . . ."

"That's it, George. This is too important."

"That wasn't what I was going to say."

"What then?"

"Just that you remember this decision. Pike doesn't believe in this mission, but sooner or later he will. I know him, and when he does—when he switches over—you'd better back him up, because he's going full bore."

President Hannister said, "That's exactly what I want."

Wolffe smiled for the first time, saying, "That's what you want *now*. We'll see about later."

CHAPTER 17

Perun drank his coffee in the hotel's breakfast area, waiting on Dishka to arrive, an hour late. He kept his eye on the escalator, then saw the sandy hair and unkempt beard of Dishka coming down. He reached the bottom, turned away from the reception desk, and Perun held up his hand.

Dishka took a seat, his eyes bloodshot, a sheepish grin on his face, saying, "Sorry I'm a little late."

Perun smiled and said, "Doesn't worry me. You're the one who missed breakfast, but we still have time for coffee. So, you went out last night?"

Dishka grinned again and said, "Of course I did. You think I wouldn't? We both might be dead in a week." He waved his hand around the lobby and said, "And this is a hell of a lot better than a bombed-out hut in Ukraine, eating stale bread while warming our hands over a campfire."

They had been put up in a hotel called Skt. Petri near the old Latin Quarter of Copenhagen. Once a department store, it was now a quirky boutique place that was a world apart from where both men had just come, as was Copenhagen itself—something Dishka was taking full advantage of.

He continued, "At the least, I got a bunch of new socks. One thing NATO can do is spend money."

In addition to extracting Perun's entire team, NATO had outfitted each of them with new clothes so that they would blend into the ebb and flow of pedestrian traffic in Copenhagen, without looking like resistance fighters who had just been pulled from the woods of Ukraine.

Truth be told, while the other members of the conference were official, and could actively talk about why they'd come to Copenhagen, Perun and his team could not. The NATO allies wanted their participation kept secret, and so, unlike the rest of the military attending the conference, all staying at a much larger establishment, Perun and his team had been put up in this kitschy hotel.

The team certainly didn't mind.

Perun said, "We have about forty-five minutes before the introductory meeting. We could walk, which takes about thirty minutes, or we could take the metro and sit here for a little longer. Your choice."

Dishka stood up and said, "Let's walk. I could use the air."

They took the escalator down to the ground level and exited, taking a left and entering the flow of people swirling about, a world away from where they'd come. Walking down the narrow alleys and avenues, past the cafés and small stores, Dishka said, "This isn't too much different than Kyiv. Back in the day."

Perun laughed and said, "By 'back in the day,' you mean before it was hammered by the Russians?"

"Yes."

The air was crisp, but not unduly so, as the sun fought to provide some heat in the morning dew. They meandered in silence for a little while, lost in their thoughts, passing squares full of people shopping and street vendors attempting to sell them tours. Something that used to happen in Kyiv as well.

Without even meaning to, they went down a short tunnel and entered the giant plaza where the royal family of Denmark lived, Perun amazed at the lack of security. Ukraine had no royalty, but its president was constantly under threat, and he longed for his seat of government to earn a time when they, too, could live like this.

Today he might just find out if he could be a small piece of making that happen. Not in the conference he was attending, but in the meeting afterwards.

They continued north, strolling like everyone else, leaving behind the cloistered shops of the old town and entering more hectic, modern thoroughfares. Dishka said, "You never told me the plan for today."

Perun knew what he was asking, and was willing to talk now. He had his entire five-man team here, and they'd be attending the conference after the weekend, but Friday's meeting—today's meeting—was simply introductions of the leadership, letting everyone know who's who in the zoo. He had kept them all in the dark on the secondary meeting.

He said, "My phone initiated last night. I got a message."

Dishka snapped his head to Perun and said, "So we're in play? It was real?"

"Apparently it was. We'll see. I didn't tell the team because I don't know. It'll be you and me making the meeting."

"When is it? I mean, we might be in this thing all day long."

"It's immediately after our meeting with NATO."

"But we don't know when that will end."

"We don't, but Daniel said he would know. I don't know how, but after seeing where this conference is going to be held, I'm pretty sure he'll just have surveillance on the entrance. He'll see us leave, and initiate the meeting."

Dishka took that in, then said, "Is there risk here? I mean, do you trust him?"

"I don't trust him yet, but there's no risk in this setting, other than giving him more information about us. That's a risk, but one I'm willing to take. Worst case, nothing comes from that meeting and we learn what these NATO guys know, go home, and use it."

Dishka scoffed and said, "What can they teach us about fighting in Ukraine? I'm glad to be here, no doubt, but really, we should be teaching *them*."

Perun stopped in the street and said, "Don't feel arrogant here. The men we're going to meet are hard. They've fought, too, just not in Ukraine."

Dishka saw the disapproval on Perun's face and said, "I didn't mean that. Just that we've been doing the fighting at home. Not them."

Perun started walking again and said, "That's true, but like I said, if Daniel doesn't work out, we're going back to Ukraine, and we always need munitions, communications, targeting, intelligence, and everything else. This will help, and they're good at what they do."

"Who are 'they'? You've never said."

"Honestly, I'm not sure who's going to show up. I know that the Jaegers here in Denmark are hosting the event, and it's chaired by the United States Special Operations Command in Europe. The U.K. SAS will be there, along with the German KSK. All of them have fought in Iraq and Afghanistan. Not our fight, but nothing to sneeze at, either. The United States has come up with something called the 'resistance operating concept,' with a focus on solidifying people like us for the fight. It sounds good to me."

"No Ukrainians other than us?"

Perun laughed and said, "Of course there will be other Ukrainians. The primary reason they're doing it is for our own special operations command. They'll be here as the number one reason for the meeting. We're number two, here to offer on-the-ground experience and advice."

They reached a major road intersection with tour buses coming and going out of a circle with a large fountain at the top, a waterfall spilling to a second level. Dishka said, "Wonder what's up there?"

Perun said, "Some statue of a mermaid. I don't get it. It's apparently like four feet tall out in the water, but has become famous for some reason. Come on, we go to the left."

They did and passed a round building with a sign that said, "Danish Resistance Museum," a park spilling out behind it.

Dishka saw the sign and said, "We should check that out. See how these guys worked in World War Two."

Perun kept walking, saying, "We will. That's the meeting site."

Surprised, Dishka said, "Seriously?"

"Yep." Perun turned inward to the park, following a gravel path until they reached a wooden bridge over a span of water, a fortress from the seventeenth century beyond, complete with bastions and rock walls.

Dishka said, "This is it? We're doing the conference at a tourist site?"

Perun smiled, watching the joggers and bikers coming and going across the bridge, families with children throwing food to ducks in the water, and said, "Yes. Believe it or not."

They started walking across the bridge and Dishka said, "Why here?"

"Denmark's special operations command and the Jaeger Corps are stationed at an air base about four hours from here. It's constantly monitored by the Russians. This place has been here forever, but apparently still has an active military intelligence brigade assigned. It was picked for the conference."

Dishka said, "Yeah, I bet it was because of the Russians and not because all these NATO boys would rather be in Copenhagen instead of some air base out in the tundra."

Perun chuckled and said, "I'm sure that works for you as well."

They reached a stone portal manned by two people in military uniforms, but there were no entrance requirements, as civilians were coming and going, some jogging, some pushing strollers. They passed through it and entered history.

Called Kastellet, it was shaped like a pentagon, with bastions in all four corners, complete with a moat, and it had defended Denmark since 1663. Its loss in World War II led to the occupation of Denmark by the Nazis, and in fact Germany occupied it for the duration of the war. Now it was a quasi–tourist site, quasi–still operational military base.

They went down a cobblestone road and saw barracks off to the left, a flurry of activity and sawhorse barricades in place, several men in uniform standing about a vehicle checkpoint, bored.

Perun said, "That's the place."

They went down to the checkpoint, the only people not in uniform, and were stopped. The guard said something in Danish, pointing back to the tourist area, and Perun said in English, "We're supposed to be here. We're here for the Jaeger conference. With SOCEUR."

Taken aback, the man got on a radio, and soon enough, two men in American uniforms came out, both wearing U.S. Special Forces insignia. Perun recognized them as the ones who'd picked them up in Germany and flown them to Copenhagen, and he saw them break into broad smiles, the first saying, "I was worried you'd still be out partying."

Perun shook his hand and said, "That's Dishka's job."

That brought out a laugh from everyone, and they were led into a large conference room, complete with audiovisual aids and full of people in different military uniforms. They were stared at for a minute, and then the Ukrainian SOF commander saw them, coming over and shaking their hands. He said, "Thank you for coming. Your contributions will be invaluable."

Perun said, "Thank you for having us. And I hope so." Not letting on what he really meant.

The meeting was called to order, and Perun quickly grew bored. One introduction after another, with speeches by all. Eventually, after a schedule was posted and more pontificating, they were allowed to leave, asked to bring the entire team back on Monday for tabletop exercises and something called "breakout sessions" where the team would split up among the groups, giving their expertise.

Before he left, the U.S. Special Forces officer said, "Enjoy the weekend."

Perun said, "Maybe we will, maybe we won't. We'll see in the next few minutes."

The officer looked at him strangely, but assumed it was a language barrier thing. Perun and Dishka left, walking back across the bridge. Dishka said, "Man, those guys can blab. Maybe that's the resistance theory. Talk Russia to death."

Perun chuckled and said, "Maybe so. Look, when we get in here, let me do the meeting. I want you to be looking around. Just in case."

Dishka nodded, saying, "You feel a threat here?"

They reached the door of the museum and he said, "No, but I didn't in Ukraine early on, either."

They purchased tickets and entered, going down a darkened stairwell for two flights until they were completely underground. They turned the corner, showed an usher their tickets, and she gave them two headsets, pointing the way for the unguided tour. Perun didn't have any other specific instructions, other than to take the tour, so they set out.

The museum itself was a maze, and very dark, with video silhouette reenactments at each station describing the various resistance activities of the Danish forces in World War II. Dishka listened intently, so much so that Perun had to chastise him to pay attention. On the third station, Dishka nudged him. Perun looked up and saw Daniel, his own headset on.

Daniel said, "So you made it."

"I told you I would. I do what I say. How about you?"

A group from the last station entered theirs and he said, "Let's keep moving."

They went to the next station, hit the play button on the display, and Daniel said, "Yes, I do what I say as well. I'm not there yet, but I will be."

"What's that mean?"

"I'm meeting some Israelis this weekend for the method of engagement. If that fails, I have another way."

"So what do we do? We have to be at the conference on Monday."

"How long is the conference? How many days?"

"I think it ends Wednesday."

Daniel thought a moment, then said, "That will work." He said, "Find a place here in town to get passport-sized photos for each of your team." He reached into his pocket and said, "This is the code for a locker at the Queen's Library. Go there on Sunday. Put the photos inside it. You'll find further instructions on when to return to the locker."

Suspicious, Perun said, "Passport-sized photos? For what? Why do you want our pictures?"

Daniel smiled and said, "For passports. You can't be running around as Ukrainians for this mission."

Shocked at how much support and trust Daniel was giving, Perun grew suspicious, saying, "Why are you doing this?"

"The same reason you are. For my country. Don't read into it. Just do it. If I wanted to kill you, I could have done it in here."

Perun nodded, starting to believe, and took the slip of paper. He said, "The next meeting will be here, and I'll get the time from the locker?"

"No. Never the same place twice. I have to figure out some things before I give you the full mission profile. Now get out of here. You go first. I'll follow."

Perun nodded, liking the tradecraft, but still said, "If you set me up, if you set up my team, I have others who will find you."

Daniel smiled and said, "Trust me, I have more dangerous men than you trying to find me right now." And he wandered away, deeper into the museum.

Perun and Dishka took the elevator to the top, exiting the museum into the November sunshine, the brisk air bracing, the cold welcoming, unlike what he'd experienced in Ukraine, when the elements were an enemy all their own. Perun took a deep breath, enjoying it, yearning for the same in his own country again.

And for the first time, he began to believe he might be able to make that come true.

CHAPTER 18

I heard the knock on my bedroom door and knew who it was. Jennifer saw my face and said, "You expecting someone?"

I said, "It's Blaine. He's pissed about the hotel. Or more likely pissed that nobody's listening to him. Why don't you rotate someone out of the lobby? I'll call when this is over."

She nodded, saying, "Well, you have to admit, this choice was a little bit nonstandard."

She grabbed her purse, saying, "Don't get in a fight here, Pike. He's in charge."

I said, "Yeah, yeah. That's what he's here to tell me, I'm sure."

She opened the door, saying, "Blaine, hey. I'm headed to the lobby to rotate. You want anything from the restaurant?"

"No thanks. Already eaten. Pike here?"

"Right behind me." She walked out and Blaine entered. He closed the door and said, "Pike, we need to talk about this hotel."

I said, "Sir, we already did. We don't have a lot of time to plan for some long-range surveillance effort, and this was the best choice, given the circumstances."

That was true, as far as it went, but I'd also picked it because I was aggravated that the Oversight Council had ordered us to continue—after we'd had a gunfight—and I knew it would piss off Blaine. I was adamant we should be flying back across the pond, and I was the man on the ground, something that should have been sacrosanct, given the potential blowback from our compromise.

Usually it was me thumbing my nose at the Oversight Council, pushing the boundaries for what was permissible while they wrung their hands at my antics. This time, after I told them we need to leave, they ordered me to continue. For the first time, I was the one being told to complete the mission, compromise be damned. It galled the hell out of me.

Should have never told them about that OnStar thing . . .

It wasn't really OnStar, but it worked the same way. It was some fleet-tracking device the rental company used to make sure the terms of the rental contract weren't being exceeded—like driving too fast or crossing a border you said you wouldn't. I knew it would have a history of wherever the SUV had been, and so I'd been ordered to help Creed crack the cloud service where the data was stored.

We'd fled the scene of the crime after the shoot-out, found a little hotel about twenty minutes away, and sent the SITREP, then waited on a response. The decision wasn't what I wanted to hear. Going back to the vehicle was the last thing I wanted to do, but it was the only way that Creed could get the geolocation data.

Veep and I went back, him because he was pretty good with all things digital, and me because I wasn't going to let anyone else do it. If I saw a single police vehicle, we were aborting. Unfortunately, we hadn't. The SUV was still sitting there in the darkness and cold, nothing around to indicate anyone had heard anything from earlier.

By the time we'd gotten there, Creed was already inside the company cloud. He just needed the specifics of our vehicle. We sent him the VIN, which did no good, frustrating the hell out of me. The data wasn't tied to the vehicle, but to the device transmitting the data. We were forced to dig around until we found the actual computer widget mounted in the rear of the vehicle. A literal black box. We sent him the serial number, and we were in business. As soon as he had the jackpot, we left again.

By the time we'd returned, Jennifer had the track of the vehicle up on a laptop screen and everyone was arguing about what we should do. It turned out the nest for the thing was back in Stockholm, but it was a public parking garage—not anything associated with a hotel or other bed-down site. So the argument was to search the garage for a similar SUV from the same rental agency—the thought being these guys weren't alone—or do a search of hotels within a one-mile radius.

Neither one of those was appealing to me. While the team hashed it out, Veep took a deeper look at the GPS track, and then called me over, saying, "Hey, I have one anomaly here."

"What?"

"Three times, the vehicle pulled over and sat for between four and eleven minutes before moving again. Same location each time."

"And?"

"It's the front of a hotel in Gamla Stan, right on the water, and that hotel has no parking."

He pulled up a website for a place called Hotel Reisen, and it was just as he described. I was convinced the vehicle was going there to pick someone up or drop them off, and that target was a hell of a lot more precise than running around parking garages looking for rental cars.

So I'd reserved rooms for all of us in the target hotel. Which, of course, was the last thing one would want to do if you wanted to track someone staying there. It was asking to get burned, quite probably right at check-in, but we didn't have time to screw around, and I was seriously pissed about being given the mission in the first place.

And now Blaine wanted to talk.

I saw his face and said, "Sir, so far it looks like it's working out. I still think this is like a fart in the wind, but it might actually be something. You ordered me to continue, and so I did. We couldn't rotate people in and out of this place from a different hotel trying to find the targets, so I opted to come here."

"*Here* is exactly where the targets might be. We'll blow this mission before it even gets off the ground."

"*Might be* is right. And my team are the ones that found that as well."

Once we'd relocated to the hotel, I'd put Creed to work again. Every respectable hotel in Sweden—Europe, actually—required one to show a passport at check-in. Since we had the location, but not the target, I'd let everyone grab some shut-eye and then called Creed again, having him penetrate the database of the Reisen.

First, we'd checked for Russians, but had come up empty, which really stood to reason, since Russians were decidedly unwelcome in Sweden now. It really would have been nice to see five passports labeled "Russian Assassin," but apparently, they weren't that stupid.

What we did find were six Belarusian businessmen who'd checked in at the same time three days before. I'd decided to focus on them because Belarus was a Russian client state, full of the same bad guys we were hunting. It could be Russians using Belarus passports, or it might be bad guys from Belarus paid by Russians. I didn't care either way; it was the closest thread we had.

We downloaded their pictures, passed them around, and now were basically rotating people inside the lobby waiting to spot one. Once that happened, we'd start a follow to confirm or deny that they were up to bad things.

Blaine said, "Okay, Pike, we'll stay here, but you need to get your head around who's in charge here. I'm not saying that as a glory hog.

I'm saying it because you doing your own thing isn't going to be allowed. I was sent here because of the sensitivity of this mission, and I'm the guy who's talking to Wolffe—and by extension, the president."

I actually felt sorry for him. Blaine Alexander and I had worked plenty of missions together, and I trusted him, but he was in a serious shit sandwich here, with Wolffe on one side and me on the other. He was missing a key component, though, and I let him know what that was.

"Sir, you get to give me operational control. That's it. It's just like the Oversight Council writ large. They tell us if we can execute, and then we do, but they don't tell us how. It's the same here. This is *my* team. You order me to execute, and I will, but don't start telling me how the tactics are going to work. In my mind we should be about six hours over the Atlantic right now."

He held up his hands and said, "Okay, okay, I get you don't like this mission. I don't like it, either, but we get orders."

I got angry and said, "*You* get orders and you take them lying down. You know this is a bad thing. This is what's going to compromise us."

I shook my head and turned away, looking out the window. "I can't believe I'm saying this . . . I can't believe I'm the guy saying we should flee, but this mission is wrong here. The world isn't going to end if this guy gets smoked, and this isn't our mission set."

Blaine said, "Pike, there are a lot of people in the administration who disagree. They think this is pretty important."

I snarled, "They're not on the goddamned ground! You are."

He held up his hands and said, "Okay, I get it. Look, you went to the SUV and nobody was around. No cops, no investigation. No chance of compromise. It's as if we just landed here completely clean, and I'm wondering why you're getting so pissed about everything."

He was right. The truth was we had a gunfight, but like a tree falling in the forest that makes no sound, nobody had heard it, and nobody seemed to care. I realized I was just aggravated because nobody was listening to me. My ego was getting the better of me, which was the last thing a team leader should do. I also realized that Blaine was being the real leader, letting me know that without outright telling me so.

I shook my head and said, "Touché. I get it. Sorry about being a prick, but you know this mission is shit."

He laughed and said, "Well, sorry I didn't tell the command more forcefully, but I thought your SITREP would do the work."

He looked at his watch and said, "It's close to four P.M. now. It took us so long to work this thread, we probably missed them anyway. They probably left this morning while we were still trying to figure out who they were."

And then our radios came alive. "Pike, this is Koko. We've got three of the targets leaving together."

I smiled at him and said, "Execute the surveillance plan."

Blaine said, "I'll start shacking up a SITREP in case this needs to go kinetic."

Slapping on gear, I said, "No you won't. Fuck those guys. They gave us our orders, and now we execute."

He said, "Pike, this is really sensitive."

I paused and said, "What? You afraid of going out?"

"Huh? No, what do you mean? I'm the control."

I said, "Not today. I'm the control, and it'll be from on the ground, not in this hotel. Get some kit on. We're going to need everyone for this."

He didn't assimilate my words at first. He paused for a moment, thinking about his duties as the Omega leader, then thinking about what I'd said. I knew which way he'd go.

He shouted, "Be right back!" and raced out the door.

CHAPTER 19

Dmitri took the menu from the waitress, waited until she walked away, then said, "Alert the team. This is our chance."

Yuri said, "Here? In this restaurant?"

"No, when they leave. They came here on foot, and they'll leave on foot. They came down here to do more than just eat."

"Why do you say that?"

He waved his hand at the interior and said, "Because this little café is nice, but it isn't special enough to walk all the way from the Foreign Ministry building. There's nothing in this place that would lead them to take the lead diplomat from Turkey here."

They were sitting at an outdoor patio in a restaurant called Glashuset, a gas station in a former life that had been retrofitted into a boutique establishment sandwiched between the main avenue and the water. Sporting white linen tablecloths and catering to the yacht set that could pull right up to the dock, it was a better-than-average place for lunch, but Dmitri knew he was correct, even given his lack of sleep: this place wasn't unique enough for the half-mile walk it took to get here.

Last night hadn't been kind to him. He'd found out about the disaster of the firefight and then had spent the rest of the night getting his men back to the hotel. They'd ditched the boat with the dead bodies on the far side of the lake and Dmitri had been forced to send out an extraction team. The only good thing about the fiasco was the men had obtained the weapons, and the boat with the bodies was in no way attached to them.

Luckily, the event was so far away from Stockholm that no connection would ever be made to his team. The only concern was the rental SUV they'd been forced to leave behind, but he was confident that they'd be out of the country before anyone decided to check it out.

That hope had been dashed after he'd reported back to Victor. He'd been ordered to continue over his vociferous objections, convinced that some Western intelligence organization was on to them. Victor was equally sure the element wasn't some undercover Western sting, but members of their own GRU. The same cell the other SOBR unit was hunting in Copenhagen.

Dmitri had acquiesced, but again asked to allow his team to take out just the Swede, because his team could do that relatively easily on the Swede's early morning walk to the ministry. He was denied again, being told both the Turk and the Swede needed to go.

And so he and Yuri had staked out the ministry building, waiting most of the day. Finally, in early afternoon, the Swede exited with the Turkish envoy, this time with only the one remaining security man.

They'd followed the team as they'd strolled along the Strandvägen waterfront, the diplomats talking and laughing, until they'd stopped at the restaurant. When they'd settled in to eat, Dmitri had decided to alert the team. They may only get one chance at this, and as much as he'd earlier fantasized about having to solve a bigger problem than just killing the Swede, he now wanted nothing more than to leave this country before they all ended up in jail.

He told Yuri to order a quick appetizer, wanting the ability to leave at any moment, but also needing a reason for their table. He needn't have worried. The diplomats ordered a full meal and settled in to eat. The lone security man kept his eyes about, watching anyone who came and went. Dmitri could tell the killing the night before had caused the man to become more cautious than he had been on the previous outing. Almost paranoid. He stood up every time someone entered, clearing his hands from the table as if he was preparing to defend himself.

The fact that they hadn't beefed up the security told Dmitri that the powers in charge believed it to be random crime, which was good. But he could tell the last man standing didn't believe it, which was bad. He would have to go too. Probably first.

Konstantin called him from outside the restaurant, saying, "We're here. What's the status?"

"They're in here eating. Take up a position outside for a follow. They're going somewhere else, and we might only have a split second to make a decision on the hit. When the opportunity presents itself, we strike. Take the security man first, then the other two."

"What if they get in a vehicle?"

"Then we're fucked. We try again tomorrow. But they aren't taking a vehicle. They would have done that to begin with. The Swede is trying to sway the Turk with some strolling and fancy food. No, they'll walk out of here."

"Roger all. Standing by for the trigger."

I hit the street with Blaine and said, "Koko, Koko, give me a lock-on."

Blaine smiled at the callsign, because he knew Jennifer hated it, saying off the net, "I thought for sure she'd have gotten you to change that to Spider-Woman or Wallcrawler or something."

I laughed and said, "It's the one thing I have on her. She can't change it without my permission, and I'll be damned if I'm doing that. Knuckles would kill me."

Knuckles was the one who'd anointed her with the callsign, as I was the one who'd anointed him with his.

She came back, saying, "They are moving with an absolute purpose. They're on the Strandvägen now and not enjoying the stroll."

"Pace?"

Brett came on, saying, "This is Blood. They're moving like they're on a timed ruck march. Eyes straight ahead and leaning into the walk."

That would mean nothing to about 99 percent of the world, but I knew exactly what he meant. They were walking at a pace that was just below breaking into a jog. Meaning they had a mission, and also meaning it was going to be tough to stay on them. They'd see us moving at that speed behind them, brushing past all the other pedestrians.

I said, "Can you track without burning yourselves?"

Veep came on, saying, "I'll get ahead of them. Knuckles is working it now."

"What? An Uber? Come on."

Knuckles said, "No. Lime scooters. We're on them now. Getting ahead."

Lime scooters?

"What are you talking about?"

When he came back, I could hear the wind in his earpiece. "It's a rental scooter. They're everywhere. Veep and I are on two. Stand by."

I can't wait to claim the charge as an expense. Only Knuckles would think of that.

He said, "We're beyond them now, still moving. Going to stop at the waterfront for some sightseeing."

"Roger. Koko, Blood, tell me you aren't also on scooters."

"Still walking."

Knuckles came on: "They've stopped. They're outside a restaurant called Glashuset, sitting on the quay looking like sightseers, but they sure as hell didn't walk like one."

And that was it. Their target, whoever that might be, was inside that restaurant. I said, "Okay, this is it. Someone is inside that restaurant controlling this team, which means the target is also inside."

Knuckles said, "Want us to penetrate?"

I thought about it. The Lime riders were closer, but I wanted to take a little edge off the surveillance. Since it was a restaurant, chances were they were midway through a meal and we had some time. If these guys were any good, they'd be looking hard at anyone who entered, and Jennifer gave me that soft touch.

I said, "No, hold what you've got. Keep eyes on the outside team. Blood and Koko go in. Get in position and give me a read."

CHAPTER 20

Jennifer and Brett walked by the three men sitting on a low wall overlooking the water, the one in the middle giving them a hard stare as they went by. Jennifer took Brett's hand, and he said, "We dating now?"

She chuckled and said, "We are today."

"Can you tell Pike? I'm not sure I want to do that . . ."

She said, "Did you catch the stare from those guys?"

"Yeah. They're here to hunt. Too bad they let us slip through."

They went into the restaurant, talked to the hostess, and were led to the outdoor patio near the water. They were seated at a four-top table, both acting like they had no interest in the people scattered about, but they actively scanned.

Brett was first, saying, "See that table of three, with the one not dressed like the others?"

Jennifer did a quick glance behind her and said, "Yeah?"

"He's security. One of those guys is the principal. He's dressed in loose-fitting clothing with a light Gore-Tex jacket. They're both in coat and tie. He's hiding a gun in those clothes. The other two are bullshitting like they're on a date."

"Get some photos. Send them to Pike."

He did that, and Jennifer said, "Two other guys at your four o'clock. They're doing nothing but staring at the target table."

Brett casually glanced that way and said, "Yeah, I'll bet he's the team leader. The one controlling the guys outside. Something is going down today."

"So what do we do? Create a scene? Break up the profile until they'd be foolish to continue?"

Brett said, "No. If we did that, they'd be foolish to continue *today*, but they'd come back, and we might not have a handle on them anymore. This is a Pike call."

"You mean a Blaine call."

He laughed and said, "Yeah, a Blaine call. With him standing next to Pike."

He got on the net and said, "We have them. Target cell is three men, one security and two suits. They're being tracked by two inside and the three outside."

Pike said, "That leaves one on the loose. Probably in the hotel as control."

"What do you want to do?"

"Stand by. Getting something from the Taskforce on your photos."

Brett relayed to Jennifer, and they waited. Pike came back on, saying, "That's the target. No idea who the Swede is, but the Taskforce has identified the other guy as a Turkish envoy named Ahmet Yimaz. He's the man doing the NATO negotiations for Turkey. That's definitely the target."

"So, what now? Take out the guys on the street? Have Knuckles and Veep take them off the board?"

"No. As much as I'd like to, we can't attack three guys on the street because they fast-walked to this restaurant. We continue."

"Pike, an ounce of prevention here. There is no way these guys aren't out for blood. This is it. It's not a simple surveillance effort. Three pipe-hitters show up and we're going to let them take a swing?"

"I hear you, but Blaine here says we need to make sure. No Omega until we witness a hostile act."

Brett scoffed and said, "That worked out well for the Marines in Beirut in '83."

Jennifer poked his shoulder and he said, "Hold on."

He looked where she wanted, then said, "They're moving. Bills paid. This is it."

Dmitri saw the Swede hand over a credit card and called on the radio, saying, "They're going to exit. Let them go and pick up a follow. We'll be right behind."

Konstantin said, "Mission?"

"You get a chance to smoke them and get away, do it. But make sure you can get away. No shoot-outs on the street."

He let them leave, paying his own bill at a leisurely pace, not wanting to look anxious. He and Yuri hit the street, him on the radio saying, "Which way?"

"They continued down the promenade and are now at a crosswalk. Going across to an island of some sort."

"What is it?"

"It's called Djurgarden, and it has a bunch of greenspaces and museums. The ABBA museum, a Viking museum, some place called the Vasa Museum."

Dmitri patted himself on the back, thinking, *I knew they were going to continue to something else.*

"Keep on them. We're right behind you."

He and Yuri stayed five hundred meters back, hearing that they were across a bridge and moving into the interior of the island. He reached the same span over the water and waited, saying, "We're about to come across. What's the status?"

"They're headed to that Vasa Museum. No idea what it is."

"Follow them in. We're right behind you."

They sprinted across the bridge, took a look at a map on the far side, and then ran to the entrance of the museum, threading their way through paths that wound around the greenspaces like spaghetti that had been thrown from above.

They reached the entrance, went inside, paid, and Dmitri said, "Where are you? What's the status?"

"They've got the headphones on. Just walking around. We have them in sight."

Dmitri saw an enormous wooden ship, the focus of the museum, the entire place lit with subdued lighting, the dim cavernous displays illuminated only by eyeball LEDs.

He said, "Where are you?"

"Second level. We're walking through some displays. It's a maze in here. We could take them right here."

"Chance of compromise?"

"Good. We'd have to run. There are other tourists about."

"No. Stay on them. Wait until you can get them alone. Did they take an elevator?"

"Yeah. For this level."

"Let them get in the next one. If someone comes in behind them, kill them too. Then get out."

"Roger all.

Dmitri waited, then heard, "They're headed to the third level."

"In an elevator?"

"No. They're taking the stairs."

Dmitri found the elevator at the back of the floor and said, "We're coming up. Keep on them. This is it. When they get somewhere alone, smoke them."

CHAPTER 21

Blaine and I caught up with Knuckles and Veep, but we ignored both them and the pipe-hitters on the boardwalk. I slowed down before we passed the kill team and saw the targets leave the restaurant, the Russians picking up a follow. I looked at Blaine and said, "We should really take them out within the next few minutes."

He said, "We can't. We don't know they're bad. Correlation is not causation."

I said, "If we wait until they execute, we're probably not going to prevent this hit, because they know a hell of a lot more than us. When those guys enter whatever kill zone is planned, it might be too late."

I could see he was absolutely torn, on the verge of telling me to take them out, wrestling with the decision. I stopped him, saying, "Look, we can't do it on the street anyway. Just give me authority to do it when I can."

They stopped at a crosswalk ahead of us, looking to go over a bridge to an island. He finally decided. "Okay, Pike. You get a shot at them without compromise, then take them out—but nonlethal only. I don't want to have to explain killing a bunch of tourists."

The last two men inside the restaurant popped out, walking the same way we were. I got on the radio and said, "Lime scooters, Lime scooters, you still have your steeds?"

Knuckles came back, saying, "Yeah, we have them."

"They're crossing a bridge to an island. Get ahead of them. If you get a shot at the pipe-hitters, take them out, but no lethal action unless they escalate. We'll handle the control."

"On the way."

Blaine said, "That's it? You aren't going to give them any further ROE?"

Jennifer and Brett arrived and I said, "I just did. Let them work their magic."

We crossed the bridge to an island called Djurgarden. I turned to Jennifer, knowing she'd done the research, saying, "What's this place?"

"It's the royal gardens. There are a bunch of museums and green-spaces."

"So a ton of kill zones to eliminate the targets?"

"Pretty much."

The light went green and we crossed over right behind the control. I could see his mouth moving with no phone to his ear and knew he was giving instructions. It made me want to silence him right here in the open air, on the bridge. But of course, I couldn't do that.

We reached the far side and Knuckles came on, saying, "They're in the Vasa Museum. We're right behind them."

I looked at Jennifer for information, saying, "Stay on them. We're coming up now. Their control is leading us right there."

Jennifer said, "It's a famous warship. The most preserved warship from the seventeenth century. It spent three hundred years on the sea-bed and then was painstakingly recovered."

We kept walking and I said, "Like it sunk in battle in the middle of the ocean, and they managed to pull it up intact?"

She laughed and said, "No, like they built it right here and on its maiden voyage it literally sank a hundred meters after leaving the dock."

We reached the entrance, let the control go through, and I said, "You're kidding."

"Nope. They spent a fortune building it, and it sank within thirty minutes."

We went in, me saying, "Man, that had to have hurt. No wonder they're selling tickets to see it. Probably still trying to pay it off."

We paid the entrance fee, and on the net I said, "Knuckles, what's the status? We're inside."

"They're on the third floor—which is the seventh floor on the maps. You entered on the fourth."

I said, "Makes perfect sense. I love Europe. What's happening?"

"The targets are still wandering around, and the pipe-hitters are still behind them. Too close to do anything, and there are too many tourists combing through this place."

"You mean too close for *you* to do anything, or too close for them?"

"Both. But this place's lighting is perfect for a hit, and with the maze that runs through these exhibits, this is it. I don't know the kill zone, but it's here."

I said, "Stay on them. I'm going to the third floor with Blaine. Jennifer and Brett will stay on the first—floor seven and four on the map. Get ready to interdict."

He said, "Interdict how? This isn't going to be clean."

"Prevent the assassination of the targets. If anyone shows hostile intent, take them out. We'll worry about the fallout later."

He said, "Why do I always end up in the hot seat on these things?"

My eyes still on the control, I said, "It's your good looks and charm. Gotta go."

We entered the main hall, the ancient ship dominating the space, the keel running two floors below and the masts rising up to the ceiling far above.

I turned to the group and said, "Okay, Brett and Jennifer are on the control. Blaine and I are going to back up Knuckles and Veep. You guys give a heads-up whenever that guy talks on the radio. I don't need to know what he's saying, but I do want to know when he's talking."

Jennifer nodded, and I let them follow their control deeper into the exhibit. I went to the elevator to go to the seventh floor. Blaine and I got in, and then Knuckles came on, saying, "They're on a viewing platform away from everyone else. I'm following . . . Oh shit. It's on."

"What's that mean? Knuckles? Knuckles, come back."

"They're alone, they're alone, they're alone."

Dmitri heard the call and said, "Where? Can you take them?"

"On an observation deck above everyone else. It has a half wall to prevent someone falling. I can take them, but I have to commit to the deck. If I go up, I either execute, or I'm no longer useful for any further surveillance work."

Dmitri said, "Do it. Kill them all."

CHAPTER 22

Lars Karlsson led Ahmet Yimaz up a set of stairs to the very top level of the museum, saying, "There's a photo deck up here. You can get the best pictures of the ship, where you can see it all instead of just a piece."

Ahmet followed, but Lars could tell he wasn't impressed. Ahmet was growing tired of the museum, and he didn't fault him, honestly. He patted Ahmet on the shoulder, saying, "Come on, man, you have to get a little bit of Sweden in your trip."

Ahmet said, "I'd rather be back at the restaurant. No offense, but there's only so long I want to spend looking at an old ship you people pulled out of the water."

Lars laughed and said, "Just come up here. We'll take a couple of pictures and then go. We can do karaoke again tonight if that's more to your liking."

Ahmet shook his head, looked at his security man, and said something in Turkish. Lars knew they were talking about the death of the other security man and realized he'd screwed up again. He shouldn't have mentioned karaoke. The security man gave a grim smile at whatever was said, and they both climbed the small stairwell to the observation deck.

A small platform with a simple wooden bench that ran for about twenty feet, the sole purpose of the location was to get Instagram-worthy photos of the stern of the ship in all its glory. The two men went to the low wall, Lars pulling out his phone and encouraging Ahmet to do the same, the lone security man standing at the entrance to the stairwell.

Lars turned on his charm, trying to recover from his misstep. Trying to get back to what had made him so successful in Turkey. "Let's get a selfie with the ship in the background."

Ahmet shook his head, and Lars said, "You know you want to. Don't let playing diplomatic hardball cause you to lose something you can show your daughter."

Lars saw a small grin leak out and said, "I knew it. Take a picture and we'll go back to being adversaries."

Ahmet brought out his phone and Lars caught motion near the stairs. He turned his head and time slowed down to nothing, the world shrinking.

He saw the security man draw his weapon, getting it out of his holster and halfway extended, and then his head exploded in a shower of brain matter. He collapsed on the ground, his lifeless corpse slapping the wood, and the gunman kept coming.

Lars screamed, Ahmet turned, and then the Turk's head exploded as well, spraying blood and brain matter all over Lars, the gunman now on the deck, marching forward, the barrel pointed right at him.

He lined up the barrel, Lars raised his hands in an ineffectual attempt to save his life, and then the gunman's own head flew apart, the bullet splitting a gap between his eyes from the rear. The gunman dropped and Lars saw another man with a suppressed pistol, now searching the rest of the deck, the barrel following his eyes, looking for a threat.

The adrenaline coursing through his body like an electric current, he saw his chance and sprinted to the stairs, the man with the gun shouting, "No! Stop! I'm here to help!"

He ignored the words, jumping down from the platform and racing past the elevator, choosing the winding staircase to get the hell away from the men with guns.

I exited the elevator shouting into my radio, "Knuckles, status?"

Jennifer said, "This is Koko. Control is going batshit. Running down the stairs to the lower level. There's an exit down there. Not the entrance we came in."

Knuckles came on, saying, "I have two friendlies and one hostile down. Both of the Turks are dead. The Swede is on the run. Only took down one up here, so there's four others out hunting him."

Veep said, "Target is on the move. Running. He's going to get out of here. I do not have control."

Jesus Christ. Should have hit those assholes earlier.

"Where is he?"

"I lost him. He's going down, though. The other two pipe-hitters are still with me. I have them and can interdict."

"Koko, Koko, what's the control doing?"

"They're moving to the back of the museum, two floors down. They know something we don't."

I looked at Blaine, feeling impotent. I said, "Veep, what are the pipe-hitters doing?"

"Holding fast. They're confused because of Knuckles. They didn't see him go up and don't know what happened up top."

"Knuckles, what do you have?"

"Three dead bodies and a couple of guys who want to ambush me if I leave."

"Hold fast. Don't move. No more gunfights."

"What if they come up here?"

"Then you can have a gunfight. Did they see the target leave?"

Veep said, "Oh, yeah. They saw it. They're now running the other way. Someone told them to leave. Should I follow?"

"No. Hold what you got. Let them go. Break—Break—Koko, Blood, what do you have?"

"Nothing yet. Still have control in sight. They're pacing at the exit."

"Where's the target?"

"No idea."

Shit. "Okay, listen up. Koko and Brett maintain eyes on the control element. Knuckles, Veep, me, and Beast are going to start searching for the Swede. He's in here somewhere."

No sooner did I say it than Brett came on: "He's here, and he's running. He's out the back. I say again, he's out the back."

The shit sandwich was about to get as bad as possible. I said, "What's control doing?"

"They looked shell-shocked. They're letting him go."

"Get on him. Stop him."

"Pike, he's gone. He's running flat out."

"You saying you can't catch him? That would be a first."

Brett said, "Okay, I'm out."

Brett was something of a freak on foot—one of the fastest men I'd ever met, and that was saying something. If anyone could catch the Swede, it was him.

Koko came on, saying, "The control is fleeing out the front. Should I follow?"

"No. Let them go. Let them all go. Focus on the Swede."

CHAPTER 23

Dmitri exited the museum and called on his radio, saying, "Hold what you got. Let us catch up." In short order he and Yuri found Konstantin and the other assassin, Dmitri immediately saying, "What the hell happened?"

"Boss, I don't know. We sent Boris up alone. The deck was small, and he only had to kill three people. I heard the suppressed shots, but was keeping an eye out for reactions from the tourists. I wasn't focused on the observation deck. Next thing I knew, the Swede was running flat out by us."

"So the Turks are dead?"

"Yeah, I'm sure they are. My best guess is the security man got off a shot and took out Boris."

"You didn't check on him?"

Indignant, Konstantin said, "You ordered me to leave immediately."

"So we don't even know if the Turks are dead? If Boris is dead?"

"They're KIA. No doubt in my mind. There's no way that Swede would come running out if Boris was alive, and by the same token, there's no way the Swede would leave the Turkish envoy if he were simply wounded. He didn't stop to get any help from anyone. He ran like a scalded dog. No, they're all dead up on that platform."

"And the Swede is in the wind. Probably running to the police right now. Shit."

"We can stop that. Give him a call. You have his number. Call him and tell him if he talks to anyone, we'll kill his family. It doesn't have to be true. Just get him under control."

Dmitri thought about that, then said, "Good idea, but let's go one step further. Let's make it true. Get Maksim out of the hotel. Get him over there and *really* get them under control. We'll bring the Swede to us."

Lars went down the steps so fast he almost fell over, going from one level to another, the image of the exploded heads ricocheting like a bullet in his own brain. He reached the bottom and began sprinting, running through a coffee shop to a back exit, causing the patrons to stare at him as he went by.

He wasn't even conscious of the attention, simply wanting to get away from the men upstairs. He looked behind him, saw no one coming, and exited the museum onto a gravel walkway circling a small pond. He let the door close and began jogging down the path, finding it split in half, one leading down to the front of the museum, and one leading up a hill to something unknown.

He most certainly didn't want to return to the museum. He went on the path leading up the hill, his brain finally beginning to engage after the horrific events, the fight-or-flight response beginning to subside.

Call the authorities. Call them immediately.

He pulled out his phone, and then thought better of it. *Call them when you're safe. Get to somewhere safe first.*

He reached the top of the hill, saw the path snaking away through an iron grate into a cemetery, and began jogging down the gravel, beginning to calm down. He started passing the tombstones, all alone, and saw the entrance to the cemetery ahead. He heard something behind him and saw a black man crest the hill he'd just come from, running flat out. He was eating up the ground like a cheetah.

Lars panicked, sprinting as fast as he could to the gate a hundred meters away. He looked behind him, seeing the black man gaining on him as if he were standing still, and redoubled his efforts, refusing to look behind again, like a child hiding underneath a blanket to make the bad man go away.

He got within forty meters before he was hammered in the back and laid out on the ground. He started screaming and fighting, flailing his arms about, and the black man snatched him from the path and threw him behind a giant statue celebrating the death of someone rich enough to buy the homage. The black man slapped a hand over his mouth, rotated around, bringing his legs around Lars's waist, and then cinched his arm across his neck.

Lars knew he was dead. He began to spasm in an explosion of fear, and the man sank in his hold. Lars could breathe fine, his lungs huffing like a bull, but felt a curtain descend over his eyes, his brain becoming sluggish. And then he passed out.

He woke up behind a building next to the church, four men standing above him, one of them the black man. He recognized the threat and rolled over, trying to crawl away. He was stopped by a female. She said, "Lars, hang on. We're on your team here."

He rolled over and said, "What team?"

A man with ice-blue eyes and a scar tracing a path down his cheek leaned in and said, "*Your* team. We're here to help you. That's all. We mean you no harm."

He sat up and said, "Then let me call the police."

Sure that would be the end of it, he waited. The man said, "My name is Pike Logan. And as you can guess from my accent, I'm American. I will let you call the police, but we have to have some ground rules here. We saved your life, and I need you to pretend you saved it yourself."

"What?"

"Look, there are Russians trying to kill you. They almost succeeded tonight. We happened to be in the right place at the right time, but we really don't need the headache of what's going to come from the assassination attempt. You don't work for the government—well, you do, but you didn't. I need you to say that the Russians attacked you—which they did—and you escaped. And you need to tell your government they're still out in the wild. They're still on this soil. And they're still hunting."

"What on earth are you talking about?"

"Do you think it was a criminal element that followed you to the Vasa Museum and killed the Turks while trying to kill you? Someone who wanted a discount at Ikea?"

His head spinning, Lars said, "I . . . I don't know what to think right now."

"Look, it's pretty simple. The Russians tried to kill you to prevent Sweden from joining NATO. We interrupted that. Unfortunately, we couldn't do it before the Turkish guys were killed, but we did manage to save you. Just tell the authorities that you fled and escaped, and that Russians are trying to assassinate people on Swedish soil. There are bodies in the museum to prove it. Can you do that?"

Gaining confidence that he wasn't about to die, Lars said, "I'm . . . I'm not sure I can do that. Who are you?"

He saw Pike take a breath, then turn to the man next to him, someone who looked like a rugby player, and mutter, "I told you this was going to shit. We're flying out of here tonight. You guys can deal with the fallout you made me do."

Lars stood up, saying, "I appreciate the help. I won't talk. I won't tell anyone what happened. I just want to go home. Can I do that now?"

Pike returned to him and said, "No. That's not how this works. You *need* to tell the authorities what happened here. The Russians screwed this up, and they're probably all dead men walking right now unless they succeed. Trust me, they don't want to die. They'll do anything to prevent that from happening, and they're still on the loose. If you leave now, you're dead. You need to call your people and tell them everything—except that we were here."

Lars said, "I can't do that. I work for the government now. I have to tell the truth."

Exasperated, Pike said, "It's not that hard. Nobody's going to believe you anyway. We're going to disappear like vapor, and we'll deny any involvement. All you have to do is tell the truth without telling the whole truth. I'm not asking you to lie."

Lars hesitated, and Pike said, "We *did* save your damn life tonight. Consider it repayment."

Lars's phone began buzzing in his pocket and he pulled it out, hitting the answer button. What he heard collapsed his entire world.

A disembodied voice said, "We have your family, but we don't want them. We want you. Meet us at the Royal Armory in thirty minutes. If you've called the authorities already, they're dead. If you call them from this point forward, they're dead. Royal Armory in thirty minutes. Second floor. Come alone."

Lars hung up the phone, his face ashen, and said, "They have my family. I have to meet them in thirty minutes. They said if I contacted anyone, they'd kill them." He started to cry, slapping his head with the phone and turning in a circle.

He looked back at Pike and said, "What do I do?"

Pike looked at the rugby player and said, "Well, shit. I guess this isn't over yet."

The man led Pike away.

———

Blaine said, "Pike, we can't help here. This is now for the authorities to sort out. We've done what we came to do. We saved his life, and now they can protect him."

Lars was out of earshot, leaning against a wall of an old storage shed next to the cemetery, rocking back and forth.

I said, "He has no time for that. He has thirty minutes. If he's not at that meet site, they'll kill them and then just leave. I've dealt with Russians like this before. They absolutely *do not* care."

"Not our problem. Not a Taskforce issue. We did our mission."

"Yeah, well, you should have said that earlier. It's our problem now."

"No, Pike, it's *not* our problem. We don't want to get compromised over the family. We'll alert the authorities through Taskforce assets, make sure this guy is protected, and we're done."

I leaned back against the wall and said, "He has a wife and a small son. The only reason they're in jeopardy is because we saved his life. If he were dead, they'd be waking up tomorrow learning some horrible news, but they'd be alive."

"Pike, let me talk to the Oversight Council before we do anything. Get authority."

I looked at him and said, "You do what you need to do. I told you I wanted nothing to do with this mission, but you made me execute."

"What's that mean?"

I turned away, walking back to Lars, and said, "It means I'm going to follow through."

CHAPTER 24

I squatted down next to Lars, glanced at my watch, and said, "Look, you no longer have time to call the authorities. You barely have time to get to the Royal Armory. That's on purpose. They think you're alone."

After talking to Blaine, I was waffling on the correct course of action, but the sheer terror on his face cemented what I was going to do. There was no way these fucks were going to take his family.

He said, "And? What do I do? I can't do anything but go. And then they'll kill me and my family."

I said, "You can listen to me. Do exactly what I say. I'll get your family out alive. I promise."

He looked around at my team, all dressed like tourists, and said, "How? What can you do? You don't have the capabilities for this."

He sagged into the wall and began sobbing. I tapped his head and said, "We're running out of time."

He just looked at me, slobber on his face and tears rolling down his eyes. I glanced at Knuckles and he shook his head, telling me this guy was no help. But I *needed* him to be of help, or all was lost.

I leaned in, put my hands on his shoulders, and got face-to-face. I said, "We have a saying in the United States: I'm not the killer man, I'm the killer man's son, but I'll do the killing till the killer man comes."

He looked at me in confusion and said, "Who the hell has a saying like that?"

"That's me. I'm the killer man's son."

Knuckles scrunched his brow, wondering what I was doing using an old Ranger Battalion saying on some guy from Sweden, but it worked. His breath hitched a time or two, but he quit crying. He bored into my eyes and said, "What's that mean?"

"It means if you play with me today, you'll play with your son tomorrow."

He nodded and stood up, saying, "What do we do?"

"Unfortunately, you're the bait. But you won't die, I promise. Is there a way out of this park where we don't have to walk to the bridge?"

"There's a taxi stand deeper in. It works with Uber and Lyft now, but we still have to go across the bridge."

I said, "Okay, Veep and Knuckles, take your Lime steeds to the armory. One go in, one stay outside. Get there before we do."

Knuckles said, "ROE?"

"Let them get control of Lars. They'll make a call, saying they have him. Don't do anything until that happens. Once it does, rip those fuckers off planet earth."

They left, and I turned to Lars, saying, "Where's this taxi stand?"

He pointed away from the museum and we started walking. I said, "Where do you live?"

He gave me the address and I said, "Shit, that's literally a block away from our hotel. Which means it's a block away from *their* hotel. What's the floor plan?"

"It's a four-story unit. The bottom floor is a separate apartment. Ours takes up the next three floors."

"So it's a big thing?"

"No. Not really. It's actually pretty small. Two bedrooms in a building built a long time ago. It's really tight. When I say it has three floors, the top one is a deck overlooking the old town. It's not really a floor."

"You own the roof of the building?"

"Yes. Is that important?"

"Can we get into your apartment from the roof?"

"Yes. I said yes. Is that important?"

A minivan taxi rolled up and I said, "Everyone in but Lars and me."

Jennifer said, "What are we doing?"

"You're going to get us to the roof. I'm going to get Lars to his appointment."

She looked shocked, and I turned to Brett, saying, "When I get back, I want an assault plan. And it's going to be from the top down."

He nodded, and I pushed Jennifer into the vehicle, her protesting all the way. The vehicle pulled away and I said, "Next one is ours."

We got in and Lars looked at his phone like it had an explosive device inside. He was waiting to hear his family was dead, but that wasn't going to happen.

He said, "I should call the police."

I looked at the driver and said, "You should just let us do the tour. Losing your camera isn't worth our vacation."

He remained silent for the rest of the drive. We pulled into the plaza for the Royal Palace, and he grew agitated again. Like four football fields large, it was packed with tour buses and others on foot. I got him out of the car and away from the driver.

He said, "I should call the police right now."

"No, that's the worst thing you could do."

"Why should I believe you? Why should I believe you're here for me?"

"Well, there's that one thing when I saved your life."

He sagged and said, "This isn't what I signed up for. My wife and child are my entire life."

I said, "I know. I was you once before."

He turned to me and said, "What happened?"

And I really wished I hadn't said that. "Nothing."

He grew agitated, saying again, "What happened?"

I turned to him and said, "Don't ask me that. You don't want to know. You're going into the Royal Armory. My men will protect you, and we'll eliminate any threat. That's it."

He nodded, not liking the answer, and I said, "You go in to the second floor and do what they say. It'll be over soon."

He said, "The second floor of that place is dark. It's like a cave. They might just kill me there."

"They won't. If that's what they wanted, they would have told you to meet them in a back alley. They called that place because they don't know this town. They pulled that out of their ass as a known place. One of them has been there, and they decided to use it. They aren't going to kill you in the Royal Palace. They're going to get a handle on you and take you back to your place. *That's* where they're going to kill you."

He blinked and said, "Then why would I go inside?"

"Because your family is in the balance. Look, these guys aren't that smart. They think they are, and they think you're on your own. You are not. Trust me here. Please."

He started walking, then turned around and said, "What happened to your family?"

I looked away, then returned to him. I said, "They were murdered."

I saw his face blanch and grabbed his arm, saying, "I made a mistake then. I wasn't there. I'm here now. Trust me on this, nothing is going to happen to your family."

He faintly nodded, and I worried if he could execute the plan. I said, "Go inside and do what they said. You are not under a threat. You're just meeting them."

He said, "I'm *not* just meeting them. I'm killing my family."

I bored into his eyes and said, "I missed my chance for my family, but I won't for yours."

He saw the absolute conviction and gained some courage, turning to the entrance. I got on the radio and said, "Lars is inbound. What's the status?"

CHAPTER 25

Knuckles heard the radio call and said, "This place is ripe for a killing. It's all dark lights and hidden passages."

Pike came back, saying, "He's not going to get smoked in the Royal Palace. Makes no sense. They're just trying to get him under control."

"Well, they picked a perfect spot for it. The second floor is a maze of hallways. They want to kill him here, and they could do it and get away."

"Look, don't let Lars know that. He's skittish as it is. Let him go up and watch him. Wait until he's under control and the man makes a call. We need that call. Once it's made, eliminate the threat."

"ROE?"

"Lethal force. Break them in half."

"Roger that."

Knuckles began wandering on the second floor, able to see the floor below from a balcony rail. The armory was situated along a timeline, with the first room showing the origins of the royal family, complete with weapons from that time, then the second room showing the next generation or epic jolt in the lineage of warfare, and so on. One room had a horse in antique armor, and Knuckles actually found it fascinating, but he had to remain on the second floor. The entire area was dark, with subdued lighting, the strong arcs of illumination focused on the displays themselves.

Veep came on, saying, "Lars is inbound. Walking with a purpose."

Knuckles said, "Trailer?"

"Not yet. Wait . . . wait. Yes. Pipe-hitter going in right now. Right behind him. What do you want me to do?"

"Only a singleton?"

"Yep. One guy. Nothing else."

"Stand by out there. I'm not sure they'd just send in one guy."

"Do you see anything inside?"

"No. Everyone in here is a couple. No singletons."

"Maybe they think he's compliant."

"Maybe. We'll see."

Knuckles saw a shadow on the stairs, and then Lars came into view, walking hesitantly. Knuckles faded back into the shadows, watching.

Lars stood for a minute at the rail, then turned to go, and another man appeared, walking right up to him and shoving something into his gut, hidden by a jacket. Lars stiffened, and the man whispered something.

On the radio, Knuckles said, "It's a singleton. Lars is captured. Come inside. Stay on the lower level. We're coming to you."

He saw the man pull out a phone and dial a number, then say something. He said, "Call's in. We're on."

The man pushed Lars to the stairwell and Knuckles began to follow. He let them enter, knowing he had to execute before they left the cloistered space. He saw the hallway below and said, "Veep, Veep, block the stairwell. Get in front of it right now."

He heard "Roger" and saw his body appear at the entrance, looking away. He started down the stairs, seeing the man with Lars pause, whispering in his ear. He whispered as well, saying, "Lars is coming to you, probably on the run. Don't let him get out of here."

"Roger all."

Knuckles kept going down the stairs, seeing the man look up at him. He said, "Excuse me, looking for my wife," and began to push past them, ostensibly in a hurry.

Lars's eyes were wide open, his breath coming in hitches. The pipe-hitter's were slits, tracking his movement. Knuckles flattened his body, acting like he was just going to pass them.

He came abreast of the pipe-hitter, keeping his hands low, showing no threat. He slammed his head forward, shattering the nose of the Russian while simultaneously grabbing his wrist, feeling the steel of a weapon. He torqued the wrist upward, causing the pipe-hitter to scream, and Lars broke free, running down the stairs.

The man tried to fight back, but it was too late. Knuckles rotated his wrist violently, causing the man to flip in the air, slamming into the stone of the stairwell. Knuckles let go of the pistol, grabbed the man's hair, and slammed his head into the granite, hard enough to crack his skull. The man folded, dropping the pistol and staring upward with his eyes half-lidded. Knuckles stood up, then went bounding down the stairs.

He caught up with Veep outside, his hand on Lars's elbow. Lars saw him and said, "What now? What do we do now?"

Knuckles continued leading him out of the plaza, saying, "*We* aren't doing anything. You hold fast and this will all be over."

Outside of Lars's apartment, sitting on the alley with a statue of Saint George above me, I got the call and relayed, "Lars is free. I say again, Lars is free. Call has been made. They think he's on the way. Execute."

Jennifer came on, saying, "Pike, it's still daylight. I can't get up in daylight, and the men behind me surely can't do it."

I said, "Sun is setting, and it's going to get a lot more crowded at night when the tourists come. Get your ass up that wall."

We'd left the Vasa Museum in two Ubers, and while I was coaxing Lars to continue the mission, Jennifer and her crew had retrieved the gear we needed for the assault—namely four SIG Sauer MCX rifles and a knotted rope that the follow-on force could use to scale the wall to the upper deck.

Jennifer had a talent none of us did, which is that she could climb just about anything. It didn't matter the surface, she could get up it. In this case, we had some lower scaffolding and rough stone. I knew *I* could get up it, but it would be a twenty-minute climb. Jennifer could do it in under five.

The key was a top-down assault. Hostage rescue was all about saving the innocents inside, focusing on eliminating the threat only as neces-sary to accomplish the mission. Get a mission to hit a terrorist holdout in Syria? Yeah, the focus was most definitely on killing and capturing the bad guys. Hit a house holding hostages? I didn't give one rat's ass if the perpetrators got away. All I wanted was the hostages, which is why I wanted to go top down.

If we went from the bottom, with an explosive breach and then an onward assault, we'd corner the bad guys, necessitating a shoot-out. With nowhere to go, they'd fight, possibly killing the hostages in the process. Go from the top, though, and they'd have a way out—namely, running out the front door. If they chose that option, I was okay with it, which is why I demanded a top entry, and why Jennifer was now on the hook.

Jennifer came on, saying, "This is Koko. Starting to climb. Catch me if I fall?"

I stood up, looking left and right in the alley, and said, "You're good. No catch. I'm spread too thin."

Brett said, "This is Blood. I'll catch you."

She came back, "Good to hear someone has my back."

I grimaced, wanting to smack Brett for his little chivalry. But he was going up the rope with me, so that would have to wait. I turned to Blaine and said, "We're all going up soon. You stay down here for the squirters. They'll come, I promise."

He said, "I think you should leave Brett down here and let me go up."

I chuckled and said, "Sure, boss, like that's going to happen. He'd be a little upset about that. You're staying down here. That's just the deal. Guys run out, let them go. Guys try to get in—stop them."

Jennifer came on, saying, "Off the scaffolding. On the wall. Ten minutes and you guys can use the rope. Start staging."

I slapped Blaine on the leg and said, "Whelp, that's my call. See you in twenty."

I walked down the alley, seeing Brett stand up, his folding-stock AR printing a little through his jacket. I had two, one for me, and one for Jennifer. We went to the scaffolding together, me saying, "We get up top and we clear as fast as possible. If it's not a child or a woman, it's dead."

He smiled and said, "Easy day."

I grabbed the rung of the lower scaffold and Jennifer came on, "Pike, slip, Pike, I'm . . ."

I looked at Brett and then we heard a thud a story above us, on the scaffolding. I started climbing the pipes like a monkey, Brett right behind me. We reached the top of the aluminum planking and found Jennifer looped with rope, rolling around. I crabbed to her as fast as I could, checking out her vitals.

She was okay. A little banged up, but okay. She looked at me, the embarrassment seeping through, and said, "I thought you were going to catch me."

I said, "You fell?"

She nodded, then stood up.

I said again, "*You* fell?"

She said, "Yeah. I did. Give me the rope. I'm going back up."

"Jennifer, let's rethink this. Are you okay?"

"I'm fine, and we're running out of time."

I looked at Brett, and he just shrugged. I turned back to Jennifer, but she was back on the wall, scrambling up it like a gecko.

I watched her go, saying, "She's never, ever fallen before. Bad omen."

Brett said, "Had to happen sooner or later. I mean, if you shoot one hundred rounds, one or two are going to be out of the black. That's all this is."

Two minutes later, she was out of sight, and then the rope came down. I said, "Well, at least she made it the second time."

I grabbed the rope and started climbing, reaching the deck in minutes, flipping over the side, and saying, "Blood, Blood, rope is clear."

I saw it go taut and turned to Jennifer, noticing a large bruise on her left eye, her socket swollen. I leaned in, touched her face, and said, "You banged the shit out of yourself."

She brushed my hand away, saying, "Happens to you guys all the time. I'm fine."

She glared at me, wanting to hear me treat her like any other member of my team. Wanting me to rib her over the fall—and absolutely *not* wanting me fawning over her because she was female. But she was my *wife*, not just a female. Even so, I recognized what was happening, and we were about to get in a gunfight. She could be my wife later. Tonight she was a team member, so I obliged, saying, "You're right-eye dominant, correct?"

"Yeah? What's that mean?"

I handed across her weapon, saying, "Just making sure you can still aim."

She turned away, shouldering the weapon at the door leading down, saying, "You are one coldblooded asshole."

But she was smiling.

Brett came over the rail, sidled up to us, bringing out his SIG MCX rifle. He took one look at Jennifer and said, "We get done tonight, and you can write your ticket at the ER. Pike here will be in jail for years."

She chuckled and said, "Maybe I will. Depends on what happens next."

CHAPTER 26

I called Blaine and said, "At breach. Status?"

"Nothing. Alley is empty."

"Roger all. Going to be some shooting here, so stay on your toes. Remember, if they want to leave, let them go, but *do not* let anyone else enter. We have four left from the original count, and that's about all I want."

"Roger all. But this being all by myself is a little bit dicey."

"Welcome to my world. Breaching now."

I looked at Jennifer and she scuttled to the door. She took a look at the lock, saw it was a Schlage, and dug into her buttpack, pulling out a Lishi pick—a combination tool that was designed for that specific brand and had both a tension wrench and pick all in one. She stuck it in, working the pick lever gently until she found the binding pin. She hit that one, and then ripped through the lock.

She looked at me and said, "It's open."

I said, "Okay, here we go. I'm leading. Hopefully, they're on the next floor. We'll get them out from the roof."

Brett said, "That's not happening. They wouldn't leave them with the ability to escape from the roof."

I said, "I know. But one can hope." I raised my weapon, nodded at Jennifer, and she swung the door open. I entered, seeing a circular metal stairwell leading down. I felt Brett bump into me and whispered, "Fucking small stairwell. Worst thing ever."

He whispered back, "I'm going around. I'll get a gun on the bottom."

I nodded, and he did. I started going down the corkscrew stairwell as silent as I could. It was excruciating. Anyone from below would see me. Could shoot me. But I couldn't shoot back because I was going in a circle every five feet.

I reached the landing, put my gun out, and saw nothing but an empty bedroom. I said, "Come on down,"

They reached my level and we waited for a moment, hearing the people talking below. I said, "Well, this is a shit sandwich. There's no way to get down there without them knowing. Ideas?"

Jennifer said, "Let me go. It will confuse them, allowing you to assault. I appear, and then you shoot them."

"That's insane."

"No, it's not. They won't shoot me for appearing. They'll think they missed something. I'll act like I just woke up or something."

"You know they've searched this place."

"Yeah, but they won't know if they've missed something. They won't shoot me just for appearing."

"They might."

Brett said, "There's a gap in the wall for the stairs."

I said, "Yeah? So?"

"We could just drop through."

"Are you kidding me? You want to drop a floor, hit the ground, and start slinging lead?"

"It's an option."

"Shit. We should have come up from the bottom."

We heard a man shout, then the wife start crying from below. I heard him slap her, then her scream, which tore into my soul. I said, "Okay, we're going to do both. Jennifer, you go down the stairs. When you get seen, we're coming down."

Jennifer thought about what she'd said earlier. "Maybe that's not such a great plan. I can't have a weapon coming down."

I took her rifle and said, "You've got your pistol. Just get their attention. When they see you and start shouting commands, we'll come down."

She looked at the stairwell, and the small gap next to it, and said, "This has got to be the dumbest thing I've ever done."

"Yeah, I'm with you, but it was your idea."

She shook her head and said, "Catch me if I fall?"

I said, "Brett will."

Brett, standing over the hole we were going to drop through, whispered, "I think we'll hit the couch."

Jennifer turned to the circular staircase, and I said, "Get that pistol out the minute they see you. Not before, but get it out, because this is turning into a gunfight immediately."

She nodded, and then started down the stairs, walking like she was getting a can of Coke from the fridge. She went halfway down, and then screamed. There was shouting from below, with Jennifer saying, "Who are you? What are you doing here?"

Brett scrunched into the hole and dropped through, falling from the floor above onto the couch. I immediately followed him, holding my arms up to my face and dropping through the hole. I landed right on top of Brett before he could get off the couch, driving him into the floor. He grunted. I rolled off him, brought up my weapon, and started shooting.

There were four men in the room, three looking at Jennifer, and one looking at the clown car of our assault. I hit the man looking at us, then saw one of the others turn my way. He spun his pistol toward me, fired a round, and I heard Brett shout, dropping behind the couch. I returned fire, hitting him twice in the chest. The last two drew their weapons and Jennifer achieved a sight picture, punching a hole in the head of the one on the left.

The last man took off running, ripping open the apartment door and bounding down the staircase to the alley below.

Everything grew quiet, with the exception of Brett bitching at me and holding his ribs. I went to him, saw he'd been grazed with a wicked bit of metal. The bullet hadn't penetrated, but it had torn open a path through his muscle right next to his chest.

"You okay?"

He had copious sweat on his forehead, realizing he had been about a half inch away from being dead. He nodded, saying, "That was close."

I said, "Keep the pressure on. We'll be out of here in minutes."

I started to turn away, but couldn't resist one jab. "When we do the AAR, remember, this was your plan."

He said, "Yeah, yeah. I get it."

The woman in the room had grabbed her son and collapsed into a corner, looking at us in fear. Jennifer went to her, saying, "We're with Lars. You're okay."

I called on the radio, saying, "Jackpot. PC secured. Knuckles, Knuckles, what's your status?"

"About a block away."

"Bring in Lars. Let him know he's good."

Blaine came on, saying, "I got one squirter out the door. He's running to the water."

"Let him go. Get up here. We need to secure this site and get out."

Ten minutes later we were sitting in the den of the small apartment, me trying to convince Lars to let us out of this mess without talking about it.

"Hey, all you need to do is say there was some sort of gang fight between the Russians. Someone on one side of the Russian state didn't like what the other side was doing."

"Nobody will believe that."

I looked at Blaine, wanting some help. He said, "It's actually how they operate. All we're asking is that you don't mention Americans. It was a gunfight, an attempted kidnapping, a killing at the Vasa Museum, but it was all Russians. It's only half-true—but it *is* half-true."

I said, "Remember what we talked about, before I saved your life?"

He nodded, then said, "It won't remain secret forever. It's going to get out."

"Only if you let it. I'm not asking you to create a huge story. Just misdirect and then say you have no idea. That's it."

I looked at his wife, sitting on a couch with Jennifer, her giving soothing nothings to both the wife and the child. I said, "Talk to your wife and let me know."

"What's that mean? Is that a threat?"

I laughed and said, "All that means is that I have to let my people know what shit storm I'm going to take a bath in because I chose to save your family instead of fleeing this continent. Makes me wonder if I'd be better off just letting all of you die."

He heard the words, rubbed his face, then said, "Okay, okay. I owe you my life. My family's life. I'm sorry. I'll do as you ask."

Blaine said, "At the end of the day, nothing is altered. You continue with Turkey, and that's it. Just leave us out of it."

He said, "I can do that."

CHAPTER 27

While I was packing my bags inside the hotel, trying to get the hell out of this country because I wasn't sure that Lars would hold his word, Blaine entered.

I said, "You ready to go? We're out of here right now."

He said, "I'm with you, but George Wolffe wants a SITREP."

"I sent it. He has it."

"He wants to talk."

I stopped packing, looked at Jennifer, then at him. I said, "Why?"

Blaine held up his hands and said, "I don't know. I didn't call this."

I stopped my packing and said, "Am I going to get burned here? What's he want? We did what he asked."

"I honestly don't know. Something to do with Russia."

"Now? Or later? Once we're out of this place?"

I saw his face and believed it wasn't him. He said, "Right now."

I tossed the pair of socks I was holding, said, "You fucks really want it both ways. Save this guy's ass, then go crazy about how that happened."

He said, "Pike, this isn't me. I've already told them it went fine."

I tapped my computer keyboard, turning it on, and said, "Well, if you need to burn someone, I guess I'm the best bet."

He said, "Pike, come on. That's not what this is about."

I looked at him and said, "You still believe. Which is good. But you don't know how these guys on the Oversight Council operate. They care more about their own lives than they do about the mission. They'll burn you in a minute if it serves their purpose. The key is to under-stand that, and still work for the national security of the United States."

I didn't really believe what I'd said. I knew the Oversight Council was skittish, but they were patriots at the core, but they really pissed me off sometimes. And then I was shown how wrong I was.

I initiated the VPN, and saw Creed on the other end. Blaine said, "Pike, this isn't like that. The Oversight Council has been frozen out of this op. It's just us."

Incredulous, I hit mute, turned around, and said, "What? We're freelancing here?"

"No. Not really. POTUS is read on, but he's one of the few."

"What the fuck are you talking about? I said I didn't want this mis-sion, and now you're telling me neither did the Oversight Council?"

He said nothing. I spit out, "So I didn't get orders from a sanctioned entity. I got orders from *you*."

I started to advance on him, and Jennifer saw it was going bad. She leapt into the breach, pushing me back, saying, "Stop, Pike. Talk to Wolffe. He's not going to sell us out. That's not his way."

I stopped moving forward and said to Blaine, "Get the fuck out of my room. Pack your shit. If you want on my plane, you'll be there with Brett. The one that took a bullet for this mission."

He left. Jennifer said, "Talk to Wolffe. See what's going on here."

"Fuck that guy. I'll talk to him over the Atlantic Ocean, before he can get a police force here."

She went to the computer, initiated the VPN, and said, "Hey, Creed. Pike's right here."

"What was that I just saw? Where did Blaine go?"

"Nothing. Just a little disagreement."

I got in front of the camera and said, "Wolffe's got two minutes and then I'm gone."

He saw my face and recoiled from the screen, saying, "Stand by."

Wolffe took his seat, saying, "I got the SITREP. The president wants to know the damage."

"Damage to him? Is that what he wants to know? I just learned that nobody sanctioned this mission."

Wolffe exhaled and said, "Yeah, this one was close hold. It's just me, Kerry, and POTUS."

"What is going on back there? Kurt would have never allowed this."

At the mention of the previous commander, Wolffe bristled, leaning into the camera and saying, "That's bullshit. He allowed it when you met Jennifer. He allowed you to run amok in Bosnia because it served the greater good. Don't put that on me."

I backed off, knowing he was right. I said, "Okay, well you have the SITREP. What else do you need? We're leaving here tonight."

"You didn't do any SSE of the crisis site. You didn't take any phones, SIM cards, computers, passports, or anything. We needed that."

"Sir, that was outside the scope of the mission profile. You wanted me to prevent the assassination of the Swede, and I did so. If I'd have taken all the electronic devices or searched the bodies, it would not hold up the cover story we've concocted—which is weak shit to begin with. Let the Swedes do the extractions. Let them make the connections to Russia. It'll strengthen our cover."

I saw him consider my argument, then nod. He said, "CIA really wanted to know what Russia is up to."

"I'm sorry, sir. It was a judgment call I made, and I stand by it. Now, we really need to get the hell out of here. I only have about fifty percent confidence that Lars is going to stick with our agreement. If he implicates us, I want to be over the Atlantic when that happens, especially since Brett's been shot. Give me that."

"How is he?"

"He's fine. A ditch in some muscle. He'll get a scar, but he's going to be fine. I just don't want that scar to be from a Swedish hospital."

He nodded, and what I said held weight. He had to push against POTUS, but he also had my team's life in his hands. He said, "Okay, Pike. Get in the air. Give me a call when you're off the continent."

"Will do."

I disconnected, turned to Jennifer, and said, "We need to go. Right now. Don't check out. Let's pay for the rooms for another day, leaving the 'do not disturb' sign on the door. Won't do much, but might buy us some time."

She nodded, then said, "Maybe we should have searched those Russians."

"Didn't want to. My call. Go get your stuff. The rest of the crew is already headed to the airport."

We dragged our bags to the elevator, waited on it to arrive, Jennifer looking at me. I said, "What?"

"Maybe we're not done here."

"What's that mean?"

"They wanted the information from the Russians. We should have gotten that. I sort of feel like we failed. I could have done that while you were with Lars and his family."

"Well, we're not going back to the apartment, so let it go. We don't work for the CIA, and I don't care about the geopolitics involved with Sweden and NATO. If they wanted to extract all that intel from the dead Russians, then they should have done the mission."

She nodded, and the elevator door slid open. We entered, me thinking about what she'd said. In any combat action, you're never sure if you made the right decision, and there was always introspection. Maybe I *was* wrong. But it was done.

We went down one floor and stopped. The door opened again, and

I was facing the Russian who'd fled the house the night before, a roller bag behind him, his hand on a cell phone held to his ear.

He took one look at me and dropped the phone, snaking his hand to his back. I jumped forward, slamming my forearm into his head while using my other hand to trap his arm. He got the pistol out, and it fired into the air. The sound brought home how close I was to dying.

I twisted his arm and swept my legs behind his, flipping him onto his back. He rotated the gun, desperately trying to get it to my head. I punched his throat, hard, and his eyes bulged. The gun went off again. I batted his weapon away and began fighting him, the desperate sounds belying the arena we were in. Nothing but low-level grunts from two people who knew someone was about to die.

Both of us knew this was the endgame. Only one was walking away, and when it's a life in the balance, it becomes something else. He slapped his arms around my spine, rotated his hips, and I ended up beneath him. He snarled, punched me in the temple, and then Jennifer entered the arena, wrapping her arms around his throat and her legs around his body.

She seated her hold and then pushed with her feet, falling backwards, stretching his body between her legs and arms. His neck snapped, an audible sound. His body fell onto mine and I kicked it off, breathing heavily.

Amazed that her move had worked, she glanced left and right up the hallway, then at the body. She looked at me and said, "Jesus Christ. What do we do now?"

I rolled upright and said, "Find that phone he was on. Looks like we're all going to win today."

CHAPTER 28

Perun looked at Dishka and said, "You think this is a trap?"

"If it is, it's a pretty elaborate one."

Standing outside the entrance of an ultramodern structure looming over the waterfront, Perun said, "I guess there's only one way to know. That'll be inside." Still, he hesitated.

Called the "Black Diamond," it was the final extension of the Royal Danish Library. Completed in 1999, the extension was built out of black granite mined from Zimbabwe and subsequently polished in Italy, leading to a stunning architectural display that was the complete opposite of its heritage next door. Full of glass and steel, perched on the water of a canal, it had a skybridge stretching over the highway that Perun was on, leading to the original library made of old-fashioned brick and stone behind him.

Finally, Perun said, "Let's go."

They jogged across the street, then entered the glass building, the lower floor wide open with a coffee shop and art displays. He ignored the art, finding an elevator and traveling to the second level. It was also open, with various reading rooms situated overlooking the canal. Perun started wandering the floor, finally finding a bank of lockers, a note in English saying they were available for rent, but anything in them would be removed at the end of each business day.

He assumed the Russian knew that, and scanned until he found the locker number he'd been given. He looked left and right, the glass of the building allowing him to see throughout the floor. He saw nothing indicating a threat. He typed in the code and the locker opened, showing nothing but an envelope with his name on it.

He pulled it out, opened it, and saw instructions for the passport photos, along with a new, unused envelope. He handed it to Dishka and said, "Put in the pictures."

Dishka opened the envelope, put in the passport photos of the entire team, but held back from handing it across. He said, "Do we really want to give them our pictures? Lord knows how they'll be used."

Perun said, "We have to give up some trust eventually. It might be a mistake, but I'm willing to risk it. Otherwise, we'll just go back to Ukraine and die in a trench."

Dishka handed him the envelope, and he put it inside the locker. He said, "We return tomorrow for the passports and follow-on instructions."

"How are we going to do that? We have to be at the conference."

"We'll figure it out. A quick stop. That's all it will take."

Dishka looked around the area they were in and said, "We're on at least thirty different camera systems from the time we've entered. Anyone who wants to reconstruct our steps can do so."

"If they reconstruct the activity after Putin is dead, I do not care."

Oleg heard his phone buzzing and picked it up, seeing a call from the other SOBR team in Sweden. He answered, getting a fraught voice on the other end of the line.

He said, "Dmitri? Is that you?"

"Yes. Listen, things haven't gone well here. Someone is thwarting our efforts. Victor thinks it's the GRU guys you're after, and he might be right."

"How does that affect my mission?"

"I don't know. I just wanted to warn you. If they were on to us, they might be on to you as well. My mission has been interrupted three separate times. When we tried to get our weapons, we ran into an ambush. We managed that, but then when we tried to execute the mission, it failed. I seized the family for control, and then tried to bring the Swede in for execution. Someone prevented that, assaulting the house. He's still alive, and I'm moving out, back to Kaliningrad."

"What about your team?"

Oleg heard nothing for a moment, and repeated, "What about your team?"

"They're all dead. I'm on the way to the airport right now. I haven't even told Victor yet. I'm getting out of here and just wanted to let you know what had happened. Be careful."

"Do you have any leads besides 'be careful'? What should I look for?"

Oleg heard a shout, then the phone dropping to the ground, the connection still open. He heard what appeared to be a fight, then nothing. He disconnected.

He went to the next room, seeing the members of his team all splayed out and sleeping, like a pack of dogs on a porch. Unlike Dmitri, staying in a swanky hotel, they were holed up in a place called Freetown Christiana.

An old defunct Army base, it had been seized in the early seventies by a bunch of free-love hippies, who declared that the base was now outside the jurisdiction of Copenhagen itself. It had existed ever since, with various attempts by the government to evict the squatters, all failing. Its most famous trademark was the so-called Pusher Street, where marijuana was sold freely.

Built and overbuilt time and time again, mostly with salvaged and stolen material, it was a rat maze of tiny houses and established businesses that was outside the scope of the Copenhagen authorities, catering to a slew of different malcontents, from hard-core bikers to peace-and-love couples looking for nirvana.

Copenhagen had tried at various times to reclaim the land, usually when overdoses and crimes like murder made the news inside the compound, but each time they did, the people inside the commune rose up, saying they'd police themselves, and it invariably generated local support. And police themselves they did, banning hard drugs and kicking out people they deemed dangerous.

It still existed outside of the authorities of Copenhagen to this day. While the police raided Pusher Street quite often, they did it in a lackadaisical way, as if they were just going through the motions in a continual game of cat-and-mouse. As long as there were no murders or violence being conducted inside the commune, the authorities were happy to look the other way. It just wasn't worth the fight, which made it a perfect location for a crew of Russian assassins looking to infiltrate Copenhagen.

By its very definition, Christiana eschewed any authority figures, allowing the Russians free rein. They could come and go as they pleased, washed from the usual security protocols at every single hotel in Denmark.

Oleg kicked the first man he saw, saying, "Get up. Get everyone up. We need to talk."

The man groaned, hungover from the night before. He sat up and said, "What's new now? We have the meeting site. What else do we need?"

Oleg went through the room kicking the men and ignoring the graffiti on the walls, hating that he had to live in such squalor. The den they were in was used by addicts a day before, and while it gave him cover, he despised it.

"Get the fuck up. We have the mission in seven hours."

The first man he'd kicked, Misha, rolled over and said, "What's the big deal? We have the targeted location. Either the guys from the GRU are there, or they're not. If they're at the site, we kill them. If they're not, we don't."

"It's changed. Someone is hunting SOBR people. The team in Sweden was thwarted on their mission."

Misha sat up, saying, "How do you know that? We're supposed to be compartmented."

"The leader of the SOBR team is a friend of mine. He called, giving me a warning."

"What was the warning?"

"Just that his mission didn't go as planned, and ours might be compromised. The GRU has long tentacles."

Misha scoffed and said, "Are you telling me that the GRU is attacking SOBR agents? That makes no sense."

"Really? Is that logic coming because we're here precisely to attack the GRU?"

Misha paused, thinking, then said, "You have a good point, I guess."

Oleg said, "Get everyone up. We need to prepare for today. If we're lucky enough to find the Valkyrie team, we can't lose them again."

They only had one clue about the elusive Valkyrie team: they were meeting some Israelis at the gravesite of Hans Christian Andersen. They had no idea what the meeting was about, or why the location was chosen, but it was supposedly a hard fact straight from President Putin himself.

In truth, Oleg thought the entire idea was insane, but he'd flown a team into the country and was prepared to execute. Once they located the Russians—if they did in fact exist—they were to kill them, then flee the country.

Why the Israelis were involved wasn't his problem, but this new information most certainly was. Originally, all he needed to do was separate them from the GRU, and then kill the Russians, but if there was a crew out here hunting him, he'd have to be careful.

He had five men for this, most of whom were now passed out drunk on the floor at his feet. It didn't give him a lot of confidence, but they had seven hours. Enough time to instill just a smidgeon of discipline.

CHAPTER 29

Out over the sea, flying away from the debacle of Sweden, the pilot signaled me that he had an incoming message. I went to the cockpit and said, "Who's calling?"

"Taskforce. I don't know. They just cut in on the SAT, telling me to get you on the VPN."

Shit. That wasn't a good sign. I said, "What did you tell them?"

"That I'd get you on the phone. What did you want me to say?"

I glared at him and said, "Something like the atmospheric conditions over the Atlantic preclude such a conversation. Or that you couldn't hear them in the first place."

He looked at me and shrugged, saying, "I get the call, I pass the information."

I said, "I'll remember that the next time you're stuck in a country that doesn't allow alcohol."

I went back to the cabin and said, "Jenn, get out the computer. Taskforce wants a VPN."

She started pulling it out, and Veep said, "Why?"

"Because I found a thread they don't want to pull. They want to jerk our team off the threat. But that's not happening."

While I was dragging the body of the Russian we'd killed to a laundry closet, I'd had Jennifer race back to our room with his phone, because that's what I believed Wolffe wanted. He was the one who'd told me I'd screwed up by not doing a sensitive site exploitation of the apartment complex where we'd rescued the family.

She'd contacted Creed, hooked it up, and by the time I'd returned, he'd already downloaded it for analysis. We'd skedaddled to the airport, meeting the team and taking off. I was in the process of shacking up an addendum to our SITREP—because killing a Russian national after sending the first one warranted an update, to say the least—when Creed had come back with the analysis of the phone, and what it said made me do a complete reversal of my earlier position on the threat. It wasn't Sweden and NATO.

Creed had uncovered a bunch of calls inside Sweden, which wasn't surprising, but he also found a couple of calls to Copenhagen, Denmark, including the final one he was on right before he'd been killed, which told me we weren't done. It most certainly wasn't something I wanted to learn, but I had to react to what the intel laid bare.

There was another team out in the wild, and while we'd stopped the assault in Sweden, we hadn't stopped whatever Russian plan was in play. I'd dealt with them in the past, and if this guy was talking to someone in Copenhagen, it was a coordinated effort for something larger than just a single killing. We had the geolocation of the phone, but literally nothing else. In truth, for all I knew, it was some woman he'd slept with on the way in, and now he was trying to hook up again as he flew home, but I didn't believe that.

Something else was going on, and the only reason for this call was George Wolffe pulling me off, which was aggravating, given how he'd flagrantly smashed the Taskforce charter ordering me to do what I'd done.

Jennifer booted up the VPN and gave me the seat. I sat down in front of the camera, saw it clear, and was facing George Wolffe. I said, "What's the emergency? You got the SITREP."

"Yeah, we did, and it says you're going to Copenhagen, Denmark. That caused a little bit of consternation here."

"Why? You sent me here to eliminate a threat. That's what I'm doing. Copenhagen will be Alpha only. Just checking out who that killer was talking with."

"That's not going to happen, Pike. You need to come home. You completed the mission."

Aggravated, I said, "The *mission* is preventing Russia from affecting Western interests. The mission is the national security of the United States. The mission wasn't some single guy in Sweden."

"I hear you, but we're throttling back here. You did what you did, and it was successful. Now the thinking is that the intelligence community takes over. Let them have a hand to sort this out. No Taskforce activity."

"Seriously? The last time I spoke to you, they couldn't do shit. It's why you pushed me. You were mad that I didn't rip apart the flat with the dead guys because you were worried about what the Russians are up to. I left that alone to preserve our cover, and now, when I find a reason to continue, you say it's time to stop. Who's calling the shots back there?"

I could literally see the pain on Wolffe's face. He didn't like what he was telling me. He said, "The president of the United States. You did what you needed to, and he's grateful."

"Grateful? Is this POTUS, or Kerry Bostwick and CIA? Did you read Creed's report? We don't have time for that shit. There's an unconventional warfare roundtable happening right now in Copenhagen, all of it about Ukraine. That's not a coincidence. It'll take you a week to wash our intel into the formal channels, and then another week to get those assholes to even check anything out. By then, whatever they have planned will have already happened."

I saw him rub his face on the screen and pushed the blade home. "This is exactly why the Taskforce was created. We can flex on intelligence much more rapidly than that bureaucratic bloat of SOCOM or the CIA. It's literally why we exist."

"Pike, this is from the president. Come home."

I looked at the people around the cabin, thinking about the risk to both me and the team. Nobody said a word, but I got a nod from Knuckles. They were in.

I hadn't wanted this mission in the first place. I wanted nothing to do with it, but he'd made me execute. I was the one who said the entire thing was outside the scope of our charter, and after it was all done, I'd found a threat. Of that I was sure. I was also sure that nobody else would be able to thwart it.

I should have just flown home, taking my orders, but my gut was telling me this threat could be one of the defining moments in world history, like the assassination of Archduke Franz Ferdinand before World War I. I should just stand down, as I'd been ordered—but I felt it was worth exploring deep inside, even if the Taskforce didn't. It wouldn't be the first time my judgment had been validated when everyone else said I was wrong.

Just go home. It's not your fight. You serve at the pleasure of the president. You solved the problem they sent you on.

But in my heart, I knew I hadn't solved the problem. What I'd done was just a sliver. There was a greater threat the president wasn't seeing.

I looked at Jennifer, my moral compass, and she nodded as well, telling me to go forward. I returned to the screen and said, "No, sir. I'm not doing that. Something is brewing—something bigger than a killing in Sweden, and I'm going to find out what it is."

"Pike, that's not going to happen. You're coming home. The consensus is to stop Taskforce activities."

I took a deep breath and said, "Consensus from whom?"

"From all involved."

I leaned in and said, "The same assholes who said there was WMD in Iraq? The same assholes who said Afghanistan would hold for a year after we pulled out? Those guys? That consensus holds no sway with me. I've learned through blood what that means. There's a threat in Copenhagen, and I'm going to find it before we get in a shooting match we can't win. Something we could have prevented."

Exasperated, he leaned forward and said, "Pike, that might be true, but someone else is going to solve the riddle. It's not a Taskforce problem."

I saw my arguments weren't working. So it was time to go kinetic. "I told you I didn't want this mission, but you sent me anyway. I told you this was a mistake using us like this, but the president said I should execute. I *did* execute on the tactical side, but the strategic side is still in play. Sir, the pilots are flying me to Copenhagen, and you're going to support my mission. I didn't ask for this shit sandwich, but you made me take a bite, and now you don't want the whole thing. I'm going to Copenhagen."

He pulled his final shot, not wanting to, saying, "Pike, the pilots have their orders. They aren't going to Copenhagen. The U.S. government owns that plane. I'm sorry."

I laughed, and he said, "What's so funny?"

I leaned in and said, "Sir, I have a pistol. The pilots don't. We're going to Copenhagen. Let the president know."

CHAPTER 30

Daniel took a sip of his coffee, enjoying the crisp morning air, glad to be out of the cauldron of Ukraine. He said, "I wish we had a bigger team here. I don't like running this loose."

Stepan said, "It is what it is. I have to do the dead drop with the passports at the library. You have to meet the Israelis. We have no one else."

Daniel took another sip and said, "I know. Perun has been spot-on with the meets and instructions, which gives me a little courage, but make no mistake, we're being hunted. At this very moment, someone is hunting us."

"Nothing we can do about that. Like I said, it is what it is."

"Well, if this doesn't work out with the Israelis, we're stuck with the damn drones from Iran. And I need to tell Perun the next steps. He'll get the passports today, but I don't know what to tell him."

"Just give him the next meet. You'll know by then."

"We only have a couple more days before he's flying back to Ukraine."

"You'll figure it out. You always have. I can't predict the next steps, but I know you'll figure it out. Drone or gun, one of them will be in play."

Daniel had two different ways to execute this mission. In 2021 Israel had killed the head of the Iranian nuclear program with a remote-controlled machine gun, operated from outside the country using satellite communications. The method of attack had initially generated enormous controversy because nobody could figure out how Israel had done it, and it was perfect for this mission, but he needed the technology in order to execute, which was why he was meeting the Israelis.

It would take much longer to get the weapon into Russia, as, like the Israelis in Iran, he'd have to smuggle it in piece by piece, but it had the ability to ensure success. The weapon used in Iran was a simple belt-fed machine gun, used to penetrate a non-armored car. His problem was different. Putin would most definitely be protected by armor, which meant he'd have to up the ante. He'd decided on the American Vulcan, a Gatling gun that fired 20mm bullets at a rate of 6,000 rounds a minute. It was a fire hose of death, and would shred anything in its path, and if he could control it from outside the country, it was perfect.

The other plan was simply a drone. Iran had given plenty of Shahed 136 or 131 drones to Russia for its assault in Ukraine, and Daniel had selectively siphoned off a few. Both were basically flying bombs, with a payload of explosives designed for one function: fly to a target and kill it.

It had been fairly successful at the start of the war, but had since become sort of a flying albatross. Ukraine had learned how to thwart the weapon, and Daniel was sure the same had been learned in Russia. Russian air defenses were state-of-the-art, and trying to kill Putin with a Shahed was a smaller probability. The best he could hope for was that since Russia hadn't experienced what Ukraine had, their learning curve would be much lower. There was a better-than-even chance the drone would reach the target, especially given that his chosen launch point was from a direction Russia would never suspect. All of its air defenses were focused on Ukraine, and he didn't plan on launching from there.

Hopefully the drones wouldn't be needed, especially if this meeting went as he planned. He'd already infiltrated both the Vulcan cannon and the Shahed parts into Finland for onward travel to Russia, but at this point, the gun was just a gun. Without the secret sauce of the Israelis, it was worthless. He'd be forced to use the drones from a standoff attack outside the borders of Russia.

He said, "You think the Israelis will have any counterintelligence assets on the ground?"

"More than likely. Wouldn't you? I'm surprised they're even meeting us, given the pressure from the United States."

"Yeah, that is weird. Gives me pause. I'm wondering if this isn't a setup."

"From Putin?"

"No. From the United States. I need that satellite control for the Vulcan, but why would Israel agree to meet me? They know I'm Russian. They know what they're dealing with."

"It's not the Israeli government. It's the private sector, and if the Israelis have shown anything, it's that they want to make money. They always talk a good game about being upstanding world citizens, but at the end of the day, they'll sell their shit to whoever is buying. Just look at NRO and Pegasus. 'We'll only sell that surveillance software to accredited states systems.' And then Jamal Khashoggi gets killed by Saudi Arabia using that program. They don't care."

"Yeah, I know. It still makes me worried. I'll be all by myself out there. If Putin *is* involved, I'll be dead."

"Israel has no love of Putin. They straddle the line between him and the West, but they would never be leveraged to kill a Putin enemy."

"I know, but that doesn't mean the Israelis haven't slipped up, letting something leak. If this meeting is known to anyone outside of our circle, it's a threat."

———

Oleg looked at each member in the room, saying, "Okay, look, this isn't that hard, but it might be dangerous. All we have to do is separate the bad guy from the others he's meeting."

He pointed at the computer screen and said, "According to the intel, there's a meeting happening between the GRU traitors and some Israelis. In the end, we want the Valkyrie team complete, but not the Israelis. That's the mission. So, this op isn't an endstate. It's a follow-on. We find the GRU traitor doing the meeting, and he leads us to the Valkyrie team. We stay away from the Israelis."

He tapped a Google Earth view on his laptop, showing the expansive Assistens Kirkegård cemetery. Dating from the late 1760s, it was probably one of Copenhagen's most famous burial places, and for some reason was the chosen place for the meeting.

He said, "The linkup location is the burial plot for the Danish author Hans Christian Andersen. Whether that's where the meet will go, or whether they're just making contact there and moving somewhere else, I don't know."

He zoomed in the view, saying, "You can see why they picked the cemetery. It's impossible to control that area. Much too large, with too many escape routes. Nobody's going to attack them in there."

He turned back to the men and saw them languishing about the room. He snapped his fingers and said, "Hey! Everyone listen up. This isn't a cake walk. Get your head in the game. There might be GRU men out hunting us here. They've already affected the operation in Sweden."

Misha said, "What's that mean?"

"It means keep on your toes. Just because we're hunting them doesn't make us the predator here. They might be hunting us in return."

He began snapping out orders, detailing where he wanted the countersurveillance teams to position, along with the follow-on surveillance forces, saying, "We have to assume they'll show up on a metro, but if they have a car, we need to be able to flex to that. The bottom line is to stay on your radios and be prepared for contingencies. We might have to follow them to another established meet location. The endstate is to keep on the GRU guy until he leads us to the full Valkyrie team."

He looked around the room and said, "Understood? No screwups here. If we lose him today, we have no other thread. We cannot afford failure."

Anton said, "What are the odds that the Israelis have their own teams out here?"

"Slim. The Israelis are from a private company. They're trying to make a sale. They aren't thinking about anyone trying to kill them. They're thinking about how to keep this off the balance sheet if it goes wrong."

"And the West? What about them?"

"What about them?"

"What if the West is on to this. The Americans?"

Anton smiled and said, "There are no Western interests here. They're all petrified about the Russian bear, as they should be. This is between Ukraine, Russia, and Israel. If they're here right now, we wouldn't even be sitting in this room. They'd just hit us with a Reaper strike, because they have no courage for a stand-up fight."

CHAPTER 31

I couldn't believe the geolocation of the phone we'd tracked. It was an absolute dump, like something out of a zombie movie after the apocalypse, and that was giving Hollywood zombie shitholes a bad name. I mean, we were literally walking through a cesspool of human detritus. Called "Freetown Christiana," it was some sort of commune run by people who apparently refused to bathe. Or maybe they had to make a choice between bathing and marijuana, and chose the latter.

In my mind, the area was the lowest common denominator of the human condition, but to hear them tell it, they were sticking up for the rights of the oppressed around the world, taking it to "The Man."

I looked around at the graffiti, threadbare buildings, and general lack of sanitation and said, "No way are the Russians living in this place. Someone stole that phone."

Jennifer said, "Honestly, it's the best spot for them. There's no official authority here, which means they can run free. If you'd given me the research job for an infiltration to Copenhagen, I'd choose this area."

It had been close to eighteen hours since we'd freed Lars and his family, and was clearly too early in the day for anyone at this place to wake up, even as it was closing in on 2 P.M. I said, "Well, they're better men than me." I looked at her and said, "Or women." I got on the net and said, "All elements, all elements, any indicator from the Growler?"

While we'd geolocated the phone to this compound, the over-the-horizon fidelity of the technology we'd used was only precise enough to get us within a half-mile circle, which meant we still had to pinpoint it on the ground. We had a more precise tool we called a Growler, which, if the phone was on and operational, would lock on and guide us right to it. I'd equipped everyone on the team with one, and now they were fanning out and searching while Jennifer and I provided control for the effort.

I got a negative from Knuckles and Veep, then Brett came on, saying he had a signal.

So they are *here. Somewhere. Or, at least that last phone is here.* Which I was pretty sure meant the Russian team was here. Unless it was some random drug addict with the handset.

Brett was still sore from the gouge he'd gotten on the Sweden op, but had refused to stand down on the mission. He sent me a location via an encrypted app on our phone, and I'd started vectoring in the team.

Jennifer and I began moving, and I had a hard time hiding my incredulity of what I was seeing: a mix of tourists coming to watch the zoo and commune dwellers that looked like they regretted missing out on Woodstock, it was one of the weirdest places I'd ever experienced. One alley was called "Pusher Street," with signs saying no photography, where one could walk up to any table and buy whatever type of hash or marijuana one wanted. No hard drugs, apparently. They'd flushed that out after a fight a few years before. Even a hippy commune has to have some standards, I suppose.

Outside of selling marijuana, there were craft shops, bars, and restaurants, and apparently the place had its own city council to run things, so I supposed it functioned. Even so, it looked a little bit like a few refugee camps I'd seen, with plenty of people sitting on the side of the streets like dogs who wanted a place to get out of the sun.

Brett said, "Got a lock on. Two-story wooden building to the south.

Looks like a barn. It's next to a bike shop covered in graffiti. Appears abandoned, but I can see lights on inside."

I found the bike shop, then the building. I looked around the area and saw a bunch of different cafés with peace and love names. I said, "Okay, plenty of places to relax without compromise. Set up a perimeter. We have the north exit. Call your bumper positions to Jennifer. I'm getting reach back with Creed."

One by one they gave Jennifer where they were stationed, and she mapped their locations on her tablet to make sure we hadn't missed an exit, which is what a surveillance control does. Veep came on, saying, "Since I'm at a café, you think we have time for lunch?"

I dialed Creed, hearing Jennifer say, "If you trust one of these kitchens, go for it." I chuckled, hearing the phone connect. "This is Creed."

I said, "You getting a feed on that phone? You still have it through the network?"

"I got it. I'm reading it."

By "feed," I simply meant if he was tracking the cell on the network. It aggravated the hell out of me, but by the Taskforce charter, we weren't allowed to intercept conversations between handsets. That was the NSA's purview, and we weren't allowed to duplicate it. Never mind that we were breaking every bit of the charter with this mission anyway; we simply didn't have the technology to do so—by design—but we *could* see the other phones it talked with through the cell network. I said, "I want to know every other phone it contacts. Every one."

"Easy day. I'm on it."

Brett came on the radio, saying, "This is Blood. Growler shows it on the move. They're leaving."

Knuckles said, "Nothing on my side." Veep came back, "Same here."

I said, "Beast?"

Blaine came back, "Nothing."

Jennifer hit my arm and I watched a group of fit guys leave the wooden shack next to the bike shop, completely different from the people they were walking through. No scraggly hair, no wispy beards, all full of muscle. They had the same vibe as the guys in the Vasa Museum. They were definitely pipe-hitters.

So it's not a woman he was hooking up with on the way home.

To Jennifer, I said, "That's them. Get some photos." I got on the net, saying, "We have them. Photos coming. Six men, all hitters. Blood, Veep, stage at the car. I'm betting the metro, but if it's a car, you have them. Beast, Knuckles, they're heading to the main entrance, the one with the arch. Pick up the follow. They're walking right by us and I don't want to trigger them."

We watched them pass, threading up the narrow lane to the overarching gate, proclaiming the "Free World of Christiana." They left in a group, moving rapidly up the road.

Veep said, "They just went by me, walking with a purpose, took a turn at the road leading to the Christiana metro station."

I said, "It's the metro. Beast, Knuckles, you on that?"

"We got them. Watching now. Five men, all positive ID from the photos. We're right behind them."

"Five? We lost one."

Veep came on, saying, "I've got the straggler. He's headed to an SUV."

"Veep, you and Blood take the singleton. We'll take the rest."

I really didn't want to split the team like that, but I had no choice. The entire point was determining what these guys were up to, and it would do no good to follow the main element to a pub for dinner while the singleton executed some secret mission.

We exited the sleazy compound, entering the real world of Copenhagen, and walked up the street, trailing behind the group. We watched them take the escalator down to the Christianshavn metro station, gave them a moment, then followed, Knuckles and Blaine first, then me and Jennifer. We found them standing on the platform for the western train. Jennifer and I loitered, not acknowledging the other members of my team. The train arrived, and we boarded, Knuckles' team a door ahead of them, Jennifer and me a door behind.

One stop later, they exited, leaving the M2 line and waiting on the northbound M3. Luckily, it was a major transfer point, or we'd have been compromised right off the bat as the only ones standing next to them on the platform. We blended into the crowd and followed the same procedure we'd done previously, me saying, on the net, "So far, so good. Stay away from them. Don't get burned."

The train arrived, and we all boarded, along with a throng of other people. When it left, I kept our eyes on them, watching for any indication that they were about to exit. We continued until we reached a stop called Nørrebros Runddel, and I saw the men move to an exit door. I called Knuckles, knowing he didn't have eyes on the target in the crowd, saying, "This is it. Exit this stop. Get in front of them."

The train pulled in and I let them go, then followed Jennifer out behind them. We went up the long escalator to the top, separated by a mass of people, and I called Knuckles again, saying, "You out?"

"Yeah. Up top."

"They're about to hit daylight."

"I see 'em. We got 'em."

"Don't get too close."

I called Veep, saying, "What's the trailer doing?"

"Coming the same way, just slower because of the surface streets."

"Okay, all elements, all elements, that SUV is some sort of escape valve for whatever is going on. Veep and Blood, keep eyes on it when it stops. Send me a location when it does. Knuckles and Blaine, follow them in. Give me a call when they commit to a direction. We'll provide backup, paralleling you."

I got acknowledgment from the teams and turned to Jennifer, saying, "Where are we?"

"Giant cemetery. One of the biggest in Copenhagen."

"Why here?"

"No idea."

She showed me her phone, displaying the cemetery map. It was huge, with a multitude of trails and paths, all wooded and looking like a miniature Central Park. Knuckles came on, saying, "Two split off. They're all heading east, deeper into the cemetery, but on separate paths."

I said, "We're in. We'll take the southern team. You stay on the northern one. Remember, the sole function is finding out if this matters. If it doesn't, we simply go home. Keep your eyes peeled. They aren't looking for gravestones."

We quickened our pace, cutting into the cemetery and looking for the wayward team. We went by a group of elderly people performing tai chi, then found the team, two guys walking in a rapid pace on a path threading through foliage, passing up families with strollers and couples out for an afternoon walk. It was surreal, but I guess this forest full of gravestones was a place for the family to come visit.

They cut to the south, exiting one part of the cemetery, circling around a church, and entering a second part. I called that in and heard, "Our guys are doing the same thing, only further east. They're setting up a box."

I thought, *A box for what?*

We kept on our team, and they eventually stopped their rapid pace, now walking much more slowly, one talking into a phone. I relayed that, asking if someone on Knuckles' team was also on a cell. He said, "Yeah, one's talking, and they're slowing movement. They're spreading out on the path."

Our guys did the same. I said, "Give me a lock on to your location, I'll send one from ours. Whatever it is, it's in between."

My phone pinged. I saw his location while Jennifer sent ours. I zoomed in on the map and saw the burial site for Hans Christian Andersen smack dab in the middle.

Looks like they are *looking for a gravesite.*

I said, "Okay, Jennifer and I are going to let these guys go unsighted for a moment and start walking to you. Whatever they want is in between us. Keep your eyes on your team. With three men, odds are you have the commander."

"Roger all."

We went down the path, threading through the bushes and trees toward the Hans Christian Andersen gravesite, and Knuckles came on, saying, "One of the pipe-hitters is coming your way."

We passed him unnoticed on the path. We continued on, and I thought, *They're doing the same damn thing we are.*

I started to reconsider my plan, wanting to circle around and keep eyes on the team we'd left, when Jennifer nudged me.

I said, "What?"

She pointed at a square opening forty meters away and said, "That's what they're here for."

I looked at the area, seeing a couple on a bench scattering seeds for birds, another older couple next to them on a separate bench, and the obelisk for Hans Christian Andersen in the middle, with what looked like a school outing of children half-circled in front with a teacher at the head talking.

I said, "They came to watch some school field trip?"

"Take a look at the pigeon feeder."

I did, and it rocked my world.

What the hell is Shoshana doing here?

CHAPTER 32

Oleg, Misha, and Ivanov exited the easternmost wall of the cemetery, spilling out onto an avenue lined with apartments on the far side. He looked at his phone and pointed south, saying, "Past that church. We'll go through the next gate."

They walked down the avenue, acting like they were out for an afternoon stroll like everyone else, but Oleg was beginning to feel the heat. The meeting time was within the next ten minutes, and if anyone was sweeping the area, now would be the time. He'd purposely dragged his entire team through the length of the cemetery precisely to determine if he was being followed, but the team had seen nothing abnormal—outside of a group of geriatrics doing tai chi, that is. Who does Chinese martial arts in a cemetery?

That didn't mean they weren't here. It only meant they were good. Absence of evidence was not evidence of absence. He'd learned that the hard way on another operation.

He radioed Anton, saying, "Are you north?"

"Yes. We're slowing. We're within a hundred meters."

"Hang on. We'll close the box from the south here in about two minutes. You see anything like countersurveillance?"

"Nothing. Just couples moving around in here. I suppose they could be putting cameras in baby strollers, but if they are, it's not GRU. They don't use women."

"True. Okay. We're penetrating back inside now. Hold what you have."

They reentered the cemetery, now walking much more slowly. They reached the path that led to the Andersen gravesite and Oleg said, "Misha, you're up." He pointed at a couple of benches, saying, "We'll be right here. If trouble comes before you make contact, come back here. If something happens after, go to Anton."

Misha left, and Oleg called Anton, saying, "Misha's on the way."

Two minutes later, Yuri called. "Misha's here, and he's not sure of a meeting. There's a group of schoolkids, an old couple, and a younger couple feeding birds. Nothing looks out of the ordinary."

"That was at the gravesite?"

"Yes. I mean, there are people wandering all over in this place, but the only ones stationary at the gravesite are those."

"What does the younger couple look like?"

"Man of about thirty-five, maybe forty. Woman about the same age."

"You come back this way. Focus on them. Tell me if you see anything that doesn't fit. Check their dress. Check them both. Do they look like they're a couple? Or is something off?"

Two minutes later, Anton appeared, taking a seat. He said, "That's them."

"How do you know?"

"The woman has on a North Face jacket and cargo pants. The man is wearing a Jack Wolfskin jacket. She's wearing American clothing, he's wearing all European."

"That's pretty thin."

"Well, it's what we have. Why would she be wearing cargo pants on a walk through the park? That's not what wives or girlfriends do. And couples buy their clothes together. She's not going shopping at North Face while he goes to Jack Wolfskin."

"Maybe she just likes American shit."

"She was also showing him something on a tablet. Who brings a tablet with them for a walk in the park? There's no Wi-Fi here. Whatever she's showing him is on the hard drive. She could have done that anywhere. Why do it here?"

Oleg nodded and said, "Okay, that's better. That's more like it."

Anton said, "I know *she's* not GRU, but he might be."

Oleg said, "She's Israeli. You guys spread out. We need to be able to pick up the follow wherever he goes."

He called Misha and said, "Can you get close enough to the young couple for an extended stay, keeping eyes on?"

"Yeah. There are bushes, trees, and benches all over the place. I can plop down right behind the Andersen marker on a bench."

"Do it. We might be here for a while."

He pulled out his cell phone and called Mikhail, the man in the SUV, saying, "We have them, but they might be here for an extended meeting. What's your status?"

"I'm in a parking garage just northeast of the cemetery, next to some sort of library. I'm good for as long as you need."

"Okay. Just stand by. I don't know how the target got here, so you might be in play if he enters a vehicle."

"No problem. Just give me enough warning to pay to get out of here."

"Will do my best." He heard a beep from his radio and said, "Gotta go. Misha's calling."

He clicked on the net and said, "What?"

"Meeting's over. Target is headed to you. Woman is remaining on the bench."

"Roger. Hold what you've got until we make contact, then you and Alek exit out the northern side. Keep eyes on the woman until then. All elements, you copy the last?"

He got confirmation and said, "First one to spot him call it out."

Anton said, "I have him. He's exiting the cemetery next to the church, headed north up the avenue."

Oleg said, "Keep eyes on him. Misha and Alek, you have parallel. All others, let's go."

From there it was an intricate dance of following their rabbit, with Oleg running men ahead of him, rotating teammates out of the follow behind him, and keeping men parallel of him on side streets to put into play. It was extremely hard to do with only a five-man team, but given the skills of his target, it was the only way he felt confident of not burning his team. All the while, Oleg was trying to think two steps ahead. The rabbit had gone deeper into the neighborhood, away from the metro, so he was sure he was moving to a pickup.

He gave Mikhail a warning order in the parking garage and continued working the problem, growing less confident the longer it went on. There was only so long you could follow someone who was skilled at detecting such a thing, and for all he knew, his target was conducting this route precisely to smoke out surveillance.

He was about to pull the team back when Anton called, saying, "He's taking a seat at a restaurant. A place called Brus. Sending location. I'm moving past it."

Oleg got the pinpoint on his phone and said, "What is it?"

"It's a brew pub. They make craft beers. It's surrounded by long wooden tables on the outside, with some seating inside. The rabbit is seated outside."

"By himself?"

"Right now, yes."

"Did he order anything, or is he just stopping to check out if he's being followed?"

"I couldn't tell. I'm around the corner now. I can't penetrate without him possibly remembering I was behind him."

Oleg called the team, saying, "Who's closest?"

Misha said, "I'm close. I can go in."

"Not as a singleton. It'll spike."

Alek said, "I'm there. Misha, where are you?" Misha told him, and then Oleg heard, "We're together. Should we penetrate?"

"Yes, but stay far enough away that he can't hear you talking. If he hears Russian, or you speaking English with a Russian accent, he'll know.

CHAPTER 33

I took a left on a path, moving deeper into the cemetery, outside of the box set by the Russians, saying, "What the hell is Shoshana doing here?"

Jennifer said, "I don't know, but whoever she's with is probably the reason the Russians are here."

"Or maybe it's her. Wouldn't be the first time."

Shoshana was an Israeli ex-assassin who used to work for the Mossad. We'd crossed paths on a mission years ago when she was a member of a group called Samson that had grown out of the fabled Wrath of God missions against Black September during the 1970s. On that initial mission, she'd tried to kill me—and I'd tried to return the favor. We'd both missed. Since then, we'd become pretty close—so much so that Jennifer and I had been in her wedding, and she had been in ours. Hers, of course, had turned into an absolute shit show, because that's what always happened whenever she was around, but she was a genuinely good person. As far as I knew, she was now in the private sector, but I also knew, once in the Mossad—always in the Mossad.

I got on the net and said, "We found the target, and you're not going to believe it even if I tell you."

Knuckles said, "What?"

"Shoshana's at the gravesite."

Blaine said, "Shoshana? The assassin?"

He'd only met her once, whereas my team had worked with her on a number of missions. I said, "Yeah, 'Shoshana the assassin.' She's here."

Knuckles came on, saying, "With Aaron? Is he here too?"

Aaron was Shoshana's husband—and the previous leader of the Samson kill team. I said, "No. She's with an unknown."

From our vehicle, Brett said, "This is Blood. You sure it's her?"

"Oh yeah, I'm sure. It's most definitely her."

"What the hell is going on? What's this got to do with a hit team in Sweden?"

"I have no idea, but we need eyes on that meet site. Knuckles, Beast, you guys still good?"

"Yeah. These guys telegraph their intentions like children. They think they're all sneaky, but they're not very good at countersurveillance."

"Penetrate in and confirm, then stage somewhere with eyes on the site."

"What about the pipe-hitters out here?"

"Jennifer and I are headed out of the cemetery. We'll pick them up. We'll lose sight of the guys to the west, but the commander is on the eastern edge, so if we get him under control, we'll know what's going on."

"You know what he looks like?"

"No, but I still have a Growler, and he's still got his phone."

"Roger all. Moving now."

We left the cemetery at the church, then circled back around, entering at the same point Knuckles and Blaine had used. I clicked on the Growler hidden in my jacket and we strolled down the path, holding hands. I spotted the first hitter and went past him, getting no notification. We kept going. We passed the second guy, and the Growler vibrated. I squeezed Jennifer's hand and we stopped about twenty meters away, taking a seat on a bench next to the wall of the cemetery.

I said, "Knuckles, we have him, what do you have?"

"It's most definitely Shoshana, and the meeting is breaking up. The unknown is leaving, Shoshana is staying put. Found the western team. They're eyeballing what's going on."

I saw the leader get on the phone, and then the unknown from Shoshana's bench exited the cemetery. The Russian team waited a beat, and then they left the park like water from a split bucket. Knuckles said, "Western team is moving away, going north into the cemetery."

"What about Shoshana?"

"She's staying put on the park bench."

So she's not the target.

And then I realized she might just know what the hell is going on. I said, "Knuckles, Beast, get on the street right now. Follow the unknown. See what the pipe-hitters want with him."

"What's the mission? Are we going to protect him now?"

"No. Still just Alpha. No kinetic action. We're still building the picture."

"What are you going to do?"

"Pay a visit to Shoshana."

He laughed and said, "Good luck with that."

We left the bench, seeing Knuckles and Blaine jogging down a path forty meters away, exiting the park next to the church.

We reached the tiny square opening with the Andersen obelisk, the student group still there but the older couple now gone. Shoshana was looking at a cell phone, typing in a text. I muttered, "Here we go. Let's see how Carrie reacts." Jennifer chuckled, saying, "She won't kill you if she sees me with you."

Carrie was the callsign Knuckles had given her because she had some preternatural ability to see things others did not. That, and she was crazy, just like Carrie from the Stephen King novel. While she *had* been in our wedding, she was a little off, to say the least. Surprising her like this was like petting a feral bobcat. Sometimes it would purr; sometimes it would start ripping into you with its claws.

We casually walked up to the bench the old couple had used, taking a seat. Shoshana looked up, and to give her credit, she barely showed any reaction. No surprise other than a tic of her eye.

I said, "Hello, Carrie."

She slowly put her phone away and said, "Hello, Nephilim. I wasn't told the Taskforce was playing in this game."

Her using my given name gave me hope that she wasn't too aggravated that we'd managed to sneak up on her. She knew I hated it and was poking me in the eye by using it, which meant she had some humor about the situation.

I smiled and moved to her bench, fairly sure I was getting the purr instead of the claws. She raised her cheek, and I knew I was good. I kissed it, then said, "Good to see you. I know you're surprised, but trust me, no more than we are."

She looked at Jennifer, then back to me, saying, "The Mossad didn't read you into this?"

"Nope. I had no idea you were operational. We're here on another thread and you happened to be in the middle of it. I have no idea what 'this' is. I was hoping you could help with that."

CHAPTER 34

Daniel ordered a craft beer, surreptitiously taking an inventory of everyone who entered after him, watching to see if anyone paid him any undue attention. Not because he thought he had been compromised as an agent of the GRU, but simply because it was a reflex. Habit from years of living undercover in foreign lands.

The fact that nobody had interrupted the meeting at the cemetery told him he was secure. If he'd been made as a foreign agent, both he and the Israeli would have been rolled up by Copenhagen authorities right then and there. There was still the threat of his brethren in the GRU, but that was remote. As far as his command knew, he was here gathering information on the unconventional warfare conference—like Perun, it was the reason he'd been sent to Copenhagen in the first place, and was his cover for action with regard to the Russian security state.

Even given that, he'd run a short surveillance detection route from the cemetery to get to this location, and had seen nothing of note. No repeat sightings of individuals behind him, no signatures of someone tracking him. If the GRU suspected him, they'd have only risked sending a single man, and he would have stood out.

Daniel had seen nothing to indicate that, and he'd looked. The key to surveillance detection was repeated sightings over time and distance. That was truly it. Go places that made sense, but stretch it out over time and distance, and if the same guy keeps showing up—you're under surveillance.

His route had been short, but the only way he'd be under surveillance was if there were a team of at least six on him—and that was a ridiculous thought. If the GRU were going to put that much effort against him, they'd just come to his hotel room and kill him.

He saw Stepan coming around the corner and waved his hand. Stepan took a seat across from the wooden table, saying, "Good choice. This place has the best beer in town."

Daniel said, "How would you know that? You've never been here."

"TripAdvisor. Best online help for spies all over the world."

Daniel laughed and said, "How'd the transfer go?"

"No issues loading the site. I put in the contact information for Finland, the weapons package, and the passports. I didn't stick around to see if they retrieved it, but they've been pretty good so far."

"So they now can travel without suspicion, and have the weapons to protect themselves if they run into trouble. Let's just hope they have the will to see it through."

"Are you going to Finland, or leaving it to Kirill and Luka?"

"I don't know. What do you think?"

"They're good men, but it's your plan. If it were me, I'd want to be there."

"Maybe I will. We'll see. Maybe I'll send you."

"My rotation is up. GRU wants me home. No chance I'm going, unless you want to compromise the Valkyrie."

"I know, I know."

Daniel was lost in thought about the future and Stepan finally couldn't wait any longer. "So? You're going to make me ask?"

"What?"

"What the fuck happened at the meeting? With the Israeli?"

"Oh." He chuckled. "Sorry. Yeah, it went okay, but I don't think they're going to be able to execute in our timeline. She asked too many questions."

"She?"

"Yeah, the rep from the Israelis was a woman, and I mean to tell you, she was weird."

"What's that mean?"

"I don't know. She just floats her eyes on you, and it's like she's reading into your soul. I can't explain it, but it was creepy. Like she knew I was lying even as I talked."

"What did you tell her?"

"I gave her the cover story about being from a Russian defense contractor looking to expand our wares for sale outside of Russia. I'm not sure she bought it."

"Why?"

"She focused on the weapon itself, asking why I wanted that specific piece of technology. She offered me several other things, like small bomb drone swarms, saying she had some samples, but was reticent to talk about the tech for the remote-controlled machine gun."

"Well, that sounds legit. That's what she's supposed to do. Sell you stuff."

"Yeah, but she really pressed me on why I wanted the remote gun. What the purpose of it was and why my 'company' had asked for it specifically instead of asking for a catalog. Which was a mistake on my part."

"Yeah, but that remote gun isn't *in* their catalog. The only way we know about it is through GRU contacts with the Iranian IRGC. You had to ask somehow. It was worth a shot. We still have the Shahed drones."

"Well, it's not over yet. She's agreed to a separate meeting, where she'll bring a little suitcase with some wares to show off. Dummy stuff, but same size. She said she'd take my request back to her bosses and ask them."

Daniel glanced across the restaurant, then did a little double take, pausing on a table more than twenty meters away. Stepan said, "What?"

"I think those two guys were in the cemetery with me today. They were on a bench right as I exited."

"So? Probably tourists. They went to see the Hans Christian Andersen gravesite, and then came here. I wasn't kidding about this being a TripAdvisor favorite."

"Yeah, maybe so, but I want you to leave here now. When you do, keep an open line on the phone. If they get up when you leave, I'm going to let them walk for a minute, then let you know. Stay on an open line."

"And if they don't leave?"

"I'll let you know. You can hang up, then walk to the metro, but don't get on. Circle back to here but don't come in. Find a vantage point, and when you're set, let me know. I'll get up and leave, and you look to see if they follow me."

"You really think this is something?"

Daniel smiled, saying, "No, I don't, but I haven't lived this long ignoring my instincts."

CHAPTER 35

Oleg heard the call on his radio and said, "Say again? Someone's with him now?"

"Yeah. A separate guy just showed up. They're drinking beer and talking."

The Valkyrie cell. But if it was, it was only two men. The plot had to be bigger than that.

He said, "Okay, so we have two of them. Somewhere is the beehive. We need to find that. Stay on them. When they leave, we'll locate where that is."

Misha, on the patio at the restaurant, said, "Maybe we just smoke these two and short-circuit the entire thing."

Oleg said, "No. That's not good enough. We need to find the entire team. The president wants them all dead, not running away and hiding."

Anton, on the far side of the block, patiently waiting on orders, said, "Well, maybe we rip one of these guys off the street and interrogate him."

Oleg thought about that, seeing it had merit, but it was a great risk. Take one, and the others could scatter, having to be found yet again. He said, "Stick with the plan. When these guys go to a bed-down location, we'll have them all. Then we attack."

Sitting on a bus stop bench, watching the public transportation come and go, Oleg thought about what Anton had said. If they could get one of them under control without the others knowing, maybe they could find the beehive on their own, and execute the mission before the others were aware.

But that would require serious planning for exfiltration and interrogation. Today wasn't that day, as doing such things on the fly was asking for compromise or relying on extreme luck.

Better to stick with the plan.

Misha said, "One of them is leaving. Not the cemetery subject. The one who came to meet him."

Anton said, "I have him. I have him. Going south on the avenue, talking into a phone. What do you want to do? Follow him, or stick with the original?"

Oleg hated making that choice. He knew the original subject was the main one, precisely because he'd met the Israeli like his commander's intelligence said would happen, but this guy could lead them to the beehive right now. He was on the move. Oleg didn't have enough of a team to do both.

He said, "Ivanov, are you in play?"

"Yeah. Just down the street from Anton."

"Okay, we stay on the original, but keep an eye on that guy until he's out of sight. The original is the main target. Misha, Alek, you copy?"

They gave him confirmation, and Anton said, "He's headed to a tunnel next to a parking garage. I'm on him."

Oleg thought, *Tunnel next to a parking garage?*

"Ivanov, Ivanov, this is Oleg, is that tunnel under a library?"

"Yes. Yes, it is. Some university thing. Why?"

Sometimes it's better to be lucky than good.

"Are you ahead of him?"

"Yes. I'm in the tunnel. It goes underneath a building before exiting back onto the street. A flight of stairs down, and a flight of stairs up."

Time started to speed up, as it always did on operations when he had to make tight decisions. He called Mikhail, saying, "Get your car ready. We're coming to you with a body."

He returned to Ivanov, saying, "Is there an exit to the garage from that tunnel?"

"Yes. I'm right next to it."

"What are the atmospherics? How many people?"

"None. Why?"

And he committed. "We're going to take that guy. Misha, Alek, stay in the restaurant until I tell you we've got him. If we abort, we go back to the original plan. Anton, are you on him?"

"Yes, but he's still on the phone talking."

Shit.

"Okay, okay, we can't take him while he's talking. That'll trigger someone. But get ready. I'm moving your way now. Ivanov, no lethal action. Use a sap and knock his ass out when he's abreast of the door. Anton, follow in and help if needed. Mikhail, get that vehicle up next to the exit for the tunnel. Everyone give me a confirmation."

He began running down the street, crossing over to the avenue they were on, skidding past the Brus brewery and realizing he was in full view of the patrons on the patio.

Alek came on, saying, "I see you. You're drawing stares."

He slowed to a walk, saying, "Did the target see?"

He waited a pregnant second, then heard "No. He's looking the other way."

Oleg picked up his pace again, leaving the brewery behind and saying, "Anton, what's the status?"

"He's going down the stairs now. I'm right behind him. I see Ivanov."

"Atmospherics?"

"Nobody around."

"Mikhail?"

"I'm staged. Waiting right inside."

"Is he still on the phone?"

"No. He hung up when he reached the stairs. He's going to cross under the building and go to the metro."

Perfect.

Oleg reached the top of the long staircase, seeing the underground walkway reaching below the building to the stairwell on the far side, Anton in front of him following the man down. He looked left and right, saw no one around, and said, "Take him."

The next thirty seconds happened so quickly it made Oleg proud. The man passed right by the entrance to the parking garage, not even seeing Ivanov. Ivanov stepped in front of him, the man gave one quizzical look, and Anton hammered him in the temple with a leather sap filled with lead. He crumpled over, shielding his skull, and Anton hit it again, dropping him to the ground. By the time Oleg met them, he was unconscious.

Oleg grabbed a leg and said, "Get him out of here, now." They hauled him to the garage exit, opened the door, and, like a miracle, Mikhail was right there with his Land Rover.

Oleg dropped the leg he was holding, letting them do the work, getting on the radio, saying, "Alek, Misha, exfiltrate now. Get out of the brewery and meet us back at the safe house."

CHAPTER 36

Still in a little bit of shock, but not showing a thing, Shoshana said, "I'm not sure what you mean about not knowing what's going on. Surely, if the vaunted Taskforce is here, there's *something* going on. Since you didn't know I would be here, maybe I shouldn't know *you* are here."

I said, "Oh, come on, Shoshana. Give me a break here. It's us. Not some conspiracy against Israel."

I knew she trusted us, but she loved her country more, and she was always looking for something hidden in the bushes when what was happening was staring her straight in the face.

She floated her weird glow on me, the disconcerting stare she used when she was boring past your eyes into your soul. I always told anyone who listened that her abilities were bullshit, because, well, it had to be—but I sort of believed, and when she did it, it scared me.

I said, "Cut that shit out. Jennifer is with me here. She wouldn't do anything untoward."

She turned to Jennifer and said, "You, I trust. This guy, not so much."

Jennifer came to the bench and gave her a hug, saying, "So you know what we're saying is true. I saw that look on your face. You know he's telling the truth."

Shoshana gave her a fierce hug back, saying, "I missed you. We should get together more often, outside of work."

Like we'd just seen each other after a soccer game with our kids.

Which was Shoshana predictably being batshit crazy. Jennifer glanced at me over her shoulder with a *what's that about?* look. I just shrugged, because Shoshana was Shoshana.

I said, "Let's take a walk. You met someone, and that someone is being tracked by Russian killers. I'm pretty sure they're gone now, but it would be better to be on the move."

She said, "Killers? Here?"

I said, "Yeah, let's go. I'll tell you what I know, and you can return the favor."

We started walking and she said, "So, you guys are still married, huh?"

I said, "What?"

She looked at Jennifer and said, "You're still married."

Jennifer said, "Of course we are. It's a struggle with this guy, but we are."

I glowered at that, but Shoshana took her hand and said, "I'm glad. Makes me happy. How's Amena? Is she still a handful?"

She was talking like we were going on vacation and had met each other in the airport after not seeing each other in a while. Not like she had just heard that some Russian assassins were watching her meeting.

I said, "Shoshana, we really don't have time for this."

She glanced up at me, showing a little anger, and said, "This is how it works when friends meet friends after a long time apart."

And I recognized something I'd learned long ago—she wanted more than anything to be normal, and she thought Jennifer and I were that. She wanted to be us, not realizing that our life was definitely not normal. She had lived in a cauldron of violence and wanted to be someone who could banter about the nothingness of living. She had no one to do that with. Except us.

I relented, saying, "She's good. Going to school and getting in trouble. Is Aaron on the ground here?"

She said, "No. He's got another assignment he's on." She laughed and said, "Don't worry, it's not in Africa."

That was a throwback to a time when we'd literally changed missions to save her husband during a coup in Lesotho, Africa, ripping through multiple factions to do so. She said it like, *Don't worry, you won't have to go pick him up again after drinking too much.*

She continued, saying, "This mission is a one-off. A personal favor to the *Ramsad*."

The *Ramsad* was the head of the Mossad, which told me a great deal without saying anything. Something big was happening.

We walked in silence for a moment, me not wanting to broach anything until Shoshana was ready. She finally took my hand, now holding both Jennifer's and mine like a schoolchild in the middle, and said, "I miss you guys. I really do. How can I help?"

Jennifer looked at me with a little melancholy, realizing that Shoshana was probably having the best day she'd had in a long while just walking in the forest. I squeezed Shoshana's hand and said, "Well, we truthfully don't know what you're doing here. We weren't trying to stop it, but know I'd like to know what it was."

She gave me a grin and said, "You told me you'd go first, Nephilim. And so you shall."

I said, "Okay . . ." and told her everything we knew, from Sweden right up until we found her in the cemetery. Technically, I wasn't allowed to do that, because it was classified beyond top secret, but I'd worked with her plenty of times and there were some things that a classification level shouldn't cloak.

She listened to it all, then said, "I have no idea what this has to do with me, but if you found me, it most surely does."

"What were you doing here?"

"Have you ever heard the name Mohsen Fakhrizadeh?"

"Rings a bell, but I don't know why."

"He was the head of the Iranian nuclear program. He was killed. I'm not saying we did it, but he was killed."

And then it clicked. "The guy who was killed by the remote-controlled machine gun? That guy?"

"Yes. That's the one."

"What's that got to do with this?"

"Well, there's a company in Israel that does a lot of security work for the IDF. They develop a lot of different assets, and they developed the ability to conduct that mission. They were contacted by a Russian company about licensing the same ability so they could develop their own systems to sell."

At those words, I realized she was telling me some of the most classified information in the Israeli arsenal. She was admitting to killing an Iranian nuclear scientist without saying so, and giving me the same trust I'd just shown her. We were on the same page now.

I said, "This guy was a Russian? From a Russian defense contractor?"

"Yeah—or so he said. But what was weird was we've never sold that to anyone on earth. We've never even admitted to having it. But he knew the exact company that had made it. Which told us it wasn't some defense contractor. It had to be someone that was in with the Iranians. Someone with power."

"So, how did you get involved?"

"Well, the Israeli company was immediately suspicious, and being good Israelis, they contacted the IDF, which contacted the Mossad. They read the request and got scared, figuring that Putin was looking to assassinate someone with a hands-off ability."

"And?"

"And they called me to figure out who that was. I'm supposed to string him along, showing him other wares while trying to determine who Putin wants to kill. That's it. That's why I'm here."

I took that in, thinking. It made no sense. I said, "Why are a bunch of Russians tracking a Russian trying to get an Israeli weapon? I don't get it."

She said, "Maybe there are some Russian dissidents who don't want Putin to get the technology. Maybe they're trying to stop Putin from whatever he has in mind."

"No. That's not it. The guys we're tracking aren't dissidents. They're trained, professional killers."

"We had that back in the day. The Irgun and Lehi. They were the best at what they did, but they didn't work for the government."

That was true then, and might be true here, except for one thing. "The only way we found these guys was because a team of assassins in Sweden tried to kill a Swedish diplomat to prevent him from convincing Turkey to drop objections for them to join NATO. That's Putin, not dissidents."

"Maybe you're wrong in the connection."

"I'm *not* wrong. We killed a guy who was talking on a phone. We tracked the guy he was talking with, and that guy was here—tracking you."

She stopped walking, turned to me, and said, "So what does that mean?"

I thought a moment, then said, "I honestly don't know. I'm not sure who's the good guy and who's the bad. Maybe your guy just went rogue or something. I don't know. Maybe it's a threat that we need to solve, or maybe we let the Russians solve it amongst themselves. I'm not sure now."

She glanced away, and I saw her thinking. I said, "What?"

She paused, then seemed to come to a conclusion. She said, "Well, I said I'd take his request to higher and meet him again. We set up another meeting. You want to go to that?"

Before I could answer, Brett came on the net, saying, "Pike, Pike, this is Blood, the mobile unit in the garage has moved to a door and they're loading a body. I say again, they're loading a body."

CHAPTER 37

Shoshana saw me stiffen, then said, "What's going on?" I held up a finger, saying, "Is it the guy from the cemetery?"

"I don't know. I wasn't at the cemetery."

Duh.

"Knuckles, Knuckles, this is Pike—" Before I could finish my question, he cut in, saying, "Not the guy from the park bench. He's still here, but he met another unsub. They had a little talk and that guy left about eight minutes ago."

"Blood, Blood, can you follow?"

"They're already moving. I can try, but there's no way I can stay on them for any length of time. I followed that car all the way here from the hippy crib. Trying to keep up with them on the way home is asking for compromise."

"Okay, okay, Knuckles, what's the original guy doing?"

"Staying put. Two of the other guys that tracked him here are sitting across the patio . . . wait, they're up. They're up and moving. What do you want me to do?"

So they didn't take the target at the cemetery. They took the one he met with. Which didn't tell me a damn thing.

I said, "Break it off. Come on back to the cemetery. All elements, all elements, clamshell. Meet at the Andersen grave. I don't have enough information to know what's going on."

Knuckles said, "What about the guy they snagged? We going to do anything about that?"

"Come on back here. Let's talk about it."

I got off the net and Jennifer said, "What happened?"

We started walking back to the gravesite and I said, "You heard what I heard. The guy that met Shoshana left here and went to a bar. He met someone else, who then left the bar and was stuffed into a car by the Russian hit team we were tracking."

Shoshana said, "My guy was part of the government. I'm sure of it. Who, exactly, were you tracking?"

"I honestly don't know, but the team was also a member of the Russian security services. That I'm sure of. Why they're hunting other Russians here I don't get."

"Well, if that guy was with Daniel—the man I met—he's not going to show up tomorrow. They'll probably roll him up soon."

"Yeah, that's what I don't get. If this were some Russian inter-agency infighting, there would be someone who's in charge outside of the country. Someone had to order this to go down, but if they really thought your guy was doing something bad—and he was operating as part of the Russian state—they'd just go to his hotel room and roll him up. Why all the cloak-and-dagger stuff?"

Shoshana said, "He *is* part of the Russian state. He's not a representative of a private Russian defense contractor. I saw that when I looked into him. He was lying the entire time."

We reached the gravesite and I took a seat on a bench, saying, "Yeah, yeah, I believe you, but I mean, when something like that happens in the United States—even if it's a defense contractor—we don't follow the guy until he's in a parking garage then thump him in the head and clandestinely haul his ass away. The FBI just meets him exiting an air-craft and says, 'You're under arrest for espionage.' I don't understand why the Jason Bourne shit is going on. There's something more in play here."

Knuckles and Blaine came into the cemetery and took a seat on a separate bench. Thirty seconds later, we were joined by Brett and Veep.

Blaine said, "What's the state of play?"

"Basically, we've got Russian-on-Russian violence. The question is if we care. Just let these guys duke it out and go home, or try to figure out what's going on?"

"What's your take here?"

I looked at Shoshana, wanting her permission to talk. She nodded, saying, "Go ahead."

I turned to the group. "Well, the guy from the bar was trying to get a specific type of technology for a precision, targeted killing through Israeli assets. The Israelis believe he's working for the Russian state and wanted to know who the target was."

Blaine said, "So they think Putin's targeting President Zelensky?"

Shoshana said, "No. Not at all. The system requires precise locational intelligence to use, along with a long lead time to set up. If Putin had that information on Zelensky, he'd just launch a cruise missile. Ukraine's a war zone. This is for more surreptitious work. We don't have any idea who the target might be. We honestly don't even know if there is a target—but I believe there is."

"Why?"

"Because I spoke with the man. I could see it."

"What's that mean?"

She looked at me to explain, but that was impossible. I'd had my life saved by Shoshana using her abilities in the past and *I* still didn't know if I believed. There was no way to explain it to someone who hadn't walked through fire with her.

I said, "Shoshana's pretty good at reading people. That's all."

Shoshana glowered at me and I shook my head, hoping she didn't go into her "seeing colors" descriptions of what she intuited. She remained silent.

I said, "So the question is, do we care about the target? And if we do, do we just let the other Russians kill the rest of the team? I mean, if we're trying to protect whoever they're planning to kill, it looks like the other Russians don't want it either, and can solve the problem for us."

Knuckles said, "The opposite might also be true."

"What's that mean?"

"If the Russians we're chasing are trying to prevent the other Russians from killing someone, maybe we *want* that someone dead."

I hadn't thought of that. He had a good point. He continued, saying, "But if we want to go that route, we need to repatriate the one they snagged. We need to go get him before they kill him."

Veep said, "He's probably already dead."

"I don't think so. If they wanted him dead, they'd have just killed him in the garage and left. They took him alive for a reason, but I'm sure he won't be alive long."

I turned to Blaine and said, "What do you think, sir?"

Blaine rubbed his forehead, then said, "I think it's time to punt this to higher."

I said, "I agree, but we need to do it quickly. We dick around with this and Knuckles is right—it'll be a moot point, because he'll be dead."

CHAPTER 38

George Wolffe met Kerry Bostwick in the parking garage that serviced Blaisdell Consulting, buzzing him in through the outer, bulletproof door into a small anteroom, then through the inner, bulletproof door to the hallway for the elevator. Kerry said, "What's that about? Why two doors?"

"Protection. If someone suspicious comes knocking, we let them in the first door, then lock them out of the second. We now have them in a bulletproof cage, and I send down someone like Pike to ask what they want."

"Maybe we should do that at the CIA."

Wolffe laughed and said, "We don't get the traffic you do, and we don't have the massive security you have. Honestly, it's never been needed in the history of the Taskforce."

They went up to the third floor, then down the main hallway, Kerry marveling at the expensive accoutrements in the offices, saying, "This is the best government gig I've ever seen."

Wolffe realized that Kerry Bostwick, the director of the CIA, had never been inside Blaisdell Consulting—aka the Taskforce. That was by design, as the head of the largest spy agency in the United States entering the firm would potentially cause all sorts of headaches if anyone had seen him.

Today was a little different, as only Kerry and POTUS were read on to the current mission set, and POTUS couldn't break away for a scheduled engagement to meet personally. They'd decided to do it virtually, with Kerry coming to Blaisdell Consulting a better choice than Wolffe going to CIA headquarters.

The Taskforce had developed an elaborate scheme to get Kerry in and out without a signature because of the chance of compromise, but Wolffe felt the risk was worth it. He wanted presidential approval before he gave his next orders, and Kerry was the only other person involved.

Walking down the hall, Wolffe said, "If you want to pretend being a global consulting firm in DC, you have to have the trappings."

They reached Wolffe's corner office, with windows looking out over Clarendon Boulevard, the Iwo Jima memorial, and Arlington National Cemetery visible in the distance. Kerry said, "Well, you certainly have that."

Creed was behind his desk, looking up when they came in. He said, "You're on encrypted VPN videoconference with the president. He's not here yet. He's in some sort of meeting, but they're about to break for lunch."

Wolffe nodded and said, "Thanks, Creed. You can go now."

He exited the office, and Kerry said, "So what's up? You called a Prairie Fire but you're not acting like anyone's in danger within the Taskforce."

Prairie Fire was a Taskforce code word for a team in distress. When it was used, all other Taskforce operations ceased and any assets available were directed to help that team.

"Yeah, I called it to get your attention. It's not a Taskforce team. It's a Russian. He's been detained by another group of Russians—the ones that Pike found in Copenhagen, tied into the killers in Sweden. Pike wants to rescue him, but unlike Pike's usual running off the reservation and just doing what he wants, he punted to us."

Kerry was flabbergasted. He said, "Wait, what? First Pike takes it upon himself to fly to Copenhagen, and now he wants permission to assault? To rescue a Russian from other Russians?"

"Yeah, that's it in a nutshell. He thinks he's found a thread to something big, and he wants to explore it. The thread goes through this guy who's been captured."

Kerry jumped to his feet, saying, "Are you literally nuts? Were you not in the room when you gave the last SITREP, where Pike disobeyed you? Was that a deepfake? You're going to bring this up to the president of the United States?"

Incensed, Wolffe said, "Pike's on to something. We should follow it. We're the ones who sent him on this bullshit, and now we're upset that he found something?"

Kerry said, "That's going to go over well with the president. It's going to look like he's forcing the president's hand."

"Yeah, I know, but Pike might be on to a threat here."

"The president isn't going to see it like that. You saw how pissed he got when Pike went to Copenhagen. He said you had no control over your men, and threatened to fire you."

Wolffe grinned and said, "Well, he couldn't do that because we're operating off the books from the damn organization that's off the books. If he fired me, he'd have to admit he was using the Taskforce outside of the Oversight Council. I knew that wasn't going to happen, and I *told* him what he was going to get by forcing Pike to do this. I explicitly told him that once Pike got on a thread, he wouldn't stop."

"And you wanted him to go to Copenhagen."

"I never said that."

"You didn't have to. You wanted it. You knew what he would do once he found a threat."

"I warned the president, but that doesn't alter the fact that he *found a threat*. That's the whole point. And yes, if Pike has found a potential risk to the security of the United States, then I want him to explore it."

"So what's this all about? What's the threat?"

Before Wolffe could answer, the computer screen behind his desk beeped, and they heard, "I'm staring at an empty chair. Anyone there? I don't have a lot of time."

They scurried behind the desk, seeing President Hannister at some undisclosed location inside the White House, looking like he had a hastily established Zoom connection for a high school presentation.

Wolffe said, "We're here, sir."

"Well, what's this about? I was told a Prairie Fire. Please don't tell me Pike not only ignored your orders, but he's now in danger of getting killed."

"No, sir. It's not a Taskforce team in jeopardy."

"Thank God. Then why the alert?"

"It's a Russian. Pike's team witnessed a man getting ripped off the street and want permission to go rescue him."

"A Russian? What the hell is that all about?"

Wolffe told him everything he knew, including Shoshana's intelligence and the threat vector from the Russian team Pike had located, ending with "Pike thinks these Russians might be doing something against the Russian security state, and it might be worth exploring, but all this hinges on the man they caught."

"Wait, wait. Did you say Shoshana, the Israeli, is on the ground?"

"Yes. She was meeting a Russian who is part of the team of the man who was snatched."

Wolffe saw President Hannister rub his face, taking that in, then he said, "So the Israelis are involved in what's going on? Kerry? Do you know anything about this? Does the CIA have any knowledge of what the Israelis are doing?"

"No, sir, but that's not odd. From what Pike's saying, they were exploring the situation, trying to determine who this supposed target might be. Once they had something concrete, they would have told us. It's the same thing we do. We wouldn't go running to them at the first piece of stray voltage indicating a potential threat against Israel. We'd confirm—or at least get more clarification—before we'd approach the Mossad."

President Hannister returned to Wolffe and said, "So you're telling me that Pike had no knowledge she was there, and that his decision to disobey my direct orders had nothing to do with her?"

Wolffe swallowed and said, "Yes, sir. That's what I'm saying, because it's the truth. If Pike had planned all of this, he most certainly wouldn't have pulled back and asked for permission to continue. He thinks we should, but he knows it's weak."

Kerry said, "Sir, I think the key thing here is that the Israelis thought there was a targeted killing being planned, and they wanted to know who the target is. I feel the same way. We should find that out. Right now, we're in the dark on what's happening."

"Why not just let the Russians kill themselves over it? Why should we get involved?"

Wolffe said, "Because we don't know who's good and who's bad. Whatever's happening could affect our own national security. What's clear is that very powerful forces inside the Russian Federation are at war, and I think it's important to U.S. interests to find out why."

"By getting involved in a fight between two Russian security agencies? We don't even know who they are. I'm inclined to say no here. Get them home. We stopped the attack in Sweden, and that was the mission."

"Sir, that *was* the mission. What's happening now is an extension of it. The men in Sweden were talking to the men in Copenhagen."

"George, I understand they were talking, but this seems like a couple of Mafia families going to the mattresses over some lost loansharking territory. Let them fight it out. It only helps us. I'm not looking to be the FBI here helping Whitey Bulger. I don't see an upside."

Kerry stepped in, now believing. "We don't see an upside because we don't know what we're looking at. The elusive man they were supposedly targeting might very well be someone we want dead. We could be helping our own national security by helping that one Russian team accomplish its mission."

Before the president could say anything else, Wolffe said, "Sir, it's close to 1800 in Copenhagen. We're running out of time here. If we keep talking, the man will be dead. Let Pike do what Pike does, and let's see what comes out of it."

Hannister thought a moment, then said, "You believe it's that important? After he completely ignored us and flew to Copenhagen in the first place? If he had followed orders, we wouldn't even know about this."

"Maybe that's a good reason to let him continue. He didn't want this mission to begin with, and now because of it, he's found something."

Hannister sighed and said, "Yeah, yeah. I remember what you told me. I should have listened then about Pike. He is a walking disaster once he's off the leash."

He squeezed the bridge of his nose, his eyes closed, and Wolffe almost felt sorry for him—but he *had* warned the president.

President Hannister said, "Okay. Do it. Give me a report as soon as it's complete."

CHAPTER 39

O leg waited for his phone to connect, dreading the conversation. Someone answered, and he heard, "Go secure."

He pulled his phone down and punched a button on the screen. While waiting on the encryption protocol to synch up with the far station, he looked at the body of the man they'd captured.

He was sitting upright in a chair, his head lolling over to the side with his eyes open, a small amount of blood coming out of his nose and both sides of his head where his ears used to be. His hands were strapped to the arms of the chair, his fingers mangled like he'd plunged them into a kitchen disposal. His toes looked the same way, the vise grips they'd used lying next to the chair, the teeth stained with bits of flesh.

It was not a pleasant scene—even to him, who'd done such things before to enemies of the state. The man had been very hard, refusing to talk despite the enormous pressure they brought to bear, and then—just like that—his body quit, his soul fleeing his mortal remains like it had someplace better to be.

Oleg knew that the man on the far end wouldn't be happy, but at least he had gleaned a little information—some of which would be explosive.

Victor Petrov finally answered the line, saying, "What's your status? Tell me you have the Valkyrie cell."

"Sir, no, we don't. Not yet. We had one of them, and I gleaned some information, but—"

"What do you mean, you 'had' him?"

"We captured one today, and were on the way to learning the extent of the rot, but his heart gave out before we could finish the interrogation. He was a hard man. A true Russian. He wouldn't talk."

He heard Victor exhale, then say, "What do you have?"

"You were right. It's a rogue cell of the GRU, but it's not only them. They've co-opted a group of Ukrainians called the Wolves. They're the ones executing the attack. The Valkyrie cell is just infrastructure support. The Wolves are the men who are going to attempt to eliminate our president."

"So you have a handle on them?"

"No, we don't—at least not currently. Like I said, the man's heart gave out before he gave up specifics. We have the leader of the Valkyrie cell's hotel, and we're headed there next. We won't make the same mistake twice."

Oleg heard the aggravation in Victor's voice. Or maybe it was fear. He wasn't sure. "How could you be so sloppy as to kill the man before getting that information? Do you at least know the method of attack or the timing?"

Chastised, Oleg said, "No, sir, we didn't get that. We tried, but I'm telling you, it took an hour to even get him to admit to being GRU. Like I said, he was a hard man."

"Did you get anything of use?"

Miffed, Oleg said, "You mean besides the fact that it's a group of Ukrainians on the hunt? Yes, we have the hotel of the leader. He was the one meeting the Israelis today."

"What was that about? Why were they meeting?"

Oleg paused, then said, "We don't know. He wouldn't tell us."

"What the fuck is your problem? How could you not get him to tell you?"

"Sir . . . we ran out of fingers and toes just getting him to admit he was GRU and working with Ukrainians. By the time we got the location of his leader, he was missing his ears. I'm telling you, he was hard."

"Tell me you know where these Ukrainians are staying. Tell me you can take them off the board."

Oleg looked at his men, keenly aware they could see the sweat pop on his brow. "No, sir, right now, we're not even sure if they're here in Copenhagen, but we know where the leader is, and he can tell us."

"Are you compromised in any way?"

"No, sir. We're still clean."

"Then why are you still talking to me? If you got the one GRU man, the other will know it soon enough. Go get him before he flees."

"Yes, sir. Doing it now."

He hung up and said, "Anton, Ivanov, and Misha, you're with me. We're going to roll up the leader. Mikhail and Alek, deal with the body."

CHAPTER 40

Knuckles called and said, "A section of the pipe-hitters is leaving. Four goons, coming out the front and slinking up the alley."

Not good.

I said, "Veep, what do you have for entry?"

Veep came back, saying, "Besides the breach in the front, there are four breaches in the back. A door and two open windows."

Sitting next to Brett and Blaine, I said, "Can they get out the back and onto the street if we go in the front?"

"Yeah, most definitely. Unless you want to use the weapon on this thing, that is."

Shoshana had brought some wares to show the Russians, what would be called "samples" in traveling salesman vernacular. One of those was a swarming drone weapon system called LANIUS, a derivative of the Latin word for "butcher."

Based on racing drones and having a sixth-generation AI engine, four of them could be attached to a mother ship from outside the threat area, flown in, then the four would detach and go on their demonic mission, flying with precise controls as fast as 45 miles an hour. Its dwell time was limited to a little under ten minutes, but it could create a three-dimensional map of a building from flying *inside* the building, send it back to us, and when called on, could detonate a small grenade with a blast radius that was tiny enough to kill only the operator's chosen target.

In this case, we didn't need the mother drone, and were only using one, but the world of warfare was truly getting scary. I couldn't imagine trying to defend a hardened structure with these things zipping down the hallways and committing suicide.

I said, "Knuckles, what are the Russians doing?"

"They're gone. Out the front under the arch."

"So at least two left inside. Shoshana, Koko, what's the atmospherics?"

One thing we'd learned about Christiana was that the police in Copenhagen raided Pusher Street about every other day, and if they were doing it tonight, it would be a threat to our operation. Once I'd been given the go-ahead for the operation from Wolffe, with the usual caveat that I'd better not be compromised, I'd staged them as early warning at a café within view of the street.

"This is Koko. We're getting hit on from the freaks in this place, but no police. You're cleared to breach."

I said, "Okay, it's showtime. Beast, Blood and I are going in the front with a surreptitious entry. Veep, you run that drone through the window in the back and find the first guy with a weapon. You detonate, and we're in. Knuckles, you go to the back for squirter control. Anyone who exits, take them down. Acknowledge."

Everyone did, except for Veep. He said, "I need a new drone. Out of battery for this one. Give me five minutes to bring it back and launch a new one."

I said, "Roger. Standing by."

Three minutes later he said, "In flight."

Blaine, Brett, and I ran to a window by the front door, hiding underneath it. I glanced inside and saw a man drinking a bottle of water, a pistol on his hip. I whispered, "Target right above us. Standing still. Just to the left of our breach point."

Brett and Blaine nodded, and I said, "Brett, get on the door."

He went to it and gently slid what looked like a baseball with a key jutting out into the lock. He looked at me, and I looked at the man through the window. He heard something and sat the bottle down, drawing his pistol.

A device that looked like an oversize bumblebee flew into the room, about the size of a fist. It flew right into his face, then hovered. He looked completely confused, and then the drone detonated, shredding his head with shrapnel, the sound just a little bit more than an M-80 firecracker.

Brett hit the baseball, defeating the lock, and we entered, flowing into the room looking for a threat. I saw a bloody mess tied to a chair, then heard movement in the back and went that way, running with my pistol out, Blaine and Brett following.

A man sprang out of a bathroom, took two shots at us, then burst out of the back door to the path next to the wall of the compound, running right into Knuckles. He clotheslined the guy, flattening him on his back, and hammered him in the head with his pistol. We kept clearing.

The place ended up being pretty small, with a den, kitchen, a community bathroom, and two bedrooms. It was empty. Well, empty of life.

The drone had done its work on the one bad guy, pummeling his face with ball bearings. The man we'd come in to save was the guy Knuckles had seen earlier at the brew pub, and his fate wasn't pretty.

He was still flex-tied to a chair, and the damage he'd taken was ghastly. Whoever had done this had no humanity in him. I'd seen a lot of heinous acts in combat, from ISIS and Al Qaida to Russian Wagner terrorists, but this was on another level. I was shocked at how bad he'd been tortured. It made my stomach turn sour, and did the same to my men.

We all lived in a world of violence, but we also lived with a code of honor that these men did not hold. Seeing his body was a reminder of our own frailty. It couldn't help but make you wonder if someday you might be in that chair.

Brett said, "Jesus Christ. Look what they did to that guy. A bunch of fucking savages."

I called Knuckles and said, "You got that guy under control?"

"Yeah, I got him."

"Koko, Carrie, bring the vehicle to the northern wall exit. We're coming out."

"Roger all. So you got him?"

"No. We didn't. Just bring the vehicle."

She knew better than to ask what had happened, and I walked out the back of the building, the growing twilight starting to darken the area. I found Knuckles pinning the guy on the ground with a knee in his back.

I saw him and felt a spasm of rage, thinking of the suffering in the room I'd just left. I went to him, grabbed his head by the hair, and jerked his neck up until I could see the whites of his eyes. I leaned down and said, "I'm going to know everything you know. I promise the man in the room will be nothing compared to what I'm going to do to you. Do you understand?"

I saw his face go white, and he said, "No English. No English."

Knuckles said, "What happened?"

I said, "You'll speak plenty of English once I'm through with you. Get him on his feet. He's got a little trip coming."

Knuckles looked at Brett, then back at me, repeating, "What happened in there? Where's the precious cargo?"

I said, "PC is dead. Get him up."

We hoisted him to his feet and frog marched him down the dirt path, the old military base's concrete wall to our left and tall shrubs to our right. We reached an iron foot gate and I radioed, "Here."

Jennifer said, "Outside."

I said, "Okay, all of you exfil to the hotel. Shoshana and I are going to interrogate this guy and find out what he knows."

Blaine had seen my anger and said, "Shoshana? Why?"

I shoved the Russian into our SUV and said, "Because she's a trained interrogator and I trust her instincts. We're going to drive away from here, get someplace quiet, and find out what this guy knows."

Shoshana flicked her eyes to Jennifer, not liking where I had gone. She said, "I'm not here to do an interrogation, Pike."

I snarled, "Then what the fuck *are* you here for? You want to learn what these guys are up to or not?"

Jennifer touched my arm, and it was like a circuit breaker tripping, cutting through my rage. She said, "What did you find in there?"

I wiped the sweat off my brow and said, "I saw pure evil. I'll never unsee it."

"And you really want to repeat that? You want to be pure evil?"

I took a deep breath, saw all of the team looking at me, wondering. They knew where I'd been in the past. Knew I'd once *been* pure evil, and I really didn't want to go back there again. I said, "No. I don't. But this guy is our link."

Shoshana floated her weird gaze on me, stabbing my soul, and I said, "Turn that shit off. Right now."

Blaine said, "What?"

Shoshana said, "Okay, I will interrogate him. You've jumped the abyss. You dodge it more than I do, and you always succeed."

I chuckled and said, "Yeah, I suppose I did. Honestly, I just wanted to deal out some punishment." I looked at Jennifer and said, "But I no longer do. He doesn't even speak English. We're not getting anything from him."

Shoshana said, "Does he speak Russian?"

"Of course. I'm pretty sure he speaks English as well, but he's going to hide behind the Russian thing."

"Well, that's not much of a hide, because I speak Russian."

My jaw dropped. I said, "You speak Russian?"

"Yes, I do. That's why I was recruited to the Israel Defense Forces in the first place. It's why I was the one sent here. I'm a little rusty, but I can get the job done."

"Okay, then, get in the vehicle and we'll go someplace secluded and have a little talk. Jennifer, Shoshana, and me. Everyone else take the metro back to the hotel and wait for further instructions. Get some sleep."

The group split up and I found Blaine next to me, saying, "Pike, I think I should stay, as the commander here."

I understood why he wanted to accompany the interrogation. He feared what I would do, but the slithering, evil part of my brain had left, thanks to Jennifer. I'm not sure what I would have done to that piece of shit before, but it was gone now.

I said, "If you want to, sir, but Shoshana leads the interrogation. Let her work it."

He nodded, and I turned to the team, saying, "Everyone go. Get out of here and back to the hotel. There's going to be a shit storm from the bodies, and I don't want to be any part of that."

Jennifer said, "And me?"

"You're out. Blaine's in. We can't do a clown car here."

She nodded, leaned into Shoshana, and whispered. Shoshana whispered back, and she smiled. Jennifer kissed me on the lips, causing Blaine's head to just about explode, and said, "You do what you do, but listen to Shoshana. She knows what's right."

I said, "You're putting her judgment over mine? She's batshit crazy."

She said, "Not tonight."

I watched her walk away, and, incensed, Blaine said, "What is going on with the fraternization? She kissed you for God's sake."

I said, "Shut the fuck up and get in the car."

We split up, me driving the SUV, Blaine in the passenger seat, and Shoshana next to our Russian. I drove until I found a suitably deserted alley, looking for cameras or the random homeless guy, and when not seeing any, I parked. I turned around and said, "Okay, Shoshana, it's all you."

She turned to the Russian and began speaking, causing him to flinch. She said a few words, and he answered. She raised her hand and stroked his face, running a nail down his cheek. He pulled his head away and said something else. It was all in Russian, and I had no idea what was going on, but trusted her.

She talked to him for about twenty minutes, then grew frustrated at his answers. She leaned into him, put her hand on his thigh, and began to drag it higher, all the while asking him questions. He slapped her hand away with his flex-tied wrists, shouted in Russian, and then did something nobody would believe.

She said one more thing and he snapped, bashing his head against my headrest, screaming in Russian. She pulled his head back by the hair, whispering something, and he jerked his head out of her hands, rocked toward her, then whipsawed to the window, smashing it open with his skull. He slammed his head down into the broken glass and sawed his neck, great gouts of blood sprouting out.

I leapt out of the driver's seat, ripped open the door, and saw Shoshana trying to provide first aid, her hand jammed against his carotid artery, the blood jetting out like a tiny fire hose around her fingers. She looked at me in shock and I slapped my hands on his neck, trying to stanch the bleeding. It did no good.

He was dead in seconds.

We both did nothing for a moment, covered in his blood, Blaine outside the door looking at the mess. Finally, I said, "We need to go back to the hippy hideout and dump this body. Let them all be found together."

Blaine said, "This is turning into a serial killing thing. The Copenhagen authorities are going to go apeshit."

"Yeah, they will, but better to go apeshit at the same place than to start making connections to our drive."

I started driving back the way we'd come, saying, "What a debacle. Who does that? What are we dealing with?"

Shoshana said, "We're dealing with men who would rather die than face what they did to the man in the room. That's all it is. They have extreme fear of failure, and not because it'll make them look bad. They fear being the man in the chair."

Blaine shook his head and said, "What sort of person does that? I mean, who would kill themselves by bashing their head out of the window?"

I said, "I guess it's better than a sledgehammer to the skull on video like Wagner does. If it had come out that he'd been captured and talked, he was dead anyway."

I turned to Shoshana and said, "Did you get anything from him at all?"

"Yes. One, he's with the new Russian National Guard, part of one of their SWAT teams. They work directly for Putin. Two, their target is a rogue group of agents from the GRU who call themselves the Valkyries. One of them was the man in the chair. They're here recruiting a group of Ukrainian partisans called the Wolves who are attending that NATO unconventional warfare conference."

"Why? What are the GRU guys and the Ukrainians here to do?"

She took a deep breath and said, "They're trying to kill Putin."

Which most definitely explained the Russian-on-Russian violence. This time Blaine said, "What?"

"That's what he said. That's why the GRU man is tied to a chair."

I said, "Where? When? What's the method of attack?"

"He killed himself at that point. I guess he figured he'd said too much. What are we going to do now?"

Honestly, I had no idea. This had gone way, way beyond my pay grade.

CHAPTER 41

Daniel walked into the lobby of the d'Angleterre hotel, wondering if he should go into five-alarm fire status or give Stepan a little more time. He passed several men and women wearing uniforms on the way to the elevator, and realized the UW conference was still ongoing.

A five-star establishment in the heart of Copenhagen, usually used by diplomats and presidents, the d'Angleterre was the host hotel for the NATO unconventional warfare roundtable, and as such, it was naturally the place he'd chosen to stay when he'd been given his assignment as part of the GRU.

In addition to the Valkyrie mission, he still had to please his masters, and had spent each night at the bar simply listening in to various conversations. He hadn't gleaned much of interest, but enough to convince his masters that he was doing what he'd been sent to accomplish. Right up until 1700 today.

He dialed Stepan's phone one more time on the elevator ride to his room, and once again, it went to voice mail. That wasn't good.

He'd waited at the Brus brewery long after the two suspect men had left, and Stepan had not followed his instructions. He'd never returned to the restaurant. Daniel had tried to call him multiple times, with each call going to voice mail. He'd left the restaurant and conducted a detailed countersurveillance route, but found nobody following him now—and maybe nobody had been following him earlier. He wasn't sure.

He exited the elevator on the second floor, praying that Stepan's phone had simply malfunctioned. Maybe he'd dropped it in a toilet or cracked it on the sidewalk. Maybe he was waiting in the room right now.

He stopped at Stepan's door, two down from his own, knocking, waiting, then knocking again. Nobody answered. He used the key Stepan had given him, an old-fashioned one that lived up to the history of the hotel. He entered, quickly finding the room empty.

Now running out of hope, he thought, *Maybe he's waiting in my room.* They'd both received two keys for each room, and had swapped the extras to make sure that each could enter the room of the other in an emergency.

He used the key for his room and found it empty as well. He took a seat, assessing the damage. If Stepan *had* been captured, everything was at risk. He didn't know where the Wolves were staying—Daniel had kept that secret precisely for this reason—but he knew the target, the various methods of attack, the passports the men were using, and the follow-on instructions in Finland. *He* was the one who'd actually loaded all of that into the locker in the Queen's Library.

It no longer mattered if Stepan was alive or dead. Daniel had to mitigate any damage just because he *might* be captured. He dialed his phone, getting Kirill—his GRU man in Finland. He explained the situation, ending with "The instructions you sent are no longer valid. Find a new time and place to meet and send it to my phone. I'll establish contact with the Wolves and pass it to them."

"That could take some time."

"Not a problem. I won't be able to meet them until at least tomorrow night."

"Okay. I'll send it via encrypted chat. You need to download it within fifteen minutes, or it will erase itself. I don't want anything like that on my phone."

"I got it. Will do."

He hung up, knowing the next call was going to be much more difficult. Perun and the Wolves didn't trust him as it was, and changing the plan at this stage would look like amateur hour. In no way did he want to intimate that they'd been compromised.

He dug through a bag and pulled out the ancient flip phone Perun had given him in Ukraine, went to the contacts, and dialed the single number there, waiting, the cell ringing out to voice mail. He hung up without leaving an incriminating message, then stood and paced the room. He decided he needed to get out of here, right now. If Stepan *had* been captured, his location was known.

He and Stepan had already made an escape plan with a different location to hole up in if things went bad. The only reason they were in this hotel was for their cover of gleaning intelligence for the unconventional warfare conference, and if that had been compromised by either the host nation determining their status as GRU, or the Russian state penetrating their true mission, they'd made alternate plans.

He began shoving only essentials into a rucksack, underwear, socks, his laptop, and other things, leaving the rest of his clothes and the suitcase he'd used when he'd arrived on the floor. He began thinking about the mission again. He had a meeting with the Israeli tomorrow, but that was probably a lost cause at this point.

And then he thought about what missing that meeting would mean. He knew the Israeli was suspicious of his activities, and not making that meeting would cause her to become more suspicious. Perhaps cause the Mossad to start investigating on its own. He couldn't allow that, because Shoshana knew his contact information, and that would be a problem. One more thing to deal with. He needed to meet Shoshana again if only to turn her off and act like he was no longer interested.

He went to the bathroom, looking for anything that could identify him later, and heard his phone ring. He raced back out, answering it.

Perun said, "Why did you call? You said no calls."

"Yeah, there's been a change of direction. I need to meet you."

"Why?"

"Because there's been a change of direction. I don't need to spell it out. I need to meet you with the new instructions."

"I'm not meeting you anywhere. I have the instructions, and if you've had a change of heart, that's not my problem. I don't know who's gotten to you, but it won't alter what's about to happen."

"Your instructions are no longer valid. I've had to deviate the team. Just listen to me—I need to give you new instructions."

Daniel heard nothing for a moment, then, "Give them to me now."

"I don't have them now. I'm waiting to get them. Just shut up and listen for a second. I want to meet at the train station downtown, in the McDonald's on the main floor tomorrow at 1800. I'll give you the new instructions then."

"We've already printed the ferry tickets. Are you sending us somewhere new?"

"No, it's still Finland, it's just that the meeting site has changed."

"Why?"

Aggravated, Daniel said, "Because I said so. Look, meet me at the McDonald's in the train station and I'll explain. I don't want to do that on the phone."

"I'm not meeting you anywhere that you set up. If you want to meet, I'll dictate the site now."

Feeling the press of time, Daniel said, "Okay, okay, tell me where. Just tell me where and when."

Perun said, "Do you have a pen?"

Daniel slid over the hotel stationery and said, "Send it. Anywhere, anytime."

"You know the Tivoli Gardens?"

Daniel scribbled that down and said, "Yes. The amusement park?"

"Yes. Meet me at the restaurant Grøften at 2000 tomorrow night. I'll make the reservations. You pay the bill."

Daniel said, "Spell it."

"G—R—O with a slash—F—T—E—N."

Daniel wrote down the information, then his in-room phone rang. He jerked his head to it, saying, "I'll be there. I have to go."

Perun said, "You'd better not be fucking me. I'll be ready. You show up. You alone. Anyone else, and there will be a situation you won't live through."

"It'll just be me. I have to go."

He hung up, lunged across the room, and jerked the house phone up, saying, "Yes?"

The phone clicked, and he instantly knew what that meant. Someone had called to make sure he was in the room, and they were on the way up. He stilled himself, listening, and heard scratches on the lock of his door. They were not *on* the way up. They were here.

He grabbed his rucksack, went to the false balcony of his room, and opened the window. He looked out, seeing an alley a story below, full of dumpsters and trash, a department store on the other side. No one was moving down the pavement. He tossed his rucksack to the ground, crawled out on the fake balcony, and heard the door burst open. He scrambled over the ledge, holding on to the cement truncheons outside his window, then dropped, falling forever. He hit the ground hard, slamming his shoulder into the pavement.

He rolled over, felt he could move, snatched his rucksack, and began running.

CHAPTER 42

Oleg glanced to his right, seeing his man at the elevator up the hallway. He nodded, and Oleg whispered, "Go."

Another man knelt to the lock, inserted lockpicking tools, and began methodically working the pins in the lock. Forty-five seconds later, he nodded, holding the tension wrench in place.

Oleg waved the elevator man to his location, they stacked on the door, and Oleg whispered, "Open it."

The man at the lock twisted the wrench and the lock sprang free. Oleg kicked the door, racing in, his men following. They cleared the small room, found it empty, and Oleg ran to the open window. He leaned out, staring at an alley below, but saw nothing. He cursed and said, "Search the room. Find something."

His men began ripping through the room like a cyclone, flinging drawers out, snatching hangers, and ripping off the bedsheets. Oleg turned around, seeing the destruction, and shouted, "Stop!"

The men did, looking at him in confusion. He said, "This isn't Ukraine. Search the room methodically. We're not on a time crunch, and we don't want to leave the impression for the maids tomorrow that something bad happened here. Just search the room like it was your own."

They began at a slower pace, replacing the drawers they'd flung about, Oleg thinking about the lack of professionalism. Wondering if he wanted to be associated with them. He was older, and, like his friend Dmitri who'd been killed in Sweden, had worked in the world of espionage before. Now he was dealing with a bunch of thugs who had gone through a ten-minute course and thought themselves experts.

He returned to the window, pulling the curtains back and gazing into the night. He knew this was how the man had escaped, but had no way of knowing where he'd gone. What he'd learned from the torture of the other GRU traitor was explosive, and he felt the weight on his shoulders to stop the attack.

The mission was well formed. Well thought out, and the team running it were true believers. He couldn't understand how the man in the chair had withstood the punishment without talking, and he had a grudging respect. He knew he wouldn't have lasted that long. The man had some inner strength he did not possess, and if the Ukrainians they were hunting had the same fervor, it would be a hard road to stop them.

It gave him pause.

A man behind him shouted, "I have something." He ran to Oleg holding a small stationery pad that was provided by the hotel. On it was a time and a word: *2000. Grøften.*

The man said, "Maybe he's going here."

Oleg took the paper and crumpled it up, wishing he had someone of worth working the room. He said, "There is no way he would use hotel stationery to write down his next meeting after hearing it on an open line, and then leave it for us to find. It's a deception."

But maybe the deception itself would provide some clues. Maybe the Israeli woman would be there. He needed anything to get a handle on the missing man, because failure was no longer an option.

He thought about the man in the chair, and thought about what would happen to him if he didn't stop the attack. He had no options, and felt the vise of this mission closing in.

The men finished their search, finding nothing else. He said, "Everyone out of the room. Leave it like he left it, but put the 'do not disturb' sign on the door. We're going back to the safe house."

They returned to a debacle. The moment Oleg had entered the room he smelled the copper scent of blood, getting furious that the man's body was still here after giving the men he'd left instructions to get rid of it.

He shouted their names, then went to the small hallway leading to the bedrooms and found his men.

It was a veritable bloodbath, with Oleg's teammates lying side by side, both clearly dead. One with his head shredded by something that looked like a shotgun blast, and the other with his throat cut, but not by a knife, like he had been intentionally executed. Almost like someone had used a rough chain saw on his neck just deep enough to sever his carotid arteries.

The stench was overpowering.

Misha took one look in the hallway and said, "Someone's hunting us."

Oleg went to the man with his throat shredded, flipped him over, and checked his pockets, finding nothing. He said, "No doubt. Dmitri warned me about this. It's the GRU. The Valkyrie team. They knew we'd taken that man and came for him."

"How, though? How did they find us?"

Oleg thought a moment, then a realization dawned on him. "It must be electronic surveillance through our cell phones. They're all given to us by the National Guard. Russia pays the bills. The GRU must have obtained access to the SOBR database."

He pulled his phone out and said, "Everyone, clean out your phones. Delete everything on them, then turn them off and pull out the battery."

The men began to do as he asked, and Misha said, "Even given that, it's too late for this place. They know it's where we're staying. We should go right now. They're probably watching us as we speak, and might be coming in."

The rest of the men heard the words, stopped work on their phones, and pulled out weapons, taking up positions to defend the building.

Oleg said, "Yes, I agree. We need to leave, but we can't abandon the mission. And I'm at a loss of what to do next."

Misha said, "The only thing we have is the note Alek found. That's it. We stake that out tomorrow and see where it leads."

Oleg nodded, saying, "If it leads nowhere, we're going to end up like our men here when we return home. Or worse, like that man in the chair."

CHAPTER 43

Sitting at a six-foot wooden table on a restaurant's outdoor patio, I called Shoshana, saying, "Nothing yet?"

"Not yet, but it's still early. Give it some time."

I called Knuckles, stationed with Brett on the outskirts of an outdoor mall area right near the entrance, saying, "You got anything?"

"Lots of people coming in, but nobody that I followed yesterday."

"Roger all." I turned to Veep across the table from me, and said, "You want to test-fire that thing?"

"Yeah, sure."

I called Jennifer on my cell, asking her how her mini-mission was going.

She said, "Pike, I don't know if we can get all this blood out. Might be better to just set the thing on fire."

The vehicle we were using was a rental, and I'd given Blaine and Jennifer the task of cleaning it up and returning it with some story about a rock coming out of nowhere to shatter the window. They were currently at a car wash, trying to prepare the vehicle for return like some businessman trying to clean the DNA after carting off his partner in a carpet.

I said, "If we do that, it gets much more complicated. We'll have to create a reason for it getting torched, not to mention in a country where we don't know the laws. Better to just have a broken window."

"I know. Let us keep working. I'll let you know what we think we should do. How's it going there?"

"Nothing yet, but the area's pretty cool. We'll have to come back someday."

Shoshana had picked a pretty unique place for her next meeting with the Russian. Located in the Vesterbro district of Copenhagen, it was called Kødbyen, and was an old meatpacking facility. Once a place that slaughtered pigs by the thousands, situated in what used to be a gritty part of town, it had evolved into an eclectic blend of galleries, restaurants, and bars.

The space was good for control, because you had to enter through a gate to get inside, but it was poor for my solution to our mission, because it was packed with people.

Shoshana had picked a Michelin-rated restaurant called Kødbyens Fiskebar for the meet, a place that had kept the industrial setting while serving what was supposed to be the best seafood in Copenhagen. Glaring incandescent lamps and stained tile on the walls gave it a little bit of retro charm, only offset by the giant aquarium they'd installed. It had outdoor seating, which was a must for our mission, and Shoshana was at a table waiting for the Russian to arrive.

If he ever did.

Veep and I were in a barbecue joint/microbrewery with the name WarPigs—a moniker that was about perfect for this shit show of a mission. It was another place that had kept the industrial vibe, with the interior looking like a gym locker room complete with tile walls and the other infrastructure left as it was, like they didn't have the time to spruce it up because they were focused on the meat they were smoking.

They actually *did* have some pretty damn good barbecue, and that's speaking from experience. I wondered if the beer was just as good, but alas, we were on a mission, so all I was drinking was water.

Veep leaned over to his bag and turned on the Growler, letting it sniff the air for cell phone signals. The device itself was designed to pinpoint a cell phone within about five feet, but we were doing the opposite here. I just wanted it to identify the Russian's cell phone so we could track it later.

Basically, once we had a number, we'd input it into the Growler, and it would start searching. It acted like a mini cell tower, tricking all the phones in the area into thinking it was the best tower to talk to. The Growler would cycle through all the numbers it sucked up, rejecting those that weren't targeted until it found the one that was, then it would give us a distance and direction to that phone.

In this case I wanted to do the reverse, sucking in the phones and *not* rejecting them so I could see what they were. My theory was that if the Russian showed up, I'd suck in all the phones, then shut off the device. Ten minutes later, I'd do it again, then shut it off. Ten minutes after that, I'd do it one more time.

From that data, we'd cull the numbers that had not changed. As the place was packed with tourists walking in and out, and the Russian was supposed to sit for an hourlong meeting, we should be able to determine which one was his once we eliminated other known numbers, like Shoshana's.

In theory, anyway. I'd have to contend with the other patrons sitting for a meal at both our restaurant and hers, but I thought I could make it work, if she could keep him there long enough to cause a rotation of customers.

The inside of the meatpacking district was basically a giant square, with a parking lot in the middle. WarPigs was on the eastern part of the square, while Shoshana's restaurant was on the southern side. She'd said she was going to eat lunch with him and would keep him as long as she could, eating as slowly as possible, but so far he'd been a no-show. Which, honestly, might be for the best, since I had no idea what my mission was now.

The last known location of the Russians we'd originally tracked was Christiana, with a final trace of about midnight last night. After that, the phone had gone dark. I was hoping that meant it had quit simply from a dead battery, but I was willing to bet he'd returned, found the bodies of his men, and destroyed the phone as a precaution.

That had left Shoshana's meeting as our only viable lead, but I wasn't clear on what that "lead" was supposed to do for our mission. My SITREP to Wolffe had caused a commotion, which was a little bit of an understatement. In truth, it had caused all hell to break loose, and after their deliberations, I still didn't have what I would call a full mission profile. It was wishy-washy "continue Alpha . . . Locate the Russian . . . Track him . . . Find the Ukrainians," but none of it had an endstate with a clear picture of why we were continuing to pursue it.

I understood why. I mean, we were sitting on an assassination plot of a world leader—who also happened to be a national security threat to our own country. I could imagine the chaos happening inside the White House.

The problems were myriad. For one, the CIA had a duty to protect. If they ever validated a death threat against a source or asset, they had an obligation to pull that guy out of the line of fire, regardless of what it did to their mission. They couldn't sit idly by and let someone be killed when they knew the attack was coming—even if letting the guy operate would give them the keys to the kingdom at the next meet. They had to warn him, and then extract him if he so chose, dooming whatever mission was being conducted.

This wasn't that—but it was close. We had information about a viable threat against a head of state. Did the president have a duty to protect? Should he alert Putin that there's a cell coming for him? Do we try to prevent it, using Taskforce assets to save that miserable war criminal because of his standing as a world leader?

On the other hand, should we simply do nothing? American assets weren't doing the mission. We didn't order anything. Putin bit this off when he invaded Ukraine. He reaps what he's sowed, so why should we do anything to interfere in their internal war? If Putin gets killed, he gets killed. Shouldn't have pissed off his own people.

Finally, what about helping the cell? Putin was a clear and present danger to the world order, and if these guys stood a chance of getting rid of him, why not help? Not in an overt way, but maybe by clearing the field of the people trying to stop them, giving them the opportunity to continue. If it works, it works. If it fails, it fails. No skin off our nose, as we had nothing to do with it other than getting rid of the men hunting the cell.

But then, doesn't that make the United States complicit in an assassination? We actually have an executive order called 12333, which states that no one from the United States—or operating on the behest of the United States—will engage in assassination. Ever. By helping these guys, are we breaking the prohibitions in 12333? Could the men be construed as operating—even unwittingly—on behalf of the United States simply because we eliminated the threat against them when we could have stopped them?

It was a shit sandwich of the highest order, but I knew where I stood: let those killers go. Putin was a mass murderer, and not just in Ukraine. I'd seen his handiwork all over the globe, and the earth would be a better place if he was gone.

But then that brought up a new problem—who would take over? Maybe the successor would be worse. Or maybe it would devolve into a giant bloodletting civil war, with all of Russia's nuclear weapons hanging in the balance.

Not an easy decision at all, and one I'm glad wasn't in my wheelhouse. All I had to do was keep track of the Russian.

If he even showed.

Veep peeked at his little experiment, then rolled his eyes. I said, "What?"

"We've got like nine hundred numbers here."

"Do it again, and then sort for the same in both snatches."

He did so, fiddled with the device, then leaned in to check it. He said, "Better, but still awful. From those two snatches we have over two hundred numbers still active."

"Well, there you go. Those snatches were about two minutes apart. We stay here for an hour, and it might work."

With little confidence, Veep said, "Yeah, sure," and then our radio came alive. "Pike, Carrie, this is Knuckles. Target just came through. He's on the way."

I couldn't believe our good fortune. Why he was coming here after his partner had been tortured to death was beyond me. I would have been anywhere else other than a planned meeting. For all he knew, Shoshana was in on his partner's capture. Or maybe he didn't even know his partner was gone. Maybe that guy was supposed to fly back to Russia yesterday. Either way, it was a stroke of luck.

I said, "Roger all. Carrie, you copy?"

"I copy. Standing by."

"Just keep him there as long as possible."

"Will do."

We waited, keeping our eyes on her table, and the man from the cemetery appeared, glancing around and then leaning over to her. He said something, then went inside the restaurant.

Checking it out for threats. I'd do the same, if I were in his shoes.

He came back out and took a seat at her table. I said, "Hit it."

Veep did his work, and then we waited, letting the ebb and flow of patrons change our snapshot. I saw Shoshana pull out a folder, presumably showing her "company wares," and they talked a bit. Then they ordered lunch, and when the waitress left I said, "Hit it again."

We sat like this for an hour and a half, taking snapshot after snapshot, hoping we could sort it out later. Eventually the meeting broke up, with the Russian leaving the same way he'd come in. I called Knuckles, who had another Growler, which was my ace in the hole. "Knuckles, he's on the way out. Hit a snatch right when he's abreast of you."

"Roger all."

Thirty seconds later, he said, "He's out. I snatched like six hundred phones, so I'm not sure it's going to be of any help."

I said, "Bring it back here and give it to Veep. He'll sort it out."

Shoshana waited a bit, then came over to our table. She said, "He's stressed. I could see it like an aura around his head. He's on the verge of exploding."

Veep started working the algorithm on the Growler, saying, "I'd be the same way, given what he's trying to do. I'm surprised he even showed up."

I said, "Did you offer the weapon to him?"

"No. He no longer wanted it. I knew that the minute he sat down. He's going feral. He met me to tie up a loose end."

"What's that mean? You think he's a threat?"

"No. I think he thought *I* was a potential threat of compromise, and only met to ensure I'd just go home empty-handed, not being suspicious of what's going on. He was trying to placate me, that's all."

I nodded, and Veep said, "After running the system, I still have twenty-four phones. Probably people who sat down around the same time as we did or waitstaff. How are we going to sort that out?"

Knuckles and Brett showed up and I said, "With his collection."

Knuckles passed over his Growler and Veep downloaded the data. He ran the numbers and I saw him smile. He said, "Only two matches."

Knuckles said, "That's great, but what does it mean? What do we do now?"

I said, "Damned if I know."

CHAPTER 44

Lost in thought of what he was going to say, George Wolffe bumped into a scrum of aides fleeing the Oval Office. He let them go and then went in, seeing Kerry Bostwick and the secretary of defense, Mark Oglethorpe, in front of the president's desk. He pulled up short and waited. President Hannister saw him and said, "Mark, I agree with what you're saying, but we're going to have to talk about this at a later time."

Oglethorpe turned, saw Wolffe, and his eyebrows scrunched up. Wolffe knew why. Oglethorpe was a member of the Oversight Council, meaning he understood that Wolffe was the commander of the Task-force. What he didn't understand was why he was here, and it caused some consternation, because he *should* have known.

He left the room with a curious glance at Wolffe, saying, "I didn't know you guys had an operation going on that required presidential attention."

Wolffe said, "We don't. I was called here about a cover company that may be too close to something the CIA is using, nothing more."

It was a lie, but all he could think of on the spur of the moment. Oglethorpe left the room and Kerry Bostwick said, "Well, that was awkward."

Wolffe said, "Sorry. I was waved in from Palmer. I didn't know there was a meeting going on."

President Hannister said, "Don't worry about it. Where do we stand?"

"The Russian had the balls to show up to the meeting with Shoshana today. We've got his phone. Actually, phones plural. One is an old-school flip phone without GPS capability, but the other is a modern-day smartphone. We've tracked him to a bed-down site called the Bed Wood Hostel, a cheap hotel downtown. He went there after the meeting, and hasn't left."

"Did we learn anything more from the meeting?"

"Not really. Shoshana thought the only reason he came was to keep her from arousing suspicion with the Mossad, but she's convinced he's on the warpath. We don't have anything definitive on that other than her intuition, though."

"Great. Just what I like to hear. What about the Ukrainians? Do we have anything on them?"

"Only that we think they're in Copenhagen attending the NATO unconventional warfare conference. We have no names or anything else."

Kerry said, "Wait, isn't SOCEUR hosting that thing? Wasn't Mark just talking about that event?"

"He was." Hannister picked up his phone, said a few words, then hung up. A minute later, the secretary of defense reentered the room. "I was headed out, was there something missing from my briefing?"

"Yes. You were talking about that NATO UW roundtable a few minutes ago. Is it possible to get a list of the invitees? Specifically, the Ukrainians who are there?"

"Yes, sir. That's easy, but why?"

"We think there's something going on with them. That's all. Specifically, from some of the partisan elements we brought in. Focus on them."

Oglethorpe glanced at Kerry and then Wolffe, understanding that the request meant more than it appeared, but he nodded, saying, "I need a secure phone."

"Talk to Palmer. He'll get you one."

Oglethorpe left the room, and President Hannister said, "So if we find them, what do we do? That's the question. Do we have the Danes arrest them?"

Wolffe said, "For what? We don't have any proof that they're doing anything wrong. We invited them to Copenhagen, and they showed up. That's it."

"But an arrest would most certainly stop the entire thing. They'd quit after that, even if they get released in a day for a lack of evidence."

Kerry said, "That would give Putin a damn propaganda coup. We can't do that, sir. It'll play right into Putin's hands, with a worldwide media frenzy once the arrest goes public. It'll end up being portrayed as NATO trying to kill him. They're at a sanctioned NATO conference, for God's sake. That's a nonstarter. No way can we do that."

"So what then? What about President Zelensky? Can we get him to pull them off? I could make a call."

Wolffe said, "Sir, I am absolutely confident that Zelensky has no idea about this. He has no control over the outcome. The men were recruited by disaffected Russians from the GRU, and those agents are good. If you go to Zelensky, it'll end up just like Kerry stated earlier. We can't do that."

"So what do we do? What's the recommendation?"

Wolffe took a breath and said, "We could pull off Pike and just let it go. If it works, it works. But we need to start planning for the aftermath. We need to be ready to respond if Putin is killed, to the point of introducing NATO troops if Russia devolves into a civil war."

"If you think it's going to be that bad, then maybe we should order him to stop it. Short-circuit the whole thing."

Kerry said, "Sir, I agree with George here. If we do anything kinetic to stop this, it'll eventually come out. We *do not* want to be on the side of Putin here, using our assets to protect his life. I'd say just pull Pike out and prepare for the aftermath. With the other Russian team chasing them, and with what they know about the team, the mission is probably going to fail anyway. They'll do the damage. There's no reason for us to step in."

President Hannister sat for a moment, and Wolffe could see the pressure on him. Hannister said, "Do we owe a duty to the man being hunted? The Russian agent that met Shoshana? We know they're trying to kill him."

Kerry said, "No, sir. For one, he's not an asset of ours, but more importantly, he most certainly knows he is being hunted. Telling him that isn't going to be a shock to his system."

"Even so, maybe we go find him and let him know what we know. Stop this without any more bloodshed. Get him to quit."

Wolffe said, "Using Pike? Is that what you mean?"

"Yes."

Kerry said, "That fucker doesn't listen to anything we say. He'll screw this up for sure."

Incensed, Wolffe said, "He's listening *now*. The only reason you know about this is because he told us."

He glared at Kerry and said, "And the *only* reason we know about the threat to Putin is because Pike ignored us and went to Copenhagen. Quit talking about him as some loose cannon. When he senses something, he's always been right."

Wolffe returned to the president and said, "Pike is *not* a loose cannon. He's asking for help here, because he doesn't know what to do. You people look at him as someone who does what he wants, regardless of what we say, but the truth is he only goes forward against our wishes when he *knows* he's right. And he's *always* been right."

Kerry said, "So let him loose here? What are you saying?"

Wolffe said, "I'm saying he's asking for an order. He never does that. He's asking because he knows he doesn't own the monopoly on what's right. We need to tell him something. Give him a direction, because if we don't, he's going to take his own direction."

President Hannister said, "If he's going on his own direction, ignoring my orders, I'll put him down. That last thing about flying to Copenhagen after we told him to come home was out of bounds. You don't order one of *my* planes to land with a pistol. I'm not sure I can trust him anymore."

Wolffe scoffed and said, "Do you really think he used a pistol on those pilots? Or did they follow his directions because he's Pike Logan? They've worked with him forever. He saw a threat, and then found the damn threat—outside of what we were seeing."

Wolffe paced the room for a moment, then said, "You people still don't get it, even after I told you. You set Pike loose in the world, and he's going to do what's right. That's it. He doesn't care about your politics. He doesn't care about the next election. He cares about our national security. And that's what he's doing now—but he's asking *you* for a direction, because he doesn't know what to do with this information."

He looked at President Hannister and said, "Because he trusts you. And he doesn't trust a lot of people."

Mark Oglethorpe came back in the room, saying, "I got the list of the folks from Ukraine at the UW conference."

President Hannister took the list, looked at it, then said, "Who are these guys without any identifying markers? Everyone else in this list has full name, addresses, phone numbers, and positions. But these guys have nothing but a first name."

"Yes, sir. Those men are part of the resistance inside Ukraine. They didn't provide any information. In fact, those names are only code names. We took a lot of effort to get them to the conference securely.

They call themselves the Wolves, and their experience is invaluable for what we're trying to do. But they've been a little bit of a problem."

"Problem how?"

"They were supposed to do a roundtable with our men, talking about the efforts inside Ukraine, but they didn't show up to the conference today."

"What's that mean?"

"Well, they aren't part of a military, so we couldn't make them come. They have no command for us to ask where they are. They just didn't show."

President Hannister said, "Thank you. That will be all."

The SECDEF glanced at the director of the CIA and the commander of the Taskforce, then said, "Sir, if I can ask, what's this about?"

"Honestly, I'm not sure. Thank you for the information, but don't tell anyone we wanted the data."

Oglethorpe left the Oval Office and the president said, "So what now? Obviously, these are the men, and they're now on the hunt. What do we do?"

Kerry said, "They aren't going to kill Putin in Copenhagen. Tell Pike to track the Russian we know. He's going to meet the Ukrainians at some point."

Hannister nodded and said, "George? What do you think?"

"I think Pike needs an answer. He's been tracking guys for days, but he needs an endstate. A mission statement. What's the purpose? Do we save Putin or do we help kill him?"

Hannister rubbed his face and said, "I don't know at this point. That's a much bigger question."

Wolffe said nothing for a second, and Hannister saw his angst. The president finally said, "Do you think he won't do that? Is that the problem? You don't trust him either? Maybe we should just pull him out now."

Wolffe said, "No, sir. He'll do as you ask, but just following this guy isn't going to stop what the Russian and Ukrainians are doing. If we don't give him an answer on what we want done, beyond just following this guy around, he'll figure that out on his own, and I'm not sure you want to see that."

"Tell him that's the mission. We follow the Russian and develop the situation. I'll make a decision after that."

Wolffe gave one more try, saying, "We don't control the environment here. If we stay on the sidelines, and something happens, Pike is leaving the bench. He'll enter the battle, and we should let him know what side he's supposed to take."

The president thumped his fist on the table and said, "Tell him not to! If they want to fight it out, then let them."

"Sir, he's not going to let people get killed just because we tell him to stand down. He's going to pick a side. What side do you want?"

President Hannister rubbed his eyes, looked out the window, then said, "I honestly don't know at this point. I need more time to assess."

Wolffe nodded, then said, "Understood, sir. I'll relay the information, but you need to understand that time is not on our side."

CHAPTER 45

The sun had set, letting the November chill start its slow attack on the patrons at the hotel's outdoor patio, dueling with the propane heaters stationed around the deck. Putting on his new Patagonia jacket, Perun said, "Where are Javelin and Sokil?"

Dishka said, "On the way down. They'll be here soon. What's the story? Why did you send me to that amusement park?"

"Did you find what I asked?"

"Yeah. The entrance has no security, other than a rotating bar at the gate. No bag checks, no metal detectors. I found the restaurant and got three reservations like you asked. One outside, two inside."

"But only one in my name, correct?"

"Yes. Why, though?"

"Daniel called me. He has a change of mission for us."

"Change of mission? Like he wants us to go after a different target?"

"No, no, nothing like that. More like our contact in Finland has changed. The information we got in the library dead drop is no longer valid. He wanted to meet at the train station, but I didn't like him setting up the location, so I told him to meet at Tivoli, which is why I sent you to the park."

"He wanted to meet at the train station?"

"Yeah."

Dishka pulled what looked like an airline ticket out of his pocket and said, "They gave us the ferry tickets, along with the weapons and the passports. Are these no good now?"

"I don't know. That's what the meeting is about."

The man to Dishka's right, code name Akula—meaning "shark"—said, "Why would we go to this meeting? It sounds like a classic setup. We go, they identify us, and then they kill us. This whole thing is starting to sound like a Russian attack plan to stop us from working in Ukraine."

Perun set his glass of water on the table and said, "I know how you feel, but up to this point, Daniel has been spot-on. He gave us the weapons. He gave us the Estonian passports, and the ferry tickets. Why would he do all of that if he just wanted to kill us? He could have done that at our first meeting."

Dishka said, "Then why the change?"

Perun glanced around, making sure they were alone. He said, "I believe that he's being hunted like us. I think he's been compromised, but he still wants to continue."

"So why on earth would we attend this meeting? Let's just go home and take our fight to the Russians."

The two missing men showed up, each dragging a small carry-on roller bag. They took a seat at the table. Perun said, "We can fight against the invaders on an individual basis in Ukraine, or we can stop the entire war. That's why I want to continue."

One of the men who'd just sat down said, "What did I miss?"

Perun said, "Nothing. Did you clean your room?"

"Yes, just like you said."

"Okay, we're going to this meeting tonight, and you'll protect me. We have the ferry tickets for six in the morning tomorrow. We'll be on that ferry. Make sure your 'do not disturb' sign is on the door of your hotel room. NATO has paid for the week, let's let that happen."

Dishka said, "But why are we even meeting him? We have the instructions. This meeting is insane. Like bringing lambs to the slaughter."

"That may be true, which is why you'll be at the tables protecting me. The bottom line is that according to Daniel those instructions are no longer valid. Something happened and he believes the original meet is compromised."

Akula said, "What if this meeting is compromised?"

"Then we deal with it." Perun glanced around the table, showing confidence, and said, "Everyone have their ferry tickets? And what they want from their rooms? Because we aren't coming back here."

He got a nod from the men, and said, "Tonight, we'll either get our instructions for the future, or we'll go back home to continue the fight, but we're not coming back here."

Perun paid the bill and they left, walking to the metro station down the street. They boarded, nobody talking. They rode the metro until they reached the primary station of Copenhagen, and then exited, walking up the stairs to the main hall.

Dishka said, "There's the McDonald's he wanted to meet at. Maybe that would have been easier."

Perun glanced at the restaurant, seeing a line of people waiting on the processed food, and said, "I'd rather eat somewhere else. Let's dump these suitcases. We'll pick them back up when we're done."

Perun led them to a stack of lockers and the men deposited their carry-on cases, Dishka saying, "You think this place is safe to leave our stuff?"

"You mean as opposed to walking into Tivoli Gardens as a group dragging luggage behind us? Yes, I think it's secure. Leave your identification and ferry tickets. Only take the guns."

They exited through the main doors of the station, crossed the street, and paid to enter Tivoli, one of the oldest continually operating amusement parks in the world.

Created in 1843, it originally held only gardens and theaters, with a merry-go-round being its most risqué fare, but over time expanded to include roller coasters and other amusement rides. It remains the most visited amusement park in Scandinavia, and a perfect place for the meeting Perun had to accomplish. Unlike the train station.

The park was public, with multitudes of families enjoying the sights, and because of that, it afforded him a better degree of survival. He needed a place with people, but not like the train station, a melting pot of every type of weirdo who could afford a ticket. He wanted a place with families, where he could separate friend from foe, and Tivoli offered him that by the very nature that someone paid to come in.

They went through the gate as a group, then split up, with Perun saying, "Be at your table at eight. I will not talk to you again."

Perun wandered through the narrow alleys, all adorned with Christmas lights and various games of skill begging for his attention. He ignored the pleas from the workers trying to get him to play, dodging the strollers of families and the teenagers out for a night of fun. He circled a lake, seeing a replica pirate ship in the water, illuminated like all the rest of the place, as if a ship such as that would merrily traverse the seven seas clad in Christmas lights.

A light rain began to fall, causing him to raise his collar. He looked at his watch and was startled at how long he'd wandered about. It was time.

He continued along the shore, eventually reaching the end of the lakeside path and reentering the plaza of the gardens, the crowds growing sparser with the drizzle. He passed an open-air theater, people in bench seats stoically holding umbrellas while the show continued. He glanced at the stage and saw a group of actors portraying a slapstick nonverbal play that appeared to have not changed since the 1800s. He went past it, turned the corner on the concrete walkway, and saw the entrance to the Grøften.

Set underneath a small forest of trees, the structure more glass than wood, it had an outside eating area, the tables empty because of the November chill and the rain. He went inside, the noise of the place assaulting him. Clinking glasses and murmured conversations bounced off the walls and the red-checkered tablecloths. He talked to the hostess and was led to a table in the middle of the room, descending some steps to get there. The roof was glass, with his table having a large umbrella folded next to it, leading him to believe that in the summer the entire place was open to the air, but now, propane heaters fired up to keep the temperature comfortable.

He took his seat and scanned the room, seeing Dishka and Sokil at one table near the front door, then Javelin and Akula at another, only two tables away. He gave no indication that he'd spotted them.

He ordered a Coke from the waiter and waited, wondering if Daniel would even show, a small part of him wishing he wouldn't. The mission he was embarking on was outside of his wildest ambitions, and he suspected—given the latest changes to the operational profile—that it would end in failure. Better to die on his feet fighting in Ukraine than on his knees at the hands of the Russian state on an ill-fated mission. And then he remembered his wife and son, the need for vengeance growing white hot, his hand gripping the glass of water like a throat he wanted to crush.

He glanced to the door, and saw Daniel enter.

On the far side of the restaurant, Oleg was beginning to think this entire endeavor was a waste of time, the effort accomplishing nothing more than to cement the futility of the information they were using, and that if he failed he was dead the moment he returned to his home. And then, like a miracle, the Russian traitor entered the restaurant. The one they'd followed from the cemetery. He felt the adrenaline start pumping in his body, but waited, wanting to see where he went. The man took a seat at a table with someone he didn't recognize, but he knew who it was: the leader of the Wolves. That's what this meeting was about.

This was it. If he took them out now, all would be good.

Sitting in the back of the restaurant, Knuckles called and said, "The pipe-hitters from the cemetery are here. They just took a seat at two different tables. What's the call?"

After leaving the meeting in the meatpacking district, we'd tracked the phone first to a youth hostel, and then to this place—a public amusement park—with the Taskforce still wishy-washy on what the hell we were doing. Now that the Russian pipe-hitters were here, they knew the same thing we did, and something was about to happen. The problem was I had no idea of who I was supposed to support, or even if I was to support anyone.

I said, "You sure?"

"Yeah, I'm sure. The same guy from Brus is here, in this restaurant."

While I'd gotten a return to my SITREP, it had basically been a big ball of "Keep your head down. We love what you're doing."

The Taskforce hadn't given me any direction at all. The entire response was a bunch of blowhard talk about democracy and Ukraine, but didn't tell me what I really needed to know: to wit, what the fuck was I supposed to do? I'd told them about the meeting, and was given the order to "assess and analyze," like that was going to be the endstate. Now I had the pipe-hitters in *my damn restaurant.* I was going to have to choose a side.

And I did. I keyed my radio and said, "If they show hostile intent, kill them."

Perun saw a shadow, and Daniel sat down. Perun glanced around him, then said, "You've come alone?"

"I have."

"You have no men with you? Nobody tracking you?"

Perun saw a shift in his demeanor, and then understood why. Daniel said, "Look, my team was hit today. I don't know by whom, but I've been compromised here in Copenhagen. Someone is hunting me. That's why I asked for the meeting."

Perun heard the words and stiffened, saying, "So you brought them to me, here?"

Daniel held up his hands in surrender, saying, "No, no. You picked this place. Not me. But I had to change the meeting location in Finland because of the compromise. The mission is still on, but I had to ensure it was secure. Your old orders are no longer valid."

Perun snarled, "Maybe the entire mission is no longer valid. How do I know they aren't compromised in Finland?"

"Because I talked to him. He's still secure. He sent me this."

Daniel slid his phone across the table and Perun saw a map with instructions on it. Daniel said, "That's the new meeting location. But I can't send it to you because your fucking phone is from the late nineties."

Perun smiled and said, "Hard to install tracking malware on my phone when it doesn't understand what malware is. I only need it to talk, and don't want its tether following me like a high school student on TikTok."

They ordered food, and settled in for dinner, Daniel doing his best to convince Perun to continue. He didn't commit until the check came, passing it to Daniel. Daniel held up his card, the waiter ran it, then passed the receipt to Daniel. Perun said, "Okay, we'll continue. I believe you about Finland, but you need to find out how you were penetrated."

Daniel started to say something, and then his head exploded, spraying brain matter and blood onto Perun's face.

CHAPTER 46

On the radio I heard Knuckles shout, "Gun!" and then saw a man two tables over draw a bead on Daniel. He pulled the trigger and I saw the target drop. I leapt up and said, "Eliminate the threat."

Knuckles was sitting with Brett, and they both started shooting, killing the man with the pistol, and then the room erupted in gunfire from all sides, like we'd turned on a switch. I couldn't believe the number of people who joined the fight. It was like a mobster movie in an Italian restaurant, with everyone drawing pistols and blazing away while innocent patrons ran off screaming.

There was no way to determine friend from foe. I said, "Avalanche, avalanche, avalanche," initiating the code word for immediate evacuation. Ordinarily used for situations like entering a building and finding it booby-trapped with IEDs, avalanche seemed to fit the shit storm we'd just found ourselves in.

I scrambled backward, dodging the fleeing guests while watching the Ukrainian and the dead Russian. The Ukrainian snatched the phone from the table and crab-walked out of the restaurant, using the chaos the shooting had caused to aid in his flight.

I duck-walked over to their table and snatched the check still holding the Russian's credit card, then dropped to the floor and began low crawling away from the gunfire, telling my team to do the same.

"Get out, get out, get out. Rendezvous at the light show on the lake. Acknowledge."

Not including our two teams, there were at least four other tables armed to the teeth and slinging lead at each other, and I had no idea who was good or who was bad. I'd let them sort it out among themselves, not wanting my team to enter the fray.

I snatched Jennifer off the floor near our table, got an up from Knuckles and Brett, but nothing from Veep and Shoshana outside the restaurant.

On the way out a side door I caught a glimpse of the Russian leader of the team from the Christiana slum jam his weapon against the temple of a man, pull the trigger, and then fall on top of him. After that, we were out and running.

We managed to escape with the crowd of fleeing service staff and innocent patrons. We jogged around a lake, going past a reconstructed floating pirate ship, lit up like a Christmas tree. We came to a viewing platform for the light show hanging over the lake, the area already filling up with crowds of tourists willing to wait for a good spot even with the drizzle coming down.

In five minutes, my team was accounted for. Brett had once again acted like a bullet trap, taking a hit through his left bicep.

I said, "You're a damn magnet, man."

He wrapped a bandage on the wound and said, "I'm fine. It's not like I knew that entire place was going to erupt."

I took a look at the wound and said, "Well, you're going home after this. Two hits on a single mission is one more than you're allowed."

"I'm fine, Pike."

"That wasn't a question. I've got enough team members to figure this out, and you're going home for some medical care."

He didn't like it, but nodded. I gave instructions to the rest of the team to get back to the hotel by twos, taking separate trains and foot routes, and we slipped out of Tivoli Gardens before the authorities could establish a lockdown that I knew was coming.

We consolidated at our hotel—a place called 71 Nyhaven, situated right on a canal, with a boardwalk next to it adorned with one quaint outdoor restaurant after another serving open-faced sandwiches and fish. I'd chosen one with a large wooden picnic table, and we all gathered around.

I said, "Okay, what do we know? Let's walk through it."

Knuckles said, "I saw the man from the cemetery—"

Shoshana interrupted, saying, "Daniel. His name was Daniel."

Knuckles nodded and said, "Daniel approached an unknown and took a seat. They had a conversation and he passed the unknown a smartphone. They appeared to have a little bit of an argument over dinner, then Daniel paid the bill. Before they could break up, one of the pipe-hitters rose with a pistol. He didn't waste any time. He was there to kill, not capture or stop activity. He pulled the trigger, hitting Daniel in the head. At that point, Brett and I opened fire. He dropped, and then two other tables started shooting."

Brett said, "What did the unknown do?"

Knuckles said, "I couldn't tell. I was facing away."

I said, "Right before you were hit, I saw him take the phone and low-crawl out of the restaurant. I managed to get their check and credit card. Not sure if it'll do any good. Jennifer, what do you have?"

She said, "At my four o'clock, one of those other tables stood up and started shooting. I realized the situation was out of control right when you called the avalanche. The leader of the Russians—the one whose phone we tracked—was across the way from me, right next to a man shooting. I don't know how I missed him earlier, but he jammed a pistol into the man at the table and pulled the trigger. They both fell to the ground, and I saw the leader rip off the dead man's jacket and start to flee. I couldn't get a shot because of all the other people running and screaming. He made it out."

Blaine said, "So what do we make of it?"

Shoshana said, "It's pretty clear to me. Daniel knew his team was compromised because of the loss of the man in the chair we found. He'd already given the Wolves instructions for completing the mission, but with the compromise he had to change those orders, necessitating one final meeting."

"But how did the other Russians know he'd be there? And why so many tables with guns? It should have been a single hit at an Italian restaurant but turned into a large-scale firefight."

"I don't know how the Russians knew of the meeting, but I'll bet the other people shooting were the Wolves. That's why they were there. The unknown at the table didn't trust the meeting. He brought his own protection, which ended up being smart."

I said, "What was the damage, as far as we know? I saw one Wolf go down at the hands of the Russian, and Daniel is most definitely dead."

Brett said, "Knuckles and I took out another guy. I can't say whether he was a Russian or Ukrainian, but he's dead."

Knuckles said, "He was Russian. He was one of the guys who pulled the body into the car at the brew pub."

"The rest got out?"

"I guess. The gunfire continued as we left, so there might be one or two more down."

Blaine said, "So what now?"

I showed the check I'd taken, a small vinyl envelope with the receipt and Daniel's credit card inside. I said, "I'm going to call back to Creed and see if he can get anything from this. May be a clue somewhere."

"But it won't matter. That guy is dead."

"Unless he was bankrolling the Wolves. He was paying for the meal. Maybe he's paying for much more than that. Meanwhile, Blaine, you call Wolffe and let him know what's up."

"Me?"

I dialed my phone and laughed, saying, "Yeah, you're the commander, aren't you? Get some clarity on what we're supposed to be doing here."

CHAPTER 47

Perun took the escalator to the main floor of the Skt. Petri hotel and saw the outside deck was hosting some type of happy hour. Crowded with guests, a DJ blaring music, he decided to stay inside, moving past the bar to a booth at the very back of the room, near the kitchen. He was the first to arrive back at their hotel, and as they'd discussed before going to Tivoli, he texted everyone in a group chat his location, waiting to see who showed up.

The shoot-out inside the restaurant had caused all of them to scatter like rats in a kitchen when the lights come on, with no plan whatsoever, and Perun blamed himself. He'd brought the entire team to the restaurant precisely because he feared it was a setup, but had not planned how they would react to just that contingency. The only thing he'd done was to tell the team that if things went bad, get out and return to the hotel. The first one there would set up the collection point, and the rest would fall in.

He waited, staring at his old-school flip phone every six seconds, with Daniel's smartphone sitting next to it. He received a text from Dishka and gave a sigh of relief. In the back of his head, he'd had a niggling, growing doubt that he was the last man standing. Twenty minutes later, the remainder of his team slid into the booth around him. He did a head count and said, "This is it?"

Dishka said, "I think so. I saw Sokil hit directly in the temple with a bullet. He's gone for sure."

"And Akula?"

Javelin said, "He was at my table. He's gone as well. I saw his body when it hit the floor. He had no face."

Perun nodded, lost in thought. He saw the men looking at him earnestly, and tried to diffuse the fear they were feeling. "Well, I guess when I said we wouldn't be back here again, I was a little off."

Dishka let out a brittle laugh and said, "Nowhere else to go."

Perun took a breath and attempted to show soothing strength, knowing that's what was needed. The men at the table were on a trip-wire, afraid of their own shadows.

He'd been here before, back when he'd first started hunting the Russians with boys who had no idea of the vortex of violence they were entering. Once they touched the flame, they needed leadership to continue. He would never have the hubris to call himself a natural leader, but he most definitely was, and he understood that he needed to calm the team now. He needed to deflect them from what had just happened and get them to focus on something else.

He looked at the man to his left and said, "Where did you get your name? Javelin?"

The man looked confused for a moment, but then Perun could see that his question had the effect he wanted. He was giving the man a chance to tout his strengths instead of the failure they'd just experienced.

Javelin said, "I was one of the first to learn how to use a Javelin anti-tank missile when I was with the army, before my unit was wiped out and I joined you. I was pretty good. One of the best with that weapon."

The men began to calm down with the conversation, the fear of being hunted receding.

Perun said, "Good. Good. Well, we're in a little bit of a quandary here. This is the next contact in Helsinki."

He slid Daniel's smartphone across the table, the last screen still showing. "He told me he'd been compromised here in Copenhagen, but the linkup was safe, because he'd changed it from what his partner knew. It's why we met tonight, so he could pass me the information, but I'm not so sure."

Dishka said, "So sure about what?"

"So sure we aren't compromised. We've lost Sokil and Akula, and not through anything we did. Through the enemy, which means they found us somehow."

Dishka said, "They didn't find *us*. They were Russian. They found Daniel."

"But how? He was good. Better than good. He'd been trained by the best. I'm willing to bet he'd killed the enemies of Russia all over the world, and yet he was slaughtered tonight."

Javelin said, "It's easier to avoid the enemy than your friends. The Russians tracked him somehow. They knew him and tracked him. It was always a risk, even when we were in Ukraine. We knew he was compromised when he called. It's why he set up the meeting, and he sacrificed his life to give us the new contact information."

Dishka picked up the phone, reading the screen. He said, "This is the new location information?"

"Yeah. That's it. So do we continue? We can always show back up at the conference tomorrow and say we slept in the day before. Nobody's controlling us, so we can go back to Ukraine without any risk. Continue the fight there."

Dishka said, "What are you asking?"

"I'm asking if you want to continue on this path. We just had two men killed in a shoot-out at a public place. Clearly, Russia does not care about the repercussions. What they care about is killing us, which means they know what we're trying to do. They wouldn't put this much effort into stopping us, which means Daniel's cell compromise told them what we were doing. They might not know the how, but they know the what. They know we're hunting."

Dishka said, "That's true, but it doesn't mean they can stop us. I don't believe our mission is compromised. Putin knows something about our mission, and that something has given him fear, but I don't think he knows about us. I think Daniel was compromised, but the mission isn't yet. If it were, they'd have simply killed Daniel at a location of their own choosing, then waited for us in Finland."

"What makes you think they aren't waiting right now?"

"Because they want the entire effort destroyed, but they don't know what that is. If they knew the entire plan, they'd have let us leave, then killed Daniel, waiting on us to show up at the new contact in Helsinki to kill us all. They didn't do that. They chose to attack because they're desperate. They know about the mission, but they don't know how to stop it."

Perun nodded, then said, "But how did they know we were meeting in Tivoli? I picked that place, Daniel didn't. It was something from me. That's what's wrong here."

Dishka picked up the smartphone on the table and said, "It's this. They were tracking this. The GRU was compromised, not us. But now we have this phone, and now they're tracking us."

In an instant, Perun knew he was right. It was the reason he never carried a smartphone. The reason he never left a digital trace. He said, "Copy down those instructions and turn that fucking thing off."

Dishka did as he asked, with Javelin looking around the room for the monster coming to kill them.

Perun said, "So, given that they know where we're sitting right this moment, and that they're probably coming in to kill us, do we continue?"

Dishka said, "Oh, yeah. If the choice is dying in a hotel bar or killing Putin? Yeah, we continue."

Perun believed the same thing, but he needed concurrence. He said, "Javelin, what do you think?"

"I think I used the missiles to devastating effect, but it still did nothing. I want something greater. If you think our mission is still valid, I want to continue."

Perun studied him, then said, "To include being captured by the Russians? I'm not talking about a bullet in the head here, or a drone strike where you look up and then die in a ball of fire. I'm talking about getting captured and suffering, like the men in my team did before I met you."

Javelin said, "The risk is worth it. My life is for Ukraine, but I promise, they won't take me alive."

Perun studied him for a moment, seeing the commitment. He said, "Okay. I agree, but the phone is just one concern of mine. The Russians aren't the only threat. What will the authorities find on the bodies of the men we lost? Did they have their Estonian passports on them?"

Dishka said, "Yeah, more than likely. But you told us to put the ferry tickets in the luggage, so that link is gone."

"Are you sure?"

"I'm sure I did as you asked. Javelin?"

Javelin nodded, saying, "I had my passport as identification, but my ferry tickets are in my luggage."

Dishka said, "We can go through the main station to get to the ferry terminal and get our luggage then, including theirs. Nothing will be left to sort out by the police."

Perun leaned back in the booth, saying, "You got that phone off now?"

Dishka said, "Yeah, it's off. You want me to destroy it?"

"No. We might need it later, but don't let it hit the cell network unless I say."

Dishka nodded, and Perun took a sip of his water, thinking of their future. He finally said, "Okay then, so here we are, a few idiots from Ukraine with the ability to alter destiny. Do we continue? Take the ferry to Helsinki?"

Javelin said, "I'm a yes. If they attack us on the ferry, then we fight back. If they attack us in Helsinki, then we fight back. If they don't know we're going, then we win."

Dishka said, "You know where I stand."

Perun surveyed both of them, thinking of the step they were about to take. He made his decision.

"Okay, I'm with you, but it's only the three of us now. We need to be out of here before the authorities make the link with the bodies they found and the unconventional warfare roundtable. When that hits the news we need to be long gone—especially if men from Ukraine are found with passports from Estonia. That's going to be a shit storm, but will probably help us, as NATO will do whatever they can to cover up our participation."

Dishka nodded, but could tell something beyond those extraordinary circumstances was worrying Perun.

He said, "Hey, sir, what else is bothering you? What aren't you telling us?"

"Nothing. I'm just thinking of the fight tonight. Something doesn't make sense."

"What? The Russians started shooting and we shot back. Thank God that Daniel provided us the means to do so."

"We weren't the only people shooting tonight. There was someone else, and they weren't Russians."

Dishka said, "Yeah, but they were *shooting* the Russians. They weren't shooting us. Maybe we have some help we don't know about."

Perun leaned back in his chair and said, "That's what concerns me."

CHAPTER 48

Victor Petrov took the long walk away from President Putin's office, shadowed by Putin's security detail, and knew he was close to being one more "trusted member" of the inner circle who found himself thrown out of a window, to be later reported as a suicide.

He'd been staying at Putin's Lake Valdai mansion since having been given the initial mission, and while Putin took his special train to travel back to Moscow every other day, Victor had been "asked" to remain to control the operation against Valkyrie, and had, of course, agreed.

Victor could see the strain Putin's "Special Military Operation" was having on him. Nothing was going right. The Ukrainians were proving a more resilient opponent than anyone had thought, and the easy victory was now in the rearview mirror. The initial stories were horrifically bad optics. Putin's divisions had invaded Ukraine with dress uniforms in the supply chains instead of beans and bullets, intending to perform a victory march three days after the incursion. That hadn't happened, and when the Russians in Kyiv retreated due to a lack of resupply, they left the uniforms behind for the Ukrainian soldiers to find.

Now they were in a stalemate, with Kyiv slowly but surely winning the war of world opinion. Putin pretended it was all part of the plan, but Victor could see the strain. Putin no longer entered an aircraft to go anywhere, fearful of the tracking. He used a specially modified armored train to travel about the country, and he no longer stayed at the presidential palace, spending all his time either here, at Lake Valdai, or his mansion on the Black Sea. For now, regardless of world opinion, he was still in the Kremlin's driver's seat, with his absolute control of the propaganda telling the population that they were winning, but the bodies coming home were beginning to cause rumblings.

It was not good, and not just because of the outside world press.

The private military company Wagner, using prisoners pulled straight out of jail, was losing men at an incredible rate, causing the owner of the organization to take the brazen route of accusing the Russian defense high command of incompetence—directly challenging Putin. Putin had responded by a continual shuffle of new high command personnel, which did not engender confidence from the population at large. Due to the propaganda, they were still on his side, but the discontent was growing larger by the day.

Victor still felt the weight of the Dead Man's Hand device in his pocket, now something he wore every day, like a pair of underwear. When he woke up, he put on his pants, and he pocketed the device. It was always with him. He didn't want to use it, but knew that was his duty should something happen to Putin.

Each night, before going to bed, he set it on his nightstand and stared at it. Part of him wanted to smash it. Another part looked at it as a status symbol. He was one of the chosen four, and that meant something in the greater dog-eat-dog world of Kremlin politics. No matter who he faced in the political world, he knew he was one of the chosen, and that held power.

The Word of the Four Horsemen had spread rapidly, and, outside of Putin, no one person knew who actual members were, and just acting with authority showed a chance that he was one of the chosen. Nobody came right out and asked, because the Horsemen were ostensibly secret, but everyone understood that it could be him, and it allowed him to open doors that he otherwise wouldn't have been able—but the reason why was something that ate at his soul.

Putin had picked him as one of the men who would engender revenge through a thermonuclear war, and Victor wasn't sure he could make that decision. Of course, he never voiced his reticence. That would be suicide—but he thought of it often, especially given the mission he was working now. He often wondered who the other Horsemen were, but never put any effort into finding out. That, in itself, would be suicidal.

On this day he had a little bit more of a pep in his step, because his SOBR team in Copenhagen had succeeded in finding the GRU traitors, and were on track to eliminate the Wolves. The mission in Sweden had only been partially successful, and that report to Putin had not been taken well.

The envoy from Turkey had been killed, stalling the effort for Sweden's bid into NATO, but the diplomat from Sweden had escaped death, and Victor's entire SOBR team had been wiped out—presumably by the GRU Valkyrie team.

It had been messy, and Putin hadn't been happy, but now they had their hands on an actual GRU traitor and had extracted information from him. And then the GRU had struck again, killing part of the team—but not before they'd gleaned the next meeting site with the Wolves.

He was expecting a report of success at his next contact. Expecting to hear that the threat had been eliminated, but when the call came, it didn't end up that way.

Late that night, lying awake in his bed, he heard his phone ring, and hoped it was good news. It was not. He picked up the encrypted receiver, saying, "This is Victor, go."

"Sir, it's Oleg. I'm at a park adjacent to the Russian embassy. I think we need to enter. I need you to let them know we're coming."

"What? Why? What happened?"

"We had a unique opportunity, and we took it. We killed the final GRU traitor and managed to kill two of the Ukrainian Wolves, but the rest escaped. Two of my own men are dead because the Wolves had their own security on-site. They began killing as well."

"You had a shoot-out? Where?"

"Inside a restaurant in the Tivoli amusement park. I had to take the chance because the GRU man was passing further instructions to the leader of the Wolves. I had to short-circuit that. We did, and we now know what the leader looks like."

"He's not dead?"

"No, sir. He managed to escape, which is why I want to enter the embassy. We left a mess. I need protection."

It took a moment for Victor to absorb the information. When he finally did, he said, "So I'm clear, you didn't take out the GRU leader or the Wolves with a car crash, a pedestrian accident on a bridge, or some sort of poison. You killed them in a gangland shoot-out at an amusement park? Is that correct?"

"Sir, things were moving fast. As you know, we captured one of the GRU men and interrogated him, gleaning the time and place of the meeting. The GRU team leader was going to give instructions for follow-on operations for the leader of the Wolves. We had them in a restaurant and I made the call to eliminate both at that time. I didn't anticipate that he would have security, but he did. They killed two of my men, but the rest were able to escape."

What a debacle. Get the team out? No doubt.

Oleg continued, "I managed to take a jacket off one of the dead Wolves. Inside was a passport for Estonia and a ferry ticket for Helsinki, so we know where they're going and how they're traveling, but I need to get my team out of here."

Enraged, Victor said, "You engaged in a shoot-out in a public restaurant? Is that what you're telling me?"

"Yes, sir. It was supposed to be a simple hit, but it turned into a gunfight. Like I said, I lost two men, and they're going to be identified as Belarusian. That will hold up for a day or two, but eventually, they're going to be pinned to Russia, just like the ones in Sweden."

Victor wanted to slam the phone down at the incompetence. He'd told Putin these men weren't up to the task. This was a GRU job, not a National Guard one. But he knew that answer would only lead to him, as the leader of the Guard. He said, "You killed the Valkyrie team leader?"

"Yes, sir. He's dead."

Well, at least that was something. He could burn this team to the ground, letting them twist in the wind, and still tell Putin that they'd accomplished part of the mission.

"And the leader of the Wolves? Did you get him?"

"No, sir, he escaped."

Shit.

"So he's on the run now? Continuing the mission?"

"I honestly don't know what he's planning now. We took out two of his men, along with his control, so maybe he's done. I don't know. That ferry ticket is for tomorrow at six A.M.—to Helsinki, Finland. Either they're going to be on that, or they're going back to Ukraine. I want to get off the street and into the embassy for future planning on exfiltration. Right now, we're in trouble. We can't go back to our hotel because the cops will probably be waiting."

What a debacle.

He thought a moment, then said, "Get out of the country. Right now. Take an aircraft to Helsinki. The first one flying. I'll meet you there at the airport."

"What about the ferry? I could put some men on it."

"You mean after you just had a shoot-out with them? Don't you think they'll be looking for you? What are you going to do on a ferry? Another gunfight and then leap over the side? Don't be any more of an idiot than you already have. How long does the ferry take?"

"Leaves at six in the morning, but doesn't arrive until six P.M. the next day. A day and a half."

"Okay, fly to Helsinki and meet me. We'll pick them up when they dock and reassess there."

"If I do that, I'm going to have to ditch our weapons. I can't risk getting caught in Finnish customs. I did the research on Copenhagen and knew we could get through, but I have no idea about Finland."

"I'll bring whatever the team needs. Just meet me there tomorrow morning."

"Okay, sir. So, head to the embassy to wait?"

"No, you idiot. Do *not* go to the embassy. Do not go to your hotel."

"Sir, it's raining here, and cold."

"Then go to a homeless shelter for all I care, but do not introduce yourself to the embassy. They are going to have enough problems when the bodies are identified, and you have no official cover. Do you understand?"

"Yes, sir."

"You made this mess, now live in it. Go sleep in the Copenhagen airport. Send me your flight information and I'll see you in Helsinki. I'm taking over the operation."

He hung up the phone and realized he needed to return to President Putin's office, something he was dreading. He had some good news but didn't think it would be enough to stop Putin's anger.

He needed to end this, now, and he needed help to do that. Some-one with unparalleled skill at killing, and he knew exactly who that was. A man he'd once served with who now did private security. In the military he'd been feared even by his commanders, but respected for his abilities. He'd once beaten a commander near to death, and his transgressions had been brushed aside because of his skill at the dirty end of the spear.

Victor had used him twice in the past, when he'd been the head of Putin's security. He picked up the phone and dialed another number, saying, "Hey, it's Victor. I have a mission for you."

CHAPTER 49

We walked through the entrance deck of the ferry to Helsinki, and I couldn't believe what I was seeing. I'd been on quite a few overnight ferries in my life, from the Mediterranean to Southeast Asia, and most were exactly what you'd expect: utilitarian boats with maybe a bar on the upper deck and a kiosk to get sandwiches, the rooms something out of a prison cell, with bunk beds bolted into the walls.

This wasn't that.

The ship had twelve decks, including an enormous duty-free store, a promenade full of shops and restaurants, and a theater that showcased comedy shows and musical reviews. It was more of a junior cruise ship than a ferry.

We showed the boatswain's mate our tickets, and then were shown a little respect, because we had the executive suite. The biggest room on the boat.

I'd like to say that was because I was important, but it was really because the damn boat was full. It was the only other room left after we'd reserved three others for my team.

We walked down the promenade on deck seven and Jennifer said, "Maybe we should give the team our room. I don't feel right taking the biggest suite on the boat."

I laughed and said, "Screw that. We need a TOC, and that's our suite. I can't be blamed for them running out of rooms."

We took the elevator to the eleventh deck, went down the small hallway to our suite, and entered. I was amazed. It was like Kim Kardashian–level opulence. We had our own sitting room, a separate bedroom, and an actual, real shower next to a Jacuzzi tub instead of a hose that you used while straddling a toilet.

I said, "Holy shit. What's this room costing?"

Jennifer said, "That's what I was saying. We should've taken the smaller room and given this to the others."

She had a point. The leader of any organization *should* take the worst accommodations. That's what leaders do, and that's why I gave Blaine a crappy little hole-in-the-wall on a different deck. I said, "We need a TOC, and this is it. We'll keep it."

She gave me the side-eye and I said, "Hey, we *do* need a TOC, and that's where I'm going to be. It won't work using one of those smaller rooms. You and I are not going to get any sleep anyway. Call the guys up here."

She did, then opened her bag on the bed, saying, "You sure this weirdo thing Shoshana has is going to work? And if it does, what are we doing about it?"

I said, "Honestly, no idea. I've done some stupid shit in the name of national security, but it was always with an endstate. I don't know what we're doing here. If it was my call, I'd let these guys go, and if they kill that fuck Putin, then they win. If they fail, then so what. But it's not my call."

"You know if that intel we got from the Russian is bad, we're dead in the water, right?"

I picked up a plate of fruit that was a gift for reserving the best room on the boat, took a bite of a grape, and said, "Yeah, but we're probably dead in the water anyway. Shoshana's weird little devices probably won't work. We can only do what we can do."

"But getting the information for her devices puts us at risk. Does the

National Command Authority know what you're about to do? Do they know what you're going to do to continue Alpha?"

I snapped my head to her and said, "They don't get to decide how I execute. They give me the mission. That's it."

I dropped the plate on the table and said, "Shit. I didn't want to do this from damn jump street. The whole thing aggravates me. Some guys want to kill Putin? Let them go. Why am I involved?"

She saw me winding up and said, "Hey, hey, that's not what I meant."

I sagged back and said, "But Wolffe won't tell me what he wants. I honestly don't know what they're thinking back home. Either tell me what to do, or tell me to back off. This whole 'continue to explore' is ridiculous. Alpha is designed to determine a threat. We've done that."

Blaine had sent our SITREP back, and it had caused some soiled panties, to say the least. The National Command Authority had freaked out, demanding information that we simply did not have, wanting to know who the various shooters in the restaurant were. I understood their angst but was a little aggravated at their ability to ask us questions we could not answer, and then get mad when we couldn't. Like we were magicians conducting a trick, and they wanted to know how we'd done it, but didn't believe me when I said I didn't know how.

There was no trick, and I'd told Wolffe in no uncertain terms that he had all our information. Russians were killing Russians, and Ukrainians were caught in the middle. Putin was a target, but how that would happen was impossible to ascertain. That's all I knew.

While Wolffe was getting his ass reamed by the president, I'd tried to find out where the Ukrainians had gone. I'd seen the leader take Daniel's phone, and so we had a track, but it had died at a hotel called Skt. Petri, either because they knew it was compromised, or because it had simply quit from a dead battery.

Creed had worked his magic on the credit card I'd stolen, doing a deep dive on where it had been used. It turned out the card had purchased five ferry tickets on a boat going from Copenhagen to Helsinki, and so we had a lead. I was pretty sure two of those tickets wouldn't be redeemed, but I wasn't sure if that lead mattered.

In the end, the president had ordered us to continue, but it was still Alpha. Still just "find out what you can find out," which was a little bit of a kick to the balls, because every time we did this, we came closer to exposure. I was getting sick of the Alpha bullshit. In the past, it was driving to an endgame, but now, it just seemed to put us at risk for no reason. Either tell me to take them off the board, or tell me to help them. Just surveying their actions was getting old, but I understood it.

President Hannister was following the oldest rule in politics—do nothing and hope it goes away. Unfortunately for him, I'd seen the bullets flying and knew that this was most definitely not going away. Someone was going to die, and I knew I was going to be pressed to make a decision on who that was, sooner or later.

But, like a dutiful soldier, I told him I'd roger on. I just wasn't sure if they'd like how I did it.

The team arrived and I said, "How did the camera install go?"

Knuckles said, "Fine. No issues. It's on the wall, but I'll tell you, someone's going to find it sooner or later. It's small, and blends in, but there's nothing in the hallway to camouflage it. It's going to eventually be discovered."

I said, "Well, then, we'd better get this done sooner rather than later."

Through the use of the Russian's credit card, Creed had found the purchases of the tickets, and then had found the receipts, showing the actual rooms the men were going to use. We had to make a guess on which one was the leader, and I'd made the decision on that. All of the rooms were the cheapest tickets available, except for one: it was one step up.

On deck nine, it was away from the others, and I figured it was the one to watch. If I was wrong, it wasn't a big deal. All we needed was one of these Ukrainians to follow, and Shoshana promised she could do that.

I said, "Veep, can you pull it up on the Wi-Fi?"

"We'll have to pay for that. It'll be recorded."

I laughed and said, "You're in the executive suite. It's included."

Jennifer passed him the code and he sat behind a computer, typing, saying, "I'm not sure why I'm doing this. Shoshana's beacon is ridiculous. If we're going in anyway, we should just plant our own."

Shoshana leaned into him, giving him her weird glow and saying, "Nobody will find my tracker. You have nothing like this."

He recoiled from her gaze, and I didn't blame him, because she was really scary when she wanted to be, but he had a point. Shoshana's beacon was almost stupidly crazy.

I said, "You sure this thing will work? Because he's right—if we're going into his room, we can plant our own."

She turned to me and said, "If you do, he might find it, or toss it. Mine will stay with him without him knowing."

"Are you sure?"

"Yes. We've used it before. It works."

As a part of her wares to convince Daniel that she was a legitimate Israeli defense company, she'd brought a tracking device called the Tick, a nano-beacon about the size of—of course—a tick. The trick was that it worked on smell and could be unleashed within thirty feet of the target. You didn't need to place it on the target—which was always the hardest part of beaconing a human being—you just had to be close.

Just like a tick drawn to a human, it would go to the target, crawl up any available appendage, then burrow into the clothing and start transmitting. It used any GSM cell network available, could triangulate to within five feet, and had a battery life of about two days.

It sounded crazy to me, but I'd seen what Israeli intelligence had done in the past—and all of that had sounded crazy at the time.

I said, "How did you guys come up with this?"

"Honestly? It came out of rescue attempts. When rockets hit our country, we use dogs to find the survivors, and we didn't have enough dogs. So we developed a technology to create a device that sniffed the air just like a tracking dog. Dogs have an incredible sense of smell. About three hundred times better than ours. It was a simple thing to take that ability and put it into a beacon."

"Yeah, but really? You made a beacon that works on smell?"

She smiled and said, "We did. If we get something of his and load it into the package, the little beacons will find him just like a bloodhound. You don't need to be close. You don't need to even be in the room, and we can track him wherever there's a GSM cell signal. Which means all over Europe."

"But we still need to get something of his for the scent. Right?"

She sighed and said, "Yes, there is that."

Veep said, "The guy's leaving the room right now."

CHAPTER 50

I saw the man leaving the camera frame and said, "Okay, there's only two of us who aren't potentially compromised. That's Veep and Carrie. You guys track him to wherever he's going and keep an eye on him. Jennifer and I are going into the room. Knuckles, you and Blaine stay here watching the video. Give us an alert if someone's outside the door. Any questions?"

None came and I looked at Shoshana, opening the door and saying, "Get on it. I'm not entering until you have him under control."

Jennifer studied the camera feed, focusing on the lock. She said, "Yeah, I can get through that in about four seconds."

I smiled and said, "Well, then, let's go."

She said, "Let me get some tools."

She went to the bedroom of our opulent TOC and I turned to Knuckles, saying, "If this goes bad, you know what to do."

"Pull your ass out of the fire?"

"Yep. Exactly."

Blaine tried to say something, like he was still in charge, and I said, "Just hold it in, sir. You'll get to say something later, when this all goes to shit and you have to talk to the National Command Authority."

Knuckles laughed, but Blaine looked a little bitter. Sucks to be the man in charge, I guess.

Jennifer came back out, and we left, jogging to the elevator, me calling Veep. "You got him? Are we good?"

"We have him. He's walking down the promenade, stopping in the stores. You're clear."

We went two decks down, then to his room. Jennifer went to work on the lock and I leaned into the button cam Knuckles had placed on the opposite doorjamb, staring into it just to annoy him. He said, "Yeah, I see you. You don't have to show me your pores."

I smiled and said, "About to enter."

Jennifer broke the lock in seconds. We went in and started searching. His room was nothing like ours. A simple space, with the bed taking up most of the room, it had very few places to hide anything, which worked in our favor.

While the mission was to find something for Shoshana's little demon seeds to sniff, I wasn't going to pass up the chance to search the entire place. Jennifer went to the small bathroom and I flipped open his suitcase, seeing a plastic bag inside full of dirty socks and underwear. Perfect.

I pulled out one sock, shoved it into my pocket, then went through the suitcase itself, finding a smartphone. It was a Samsung, which meant I could extract the SIM card. I tried to power it up, but it was dead. Jennifer came out of the bathroom and I held up the phone, saying, "Got something here."

She nodded, and started searching the closets. I flipped the phone over, about to take it apart, and heard, "Target is headed back up the promenade. He's coming home."

I looked at Jennifer and she said, "Let's go. We got what we needed."

I waved the phone and said, "But this thing is the jackpot. It's Daniel's phone. We don't need Shoshana's weird-ass experiments with this."

"We don't have time to extract it. That'll take at least ten minutes. Put it back."

"I'm not doing that. This is it."

"Is it on?"

"No. It's dead."

"So you want to sit here while it charges? If you take it with us, he'll know someone's been in his room. Let's go."

I did, cursing, and we left the room just before the man returned.

We went back to the TOC—which is to say, we went back to our swanky room—and met Shoshana and Veep. Shoshana said, "Got some photos of the men."

She pulled out her phone, showing the leader we'd seen at Tivoli with two other men. She sent the pictures to our phones and said, "So what did you get?"

"Well, I had a damn smartphone, but it was dead. So all I got was a sweaty sock." I pulled it out of my pocket, and she said, "Perfect."

I said, "Are you serious? We had a cell phone. I should have planned for that. I saw him take it at Tivoli. Instead, we went into his room and found a sweaty sock."

Jennifer said, "We didn't have any time to do anything with that phone. What were you going to do, charge it in the bathroom while you hid?"

I said, "Okay, well, we have a dirty sock. What now?"

"Now, we put the Ticks to work."

She opened up a small Pelican case and pulled out a device about the size of a brick with a small wand on the end. She said, "Lay the sock on the table."

I did, and she pushed a bunch of buttons on the touch screen, then hovered the wand over the sock for a second. She finished with that, then opened up a small container in the back of the brick handle. She dumped out two very small disks, put them in a well in front of the touch screen, closed it up, then punched some additional buttons, letting the device work.

It beeped, and she opened up the well, pouring the disks into her hand. They were so small they could have been mistaken for pocket lint. She said, "Put the sock on that chair over there."

I did as she asked, she set the disks on the table, then passed me her phone, saying, "Open the Tick app."

I did so and she said, "Hit initiate." I did, and like something from Harry Potter, the disks started moving across the table. They dropped to the floor and began moving to the sock. It was the creepiest thing I've ever seen.

The two little ticks reached the chair and one kept going to the wall; the other found a leg and began climbing. It reached the sock and burrowed into the cloth, ceasing its movement.

Shoshana said, "Check the location on the app."

I did, and saw a giant bubble in the middle of the sea we were on. I said, "Well, that's perfect. We can geolocate this guy to two thousand square miles."

She frowned, then said, "It works on the GSM cell network. We have no coverage here. When it gets to Helsinki, it'll be much more finite. And that's only one."

"What's that mean?"

"They work together. They talk to each other, using their own batteries to synchronize. The more you can get on a target, the better the fidelity."

"So we literally have to get a thousand ticks on this guy to track him?"

She smiled and said, "Not a thousand, but four would be good."

I said, "Okay, well, that's about par for the course on this mission. He's got to go to breakfast tomorrow. Veep and Carrie have the mission. When he leaves, you guys track him, then let the little demons loose. I'll pull the camera off the door next to his room after he's gone.

In the meantime, we have to set up a watch. Knuckles, that's on you. Rotate every four hours."

He set about doing that, and I went to our bedroom. Shoshana followed me in, startling me. I said, "Did I miss something?"

"No. I just wanted to talk a bit."

I sat down and said, "Okay, about what?"

Jennifer came in, saw what was going on, and said, "I'm going to shower." She grabbed her things and disappeared into the Kim Kardashian bathroom, closing the door. Soon enough, we heard the water start running.

Shoshana grinned and said, "She doesn't want to see us fight."

I said, "Shoshana, fighting with you is a losing proposition. I learned that long ago. What's up?"

"You don't want this mission. You think it's a waste of time. It's why you've allowed me to use my devices. If you believed in the mission, you would not do that."

She wasn't wrong. I said, "So? We're going to use your devices, and I'm going to keep doing this stupid tracking for no reason that I can see."

She sat down next to me on the bed, scooted over until our hips touched, and said, "This mission matters."

Honestly, when her hip touched mine, I felt uncomfortable. I wanted to move away, but I knew that Shoshana was just being Shoshana. She didn't understand how real humans interacted, and her scooting over until we had an intimate touch was just her showing me she believed in what she was saying.

Trust me, it wasn't intimate. It was downright scary.

I said, "Yeah, this mission matters just like all the other ones. Except in this case, we could stop right now and it wouldn't matter."

She took my hand and said, "No, I don't think that's right. I saw

Daniel's soul when we met in the park. This is bigger than just an attempt at Putin. There's more in play here."

"What's that mean?"

"I honestly don't know. I just saw it, and I want you to see it too."

"Shoshana, I can't do what you do. I don't 'see' things. I just execute. And this mission is ridiculous."

She squeezed my hand and said, "I know that's how you feel, and I don't like it. I need you to be *Nephilim*. Not Pike."

I pulled my hand away and said, "What's that mean?"

"It means that something bad is happening with these people. I don't know if *they're* bad, but what they're doing is going to be very bad."

"Killing Putin? Who cares?"

She took my hand again and said, "I don't know if Putin matters, but something does. Give me Nephilim. You once called me the Pumpkin King and it saved my life. I'm asking the same of you. Nephilim."

She knew I hated my given name, but it held some mystic worth in her mind. She was so earnest I couldn't look away. I thought a moment about how aggravated I was with the entire mission profile, and how I'd been cavalier about executing it, and decided she might be right. I would never admit it to anyone, but she could *see* things.

I said, "Okay, Carrie, you have my attention. Just don't tell anyone."

The shower turned off and she leaned into my face, tenderly kissing my forehead. She said, "You give me Nephilim, and I'll give you Carrie. Together we might do some good."

She stood up and left the room. Jennifer came out wearing an executive suite bathrobe, completely dry. She'd never entered the shower. She said, "What was that about?"

I said, "I have no idea."

CHAPTER 51

Veep heard his phone's ringtone and rolled over, seeing the other bed empty. He looked at the clock and saw it was six in the morning. Knuckles was in the TOC, and his shift didn't start until eight. That only meant one thing.

He groaned and answered the phone, saying, "Tell me this guy doesn't get up this early."

"Yeah, he does. He's out of the room and headed down."

"Where? How am I supposed to find him?"

"At the only restaurant that's open. That biscuit place. Everything else is closed."

"Did you alert Shoshana?"

"Uhhh . . . no. That's up to you."

"Wait, what? You're going to make me wake her up?"

Knuckles laughed at his reaction and said, "Just kidding. Pike's already called her. Good luck."

He rolled out of his bed, put on some sweatpants, a hoody, and his shoes, and left the room, walking down the hall to Shoshana's room.

He hesitated at the door, not sure if Pike had actually called. He would never admit it, but Shoshana scared him. He didn't realize she scared everyone she met, thinking the fear was his alone. He would have been shocked if he learned that Shoshana scared Pike as well.

He raised his hand to knock, and the door opened, Shoshana standing there fully dressed. She smiled at him and said, "Looks like it's you and me again."

He gave a little grin, trying to show he was ready to go, and she floated her weird gaze over him, saying, "What's wrong? You're afraid of this mission?"

He felt the penetrating stare and decided to just come clean. "I'm not scared of this mission. I'm scared shitless of you. That's all."

She drew back and said, "What?"

"Come on. Let's go find them. I really wish I'd have been in that Tivoli restaurant, so I didn't have to do this."

He felt her gaze on him again, and tried to turn away. She touched his arm and he stopped. She reached up and put her hand on his cheek, saying, "You are a good man. Unlike Pike, you haven't seen the abyss. You're still pure."

He didn't know what to make of that. He said, "So you're really crazy, just like they say."

She laughed and said, "No, I just see what I see." She grew serious. "And what I see is a good man. You will do."

He wouldn't be able to explain it later, and did not understand why, but in that moment, he felt her loyalty wash over him, and it meant something. He knew he was now inside that small circle few others had attained, and for reasons he didn't understand, he felt a moment of pride.

According to Pike, Shoshana was just a crazy assassin, someone they had to tolerate to accomplish the mission. With Shoshana's words, he realized that Pike didn't believe that for a minute. Shoshana was something else, and Pike knew it. Pike trusted her explicitly, and if he did, so would Veep.

He smiled for real and said, "We need to go. He's out and about."

She returned the smile, although it held all the joy a wolf would give, taking his hand and saying, "I'm all yours."

They walked to the elevator and he said, "You've got the ticks?"

"Yep. They're prepped and ready to go."

They went down to the promenade and began strolling at the early hour, Shoshana's hand still in his, although he no longer found it uncomfortable. Few guests were about at the early hour, with only one restaurant open—a coffee shop that also sold bagels.

They entered the line two couples behind their target and waited. He bought a coffee and a bagel and took a seat in a corner booth, right next to a window, the rising sun beginning to illuminate the archipelago. They paid and took a seat across from him, on the other side of the small room. Eventually one of the other Ukrainians met him, sitting across the table.

Shoshana said, "They're settled in. This is it." Veep agreed and let her get to work. She pulled out a Ziploc bag that appeared to have coffee grounds inside, opened it up, and dumped them by her feet. She pretended to check her phone, clicking on an app, and the little ticks began moving like they were searching for food. And they literally looked like ticks to Veep.

They woke up and began sniffing, all of them marching in the same direction, but blending in to the black tile of the floor. Veep was fascinated.

Shoshana said, "Don't stare at them. It only draws attention."

He returned to her and said, "What happens if he finds them? He'll know."

"Once they burrow in, they end up looking like a piece of lint or bramble from nature. Usually, they're just flicked off as an annoyance. Nobody thinks they are what they are."

"You guys are really ingenious with that stuff."

She smiled and said, "Necessity is the mother of all inventions. First one has made it."

He glanced over and saw the small army of ticks starting to swarm onto his boots, crawling higher.

"What if he feels them?"

"Do you ever feel a tick, or only find them after they've burrowed in?"

He chuckled and said, "Only after."

She said, "Anyway, they won't be crawling up his leg. They'll stop at his boots." She slid across her phone, the Tick app open, saying, "Inside the archipelago we have cell coverage." Veep saw the boat they were on, like a Find My iPhone application. He zoomed in, and got down to the very restaurant they were in.

He said, "Amazing. How long?"

"Two days at most. Depends on how many get on him. They work together to conserve battery power."

"Hopefully long enough to get off this ship and see where they go."

Perun saw Javelin take a seat across from him and said, "Where's Dishka?"

"Sleeping in. He spent the night in the casino. Any chance he gets, he wants to forget about Ukraine."

Perun laughed and said, "Good for him. I wish I had the same energy. Make sure he's at lunch because we need to talk about the next steps."

"And what are they?"

"Before he died, Daniel paid for a block of reservations in the Runo hotel in Porvoo. It's a small town about forty minutes away from Helsinki."

"You think using that hotel is good? They're killing us all over the place. They killed Daniel less than forty-eight hours ago, for Christ's sake."

"It's his contact in Finland. A guy named Kirill. He's apparently firewalled and clean."

"You believe it? He might be clean, but he could also be a dead man walking. Who else knows about this? The men hunting Daniel? The ones who hit us in Tivoli? The ones who killed our own men?"

"I don't think so. If they did, they wouldn't have attacked in the restaurant. They would have killed Daniel at a more secure location, then simply followed us to this meeting, killing all of us there. It makes no sense to shoot Daniel when they did, in such a public manner. They know something, but not everything. I think we're okay."

"*Thinking* isn't good enough. We're probably being tracked right now."

"If we were, we'd be dead. Nobody's tracking us here. That would make no sense. Why do all the killing at a crowded restaurant if they knew we were going to be on a ferry to Finland? They'd just wait for us on the boat."

Javelin shook his head and said, "I don't know. None of this is making sense. Maybe they're sloppy."

"Maybe they are, and that's our edge. We go to Porvoo on high alert. We meet the contact to continue the mission. If it's bad, we back off. If it's good, we continue. Understand?"

"Okay, I guess. Worst case, I got two days to enjoy this boat."

CHAPTER 52

Victor Petrov saw Oleg enter the hotel lobby, his remaining two men trailing behind him. All three looked exhausted, like they hadn't slept in days—and Victor thought that was probably correct. He raised his hand and they came over to him.

Victor said, "Any trouble leaving Copenhagen?"

"No. We paid cash for the tickets, and they were one-way, so there's probably a tick on someone's database, but nobody gave us any trouble."

Oleg glanced to the man sitting to Victor's left, seeing thick shoulders, scarred knuckles, and an overlarge brow hooding his eyes, making him look more simian than human. Oleg said, "Who's this?"

"You may call him Wraith. I've brought him to help."

The man looked up at Oleg, and Oleg felt a sliver of fear from his gaze alone. Victor said, "You mentioned you had pictures of the Wolves?"

Glad for the change of conversation, Oleg pulled out his phone and began flipping through photos, saying, "This guy is the leader. He was the one meeting Daniel."

"And the ferry?"

"It docks at six P.M. tomorrow night. It's an overnight trip. Plenty of time to set up a surveillance box and pick them up."

"What's your status? Are you burned for surveillance?"

"I honestly don't know. The gunfight was chaotic, so maybe not, but we were definitely shooting." He pointed at his two remaining men, saying, "Misha and Alek here are the best bet. They were at a table in the back. They didn't get involved."

"Okay. I brought a targeting package with me. Weapons, radios, and surveillance gear. Go get some sleep. We'll conduct a reconnaissance first thing in the morning, then stage before the ferry docks."

Shoshana's little demon ticks worked like a charm, and so we spent the rest of the trip enjoying the amenities of the boat, to include going to what was probably the cheesiest dance revue I have ever seen. It was only topped by the venue bar making the worst bourbon old-fashioned on record, adding club soda for some reason.

But in a weird sort of way, it was honestly relaxing. Jennifer and I enjoyed the night, then woke up to breakfast with the team. Of course, we couldn't just barge into the breakfast buffet because the Wolves might already be there eating, so I'd called Veep first, finding out that the ticks were still working and the location of the restaurant the Ukrainians had chosen. We went to another one.

From there, it was basically hanging out in our room to avoid compromise. While it wouldn't be strange to see the same people locked into a boat, it *would* be a problem if one of the Wolves saw us on the street later and made the connection.

We spent the time setting up rental cars upon our arrival, having Blaine send SITREPS, and conducting research on Helsinki for follow-on operations.

It was only 1730, but the sun was already beginning to drop below the deck of the ferry. Perun glanced out the portal in his room and saw a fortress slipping past as their ship glided into the port, an eighteenth-century island defensive structure that dominated the Helsinki harbor.

He heard a knock at his door and opened it, seeing Javelin and Dishka with their bags. Dishka said, "We're about ten minutes out."

Perun said, "Come on in."

He closed the door behind them and said, "Take a look at that fort out the window. It reminds me of something from home."

They went to the portal, Javelin saying, "What is it?"

"I have no idea."

Dishka turned from the window and said, "Are we good for the meeting? Nothing happened on the boat, so I think we've broken surveillance."

"We may have done that, but I'm not counting on it. Now is not the time to get lax. As for the meeting, I have the hotel, but don't have the actual meet site."

"They aren't in Daniel's phone?"

"He might have hidden the final instructions inside it somewhere, but I'll be damned if I'm plugging that thing in and turning it on. I'm convinced that's how Daniel was tracked to our meeting at Tivoli. Anyway, if it is inside, it's probably encrypted. He told me how to get the information, and that's all."

Javelin said, "How's that?"

Perun took a breath, then said, "In the hotel he reserved for us there is a step-down area off the bar with a bunch of couches and chairs, along with a wall full of books. He gave me a book to pull out and the page number to look at. Our instructions for the meeting will be there."

Javelin said, "You mean we check in and then go find an Easter egg in the bar lounge?"

"Yeah, that's it. I think Daniel was being extremely cautious after his man was captured. If we were caught on the way to the hotel, we wouldn't be able to tell them anything but that, giving his other team time to clear out of the area."

Javelin said, "Nothing like using us as the bait."

"I don't think it's that. I actually appreciate the caution. Let's just hope the car is there like Daniel said, or we're doing some serious walking."

They felt the boat slide to a stop and Perun said, "Time to see if this mission is real."

CHAPTER 53

Perun led the men out of the room and down the hall to the elevator, seeing a crowd had gathered. The door opened, revealing a tiny space, allowing only three people to enter with their luggage.

Dishka said, "This is going to take forever."

Perun smiled and said, "We have time."

Eventually, they were the only ones left. The elevator appeared, and they went down to the promenade deck, seeing a huge gathering of passengers all waiting for the gangway to open.

Perun said, "Looks like it didn't matter either way. You guys want to wait in the café, or just stand at the back?"

Javelin said, "Let's just get in line. I'm ready to get off this boat."

They joined the other passengers just as everyone began to surge forward, the gangway open in front of them. They followed the crowd, exiting the ship and winding through a long passageway that turned left, then right. They finally reached an escalator, passing by various armed men and women in uniform, all looking bored. It raised the hair on Perun's neck, wondering if they would have to go through a customs inspection at the bottom.

They went down it, and reached the large entrance hall, sprinkled with cafés, ticket counters, and rows of chairs, the area full of passengers waiting to board a ferry. No customs in sight. They were free to leave.

Perun paused, and Dishka said, "Man, I saw those police and was about to go to the bathroom and toss my weapons in the trash can."

Javelin said, "No doubt. I thought for sure we were going to get corralled at some customs control point."

Perun chuckled and said, "That thought crossed my mind as well."

He went to a map on the wall, traced around until he found the parking lot he'd been told held their car, and tapped it, saying, "Supposed to be here."

He turned his head, saw the south exit, and said, "Which means it should be out that door."

He led the way, exiting the terminal and walking past the throngs of people fighting for a taxi or searching for their Uber. He went down a sidewalk until he saw a parking lot across the street. He looked both ways, then walked across, hoping against hope the car was there. He saw a sign stating that parking was only for four hours maximum. After that it would be towed. It gave him pause.

If the car *was* here, the men leaving it hadn't done so yesterday. Meaning they were tracking his progress. They knew he'd made it.

He wasn't sure if that gave him confidence, or concern.

He crossed through the lines of cars and kept heading south until he'd reached the corner of the parking lot, doing a slow circle. Four vehicles over, he saw a Volvo station wagon and went to it. He looked in the window, seeing nothing of interest.

Dishka said, "Is this it?"

"I don't know. Check the right rear tire well for a magnetic box."

Dishka did, then stood up, saying, "Nothing here."

Shit.

On the far side, Javelin stood up, saying, "Got it." In his hand was a small box with a magnet. He opened it, pulled out a key fob, then hit the unlock button. The car chirped, and the doors unlocked.

Dishka said, "Yeah! This secret spy stuff is working!"

Perun said, "Load up. Dishka, you drive. Javelin, put the Porvoo Runo hotel into the navigation system."

In five minutes they were on the road, Perun in the passenger seat, Javelin in the back, and Dishka behind the wheel. They wound through the steel and glass of Helsinki until they hit the E18 expressway, and then Dishka poured on the gas, driving through the countryside, the road being eaten up under headlights in the growing darkness. Forty-eight minutes later, the GPS beeped, and Dishka saw the exit for Porvoo. He took it, crossed the Porvoonjoki river, and slowed down, entering the old village.

He drove right by the hotel without realizing it, Javelin from the back saying, "That's it, that's it."

Dishka circled the block, came back, and parked in a lot directly across from the hotel, saying, "I'm getting homesick."

Javelin said, "What do you mean?"

"Don't you think this looks like our towns in Ukraine?"

Javelin glanced around in the dim glow of the streetlights and tended to agree. The area had no building higher than four stories, with stone façades covered in stucco and ornate window ornamentation. They had once been grand, but now looked like the anachronism they had become. Still regal, but dated, like a debutante staring in the mirror after she turned seventy, seeing the glory she used to be.

Dishka turned to Perun and said, "How do you want to play this?"

Perun said, "I'll go in with Javelin. You stay out here for security. Keep the car running. If we have to leave, it'll probably be on the run. Give me your Estonian passport."

Dishka handed it to him and Javelin said, "Weapons?"

"Yeah, we're taking in weapons."

Five minutes later, they jogged across the street, both feeling the adrenaline rise. They entered the hotel, finding it completely unlike the outside square where they'd parked.

Fully remodeled, it was a modern interior that would rival an up-scale hotel in any large city, with burnished steel, marble floors, and modern sculptures sprinkled about. Perun glanced around and saw the check-in desk, then further on the bar area, with a concierge desk manned by an attractive blonde.

Javelin took a position near the front door, his hand inside his jacket. Perun approached the desk, gave him the name on his fake Estonian passport, and told him he should have three rooms fully paid.

The man said, "Five, actually, for four days. Do you need all five rooms still?"

Four days? That was a surprise to Perun. He said, "Yes, but only three for tonight. Two of my friends couldn't make the trip just yet, but might come later. Only three are here now."

"That's fine. We'll keep the other rooms open. Passports?"

Perun slid across his and Dishka's fake passports, turned to Javelin, and nodded. He came over and gave the man his passport. The clerk made copies, then said, "One or two keys per room?"

"One is fine."

He passed the cards through a key reader, wrote down the number on a small envelope, and slid them across. Perun suffered through the speech from the clerk about the breakfast times and layout of the hotel, then took the keys. He turned to Javelin and said, "Get the luggage and bring in Dishka."

Javelin left and Perun walked to the bar, nodding at the bartender. He said, "Drink?"

Perun said, "Not yet. Just checked in and looking around. Waiting on my friend."

The man nodded and Perun turned, looking past the concierge, into the step-down lounge. In the back of the room, he saw the book-shelf. He smiled at the concierge, then went to the bookshelf, searching for his title—a book on the history of the town.

It was hard to act like he was just killing time, waiting on his friends, when he fervently wanted to search the shelf like a bloodhound. He scanned the spines, and found his book on the fourth shelf. He glanced back, saw nobody in the lounge, and pulled it out, turning to page 174. It was a chapter on something called the Porvoo Cathedral. Written at the top of the page was, *10:00 am tomorrow. Walk. We'll make contact.*

He closed the book and put it back on the shelf, turned around, and saw Dishka and Javelin, both dragging the luggage. He took his bag from Dishka, went back to the front desk, and said, "Do you have a tourist map?"

The clerk, eager to please, said, "Of course." He pulled one from underneath his desk and handed it to him, saying, "Anything in partic-ular you want to see?"

"Nope. Not yet. Just want to explore. Thanks."

He turned from the desk, nodded to Dishka and Javelin, and they went to the elevator. He pressed the button, and while they waited, Dishka said, "Did you get the information?"

The elevator landed, they entered, and he said, "Yes. So far, so good. Anything happen outside?"

"Nothing suspicious. A few cars came and went, long after you went inside. A man and woman left the hotel, some others entered, but none seemed connected to us."

"Good, good. Maybe this will work out after all."

He wouldn't have felt such confidence if he'd seen the man who moved through the lobby after the elevator doors closed, pulling the same book off the shelf and leaving the hotel.

CHAPTER 54

I saw Helsinki getting closer, felt the ship start to slow down, and said, "Get the team up here."

Jennifer made the call while I looked out the window, seeing some gigantic old fort with corner bastions guarding the harbor. I could make out people walking around and a few old cannons facing out. Rhetorically, I said, "What's that?"

She came to the window and said, "It's the Suomenlinna Sea Fortress. Built by the Swedes, when this was their terrain. The Russians took it over in a war and occupied it, finishing the fortification, and then when the Finns declared independence after the Russian Revolution, they inherited it."

I turned to her and said, "Is there nothing you don't know when we go somewhere?"

She said, "Jesus, Pike, all you had to do was buy a guidebook to Finland in the gift shop. I did that last night when we left the dock."

I laughed and she said, "The cool part is that people actually live there. I mean they have families who have lived there for generations. I don't know how they do things like grocery shopping."

I said, "It sounds like a real romantic place to stay."

She punched my shoulder, and someone knocked on our door. She opened it and the team filed in. I said, "First things first, Blaine, did you get anything?"

"Yeah, I got the same ol' same ol'. Sorry, Pike."

I slapped my hands against my thighs in frustration, saying, "What the hell? So we're supposed to just continue following these guys while they plan a hit on Putin? Can someone in this world give me an actual mission?"

The rest of the team glowered at the news, and Blaine saw it. He held up his hands, thinking we were blaming him, like he was failing in his leadership duties, but I knew that wasn't the case. I'd done enough operations with him to know the squeeze he was under. He wanted clarity as much as we did. He said, "Yeah, I get it. I'm with you on this, but I'm not the president."

I said, "Don't worry about it. Nobody's mad at you. If I'd have sent the SITREP, I'd be the one reporting the same information."

He looked relieved and I said, "So, the worst mission ever continues. Knuckles, you got the rental cars ready?"

"Yeah. There's supposed to be a guy who meets us outside the terminal in the loading and unloading lot. Three vehicles. One SUV, two sedans."

"Okay, you get downstairs and get out first. Might as well go right now. You know how these ferries work. There'll be a crowd fighting to leave and I want you out."

He nodded and left the room. I turned to the rest of the team and said, "Okay, Knuckles will be at the front of the pack trying to leave. Jennifer and I will be in the middle. Veep, Shoshana, you stay in the back. You've got the Ukrainians. If they're with us, I'll alert you and we'll take them until you can catch up. Blaine, you're cleanup. You go to the café and just wait, last out. If we don't see the Ukrainians in the middle or the back, you pick them up."

He smiled and I said, "Yeah, you finally get to play."

"About time."

"Don't screw it up."

His smile faded. I said, "Once we have them, Veep and Shoshana will track them to either a vehicle or a structure."

Veep said, "We've got the ticks. We don't need to track them."

I said, "Yeah, I get that. I'm not worried about losing them, but I am concerned we'll miss some sort of meeting. The ticks won't give us that."

He nodded, a little embarrassed at the question, and I said, "Okay, if we have to go mobile, vehicle assignments are Jennifer and me, Veep and Shoshana, and Blaine and Knuckles."

I looked at each in turn and said, "Any questions?"

I got none and said, "Let's get to it then. We're almost docked."

They left the room and I snatched my bag off the bed with a little more force than necessary. Jennifer said, "What's up?"

I said, "That fucking Blaine. I can't believe he just took the answer to that SITREP. We deserve a damn mission statement here. We're just floating along with no direction, and I'm getting a little sick of it."

"You think that's Blaine's fault? Or is it just you thinking you can do better, like always?"

I took a deep breath, knowing she was right, but still said, "I ought to call Wolffe myself."

"So he could tell you the same thing he told Blaine? Remember, Blaine's the acting deputy commander. You think Wolffe would change his mind if it were you on the line?"

I walked to the door, opening it and saying, "No, but I could give him a piece of my mind about this mission."

We went down the hall to the elevator, waited for it to arrive, then descended to the promenade deck, seeing scores of passengers all dragging bags toward the gangway. We joined them and entered the pack, people piling up behind us. We took a minute to scan the crowd in front of us. I said, "No contact from me. You see anything?"

Jennifer shook her head and I got on the net, calling the team. "Koko and I are in position. No sighting of Wolves. Give me a status."

Knuckles said, "I made it to the front. Just standing by."

Blaine came on, saying, "In position in the café. No sighting."

Veep was last, saying, "Carrie and I are hanging out on the port side, waiting on the cattle to finish stacking up. No sighting."

I said, "Roger," and turned to Jennifer, saying off the net, "I hope the Ukrainians aren't pulling some James Bond shit here, rappelling down the side or something."

She laughed and said, "Give it some time."

We felt the boat slide to a stop, then heard clanking and pounding as the crew secured it to the terminal and maneuvered the gangway. After another five minutes of waiting, Shoshana came on the net. "Pike, this is Carrie. We have the targets."

Whew. "Roger all. Execute the plan. Beast, you still come out last."

I got an acknowledgment, and we waited a little more, the crowd patiently standing around their luggage. Apparently, they'd done this a time or two. Finally, the purser opened the portal and waved the lead elements on. We shuffled forward slowly, getting funneled into the gangway of the terminal, going from about twenty abreast to four or five.

Knuckles would be way ahead of us, and we would be way ahead of the Wolves, which was good because it would give me a chance to set up at the bottom and watch them pass.

We had just entered the passageway of the terminal proper when Knuckles called, saying, "Pike, Pike, we have a problem. I just reached the entrance hall and see one of the pipe-hitters from Copenhagen."

What?

I said, "Are you sure? You have positive identification?"

"Yes. PID. He was in the cemetery with us the day that guy was tortured to death, and he's now in a café with some big thug-looking guy staring at the escalator, checking out everyone who comes down."

Well, that certainly changes things. We kept walking, Jennifer looking at me, while my brain began steaming at a thousand miles an hour sorting through options.

I got on the net and said, "Change of mission, change of mission. Knuckles, keep eyes on the pipe-hitters. Beast, get in the crowd right now. Push your way through and link up with Knuckles for backup. Veep, you're getting the vehicles now. Shoshona, you're a singleton on the Wolves. Acknowledge."

They did, with Knuckles going last and saying, "What's the mission?"

"Same as before, but we're going to have to track them both."

"Pike, you know they aren't here for an autograph from the Ukrainians. They're here to wipe out the Wolves, just like happened in Tivoli."

I knew what he was asking. If they attacked, were we just going to let it play out on its own, or were we going to intervene? He wanted me to pick a side, and honestly, I was a little sick of the wishy-washy orders I'd been receiving ever since I'd been given this shit sandwich. I made my decision: we were on Team Ukraine.

"If they show any lethal action against the Wolves, take them out."

There was dead air on the radio for a few seconds. Then Blaine came on, saying, "Pike, we don't have Omega authority."

"I understand that, but we *do* have the implicit authority to protect the lives of innocents in extremis. I'm not going kinetic unless they do. If they choose to start shooting inside this crowded terminal, then we shoot back."

He said, "Pike, there are policemen all over the place. That's for them to handle."

I keyed my radio and said, "If it happens, it's my call. You can tell

Wolffe that when it's over, but you'd better be doing the call with smoke coming out of your barrel. You understand?"

I heard a weak "Roger all," and we reached the escalator. Jennifer and I rode it down, and I saw Knuckles in the crowd at the back of a café. We reached the bottom and kept walking, going midway down the hall and stopping in the line of a ticket counter, using the crowd for cover.

I got on the net and said, "Beast, Beast, what's your status?"

"Moving through the crowd. I'm ahead of Veep and Shoshana now."

"Okay, we need to get a count of how many there are. That'll be me and Jennifer and you and Knuckles. Carrie, you just stay on the Wolves. Veep, no change."

I saw Blaine at the top of the escalator, then Knuckles came on the net, taking over his side of the operation. "Beast, I see you. Walk straight down the hallway until you see a bar on the right. Go to the bar, I'll meet you there."

He did so, and then I saw the Wolves at the top of the escalator. Knuckles said, "Pipe-hitter just got a hard-on. He's on the phone talking to someone."

Jennifer pinched my side and leaned in, saying, "The guy we tracked in the cemetery—the one with the phone—is coming this way. He's got two others with him."

I glanced behind me and saw them. I immediately got on the net, saying, "We have three more inbound."

CHAPTER 55

We moved back into the crowd and the three passed by us, beelining to a café. Knuckles called, saying, "Thug team is moving."

My three met Knuckles' guys and I finally saw the thug—and he was one mean-looking SOB. Over six feet tall with a face like a Neanderthal, complete with a thick brow and deep-set eyes, he had tree trunks for arms.

I said, "Photos. Get pictures of all of them. Veep, status?"

"Moving to the cars now."

"Carrie, status?"

"They're looking at a map on the wall. I'm still good—wait, wait. They're on the move. South exit. Headed to south exit."

The group of pipe-hitters broke up, with three moving directly to the nearest west exit and the thug and his partner jogging toward the south exit. I said, "Knuckles, keep on your guys. Koko and I will take the other three."

"Roger."

I let our targets get through the door and then followed. We exited right into a swarm of people all shouting for taxis or searching for Ubers. I saw our targets threading through them to a far parking lot across the street, and said, "You have a beacon readily available?"

Jennifer said, "Yeah, I can get to one. Why?"

"They're headed to a parking lot. I'll bet they're about to stage some vehicles. I'd like to get one on a car."

She dropped her bag in the crowd and unzipped it, going to a pouch in the side, saying, "Copperhead or Cottonmouth?"

Both transmitted over the cell network using GPS for geolocation, but each had a different battery life and transmit interval. The Copperhead could last a couple of weeks, but transmitted intermittently, as set by the user, but the minimum was ten minutes. The Cottonmouth only lasted days, but transmitted continuously, allowing us to track it in real time on our phones.

I said, "Cottonmouth. I want real time on this."

She pulled out a disk the size of two quarters glued together, with a magnet on the bottom. She peered at the top and said, "Twelve-dash-two."

We had to know which beacon was being initiated in order to find it on our phone. I said, "Twelve-two. Got it. Let's go before they get out of sight."

She zipped up her bag and we threaded through the crowd, checked the traffic on the road, and jogged across to the parking lot, slowing down once we were in it. There were a few other people moving about, but not many, and our targets were making a beeline to their vehicles, walking at a rapid pace.

We matched it, moving parallel three car rows over. I watched them stop and enter two different cars, the leader and an older gentleman in one vehicle, and a singleton in another. I said, "They're in. Let's get past them and cut over like we're headed to the main road leading out of the terminal."

We went a little farther and then took a left, moving between the cars. Jennifer said, "How am I going to get it on without compromise? If they look in any of their mirrors they might see me."

"Not sure just yet."

I surveyed ahead of us and saw a panel van in the parking slot on the passenger side of the singleton vehicle. I swerved that way, saying, "When we get on the other side of that van, stop, drop, crawl under it, and slap that beacon underneath the passenger door."

She snapped her head to me, saying, "Are you kidding me?"

"No. Come on. You're a hell of a lot smaller than I am."

We reached that row and walked until we were lost from view on the other side of the panel van. I said, "Go."

She flattened on the ground and wormed her way underneath the van, her feet disappearing from view. I took a knee, looking back and forth. The problem with missions like this is you get tunnel focused on the opposition and forget about the third man out there—the random stranger who could see you and cause compromise.

Thirty seconds later she came rolling out from underneath the van, standing up and muttering about how I'd just ruined her pants.

We stood, grabbed our bags, and returned the way we came, keeping the van in between us and the targets. I said, "Good job there, Koko."

She continued muttering and I knew I was going to be in trouble later. I started to say something else when Shoshana came on the net: "Pike, this is Carrie, Wolves are on the move. Volvo station wagon. Leaving the terminal."

"Roger. Knuckles?"

"Thug and his buddy are watching them leave, talking on a phone."

I saw our beaconed vehicle back out of his parking slot and then race out of the lot. *He'll be the first one to get eyes on.*

Knuckles said, "Okay, they've turned around and are now jogging north."

They're coming here to link up.

I said, "Roger all. They've got a vehicle on the way as initial follow and another one to pick up thug and his friend. Veep, what's your status?"

"Ready to roll."

"All elements, all elements, link up at our vehicles. No change to vehicle assignments."

We were the first to reach Veep at yet another parking area, this one at the north of the terminal used for pickup and drop-off only. Veep gave me my keys and said, "This is going to be a bit of a challenge."

I said, "Yeah, we're going to be a conga line tracking the pipe-hitters as they track the Wolves. Check the ticks while we're waiting on the team. Jennifer, load up the Cottonmouth."

He gave me a quizzical look and started manipulating the app Shoshana had given him.

The rest of the team showed up and I said, "Okay, quick SITREP. Carrie first."

"Not a whole lot to talk about. They went straight to a Volvo, checked the rear wheel wells, found a key, loaded up, and drove off. No idea where."

"Veep?"

"Ticks are working. I'm tracking the car. The circle of probable error is fairly large—probably because they're moving—but I can see them."

"Knuckles and Blaine, what did you see?"

"Thug and his buddy simply followed those guys, watched them get in, then made a call. That was about it. They never showed any hostile intent."

"Okay, well, we now know there are five of them, most likely three vehicles but definitely two. Jennifer and I tracked the other three to their vehicle staging point and watched them get in two cars, but I'll bet there's a third for the thug and his buddy. We managed to get a Cottonmouth on one, and it's out in the wild right now."

Everyone looked surprised at that, maybe even a little impressed. I said, "What? Did you think we were getting ice cream while all this was happening? Jennifer, is it up?"

"Yeah, I got it. On the E18 headed north."

"Okay, pass around those pictures of the pipe-hitters. Make sure everyone's got them. We're going to start a loose follow here, with a focus on the Russians. We only have a single beacon between three cars, and it's on the vehicle itself, not a human, so I want to track them until we find a bed-down. I'm not really worried about the Ukrainians because that beacon is on a body, and they only have one vehicle."

Knuckles said, "What's the mission here?"

I exhaled and said, "Blaine's going to figure that out while we drive." I turned to him and said, "Sir, call Wolffe and tell him what we have. Let him know the pipe-hitters are back and ask for guidance. Don't take waffling for an answer."

He nodded, and I said, "Load up. They're getting farther and farther away."

CHAPTER 56

Misha waited in his car at the back of the parking lot, watching two of the Ukrainians go inside a hotel called Runo. He knew one man had remained in their Volvo, and because of it, he stayed in his vehicle as well—although he'd rather be anywhere than inside a car with the man called Wraith.

The drive to Porvoo from Helsinki had been made mostly in silence, with Wraith sitting in the passenger seat and grunting short quips to any questions Misha had asked. They'd spent an hour on the road and Misha still had no idea what he did for a living or where he'd come from. All he'd managed to glean was that Wraith had worked with their commander, Victor Petrov, sometime in the past. Misha wasn't too keen on spending the night staring at a hotel entrance with this man.

Misha said, "If that last guy goes inside, I'm going to move in for a closer look. Can you take the wheel?"

Wraith glanced at him, looked out the window as if he were bored, then said, "Yes, I can do that, but don't do something stupid."

"I won't. I just want to see if we can glean anything other than the name of a hotel."

Wraith leaned forward so close Misha could smell his fetid breath, saying, "I meant, don't try to kill them without me. That's what I'm here for. Putin sent me because you fucks keep screwing up."

Misha simply stared at him, now understanding why he was here. He was one of Putin's personal killers, which meant he was very, very

skilled. Misha stammered for an answer and Wraith returned to looking out the window. Like he was commenting on the weather, Wraith
said, "The other one's returning."

In the glow of a streetlight, Misha saw two men unload three sets of
luggage from the back and then begin rolling them to the hotel.

Trying to appear confident after Wraith's last statement, he said,
"Looks like they're staying at the Runo, which is good for us because we
can stage here in the parking lot indefinitely."

Wraith nodded, not bothering to reply, and Misha wondered if
leaving him alone was a bad idea. There was no telling what he'd do.
He thought about calling Oleg on his personal cell, but dismissed it.
One, Oleg would defer to that shit Victor, and two, if Wraith thought
he was doing something against him, Misha was sure he wouldn't shy
away from delivering punishment for the transgression.

Misha opened the door and said, "I'll just take a peek from the
outside window."

Wraith nodded, and he jogged through the lot and across the street,
glad to be free from the car.

He walked down the sidewalk until he could see into the hotel from
the window behind the bar. He stayed far enough from the glass to
remain in the dark, peering inside. He made out the older Ukrainian
moving deeper into the lounge area, toward a bookshelf. To his surprise, the man removed a book, flipped through it to a page, and then
seemed to be studying something.

He put the book back and Misha memorized the shelf it was on,
then counted the books to its left. He sidled over to the window behind
the reception desk and watched the man receive a tourist map, now
convinced he had found something important. He stared through the
window until the three of them disappeared into an elevator, then scur-

ried to the front door. He took a breath and opened it, nodding at the man behind the desk, acting as if he belonged in the hotel.

He tried to be nonchalant, moving through the lobby as if he were a guest, but felt self-conscious. Luckily, there were four people at the bar keeping the attention of the bartender, and the concierge desk was now empty. He dropped down into the lounge area, moved past a couple deeply entranced with each other on a couch, and went to the shelf.

He counted the books, found the one the Ukrainian was studying, and pulled it off the shelf. He took a seat, as if he were killing time, and slid his backpack in front of him.

He glanced up, saw nobody paying him any attention, and shoved the book into the bag, then stood up, walking past the bar again. The bartender gave him a quizzical look because of his short stay, but that was all he did. The man behind reception didn't even glance up from his computer.

He exited the hotel and jogged back to the car, opening the door and saying, "I have something."

Wraith said, "What? Where did you go?"

"I got a book. The man was looking at this book. I have to get this to our command and check it out. Can you stay here on surveillance? Or should we call someone to replace us?"

Aggravated, Wraith said, "What book?"

Misha said, "A book! He was looking at a book before he went to his room. I took it."

"You idiots are always looking for something that isn't there. We should just go in and kill them. Be done with it."

"We can't do that, because they're meeting the traitors. The ones from the GRU. That's who Putin wants more than anyone else. Look, just watch the hotel until you're relieved. Can you do that?"

Wraith snapped his head to him and Misha felt fear for being so bold in his orders. He stammered, "Just watch the hotel. I'll be right back."

Wraith nodded and said, "It's getting cold out here, and I can't start the car without alerting someone that I'm here. Do not take long."

Misha nodded, then turned and began jogging to their hotel, wondering why on earth Victor had brought that psychopath. Staying at a place called the Hotel Sparre, it was only two blocks north of the Runo hotel. Close enough to move on foot.

He entered the lobby, ignoring the people on the bar stools, moving straight to the elevators. He rode up to the second floor, ran down to a room, and banged on a door.

Oleg answered, and he went inside, seeing Alek and the commander, Victor. He wanted to talk without Victor in the room, but knew that wasn't going to happen. His heavy hand now hung over everything they did.

Oleg said, "What's the urgency here? What did you find?"

He dropped his bag and said, "The leader was looking at a book in the hotel. I took it." He pulled it out like it was the holy grail, and Victor said, "That's it? Where's Wraith?"

Chagrined, Misha said, "The leader of the Wolves was going through this book like it held a secret. There's something in this."

Victor said, "I repeat, where's Wraith?"

"He's still in the car, watching the hotel."

Victor grew agitated, saying, "You left him in the car watching the hotel?"

Misha began flipping through the book, saying, "Yes. He's on the hotel."

Victor looked at Oleg and said, "He can't be alone. Get someone down there."

Oleg said, "What? Why can't he be alone?"

All the men looked at him at that point, waiting. Victor backed off, saying, "He has a little bit of a problem when working on his own. He needs guidance. If he's alone, he might take action based on what he thinks is right."

"Meaning he's a fucking loose cannon? Who is this guy? Why did you bring him?"

"He's the best at what he does, but what he does is hit a target that someone tells him to hit. You can't let him make that decision on his own."

The words caused Oleg to stand, saying, "We could have done this mission alone. Why have you brought a psychopath here? Who is he? One of Putin's assassins?"

Victor faced him and said, "You men were not accomplishing the mission. You have failed at every turn. Don't question me. I have Putin's ear, and this is what he wanted."

Oleg backed down and turned to Alek, saying, "Go relieve Wraith."

Alek left the room and Oleg said, "We really need to talk about what we're doing here. The original mission was to eliminate the Wolves and their GRU traitors. Is that still it?"

"Yes. That's it, and Wraith can get that done. You men need to find them. *He* will do the mission. That's what he does. That's why I brought him."

"So we're not good enough, after all the men I've lost."

"It's not that. Look at it this way—he's like a cruise missile. Once it's fired, it's done. He's expendable."

Oleg looked at him with disgust and said, "Is that what you think of us?"

Realizing he'd said something he shouldn't have, Victor said, "No, no, not at all. Just find the traitors. That's all you have to do."

Misha looked up and said, "I found them."

Everyone looked at him, Oleg saying, "Found what?"

He held up the book, the spine splayed open, and said, "This is what he was looking for."

"What is it?"

"He's meeting the traitors at ten A.M. tomorrow at the Porvoo Cathedral. He's been told to walk to the location."

Oleg worked a computer and said, "That's about four minutes away. It's at the end of the old town."

Victor thought a minute, then said, "He's been told to walk because they'll have countersurveillance watching the route."

Oleg said, "So we drive. We know the end of the route. We don't need to follow them."

Victor nodded, and they heard a knock on the door. Misha opened it, and Wraith entered the room, looking around with his brooding eyes.

He said, "What are we doing here? I'm sick of sitting around watching."

Victor said, "We're going to end this tomorrow."

CHAPTER 57

Perun took a seat in the breakfast area at 9 A.M., the room sprinkled with hotel guests taking advantage of the free meal. He ordered a coffee and waited on his men, knowing they hadn't gone out partying the night before. Instead, before going to sleep, all three had planned out a route to the cathedral.

Dishka and Javelin came through the doorway, spotted him, and moved to his table. They took a seat, ordered coffee, and Dishka said, "Any changes?"

"Nope. I think the route we picked is the best one. Thread a little left, thread a little right, then straight in. If Daniel's men are watching like I think they will be, they'll pick up anyone following us."

"Do you think someone is? Do they know something we don't?"

"I think they're just being prudent, that's all. After Daniel's partner was lost, and then Daniel himself, I appreciate the concern."

Javelin said, "How will they know it's us? They talk about 'making contact,' but how will they do that?"

"We gave them our passport photos, remember? I'm pretty sure they'll know what we look like when we show up. Or when we begin walking, for that matter. The key thing here is not to act like we're looking for them. Just walk naturally and let them do the work."

They both nodded, then let silence settle on the table, nobody else speaking, drinking their coffee and thinking about what they were about to do. Dishka finally asked, "What do you think they're going to tell us? Why the four-day stay here?"

Perun smiled and said, "You guys keep asking me questions like I'm keeping something from you. I have no idea. Maybe there's some training we have to do before we go. Maybe it's all a ruse. I'm not sure."

Dishka nodded, looked at his watch, and said, "We should probably be going."

Perun saw it was closing in on 0940 and said, "Yeah, getting there early shouldn't be an issue."

They left the restaurant, reaching the front door of the hotel like it was a portal to another dimension and they were dreading stepping outside. Perun said, "Ready?"

Both of his men nodded, and they exited onto the street, taking an immediate right around the corner.

I watched the two cars turn into a parking lot next to a church and pulled over to the side of the road, not following them in.

I said, "What do you think? Going to confess their sins?"

Jennifer chuckled and reached behind her, getting her small knapsack, saying, "I doubt it."

Jennifer and I were currently the eye on the Russians, and because of it, I wanted someone else to penetrate and see what they were up to. I got on the net, gave the team the location, and sent in Blaine and Knuckles, the only free agents I had at this point.

Jennifer said, "What do you think's going on here?"

"No idea, but I doubt they're on a tour. I guess we'll know more if Veep and Shoshana see movement and it's headed this way."

We'd followed the entourage from Helsinki last night to this little village called Porvoo, staying laser focused on locating the bed-down site of the Russian pipe-hitters. I knew the ticks would give us the

Ukrainians' location, but was afraid of losing the Russians with only a single beacon on a single car.

We'd watched them drag their luggage into a place called Hotel Sparre, and I figured that was where they were going to hole up. The ticks told me that the Ukrainians had taken the only other big hotel in the town—called the Runo—which left us scrambling. We'd found a small place down the street in the old town called the Hotel Pariisin Ville. They only had ten rooms in the entire hotel, but since tourist season had ended, nine of them were open and they were ecstatic that we'd shown up, renting half of the remaining ones.

We'd convened in my room, one of the few that had an actual Finnish sauna in it, and had decided what to do next. Knuckles had shown up first, and then did the usual ignoring-the-mission thing, saying, "Hey, my room doesn't have a sauna."

I'd laughed and said, "I didn't ask for it, but you can get your big ass in there when we're done."

The rest of the team had shown up, with Shoshana entering last. She looked at me with her little disconcerting gaze, raised one eyebrow, and I knew she wanted to talk again. Something I didn't want to do. Alone, anyway.

I'd said, "Okay, Blaine, tell us what we're here for. We have a group of Russians clearly wanting to kill some Ukrainians, and a group of Ukrainians that clearly want to kill Putin. What are we doing about it? What did the Taskforce say?"

He'd given me a look that told me he'd failed in trying to get a resolution. I didn't blame him, and honestly expected it deep inside. The politicians in DC never wanted to make a decision that would cause them repercussions, but I was a little disappointed in George Wolffe.

He knew better.

Blaine had been told that the mission was still Alpha, but because we'd found the Russians, the mission had expanded to them, which was the last thing I wanted to hear. How these guys could sit on the sidelines like this was beyond me. There was a threat, and they were only telling me to follow it, like we were a documentary news crew instead of the Taskforce. And follow the Russians as well? Did they think I had four teams over here? How easy did they think this was? The only good thing about the conversation was that Wolffe had said the president was finally convening the entire Oversight Council, bringing this into the light of day, so to speak. It was no longer just a mission between Wolffe, the CIA, and the president.

That was something, I suppose, but it still made me cranky, to say the least.

Once we'd gotten our hotel situated, I'd told everyone to get some sleep, knowing tomorrow was going to be a long day. I'd given Veep and Shoshana the mission of keeping track of the Ukrainians, letting them sort out how they'd do that, and then had started a surveillance rotation in the parking lot next to the Russians' hotel, starting at 6 A.M.

The call had come in at 9 A.M. with Blaine on the shift, saying he had movement. The Russians exited the underground garage of the hotel with two cars, which, because it was just the fate of my life, did not include the one I'd placed the beacon on. He'd followed them for a block while we'd scrambled, and now Jennifer and I were the surveillance team focused on a group of Russian killers wandering around a church.

Knuckles came on the net, saying, "These guys are boxing in the footprint of the chapel. They're here to see someone enter."

I said, "Are they showing hostile intent?"

"Not right now. They aren't setting up for an ambush or anything, but they're most definitely printing."

Meaning he could see weapons underneath their clothing. I said, "Okay, keep them in sight, let's wait until it develops."

"If it does? Is yesterday's ROE still in effect?"

I looked at Jennifer, and she shook her head, telling me no, but I was really aggravated about the lack of direction from the National Command Authority. If they didn't want to provide it, I would do so myself.

Looking into her eyes, I said, "Yes, it does. If they try to harm the Ukrainians, you defeat them. I'll deal with the fallout later."

I clicked off and Jennifer said, "Pike, that is *not* a good call. We can't get into a shoot-out here without Omega authority. This is not what we do."

I leaned back into my seat and said, "You're right. It's not what we do. This entire mission isn't what we do, but those guys from Ukraine are fighting for the life of their entire country, and I'll be damned if I stand by while some Russian assholes try to kill them. If they don't do anything, then I won't. It's up to them, not me."

She said, "It *is* up to you, and you know that."

I said, "So if you were in charge, you'd just let them die? Is that it? It's easy to second-guess from the back seat."

She looked like I'd slapped her, then said, "You're *not* in charge of this. Blaine is. You're *in* the back seat. You don't need to make that call. Let him do it, if he wants to."

I turned to her and said, "You believe that? Is that what you think?"

She saw my stare and backed off, like I knew she would. She loved the underdog and hated bullies, whether that was a kid in the playground or a state system on the world stage.

She sighed and said, "No, I don't believe that. These assholes deserve to die if only for what they did in Copenhagen to that man. I just don't want you in the crosshairs of the decision. Let Blaine do it."

I said, "You know that Blaine's not in charge here, right?"

"He *is* in charge. That's his job."

"He's in the position of leader, but he's not in charge. That's me. I'll let him do what he thinks is best until it crosses what I think is best. And right now, he'll tell me to stand down."

She leaned forward, getting face-to-face. She said, "Okay, Pike. I'm with you, you know that. But you really need to talk to the team before you do something crazy. Get their thoughts. You aren't the end-all be-all here. We're hanging our asses out too."

And then she kissed me.

As usual, she was absolutely correct. I'd spent so much time pissed at the lack of direction, I wasn't getting my own compass bearing from the men who mattered, like I usually did.

I tasted the Carmex from her lips and said, "All right, you have a point. We'll talk to the team later today if those fucks at the Oversight Council still haven't made a plan."

She smiled, starting to say something, and our radio came alive, Veep saying, "The ticks are on the move. They're on foot, leaving the hotel."

I said, "Where? North or south?"

I heard him huffing, telling me he was running to catch up to them. He said, "South. South. They're headed to you."

CHAPTER 58

Within seconds of leaving the Runo hotel, Perun and his men exited the relatively modern square and entered the cobblestones of the old town of Porvoo. The four-story stone buildings built in the twentieth century gave way to two-story wooden ones built in the seventeenth, the narrow cobblestone alleys lined with art galleries and antique shops.

They conducted their planned route, weaving in and out of the narrow alleys, at one minute walking next to the river, at another walking deeper in the old town, until they reached the gates of the cathedral.

Sitting on a spit of high ground, the chapel itself was unassuming. It wasn't like Notre Dame or anything like that, but it held gravitas because of its past. Built in the thirteenth century, it had seen the entire history of the country of Finland, and had been destroyed by fire multiple times, but had always risen from the ashes.

Still a functioning church, it was now also a tourist site, which gave Perun and his men a reason to move past the wall that surrounded it.

They left the cobblestones and entered a grassy area surrounding the chapel, pretending to study the various plaques and historical markers plastered all over the place, but really just giving whoever was going to meet them time to approach.

After wandering around a bit, Dishka said, "Are you sure they're going to meet us here? Maybe we misread the instructions."

Perun turned to say something, and saw a man approaching. Young, mid-twenties, with a shock of blond hair, chiseled features, and an athletic build, Perun knew he wasn't the contact. He said, "Shush."

The man stopped next to the same marker, pretending to read it, and said, "Perun?"

"Yes."

"My name is Luka. Follow me please."

Surprised, believing the man was a tourist due to his youth, he said, "You're the contact? I was expecting someone older."

Luka smiled, showing perfect teeth, reminding Perun of a model in a men's magazine. He said, "I get that a lot. It'll help us when we need to blend in here. Follow me."

"What about my men?"

"All of you follow."

He walked toward the cathedral, saying, "We're glad you made it here. It's been a little trying, as I'm sure you've learned."

Perun said, "I don't want to hear about how hard it's been for you. I've seen the beast inside Ukraine."

Luka paused at the door to the chapel and said, "I'm sure you have, but it's probably going to get worse."

He led them inside, and Perun saw an ornate pulpit overshadowed by an enormous iron chandelier, the interior decorated in stamped metal surrounded by white stucco. It looked like the entire structure had been renovated time and time again, but the people doing the renovations refused to remove the old decorations. It held a history of centuries, something Perun understood and appreciated.

He led his men inside, past a few older patrons praying at an altar. Luka took them to the back, and he saw a man in a pew staring at them. Luka stopped at the entrance to the row and waved them forward. They shuffled into the pew, with Perun taking a seat next to the new man.

He said, "My name is Kirill, and I'm going to help you on the final leg. Are you still willing?"

Perun glanced around him, wondering if the church was chosen as a bit of a psychological operation because of its heritage, designed to remind him of Ukraine. He said, "I'm willing, and so is my team, but you didn't need to bring us here for that. Where are the rest of your men?"

"The rest?"

"The ones you stationed to watch us."

He laughed and said, "I don't have the manpower to do that. I had you walk because you're going to drive out of here. If anyone was following you—which very well might be the case—they're on foot now. A simple trick."

Perun nodded, a little dismayed at the subterfuge. He had been sure there were more in play to engender his success, but apparently that wasn't the case. He said, "So, what now?"

"You're going to take a boat from here back to Helsinki. We have two Iranian Shahed 136 drones that you will use to eliminate the target."

Perun only heard the first part. He said, "A boat from here? Back to Helsinki? What are you people thinking?"

Kirill turned to him and said, "What we're thinking is that you're a target. Someone captured our men in Copenhagen, and that same someone knew about your meeting in Tivoli. Daniel was my friend. My mentor. He's dead now because he thought your meeting was secure. I brought you here to make sure the next one was. If anyone is on us now, they'll be lost when you get on a boat. I'm breaking whatever the chain was between you and him."

Perun said, "There was no chain. If anyone's on to us, it's from your end, not mine."

Kirill nodded and said, "I agree. That's why you're going to go back to Helsinki on a boat."

Perun said, "We don't know how to use the drones. That's not what we do."

"I know. Your next contact will give you instructions on how to load the coordinates and how to launch them. The main thing is to get them out of here and into Estonia."

"That's where we're going?"

"Yes. It's why we gave you Estonian passports. You're going to penetrate that country and launch the Shaheds into Russia."

"Where? What's the target? He's always on the move."

Kirill glanced at the door and stiffened. Perun followed his gaze and saw two uniformed police enter, a man and a woman. He hissed, "I don't know the final coordinates yet. The man in Estonia will have that when you arrive. Putin's schedule changes day-to-day, but he'll have it."

Perun came back, speaking low, "I need more than that. Something to show me you're serious."

"When you see the drones, you'll know we're serious."

Kirill saw the police giving them more attention than was necessary and said, "Go. Follow Luka's instructions. He'll get you the drones and your next instructions, which will be a meeting in Estonia with the grid coordinates for the strike."

Perun started to say something else, but Kirill stood up, moving away. Perun stood up as well, moving in the opposite direction, his men following him. They reached Luka outside of the chapel and Perun said, "So, you have a boat for us?"

CHAPTER 59

I saw the Ukrainians enter through the gate and said, "Wolves are in the den. What's happening?"

Shoshana came on and said, "There's a meeting going on inside the chapel. We have the guys outside."

I thought about it for a pregnant second, trying to see how we could use the fact that they were all here, at a chapel. I came back on the net, saying, "Beast, Knuckles, are you clean?"

Meaning, could they pass off surveillance duties to Shoshana and Veep. Knuckles came back and said, "Yeah, we're clean. Carrie's got the same view we do."

"Get back to the Sparre hotel. Penetrate their room and find out who these assholes are."

He said, "Pike, we don't even know the room they're in. We don't have that sort of time."

I said, "Bullshit. We have some of their names from Copenhagen. I'm sure they're still using passports from Belarus just like they did in Copenhagen. Have Creed penetrate the hotel system and find their rooms, then go pick the damn lock and get in."

I heard nothing for a moment, then, "It's a modern hotel. I can't pick a key card, Pike."

And now I knew he just didn't want the mission, because there was no reason to actually need a card.

I said, "You have a slider?"

I heard a sigh, then, "Yeah, I've got a slider."

Every hotel room on earth had one requirement: if the guest wanted out of the room, door locked or not, it happened. From the inside, if you turned the door handle, the door opened no matter how many locks had been engaged. It was designed that way for hotel fires or other emergencies, and it worked for us. No hotel wanted to be blamed for a guest not being able to exit in an emergency, and because of it, we could get in. If you could manipulate the door handle from the inside of the room, it would open. The "slider" was a tool to do just that. You slid it underneath the door, raised it, hooked the handle of the door, and then opened it, regardless of whether it was locked or not.

"Then get to it. What's the issue?"

He said, "The issue is that we have no mission, and me going in there is asking for compromise. I'd do it in a heartbeat if they had a bomb targeting AMCITS, but this is just fishing."

I said, "I know, I know. I hear you. Just do it, because I think you're going to find the bomb targeting American citizens in that room."

He sighed and said, "Okay. On the way."

Jennifer gave me the side-eye and said, "Why are you doing that?"

"Alpha. I'm doing Alpha. Exploring what we're dealing with here. These Russians scare me. They knew about the meeting in Tivoli, and somehow knew the Ukrainians were on a ferry to Finland, and now knew they were meeting at a chapel in Porvoo, Finland. They were here before the Ukrainians showed up, which means they weren't conducting surveillance. They *knew*. How did they know that? There's something we're missing, and I want to find it."

She settled into her seat and said, "It could come back to bite us."

And I'd finally had enough of the bullshit. I turned to her and snarled, "What the fuck is the problem with this team? For the first time ever, we're living under the mantra of 'minimums wouldn't be minimums if they weren't good enough.' I don't do minimums. I was given a mission, and I'm executing it. You and Knuckles can take the next plane out of here if you don't want to do what's right."

She said, "Whoa, hold on. I never said that."

"Yes, you did. You've been saying it since we got here. And so has Knuckles. There's a threat, and I'm going to eliminate it. Get on board or get on another train."

For the first time since we'd met, I was willing to cut her away, and I saw it scared her.

She said, "Nobody's saying this isn't a good mission, Pike. We're just saying the mission might not be worth the pain. Maybe someone else should do it. Even you've said that."

I had, that was true. But it didn't mean I wouldn't follow through. I said, "Look, these Russians are up to no good. Yeah, it might not be the mission I want, but I was given it, and I'm going to see it through."

Shoshana came on the net, saying, "Pike, Pike, the Russians are starting to move. They're talking together outside the chapel. I think they're formulating a plan of attack."

I clicked on and said, "What do you mean?"

"They're all together now, and I think when they break up, they're going to go in the chapel and start killing. It's just a discussion right now, but it's about to happen."

Shit.

I opened my car door, checked my pistol and spare magazine, then said, "We're on the way."

Jennifer had done the same, looking at me with a little trepidation. I said, "Time to get wet. Sorry, I didn't plan this."

We started speed-walking to the gate of the chapel. "We're on the way. What's the status?" I asked over the net.

Shoshana said, "They're still talking. I don't think there's a consensus on a hit right here, but three of them most definitely want it."

"How do you know?"

"Because I can see them. I can read them."

I wasn't going to question that. I said, "Okay, it's going to be a gunfight. Get ready."

I turned to give Jennifer some instruction for the fight and saw her about thirty feet away, talking to a couple of uniformed police. A man and a woman. She was waving her arms in the air and looking like she was really incensed. The police took off running into the chapel grounds.

I said, "What the hell was that?"

"I told them a teenager just snatched my purse and ran inside the chapel."

Unable to comprehend that she'd just engaged the uniformed authorities in an area we were about to turn into a free-fire zone, I simply said, "What?"

"Pike, they won't attack if the police are on-site. It'll be too risky."

Dumbfounded, I just looked at her. She said, "We should get in now."

We did, just in time to see the Ukrainians and one of their contacts leave. Shoshana said, "Looks like they called it off because of some police showing up. Four are leaving, one is staying."

I honestly couldn't believe it. I looked at Jennifer and she just shrugged. I got on the net and said, "Okay, we know they want to kill them. Let's start tracking."

Fifty feet away, Victor was cursing the appearance of the police. He'd called off the assault—against Wraith's protests—and now had to make another decision. He was sure that this was the nuclear cell of the efforts against Putin, but couldn't eliminate them here due to the police presence. And now they'd split up, with the Wolves following a guy to a car while the GRU contact remained inside the chapel.

He made his decision, saying, "Wraith, Misha, you remain here. When that man leaves, you find a place and kill him. We'll take care of the Ukrainians, wherever they're going."

Wraith said, "We have them here right now. Let's just kill them all and leave. We can be out of this country before they can react."

Victor said, "No, we're not going to do that. You might have executed such a thing in the past, but I'm not going to be responsible for throwing raw egg into Putin's face. We'll kill them at our choosing, and this isn't it."

Wraith grimaced and said, "You men are such cowards."

Oleg heard the back-and-forth and hissed, "We are *not* cowards. We're prudent, you Neanderthal. They will die, but not here. Live with it."

CHAPTER 60

Veep and Shoshana came to my location just as the Ukrainians were moving to the parking lot, loosely followed by the Russian pipe-hitters. I said, "Okay, Brett and Knuckles are on their room, that leaves us. These roads are going to be tight, so stay far enough back to prevent us from spiking. Jennifer and I will start the follow, then pass off to you guys."

Veep nodded and Shoshana said, "What do we do if they try to interdict them?"

Lord, I was beginning to hate that question. I said, "If they try to interdict while they're still in the vehicles, then close up the follow. That'll cause them to back off. They won't do anything if there are witnesses."

"And if they stop? If they get out of the vehicles?"

"I'll assess at that time. I don't know."

Shoshana looked at Jennifer, then back at me. I knew it was a wishy-washy answer, and realized that Shoshana wouldn't let it stand. She said, "We might not have the time to call you for advice."

I closed my eyes, not wanting the decision to be placed on me. It wasn't my call, damn it. Yeah, I'd made the call to interdict earlier, but Jennifer was right—we didn't have authority to do that then, and I was just lucky nothing had happened. I was beginning to hate the Oversight Council for putting me in this position.

I looked at Jennifer, then back at Shoshana and Veep. The truth of the matter was the decision was fairly easy—it was only the repercussions that would be hard. I was still on Team Ukraine for this.

I said, "If the Russians show hostile intent against the Ukrainians, then we interdict. Lethal force."

Jennifer shook her head, but didn't say anything. I said, "But *only* if they show hostile intent. We're just observers until then, which means we need to be very careful on the follow. Do not force their hand. Understand?"

Veep nodded and Shoshana said, "Understood. Thank you for the clarity."

I saw her eyes and said, "Shoshana, I'm not kidding. Don't get in a gunfight because of something you 'see.'"

The Ukrainians left the parking lot, driving right by us, followed by a car full of Russian killers. She said, "That's only three. What about the two who are still here?"

I opened my door and fired up the engine, now regretting sending Blaine and Knuckles to the hotel. I said, "The Ukrainians take priority. With Blaine and Knuckles out of play, it's just us, and I need everyone. Stay on the net."

They began jogging back to their vehicle and Jennifer and I pulled away, driving down the cobblestone road as one more vehicle in the train of people chasing the Ukrainians. I didn't try to keep up with the lead vehicle the Wolves were in, satisfied with just keeping the Russians in my sight.

It turned out to be a short trip. They left the old town and began driving down the river road, entering the newer section of the city. We kept up with them, but not too close, as I was sure the Russians were fixated on the Ukrainians. I didn't want them to get fixated on us.

I saw the Ukrainian vehicle pull into a small marina parking lot, the river lined with powerboats. The Russians immediately pulled over to the side of the road, not daring to follow them inside the parking lot. I went to the curb myself, content to watch from a distance.

The pipe-hitters left their vehicle, jogging across the road to the marina. Now interested, I said, "Veep, can you pass us by and enter the marina? See what's going on?"

He said, "Roger," and within seconds he went by me and entered the lot. He swung around to the far side as if he belonged and Shoshana came on the net, saying, "The Wolves are getting on a boat."

"A boat? Seriously?"

"Yes. The Russians are clearly pissed. I guess they don't have a boat. The contacts for the Wolves aren't making the same mistake they did with Daniel. It's a little funny."

I looked at the Russians' car in front of me and said, "I'm going to give them a little more help."

Jennifer said, "What does that mean?"

"It means they'll be headed back to the hotel after that boat leaves. I need to give Knuckles and Blaine a little more time."

I slid out of my car not waiting for an answer, moving down the sidewalk at a normal pace. On the net, I said, "What's the status?"

"They're still watching. The Wolves are on the boat, starting to remove the lines to the dock. They're clearly leaving here, and the Russians are not happy. They might have been able to ascertain the meet site, but clearly didn't predict this."

I reached the pipe-hitters' vehicle, pulled out a folding knife, leaned down, and punched a hole in the passenger-side front tire, the air hissing out as if the tire were angry. I turned around, going back to my vehicle. I clicked on the net, saying, "Their car is now disabled. Can't wait to see this freak out."

Oleg led the way back to their vehicle, telling Victor, "We don't have any idea where they're going. What do we do now?"

"We get back to the chapel. There's still a man there who does know. We need to capture him."

"You told Wraith to kill him."

"Shit. That's right. Come on, we need to get there before he does something stupid."

Oleg slid into the driver's seat, Alek getting in the back. Victor opened his door, then said, "What the hell?"

Oleg said, "What? What's the problem?"

"We've got a flat. The tire is flat."

Oleg circled the car and Victor pulled out his phone, saying, "We have to stop Wraith. If he kills that Valkyrie man we'll never find the Wolves."

CHAPTER 61

Wraith tracked the final Russian leaving the chapel, watching his back disappear down a narrow lane. He pulled out a knife, looked at Misha, and said, "We should have taken them all right here. Go get the car. Meet me on the street. I'll leave the body there."

Wraith didn't wait for Misha to even respond, leaving the grass courtyard and beginning to follow the Russian down the cobblestone street. The man took a left, entering an even more cloistered alley not even wide enough for a car, the avenue hemmed in by wooden houses and trash bins. Wraith knew this was it. Kill him there and he could leave the body where it lay.

He hustled to catch up, then felt his phone vibrate in his pocket. He thought about ignoring it, but the pull of duty was too much. He put the cell to his ear and heard, "Wraith, this is Victor. Change of mission. Do not kill that man."

"What? Why? I have him in my sights right now. He's a dead man."

"Do not kill him. We need to capture him. The Wolves got on a boat. They're headed down the river to the archipelago, and we don't know where they're going. Your man is the final thread to that. If we kill him, we'll lose the Wolves."

Wraith stopped walking, wanting to throw the phone against the stones at his feet. He said, "I told you we should have killed them here, at the chapel. Now they're in the wind again and we don't know where."

Victor said, "Yes, okay, that was something we should have executed, but what's done is done. We need that final Russian."

"I have to go."

He hung up without another word, then called Misha, saying, "Come get me, now." He gave directions and waited, studying a map on his phone to see where the smaller alley went. He saw it spilled out into another road by the river, this one big enough for a car.

He heard a vehicle and turned to see Misha behind the wheel. He got in the passenger seat and gave instructions without providing any explanation as to what they were doing.

Misha wound down the cobblestones from the high ground, reaching the river and the wider road. He said, "Which way?"

Wraith looked left and right, but didn't see his target. He said, "I don't know. Head back to the hotel, out of the old town."

Misha did, saying, "What are we doing?"

"They lost the Ukrainians. The Wolves got on a boat and left, and we don't know where. This GRU man is the last link. We're no longer killing him. Well, not yet anyway."

Misha drove up the road doing the minimum speed, the tires bumping along the cobblestones, his left hemmed in by wooden structures built right up next to the avenue, the right with a pedestrian walkway paralleling the river. Misha said, "Maybe we should try the other way."

Wraith said, "No, there he is. Up ahead, on the river side. Speed up and get over right next to him. Pass him. I'll do the rest."

Misha accelerated to twenty miles an hour, the only car on the road, and swerved toward the pedestrian walkway. The car came abreast of the GRU agent, the man turning at the sound of the approaching vehicle, his eyes going wide at the closeness of the steel. Wraith swung open his door, slamming it into the agent's body and knocking him to the ground.

Misha hammered the brakes and Wraith leapt out, punching the man in the head with his fist, then circling his body with his arms and dragging him to the car.

He opened the back door, shoved in the agent's body, and piled in behind him, shouting, "Go, go, go!"

CHAPTER 62

George Wolffe finished his background briefing on the current operation involving the Wolves and saw nothing but stern faces and disbelief. Because of it, he was glad for two things: one, that President Hannister was in the room, and two, that only the principals of the Oversight Council were present, not the full thirteen members. He was pretty sure he was going to get roasted badly enough by the smaller circle of trust.

Comprised of the secretary of defense, the secretary of state, the national security advisor, the director of the CIA, and the president, Wolffe could almost smell the anger emanating from the members, like smoke from a burning ember. Kerry Bostwick and President Hannister were the only two who seemed to be listening intently to what he was saying. The rest appeared flustered that they were just now being informed of the ongoing operation. He didn't blame them, which was why he was glad the president was able to attend the meeting.

He said, "Currently, the element known as the Wolves have boarded a boat with the help of what we believe are disaffected Russian GRU agents and are heading south in the archipelago. We don't know their intentions with the boat, but we did manage to beacon the leader of the Ukrainians, so we can still track their movement. This leaves us with three courses of action."

He flipped a slide and said, "One, we simply redeploy, letting this play out however it will play out. Two, we actively help the Wolves on their mission. Or three, we actively thwart the Wolves on their mission."

He clicked off the screen and said, "With that, I'll open the floor up to your thoughts."

The room erupted into shouted questions, all revolving around the fact that the mission had been sanctioned in the absence of an Oversight Council vote, with the secretary of defense trying to talk over the secretary of state while the national security advisor tried to get them to calm down.

President Hannister raised his hand and the room quieted. He said, "This was my call. It was extremely sensitive, and I initiated it in the absence of your input because of that. That is all water under the bridge now, and I'm not going to rehash my choices, but it has grown into something larger. The question before us now is what do we want to do."

The secretary of defense, Mark Oglethorpe, said, "Sir, you've basically thrown out the Oversight Council charter here. I think that needs to be discussed. The only reason I agreed to become a member of the council was precisely that it still had control over Taskforce activities. Now it appears George here just does what he wants."

Wolffe started to retort when Kerry Bostwick beat him to the punch, saying, "George Wolffe did not want to do this. He didn't execute on his own, and specifically asked for council oversight. It was my recommendation to the president, and the president concurred, that we keep this tight, but that was just when it involved the Swedish diplomat. President Hannister is correct—it's grown much bigger with an assassination cell targeting the president of Russia. Can we stick to discussing that? If not, we'll be here all night."

The secretary of state, Amanda Croft, said, "You just briefed that a Taskforce member was shot not once, but two separate times on two different operations and we were completely in the dark."

Wolffe knew that statement was damning, mainly because it was true. He said, "The wounds were superficial. He's home now and doing fine."

Amanda looked at the president and said, "Maybe we should bring in the entire council for this."

President Hannister said, "We don't have the time for that. Whatever play they have is in motion. We've conducted operations with just the principals before—and for Sweden, all I did was make that circle a little smaller. What are your thoughts?"

She started to protest again, but gave up, saying, "Sir, we can't help the Ukrainians. The risk is too great. If they succeed, make no mistake the West is going to be implicated no matter what, and if there's even a whiff of our support here it will be calamitous."

The SECDEF said, "I don't know about that. If they manage to get rid of Putin it will solve our Ukraine problem."

"How? We have no idea who would take over, but we *do* know that whoever takes over will need unified support from the Russian elites and common people. They'll get that by painting this as a Western plot to galvanize support. It'll be nonstop propaganda about NATO on a killing spree, and might devolve into NATO actually getting in a war with Russia."

Kerry said, "Maybe, and maybe not. They have a team of Russians— we think from the National Guard—out hunting them right now. We know the Ukrainians are getting help from someone in the Russian intelligence world, and that at least one was captured and tortured to death. Russia knows it's an internal matter. It might just end up being a purge of 'traitors' that happens as they consolidate control."

Amanda turned to the president and said, "Who is 'they'? We don't even know. Do you want the head of Wagner in charge of Russia? Because that might happen."

"So you're saying you want to actively oppose them?"

She paused, then said, "I'm not sure I want them interacting at all, but helping them certainly isn't what I would say. This goes against your own executive order 12333 forbidding assassinations. If the Taskforce does anything at all to facilitate the operation, the Ukrainians unwittingly become our proxy force—and by extension, we're aiding and abetting an assassination attempt."

"I'm not too worried about breaking an executive order. The Taskforce and Oversight Council itself break just about every law on the books. Surely you're not suggesting we inform Putin of what we know, are you?"

"No, not that. If what Kerry's saying is true, they probably know more than we do at this stage, so telling him is just giving him ammunition against us."

The SECDEF asked, "Do we know the method of attack? Or location?"

"No, we don't. Not yet anyway. All we know is that they're planning one. They tried to get a satellite-controlled anti-armor weapon from Israel, but Israel balked. That tells me that they planned to penetrate Russia, but don't plan on being there when the attack occurs."

"So we can't really help at all anyway, can we?"

"Well, we *are* tracking them, and there *are* some Russians out to kill them."

The SECDEF turned to the president and said, "Sir, honestly, I'd need more information before I give my advice. I'd like to at least know the method of attack and the location. Amanda here could reach out to her counterparts in Finland to stop them, I suppose, but we don't even know if that boat's coming back to Finland—and I'm of a mind to just let it continue at this point."

"So bring the team home? COA one?"

"No, sir. I'd suggest a fourth COA. Let them continue to track without interference."

President Hannister thought a moment, then said, "I'm inclined to agree. George?"

"Sir, we aren't an intelligence gathering organization. We're a direct-action unit. They aren't designed or tempered for that. If it's intelligence collection, let me pass off my information to the CIA and let them pick up on it."

President Hannister said, "Bullshit. Every mission we've ever done was preceded by the Taskforce building up a targeting package first, in essence collecting intelligence. This is no different, other than the fact that we haven't made a decision on what to do with the information yet."

Wolffe said, "Sir—"

President Hannister cut him off, saying, "I'm not shifting horses in the middle of a race. You try to pass off this information and something will get lost. Let's put it to a vote."

It was unanimous—course of action four, the one that George Wolffe despised and specifically had not offered. He tried one last time, saying, "Sir, there is a threat of compromise just by collecting. Secretary Croft brought up that very problem just moments ago. Brett Thorpe was shot the second time just 'collecting.' If we don't have an endstate for why we're doing it, I think it's a risk."

"I think we understand that risk. The council has voted. Tell Pike to continue the mission, but it's still Alpha only."

"What if the Russians attack the Ukrainians?"

"Then they attack. It's an internecine fight, not our issue."

"That's not what I'm talking about. They have shown no compunction about killing innocents. They started a gunfight in Tivoli, the most popular amusement park in Europe, *inside* a crowded restaurant."

"Okay, what's your point? I can't be the world's police here."

"My point is Pike won't sit on the sidelines. He just won't. He's not going to let innocent people get killed if he could prevent it. If they attack, and it's threatening others, he's going to react. He's not going to just do 'intelligence collection' and take pictures while it happens."

President Hannister bristled and said, "Then tell him we'll replace him with someone who can follow orders."

Wolffe nodded and said, "Okay. Like the CIA? Do you want me to engage them on this now?"

President Hannister laughed and said, "All right, touché on the debate trap you set. No, he stays on it. Tell him to follow orders. Just watch and report."

Wolffe nodded and said, "So no guidance if the worst happens?"

The SECDEF said, "He has his guidance. He reports only. I swear, what sort of team are you running if he can't listen to an order?"

Wolffe said, "A team that doesn't think you people have the monopoly on intelligence. You're putting Pike in an impossible situation here. You tell him to observe and report only, but you're putting him in a situation where he might be forced to fight. I just watched all of you debating what we should do, and *you* couldn't even make a decision, so you're leaving it up to him."

Amanda Croft said, "No, we're not. We're explicitly telling him *not* to do anything. It's the easiest order for anyone. Just sit on the sidelines. How hard is that?"

Wolffe looked around the room, then said, "You're forgetting that the enemy gets a vote. They may not let him just sit, and if an attack occurs, he's going to pick a side."

CHAPTER 63

Perun rode inside the boat for about forty-five minutes before finally moving to the cockpit, Luka behind the wheel. He said, "Where are we going? I know you're not thinking of taking this craft across the Baltic Sea, and we're headed east, so you're not skimming the coast to St. Petersburg."

While it had twin outboards, at only thirty-five feet it didn't appear to be robust enough to risk the Baltic Sea, but Perun wasn't sure that Luka believed that.

Luka said, "We're going back to Helsinki. The entire purpose of meeting in Porvoo was to break any connection from someone following you. After Daniel's compromise, I was taking no chances."

"Where?"

"Did you see that fort on the way in? The one on the island outside of the harbor?"

"Yes."

"Your method of attack is hidden in an old bunker on that island. We have a vehicle on standby. We'll get there, load it up, and drive back into Helsinki."

"It's an island. There are no roads to it."

Luka smiled and said, "There is a road. It's an underground tunnel built for emergency and maintenance vehicles to access the island. It's for official use only, but it's there."

"How are we official?"

"You'll see. Don't worry."

"How long is the trip? It only took forty minutes to drive up."

"It's about three and a half hours by boat. I wanted to get there at dusk, which is why we planned the meeting when we did."

Perun nodded and said, "We still don't know how to work the Shahed drones, and we still don't know where the attack point is or where we'll launch from."

"Believe it or not, the drones are easy to assemble. Basically, you just need to put on the wings. Launching them is fairly easy as well, but your contact in Estonia will show you all of that, to include the launch point and attack grid. Have you ever been there?"

"No, but it can't be that hard to figure out. Where is the contact?"

Luka continued to drive the boat for a moment, then said, "You'll get that information after we recover the drones. If that fails for any reason, then you won't need it."

"We have three hours to study and ask you questions. I understand you don't want to put your contact in danger, but I don't want to do this on the fly, putting my men in danger."

Perun considered for a moment, then said, "Hand me that backpack."

In the passenger seat, Misha driving, Wraith looked around, seeing the highway threading through forests with little sign of civilization. He called Victor in the car behind him and said, "We're dumping the body at the next side road."

Victor said, "Okay, but make sure it's not a paved one leading to a house or other structure."

Misha saw a power line crossing the highway ahead and said, "I'll bet that's got a maintenance road underneath it."

Wraith said, "Take it."

Misha cut off the highway, driving down what was basically two tire tracks on a rough-cut utility road made for four-wheel-drive vehicles, the track causing the sedan's suspension to protest. Misha drove for about a hundred yards, until the highway was lost from view, then stopped.

Wraith said, "Give me a hand," and went to the trunk. He opened it, a body wrapped in plastic, its wrists and ankles zip-tied together, a single trickle of blood leaking out around the head.

Wraith grabbed him underneath the armpits and Misha took the feet, hoisting him up out of the trunk and dragging him thirty feet into the underbrush. Wraith said, "Good enough. Drop him."

Misha did, and Wraith halfheartedly threw some limbs over the body, saying, "He died too soon. We should have taken our time."

"We didn't *have* the time, and he was just as stubborn as the last man we questioned in Copenhagen. Those GRU guys are tough. We know where the boat is going. That's enough to end this."

They went back to the car, Wraith saying, "I don't like loose ends. He said that the man in the boat was the only help he had here."

"Why don't you believe that?"

"Because he had the Wolves do a countersurveillance route to the chapel. You only do that if you have someone watching your back trail. And someone punctured your tire. It wasn't the man we caught, and it wasn't the man on the boat. If he lied to us about that, he could be lying about where the boat is going. All we have left is the country of Estonia, because that idiot Alek applied too much pressure."

Misha didn't want to relive the interrogation. Coming out of the woods he was relieved to see that Victor's vehicle had followed them in. He went to the passenger-side door and Victor rolled down the window.

Misha said, "Are we going straight to the fort?"

"Yes. Well, at least straight to the ferry terminal. We can't drive to the fort."

"And then what?"

"We find them and kill them."

Wraith said, "Kill them on an island? How will we get off? Take the ferry back, waiting on it to arrive while the cops are searching for us?"

"We take their boat off the island once we're done."

Wraith said, "You make it sound like this will be straightforward and easy. Aren't you worried they have some help here, besides these two men?"

"No, I'm not. If they did, they would have taken action against us. All they did was run."

"Someone punctured your tire."

Growing aggravated at Wraith's pushback, liking him more when he acted as a stoic assassin, Victor said, "Look, I can't explain that. It might have just been hooligans. One thing I know is if they had more GRU men here, they wouldn't have punctured our tire. They would have killed us."

Wraith said, "Maybe it's not GRU. Maybe there's some other predator out hunting here. If so, you'd better pray they don't care about the Ukrainians."

CHAPTER 64

Veep called me over to the computer, saying, "Ticks are still in motion, but they're not giving us the same fidelity as before. I think they're losing power. Shoshana said they work together to generate a signal and the fewer you have, the worse they are."

"Where are they?"

"Still in the Gulf of Finland, still headed east. But that's not why I called you. The Cottonmouth you put on that car is booming." He pointed at the screen and said, "It stopped here and has been there for at least twenty minutes."

"What is it? A hotel?"

"No. It looks like a wharf." He pulled up satellite imagery, showing the location of the beacon in a parking lot on the edge of a quay, multiple concrete pilings jutting out into the water.

I said, "Find out what that is. If they got on a boat it means they might know more than we do about the Ukrainians' intentions."

Veep fiddled around on the system for a minute, then said, "It's a ferry terminal for sightseeing around the harbor. It goes to that fort we passed on the way in."

"Why would they be going to that fort?"

Jennifer said, "Maybe because that's where the Ukrainians are headed."

Knuckles said, "What on earth for?"

I answered, "No idea, but the better question is 'How do these

Russians always know where the Ukrainians are going to be?' They knew to be in Tivoli, they knew to meet the ferry, and they were at the church before the Wolves showed up. How do they keep doing that?"

"Maybe they've got a beacon on them like we do."

"Beacons aren't predictive. They couldn't have known to be at that church based on a beacon showing them in the Runo hotel."

I turned to the rest of the team and said, "Doesn't matter right now. Everyone get ready to move. It looks like we're heading back to Helsinki. Knuckles, call the pilots in Copenhagen and tell them to get their ass to Helsinki. We're probably going to need the Rock Star bird soon, because I doubt these guys are going to hang around long. Jennifer, find out where we can rent a boat. I'm not taking a ferry if they go to that island fortress. Veep, figure out where we can dock a boat away from the public landing on the island. Any questions?"

None came and I said, "I want to be ready to roll in less than thirty minutes."

The team started moving and Blaine held up his hand, saying, "Pike, I think I should go over the ROE here, after the phone call."

He was telling me, without telling me, that my previous ROE was now defunct, courtesy of the Oversight Council.

After I'd punctured the Russians' tires—to no small angst from Blaine—we'd come straight back to our little boutique hotel and sent in a SITREP on what we knew. At the crack of dawn this morning—Washington, DC, time—the principals of the Oversight Council had held a meeting and heard about our shenanigans for the first time. I'd shacked up a final report about the latest activities, to include the fact that the Ukrainians had left on a boat, getting it to George Wolffe before it convened.

Of course, I'd conveniently left out the part about puncturing the tire. Blaine wanted to include it, but I wouldn't let him. Not that it mattered in the end. We'd been given the death sentence of "continue to develop the situation," which was aggravating to no end.

If I'd have wanted to do nothing but collect intel in order for some egghead analyst in the directorate of intelligence to tell the president what it meant, I would have joined the CIA. My work ended up with some terrorist's head on a spike or a national security threat resolved.

The brunt of the conversation had been the commander of the Taskforce, George Wolffe, telling us—meaning *me*—in no uncertain terms that it was collection only, no matter what occurred. We were to follow and decipher what we could for the National Command Authority to make a decision that could end up much greater than the Taskforce's narrow mission profile. In other words, the rules of engagement on this one were extreme: we couldn't do anything, even if the lives of innocents were involved. Which really stuck in my throat, but I'd agreed, taking one more bite out of this shit sandwich.

I nodded at Blaine to continue, and he explained the new ROE that had been relayed to us. Everyone looked at me when he was done, waiting on what I would say.

I said, "That's it. That's the ROE, and we'll abide by it. No more picking sides. We're now like scientists watching rats in a maze. If they start to fight, we let them."

They nodded and I added, "That does not limit our right to self-defense. If you get crosswise with them like we did in Tivoli, you defend yourself."

Blaine thought I was giving tacit approval to ignore what he'd just explained. He stood up and said, "That doesn't mean you put yourself in a position to get shot at. Is that understood?"

I held up my hands and said, "I'm not saying that at all. Just that if you're about to get shot, don't sit there and take it because of this ROE. That's all."

I looked at Blaine and he nodded at me, but I could tell he thought I was sending some sort of subliminal message.

Blaine said, "Okay, let's get to work," and the team split up to accomplish their various tasks. In seconds, I was left alone in my room with Shoshana, the only one who hadn't been given a mission.

Blaine was the last out, and he noticed she'd remained. I could tell he didn't like it, because he knew the enormous respect I held for her. In truth, I trusted her more than him, and he thought she was going to use that to usurp his orders.

Which wasn't wrong, but I was on board with the new ROE, even if he didn't believe it.

She said, "Can we finally talk?"

I really didn't want to, sure she was going to tell me to ignore my commander and attack the Russians, but I either convinced her to follow my lead—a very small possibility—or she just flew home to Israel.

Honestly, letting her leave was probably the best thing, because she *was* a little borderline crazy and wasn't obligated to follow Taskforce rules, but I needed her skills on this, not the least because of the very ROE she was about to fight me on.

We could no longer risk getting caught in the crossfire with the new ROE, which meant I'd need people who could seamlessly blend into their surroundings. In the past, I'd seen her melt into a Muslim group in Jordan without compromise. Doing the same in Helsinki would be a no-brainer.

I looked around the room for Jennifer, noticing for the first time she was gone, and Shoshana smiled, saying, "I sent her to Veep's room to do their computer research together. She's not going to help you here."

I sighed, sat on the bed, and said, "What do you want?"

"I want you to understand what this is about. I've seen the people involved. I've read them."

I slapped my hand on the bed and said, "Shoshana, look, the ROE stands. I need you on this mission, but if you can't abide by our rules, then you can fly home. I'm sick of the 'seeing people' bullshit."

She sat next to me like she had before when we'd been alone, putting her hand on my thigh. Not in a sexual way, but in a way to connect. To show she was serious. I wanted to slap it away, because, well, honestly, it's uncomfortable having a female put her hand on your thigh when you don't want it. I didn't do that, because I'd worked with her enough to realize she didn't get the intimacy. She literally didn't understand the nuances of such a thing. She only knew that touching a person projected the trust she held.

She'd probably sat next to a total of three people on earth and done such a thing. One was her husband, Aaron. The second was Jennifer. I was the third. I would respect it for what it was: an action telling me she trusted me, like a lioness rolling over and exposing her neck.

Her next words surprised me.

"George Wolffe is right with the rules of engagement. We shouldn't help the Ukrainians."

That answer surprised me. I said, "What do you mean?"

"I told you I'd read Daniel in the cemetery, but wasn't sure what it meant."

"Yeah?"

"Well, after seeing the man who was following the Ukrainians to the boat, I think it's bad."

"You mean the thug guy?"

"No, the older one who's in charge. The one who followed him to the boat. He's scared. I mean petrified, and not because of his own life.

He's blinking red, and it's not just because of his failure on the mission. There is something more happening here, and it involves the Wolves' attack on Putin. If that happens, I think there will be a world of hurt. I don't think we should help it."

The words were disconcerting, mainly because I'd expected the exact opposite. "Okay, that's exactly what we just said."

"But you don't believe it. You want to fight. I'm telling you not to at this point. Let it go."

I said, "Why? What did you see?"

"I saw an inferno. I don't know why."

CHAPTER 65

Victor boarded the ferry along with the rest of the SOBR team, blending in among the few other passengers going to see the fort as tourists. Because of the weather and the fact that tourist season was long over, the boat was fairly empty, but still felt crowded. In the summertime everyone would have been outside on the deck chairs, but with the November wind and temperature, all of them had crowded into the small cabin with bench seats.

Victor saw Wraith coming to him and ground his teeth, sure the man was going to complain about the plan he'd already briefed.

Wraith reached him, opened a tourist map of the fortress, and laid it on the bench, saying, "You sure about focusing on the southern tip of the eastern island?"

Victor said, "Yes. That's where the traitor said they were coming. We don't know where they're going to land, but we know where they're going to end up."

Wraith said, "I think we should set up one observation post with some security behind it. The area to the west appears to be open, with little to hide behind, but the east has old fortifications where someone could be waiting for us."

Aggravated, Victor said, "Wraith, nobody is out here besides the Wolves and the last member of the Valkyrie team. They're coming by boat, and I'm going to need everyone to take them out. Including you."

Wraith said, "Your men have made one mistake after another. You should listen to me for once. Let me take one man to the King's Gate as rear security. We'll clear those fortifications while you wait."

Victor thought a moment, then said, "We'll clear it first, together, then set up the OP."

"Give me one man as rear security for your operation."

Aggravated, Victor said, "Okay. Take Misha, but when I call, you come running. And set up both of your phones to send me your location so I know where you are at all times. I don't want another issue like Porvoo where we were running around like chickens trying to find each other."

"How?"

Surprised at his technological ignorance, Victor said, "Just turn on Google Maps from the phone I gave you and share your location with me. It's real time and I can see it on my phone."

He could see Wraith wasn't convinced. He said, "It's what we do, and I'm going to make sure each man is sharing so I can understand what's happening in real time. Go ask Misha to show you. It's simple."

Wraith nodded and sought out Misha. Victor watched them working through the apps on their phones, Misha giving him a class that any modern preteen would have known.

They approached the small quay for the island fortress and Victor saw a Finnish naval cutter on the other side, painted camouflage colors and giving him some angst. He hoped it was not an active patrol out to stop anyone but the ferry from approaching the island. That would do them no good, as they needed the Wolves to land.

The ferry docked, the passengers began to exit, and Victor flowed out with them, his men trailing behind. They followed the crowd through a stone arch and entered the fortifications. Victor looked at a map on the wall, traced a line, and found a piece of fortification called the King's Gate.

Built on four separate islands, the Suomenlinna Fortress had two smaller islands filled with permanent residents and utility facilities off-limits to tourists, and two larger ones comprising the primary old fortifications the tourists came to see. Under extreme duress, the Valkyrie traitor had given them the southern tip of the larger, western island. Somewhere near the King's Gate they would find the Wolves.

Victor led them away from the dock, walking up a gravel road that was bounded by old stone buildings on either side, some falling into disrepair from the elements, others having been renovated into art galleries, coffee shops, and museums. They went through a tunnel, leaving the fortifications of the eastern island, reaching a narrow bridge. Victor checked another tourist map, and they crossed over to the western island, finding themselves once again inside the stone walls of the ancient fortification.

They passed through what looked like a town square, the centerpiece a tomb with the helmet of Ares, the God of War, on top, the square surrounded by museums and shops. Victor got his bearings and turned south on another gravel road. They passed through a separate stone arch, entering an open field sprinkled with ancient bunkers, the grass growing over them making the area look as if giant moles had been burrowing under the ground.

The wind hit them as soon as they left the stone walls. The frigid air coming off the ocean was bracing, the falling sun doing nothing to provide any heat. Victor surveyed the area, seeing the bastion that protected the fort at the southern end of the island.

He said, "That must be the King's Gate."

They started walking along the high ground, the bunkers clustered below them in a bowl, looking like giant turtles trying to escape the cold. They passed by one defunct cannon after another, and Misha glanced around, saying, "There's nobody here but us."

Victor swept the area and saw he was right: the bunker area was devoid of any tourists, the summer season gone months ago and the late hour—combined with the steady drumbeat of November wind—convincing the few who came to stay inside the primary fortifications, visiting the various museums, coffee shops, and galleries.

Perfect.

The ancient gravel road sloped down, and soon enough the bastion walls provided protection from the blasting of the wind. Victor saw a closed outdoor café built into the old stone of the bastion, the umbrellas now folded, the chairs stacked together. In front of him was a two-story wall with a wooden footbridge crossing a dried moat. Beyond it was a huge arch with an iron portcullis raised, a sign proclaiming in Finnish, Swedish, and English that it was the King's Gate.

They went into the gate, seeing tunnels running left and right. Victor continued through, finding the ocean lapping just beyond a concrete landing, a small dock to his left. He went back inside the gate and said, "All right, let's spread out and search the area. I don't think they've arrived yet, but you never know. Everyone make sure your phones are sending me location updates. Like I told Wraith, I don't want a repeat of what happened in Porvoo."

Each man sent him a "share location" from Google Maps, and then began to spread out, searching the nooks and crannies of the fortification. Wraith chose to go on top of the bastion itself, taking a stone staircase up until he stood on the wall.

While the wind battered him, from this location he could see all the way back across the bunker field, to the wall surrounding the town square they had left. From this height he could see a small crescent-shaped beach at the bottom of a cliff, a set of narrow wooden stairs leading down to it. Something they'd missed from their walk through the bunker field.

Just off the shore of the beach was a boat, but no dock, the craft itself apparently held in place by its own anchor, which was strange. He caught movement, and strained his eyes, finding four men walking up the wooden steps.

He studied them, sure they weren't tourists, given the weather. They reached the top of the cliff and walked to a yellow wooden shed that wouldn't be out of place if it were a barn in Russia. One of them worked a lock, and a short amount of time later opened the large sliding doors, exposing a small cab-over truck with a canvas top covering the bed, markings on the door stating it was a power company utility truck.

Why are the utility repairmen showing up on a boat at a beach?

The vehicle drove out of the shed, leaving the high ground and lowering down into the bowl with the decrepit bunkers. It parked outside of one, and the four men exited, one unlocking the bunker and waving the others forward.

He pulled his phone out and called Victor, saying, "I think I have the Wolves. They're in the bunker complex with a truck, loading it up."

Victor said, "Right now?"

He couldn't understand what Victor was saying due to the wind. He turned around and huddled next to the wall, saying, "What was that?" He put a finger in one ear and heard Victor repeat, "They're in the bunker system right now?"

He caught movement over the wall facing the sea and saw another boat arriving at the King's Gate dock, another five people inside. He said, "Yes, I'm sure it's them, but you have someone coming to your back on a boat at the King's Gate. I don't think it's a coincidence. You go to the bunker. Leave me and Misha behind. We'll handle the follow-on."

CHAPTER 66

Perun ducked behind the console of the boat, the wind battering him more than the incessant waves. He saw the fort in the distance and said, "Are we almost there?"

Luka said, "Yes. We circle that point and anchor at a beach."

He passed around the southern tip of the island, the old walls of the bastion silently overlooking their approach, and circled in where it necked down into a cove, cutting the throttle of the engines and sliding toward the shore. Perun saw a sand beach that was maybe seventy meters long, with a single wooden cross holding an ubiquitous orange circle float, as if the life support was needed on a day like today.

Luka said, "Get the anchor ready."

Perun shouted into the hold, where Dishka and Javelin had been cowering from the weather, "Dishka! The anchor!"

Dishka came out looking a little green and said, "Are we here? Because I'd rather take a bullet in Crimea than spend any more time on this boat."

Perun laughed and said, "Yes, we're close. Get the anchor up front and wait for Luka to signal you."

Dishka went to the bow, secured the anchor, and looked back at the console. Luka raised the outboards above the water and let the momentum carry them forward. He reached within five feet of the shore, the boat barely moving now, and said, "Toss it over."

Dishka did and the anchor grated on the bottom of the seabed, the boat still sliding forward. It bit into the rocks and held, causing the bow to start to swing in slow motion around it. Luka said, "Sorry, we're going to get wet."

He jumped into the surf, the water stopping just below his knees, and slogged forward to the beach. Perun looked at his men, then back at Luka reaching the beach and said, "Get over the side."

They did, slogging forward just like Luka had, and met him on the beach. Perun said, "What the hell are we doing here?"

"Getting your weapons. Follow me."

He went to the rickety wooden stairs that led to the top of the cliff and started jogging up them, Perun and his men following.

They reached the top, the wind starting to scream the higher they rose. Perun said, "What now?"

Luka repeated, "Follow me."

He went to a wood structure painted yellow, with large sliding doors. He worked a lock, then began pulling one side open. Dishka worked the other side, the ancient rollers groaning through the rust. Inside, Perun saw a mini-truck with a canvas back, a sticker in Finnish on the side.

He said, "What's this?"

"A utility truck. One that's allowed in the tunnel. Something just like it comes and goes, keeping the utilities for the people who live here functioning. Cable TV, electricity, plumbing, you name it, it all comes through that tunnel. And someone has to maintain it. That someone is you, now."

He opened the door, reached in the back, and pulled out three jackets embroidered with the same logo as on the door, saying, "Put these on. You now work for the utility company."

They did and Dishka cranked the engine, driving it out of the shed. The rest boarded on the bench seat, squeezing in to fit, and Luka said, "Drop down into the bowl, where the bunkers are."

Dishka did so, winding on paths that were barely wider than the vehicle, Luka giving directions. They stopped outside one of the bunkers, the face built of brick, but the bunker itself grown over with grass.

Luka said, "This is it. Inside there is the means for Ukraine's victory."

Perun looked at him, knowing the man didn't care one iota about Ukraine. He said, "I understand why you're doing this, but don't pretend it's for Ukraine. You and I would be enemies in another life. You believe Putin is destroying Russia, and I know he's destroying Ukraine, but don't pretend you're on my side. The minute something shifts, you'll throw us into a waste bin."

Perun kept his eyes on Luka, waiting on a response. Finally, Luka said, "What you say might be true in the future, but right now, we're on the same side. Let's load this up so you can leave."

They exited the vehicle and Luka unlocked the bunker, the wooden doors rotting away on their hinges. Perun was surprised to see it was only a simple padlock that prevented entry. He said, "You put the bombs in here? With nothing but a padlock and these ancient wooden doors?"

Luka swung them open and said, "Sometimes it's the camouflage that's the protection."

Inside, Perun saw five crates, two large ones about ten feet long, two smaller ones about eight feet long, but wider, and a single one about two feet long. Luka said, "The smaller ones are the wings. The larger ones are the bodies. The little crate is the input controller and the rockets for the assisted takeoff."

Dishka and Javelin started loading them into the truck and Perun said, "What about the explosives?"

"They're already inside. They're ready to go."

"Do we need to worry about that? Can they be detonated by shaking them or something like that?"

"No. They have a fuse that requires the drone to drive into something, and they aren't armed yet. They won't just go off."

"And how will we learn to do this? To initiate the fuse?"

"Your next contact will have that. You understand how to get out of here, right?"

"Yes. We drive from here to the final island and there's a gate. I show the guard the pass you gave me, and we get through."

"No, no. You wear the jackets, the ones that the service company uses, but that's for the camera only. The gate isn't manned. You scan the QR code on your badge, and the gate will open. You do the same at the tunnel entrance, and it will unlock. There are no manned guard posts."

Perun nodded and said, "How will I trust the man at the next linkup? We've been attacked throughout this journey."

"You do it just like you did here. We spent an enormous amount of energy and time to plan this. We got the drones in here under the cover of darkness, and we'll get them out the same way. Just make the ferry to Estonia with this truck and meet the next contact. He'll have the instructions, the final target, and the launch point."

Perun said, "You don't even know the launch point?"

Luka laughed and said, "One step at a time, one step at a time. That's how we live for another day."

Dishka closed the bed of the small truck and said, "It's done. Now what?"

Luka said, "Now you drive out of here, using the route I gave you. Go slow, make no sudden movements or speed. Just roll out of here at fifteen kilometers an hour, because that's what these trucks do."

Perun said, "What are you going to do?"

"Go back to the boat and return to Helsinki. I wish you the best of luck. I mean it, even if you don't believe it."

Perun heard a pop, then another, a small sound hidden by the wind. He turned to the bastion at the southern end and said, "Did you hear that?"

He drew his pistol, saw Lukas's eyes widen, and turned in the direction he was looking, seeing three men running at them, all with weapons out.

CHAPTER 67

The wind on the sea was a hell of a lot worse than it had been on the land, and once again, I was wondering if Knuckles—a Navy man—knew how to drive our boat. After one brutally hard landing over a swell, I gritted my teeth and said, "Do you know what the fuck you're doing?"

He said, "Slow your roll there, Commando. This is nothing like we used to do on our boats in the Navy. You want to lose a few inches out of the cartilage in your spine? You should have been there for that."

Jennifer said, "I always wondered what made SEALs so tough. I had no idea it was because you couldn't drive a boat without losing parts of your spine."

He grimaced and slowed the approach, giving us a reprieve. Shoshana looked like she wanted to throw up, and even Veep—who was Air Force Special Operations, meaning he'd spent a lot of time on SEAL boats—appeared a little green.

I said, "We might have to fight when we get there, so can you try to thread through the waves instead of bashing over them?"

Knuckles said, "I didn't rent this damn thing. It's not my fault we're in a bathtub with a motor."

We'd reached Helsinki about an hour after we'd located the beacon at the ferry terminal, and during the drive both Veep and Jennifer had come through.

Jennifer had found a place to rent a boat, but since it was after the tourist season, all the boats that could be considered "seaworthy" had been put into dry dock, leaving us with a twenty-foot aluminum hull with an outboard. It was, in fact, a bathtub, but it both floated and went forward, so I was taking that as a win.

Veep had tracked Shoshana's ticks to the southeastern edge of the Suomenlinna Fortress, which was enough to convince me that the damn Russians were ahead of us again. The ticks had finally started to crap out, their batteries dying, giving us a wide location as to their last known point, spreading out over a kilometer, but part of that circle had intersected with the fortress, and, given what we knew the Russians were doing, it was enough for me to continue.

Everything had gone smoothly for the exfiltration of Porvoo. We got out of the area within twenty minutes, with the only hiccup coming from Blaine, who cornered me about my talk with Shoshana.

He'd honestly thought we were cooking something up to get around the ROE of the Taskforce and I'd snapped at him, insulted.

He'd said, "Don't give me that shit, Pike. I've done enough missions with you to know how you operate. We can't do that here."

I'd snarled at him and said, "Have I ever gone around you? Gone behind your back?"

He'd stammered for a second, because that was absolutely true. I'd ignored his orders in the past, but when I did so, I told him up front to stick it up his ass. There was no way I'd usurp the chain of command by sneaking around getting people on my side. That was anathema to me, and he should have known it.

I'd said, "If I wanted to change the ROE, I'd do it to your face."

He'd said, "So what was that talk with Shoshana? What did she want?"

"She wanted to tell me that she thinks you're right. That we shouldn't get involved."

He'd said nothing, taking that in. I'd continued, "She's 'seen' something here and thinks that helping the Wolves will harm our interests. I don't know why, and neither does she, because she's fucking crazy. But I believe in what she can do, so no, I'm not sneaking around behind your back."

He'd said, "Hey, okay, I'm sorry, Pike. I should have known you wouldn't do that."

I'd said, "You *do* know that. Look, just run this mission like you have a team that trusts you, because we do, and quit playing like you're still in Washington, worried about who's going to stab you in the back. We don't play that game out here in the field."

He'd nodded and we'd gotten on the road, burning rubber to Helsinki.

Veep had done a deep dive on the tick location, and it was surrounded by cliffs and jagged rocks with the exception of one small beach in a cove. I figured that's where they were going, and obviously didn't want to land in the same place. Veep had found a dock outside a portal called the King's Gate that wasn't used after the summer tourist season had ended, and that was where we were headed, if Knuckles didn't kill us first.

The dock came into view and Knuckles, after getting yelled at, now pretended that he had everything under control. Which is to say he shouted for us to get the bumpers out right before we hit the dock broadside. We bounced off, Veep jumped out with a line, and in short order we were tied up.

We exited the boat onto the concrete pilings of the dock, the wind about to blow us over, and Blaine said, "Okay, what now?"

I said, "Well, we know two things: the Ukrainians are here for something, and the Russians are here to stop them, which means we're in what Kenny Loggins would call the 'highway to the danger zone.'"

I looked around the area and said, "And because of the weather and time, I think this entire place is going to be filled with only killers. No tourists are stupid enough to venture about in this wind, so it's going to be hard to act like we're the only ones who care about the history here. Let's split up."

I looked at the area in front of the bastion, seeing a path to the left, and a stairwell to the right leading to the top. I said, "Shoshana, you and Veep head to the top of the wall. Get up there and take a look-see around this place. Once you're up, Knuckles and Blaine go to the left. Jennifer and I will go straight through. The first person that spots a human, call on the net."

I got nods and, for Blaine's benefit, I said, "Do not, under any circumstances, cause a spike. Both of these crews are going to be on high alert and we do not want to become involved. Remember, we're just the scientists watching the rats. Don't fall into the maze on this."

I looked at Shoshana, and she slightly nodded at me, agreeing. I nodded back and said, "Get going."

We left the dock as a group and then split apart, each taking a sector. Jennifer and I waited until Veep and Shoshana made it to the top, and I saw Knuckles disappear around the side of the wall. When both teams were gone from sight, I started through the huge arch of the King's Gate, entering the tunnels that permeated the bastion, intending to walk straight through to the light on the far side.

I heard Veep come on the net, saying, "There's a truck out in the middle of a field, loading something up."

I said, "What kind of field?"

"I don't know. It has a bunch of mounds with grass over them. It looks like something out of *The Hobbit*, like Frodo Baggins lives here. They're at one of the mounds loading something."

I picked up my pace, saying, "Knuckles, can you see them yet?"

Before he could reply, I caught movement out of my eye and reacted from a lifetime of living with the threat of death.

It was the thug, charging forward. He tried to circle his arm around my neck, his other hand holding a knife. I jammed my own arm high, blocking the hold on my neck, and trapped the wrist holding the knife with my other hand. I held the arm around my neck in place, ducked my knees down, then sprang up, rotating violently and flinging him off me like a dog shaking off water.

He slammed into the stone wall and I drew my pistol, then heard Jennifer scream. I turned to her, seeing her on the ground, another man on top of her. She writhed for a split second, him trying to pin her down, and then she had her gun in her hand. She put it to his head and pulled the trigger, the bullet penetrating his skull and flinging him off her. I turned to the thug and saw a pistol in his hands. I fired and missed, hitting the wall next to his head and splattering him with spall. It caused him to lose his aim and the will to fight. He took off running down the tunnel, disappearing in the darkness. I assumed he knew the area much better than I did, and refrained from chasing him and possibly getting ambushed.

On the net, Blaine said, "What are the shots? What are the shots?"

I said, "We were just attacked."

Veep said, "There's a gunfight at the Hobbit house. I say again, there's a gunfight at the Hobbit house."

I started running through the arch, saying, "Thug is here, and he's on the loose. Watch yourself."

Knuckles said, "Fight's over. One man fleeing to the east. One man coming back to you. Watch out."

I heard the words and jerked Jennifer into the darkness of the tunnel. A man entered, breathing heavily and loping along with a limp. He shouted something in Russian as he came abreast of me and I hammered him with my weapon, splitting open his temple and dropping him like a sack of dirt.

I kicked his gun away, and then realized he was the Russian leader whose tire I'd punctured in Porvoo. He was the head man of the attempts against the Ukrainians.

I said, "Secure this guy," and, not waiting for Jennifer to answer, exited the tunnel running flat out, going up the road to the high ground. I reached it and saw a small lorry driving away. I said, "Knuckles, what do you have?"

"One guy running down the stairs to the beach. He's headed to a boat. The others are in that truck. Two dead on the ground."

"Veep, Carrie, what do you have?"

"Nothing. Nobody on the wall."

Jennifer came on, saying, "Pike, this guy is waking up. What do you want me to do? Leave him here and run?"

Too late for that. We were in it now, whether we wanted to be or not. I said, "No. Lock him down. I'm coming back. Knuckles, Beast, catch that guy before he can leave in the boat."

I started running back to the gate and Blaine came on, saying, "Pike, we can't take him down. We *cannot* interfere."

I reached Jennifer, saw the man at her feet had been shot in the thigh, and said, "Damn it, they just tried to kill me. We fell into the rat maze without even meaning to. Take that fucker right now."

Knuckles said, "I'm on it. I'll have him."

Thank God for my 2 IC. I said, "Veep, Carrie, get down here and help us. Knuckles, Beast, exfil using that guy's boat. We're taking the one here."

Blaine said, "Pike, we can't steal their boat."

I said, "Knuckles, do you have control?"

"He's down. I caught him at the beach."

"Blaine, you either help get his ass into that boat or take a ferry back to the mainland. We're in this now whether we like it or not."

I heard nothing else on the net, saw Shoshana running into the tunnel, and said, "Where's Veep?"

"Right behind me."

"Can you run a boat?"

"Yes, I can drive a boat."

"You and Jennifer go get it ready." They raced out of the tunnel just as Veep entered and I hoisted the man on the ground to his feet, saying, "Give me a hand with this guy."

I put one arm around my neck, he took the other, and we speed-walked/dragged him back through the gate and down to the dock. I threw him onto the floor of the boat, saying, "Jennifer, put a gun on him."

We leapt in, Shoshana hit the gas, and we spun away from the dock, heading back to the mainland. I got on the net, saying, "Knuckles, Beast, what's your status?"

"We're headed back to the marina in our stolen boat. We've got the man with us, but I'm not sure what we're going to do when we arrive with him."

I said, "Yeah, me neither, because we have another one in my boat."

Blaine came on, saying, "How in the fuck are we going to explain this in a SITREP? Instead of doing nothing, we've taken two different Russians hostage after a shoot-out."

I said, "I honestly don't know, sir. I'm glad I'm not you."

CHAPTER 68

Perun entered the tiny square, driving erratically around the tomb in the center and shouting, "How is he? How is he?"

Dishka said, "He's hit bad. It's gone through his lungs."

Perun looked over and saw Javelin, his face ghost white, his eyes scrunched closed in pain, grunting to breathe, each exhale sprouting a pink, bubbly froth from his mouth. Dishka shouted, "Watch out!"

Perun glanced back at the road and swerved to avoid two tourists leaping backwards. He passed around the circle, shouting, "Pressure! Put pressure on the wound! Seal it up with your hand before his lung deflates."

Dishka did his best, the blood flowing freely in the cab. He said, "How did they know where we were? How did they find us?"

Perun passed through the small gate of the western island fortifications, now driving at a steady fifteen kilometers an hour, and said, "I don't know. I just know if someone hadn't started shooting at the fortification, we'd all be dead. We're lucky we were quick on the draw."

As soon as Perun had heard the shots, he'd drawn his pistol, as had Javelin and Dishka, and then they'd seen the men running at them from behind the bunker. A split second earlier and they'd have all been mowed down like helpless grass under a lawnmower, their backs turned loading the vehicle. As it was, the three Russians ran into their own buzz saw, with the Ukrainians firing before the Russians could stop and gain a sight picture.

The Russians had started shooting wildly while still on the move, while Perun and Dishka took cover behind the open truck door, using it as a platform for their placement of rounds. Only Javelin was caught in the open, and he'd been hit.

Luka had stumbled backwards and had begun running, disgusting Perun. The fight had lasted less than ten seconds, with two of the Russians dead on the ground and the third running back the way he'd come. Perun had looked at Luka sprinting away and thought about putting a round in his back, but did not, instead running to Javelin.

He'd been hit directly in the chest, and it was bad. They'd loaded him in the truck and then started on their journey, Dishka frantically trying to stop the oozing blood and Perun desperately trying to ascertain how to get to the tunnel.

They reached the small bridge crossing over to the eastern island and Perun took it, still driving a slow and steady fifteen kilometers an hour. They crossed over to the eastern side and Perun began driving north, knowing the tunnel entrance was on one of the smaller islands. He said, "How is he?"

"I can't stop the blood. I'm losing him."

Perun pulled over next to a decrepit ammunition magazine, put the truck in neutral, and said, "He must have an exit wound. We need to find it."

He leaned over Javelin's body, telling Dishka to lift it off the bench, the blood now slopping onto the floor. Dishka did, and Perun raised the maintenance jacket and shirt he was wearing, finding a large hole in his back sprinkled with pieces of Javelin's rib bones. He said, "That's it. Find some plastic to put on it."

Javelin coughed, spewing blood out of his mouth, then screamed when Dishka tried to stanch the blood. Dishka said, "Hang on, hang on. Sorry for the pain, man, but we need to do this."

Javelin's eyes grew clear and he said, "Don't stop. Don't stop the mission because of me."

And then his eyes lost their spark, his head lolling to the side like someone had cut a rubber band in his neck, showing Perun he was gone. Dishka continued working, but Perun knew he was lost.

He said, "Put him in the footwell. We still have to get off this island."

Dishka held Javelin's head and said, "The footwell? Stuff him in the footwell?"

"Yes. He can't be seen on the cameras. And try to clean the blood off your face."

Perun put the truck in gear and began driving. Dishka was incensed, saying, "I'm not going to stuff him in the footwell like a bag of trash."

"Yes, you are. Do it now."

Dishka growled, but rolled the body into the well, folding the legs over the torso to get it off the cameras they would encounter. He said, "This disgusts me."

Perun said, "Me as well, but it's the only way."

They crossed the bridge to the first smaller island, encountering no resistance, the spit of land holding various machine shops and other maintenance facilities. They went to the far side and saw the bridge to the final island—a veritable rock outcropping with only a smattering of buildings. They entered the bridge, reached the far side, and rolled into a gate. Perun looked directly into a camera mounted on a stalk and held up his badge he'd been given, letting the reader scan the QR code on it. He held his breath, and after a pregnant second, the gate opened.

He wound around the rock, following the road, seeing only trucks and warehouses, but no humans. The gravel track dead-ended into what looked like a rolling door for a loading ramp at a grocery store, another stalk with a camera next to it.

He repeated the procedure, and the door opened, slowing rising in the twilight, exposing a dripping tunnel full of pipes and cables draped along the walls. He looked at Dishka and said, "I guess they weren't lying about their planning."

He drove forward, the concrete floor sloping down, the tunnel bored underneath the ocean floor for over a thousand meters. They reached the bottom and continued forward, hearing the continual noise of bilge pumps even as their tires rolled through about four inches of seawater.

Dishka said, "I hope these walls hold."

Perun gave a grim smile and said, "Yeah, me too."

They continued through the dark tube, the only lights coming from the glow of their vehicle headlamps and sporadic fluorescent bulbs, and eventually began climbing again, telling them they were on the far side.

They reached the top, the exit blocked by another gate. Perun rolled over a pressure plate and waited. The gate opened, revealing the twilight of Helsinki.

He slowly drove out, finding himself in woodlands, no structures around. It looked like he'd driven straight into a forest of rolling hills. He stopped, pulled out the smartphone he'd taken from the table at the Tivoli amusement park fight, and passed it to Dishka, saying, "Turn that on and find out where we are."

Daniel took it and said, "Are you sure? Luka said to keep it turned off until we made the meeting."

When Luka had given them instructions for the next contact, he'd asked to see Perun's smartphone to make sure it was compatible for the transfer of information. He'd been astounded that all of Perun's men only had flip phones. Perun had told him it was for security reasons, and then had mentioned that he had Daniel's old smartphone.

Luka had told him that would have to do, and had instructed him to charge it but not turn it on until the meeting took place.

"Yes. It's a risk, but we have no idea where to go from here. Turn it off as soon as you're done."

Dishka did, then said, "It's a place called Kaivopuisto. It's a national park. We're south of the city center."

Perun put the truck in gear, winding out of the outcroppings leading to the tunnel and into the park itself. "Plot a route back to the city. Find the ferry terminal for Estonia and buy a ticket for us and the truck, then turn it back off."

Dishka said, "What about Javelin? We can't board with a dead body."

Perun looked around the woods cloaking the threadbare road and stopped the vehicle. He said, "We leave him here."

Dishka said, "Just dump him on the side of the road?"

"No. We bury him. As he would have wanted."

They spent the next thirty minutes in the dwindling light scraping a shallow grave, covered the body with rocks, and then both stood above the mound, Perun giving a prayer.

They left him there, driving away, leaving one more casualty in the ongoing war Putin had engendered. Neither one spoke, not wanting to open the wound.

After thirty minutes of silence, Dishka said, "What are we going to do now? Do we continue?"

Perun said, "Yes. We have the weapons. We can kill that fuck and end his war."

"But we've been attacked at every turn. In Copenhagen and here. How can we trust them? Luka said the entire reason for the boat trip was to break us from potential Russian state surveillance, but they were waiting for us. They were there. Maybe they were supposed to be there because we've been betrayed."

Perun said, "I don't know how they found us, but I don't believe it was Daniel's team. For one, they killed Daniel. For another, why take us on a boat trip to an ambush? Why not just kill us in Porvoo? Or any other place we've been? The Valkyries knew where we'd be each step of the way, and those same members tried very hard to see the mission continue. I don't think it's a setup. It doesn't make sense."

"It might not make sense, but it is real. We just buried Javelin."

"Yes, we did, but it was only him because someone else alerted us by shooting behind us. Don't you wonder who that was?"

"What do you mean?"

"Someone interfered with the Russians trying to kill us. I think it was the same people in Tivoli. There's a third player in this, and I have no idea what their intentions are. They seem to appear at the same time as the Russians, but they never show their hand."

"You think someone outside of Russia is helping us on this mission?"

"I don't know. All I know is we're going to be on that ferry, but I'm going into the next meeting with my eyes open."

CHAPTER 69

Wraith ran up the inside stairwell to the top of the bastion wall, feeling fear for the first time. Whoever he and Misha had attacked had not turned out to be just Ukrainian farmers turned partisans. They were skilled.

He'd watched the man and woman enter into the light of the gate, whispered to Misha to take the woman with a knife, not wanting the sound of a firearm to harm the ongoing operation. Misha had nodded and pulled out a blade, waiting on Wraith's move.

Wraith had waited until the man's back was facing him, and then had struck. It should have been easy enough to wrap an arm around the man's neck and plunge in his blade, but the man had reacted instantly, like he'd had some preternatural instinct.

In a single second, instead of him standing over a dead body, he'd been launched into the side of the stone wall, crashing his skull against the rock hard enough to nearly render him unconscious.

When he'd stood back up, unsteady on his feet, he'd seen Misha was dead, lying on the floor of the stone gate with his head split open. He'd drawn his pistol, and the man he'd attacked fired, missing his head by inches and spearing his face with stone shards.

He'd turned and run, not wanting to face them both. It brought him shame and anger, but he knew it was the best thing he could have done at that moment for his survival.

He'd reached the top of the bastion wall and looked out to the bunkers, seeing the vehicle gone and two bodies lying in the grass. He'd called Victor, but it had gone straight to voice mail. He decided it was time to leave.

While many called him nothing but a ruthless targeting machine, in truth, he had managed to survive by his skill at self-preservation more than his ability to kill. He knew what people thought of him because he saw the same façade every time he looked in a mirror. They thought he had no intelligence—a brute pulled in to do the dirty work when all else had failed—but that wasn't the truth.

He might appear to be a Neanderthal, but he was intelligent, if only in a reptilian way. Like a rattlesnake, he knew when to attack and when to flee to live another day, but unlike the snake, he *would* accomplish his mission instead of hiding under a rock, letting the threat pass by.

He ran down the wall until he reached the far northern end and another stairwell, calling Victor one more time. It rang out to voice mail yet again. He sprinted down the stairs to the path that ran along the water, seeing the bridge to the eastern island two hundred meters away. He remembered that the last ferry was leaving soon, and wanted to be on it.

He jogged toward the bridge and then saw the lorry from the bunkers cross it, causing a spike of rage unlike he'd ever felt. He wanted to kill them more than anyone he'd ever targeted. For the first time, it was personal. They had caused him shame in running, and he wanted them to pay the price of that shame.

The lorry made it to the far side to the eastern island just as he reached the bridge. He ran across it, putting his hand on the butt of his pistol and slowing to a walk as he exited on the far side.

He glanced around and saw a sprinkling of tourists on this side, visiting the various art galleries and museums. He couldn't kill them here even if he wanted to. He watched the vehicle drive away along the coastal road, and then saw it pull over to the side, its brake lights coming on.

It sat for ten seconds before Wraith realized he was missing an opportunity. He pulled out his phone, opened the Google Maps application, and went through the options of sharing its location that Misha had taught him, only this time sending it to a Gmail address he owned.

Once that was done, he sidled forward on the sidewalk until he was just behind the vehicle. He sprinted to the rear, reaching the bed of the truck close enough to prevent anyone from seeing him in the rearview mirrors.

He pulled out his phone one more time, ensuring the maps application was running and accurate, saw it was, and reached between the seam of the flap covering the tail and the side canvas, peeling it open and shoving his hand inside, dropping the phone underneath a bench seat bolted into the side of the bed.

The vehicle jerked forward, literally pulling away from his arm, and he let it go, watching it cross over another bridge to a smaller island.

He had no idea what they were doing to get off the fortress, but he knew he'd now be able to find them if they were successful.

CHAPTER 70

Knuckles closed the hangar door and I turned to the pilots, saying, "How secure is this place?"

"We own it for three days. It's completely secure as far as anyone coming in to check on us, but it does have cameras. I asked for them to be turned off and they agreed, but I don't control them."

"Where are they? Just in the main bay, or in the office as well?"

"Two outside the hangar, looking at the field, and two in here, looking at the hangar space. None in the office that I could see, but that doesn't mean they aren't there."

I said, "You have an APU hooked up to the plane? Does it have power?"

"Yeah, we've got that."

"Okay, we do the interrogations inside the aircraft then. Go get it up and running."

He left and I glanced around the place, saying, "This looks more like a hospital operating room than an aircraft hangar."

It was just large enough to house our bird, but was painted white throughout, with a floor that looked newly waxed, not a stain in sight.

Knuckles said, "I guess we can't leave any blood trails in this place. We'll end up on an episode of *Dateline*."

I laughed and said, "Veep, Jennifer, take their electronics that we found and start draining them of anything that might help us. Contact lists, web searches, any residual geolocation pings, phones they've called, the usual. Use the office."

I turned to Knuckles and said, "Call Blaine and tell him to bring in the vehicle. Get them out of it and into the plane."

He pulled out his phone and said, "I'm not sure he's really going to want to listen to you at this point."

I glared at him, saying, "It's *not* my fault. I didn't ignore the ROE, no matter what the Oversight Council thinks."

It had grown dark by the time we'd reached the marina where we'd rented our bathtub boat. We'd managed to find an open slip for the stolen craft and had returned the one we'd rented, letting Jennifer finish her transaction in the small shack next to the wharf while we loaded up our two prisoners into an SUV, staying in the gloom to keep them out of sight.

We'd discussed what to do with them, and, since trying to check in two unwilling prisoners at a hotel was a little bit of nonstarter, I'd settled on taking them straight to the Rock Star bird. They'd landed earlier in the day, renting a private hangar at an FBO called Jetflite at the Helsinki airport. The management there was used to dealing with the vagaries of real-life rock stars, so our requests for the hangar didn't seem out of place. I was sure it was costing a fortune, but as we said with the Taskforce, "Money is no object."

Jennifer had finished her transaction and I'd let Knuckles drive the prisoner-mobile with Veep as security while Blaine and I, along with the rest of the team, took another vehicle. It was about thirty minutes to the airport, and Blaine wanted to make a verbal SITREP, which was probably a good idea, given what had happened.

Blaine called the Taskforce priority line, waited on the encryption to synch up, and then put it on speaker. When George came on, Blaine gave him a truncated situation report, and that just about caused Wolffe to lose his mind.

He was literally shouting into the phone, the encryption making his words come out distorted, which was probably for the best. All I made out was, "What part of 'don't get involved' do you shitheads not understand?"

I broke in and said, "Sir, it wasn't like that. Jennifer and I were attacked out of the blue. A guy tried to gut me with a knife and another Russian tried to break Jennifer's neck. We had to engage."

"Why is it always *you* that has to engage?"

Now a little pissed myself, I said, "Well, next time I'll let them kill me so you can tell the fucking Oversight Council I followed their orders."

That broke his anger a little bit, and Blaine was able to tell him what we had in the car behind us, which caused Wolffe to ramp back up.

"You have not one, but two fucking Russians as prisoners? Did I hear that right?"

I said, "Uhhh . . . yes, sir."

"What the hell are you two doing over there? You're supposed to be collecting intelligence, not leaving a trail of bodies while conducting an extraordinary rendition of Russian agents."

Blaine looked at me, then said, "Sir, I know it looks bad on the surface, but it literally could not be helped. They attacked us. We had to defend ourselves, and at the end of it, we had two of them in custody."

Wolffe said, "Don't hand me that shit. I'm not a fool. Pike made a decision on this."

Blaine pursed his lips, thinking about my call with the guy in the boat, and I broke in again, saying, "I guess the Oversight Council would just prefer it if I'd have put a bullet in their head, but at the time I was thinking about collecting intelligence, so I let them live. If you want, we'll pull over right here and eliminate them."

I heard him exhale, knowing his shouting wasn't going to change anything. To get Blaine out of the hot seat, I said, "Sir, once we were engaged in combat, all bets were off. We were in it then, through no choice of Blaine or myself. They chose to attack us, and once shots were fired, yes, I made a decision to take the guy helping the Wolves. The other one is a Russian who was trying to stop them, so we have one of each. I think they'll be invaluable in telling us what's going on over here."

"What about the Wolves? The Ukrainians?"

"They're in the wind, but one of these guys will know where they're going."

"Okay, that's good news, what's your next move?"

"We're going to interrogate them inside the Rock Star bird at the airport."

He said, "I'm not going to the Oversight Council until you're done. Give me something to bring to them that'll take the sting off this debacle."

Blaine said, "Will do, sir."

That had been twenty minutes ago, and now we were bringing the prisoner-mobile inside the hangar. Knuckles opened the doors, and Blaine rolled in. I motioned to Shoshana and said, "Which one do you want first?"

"Boat guy. He for sure knows the who, where, and what for the Ukrainian mission."

I said, "You got it," and nodded to Knuckles. He opened the door and dragged out the man who'd taken the Wolves on the boat from Porvoo, his head now bagged in black sackcloth. Knuckles walked him up the stairs of the aircraft, took him to the back, sat him down, and then flex-tied his arms to a couple of rings down low on the chair, special built for just that purpose.

I turned to Shoshana and said, "You want us in or out?"

"Out. I want him alone."

I nodded and flicked my head to Knuckles, saying, "We'll be right outside. No permanent damage, you understand?"

She smiled and said, "That's not how I work, but yes, I understand."

Knuckles and I went down the stairs and took a seat with Blaine. He said, "Man, I hope she can get something out of that guy."

"If anyone can, it'll be her."

"Pike, any thoughts on what we're going to do with these guys when we're done?"

I'd been thinking about that since we'd captured them, and honestly had no idea. It wasn't like we'd rolled up a couple of ISIS assholes and could ship them to GITMO. They were Russian members of official state organs, which made things a little problematic.

I gave him the truth, saying, "Right now, I have no clue what to do with them."

He nodded, saying, "Me either."

Forty-five minutes later, Shoshana came down the stairs, saying, "He's not giving me anything. I got his name and that he's in Russian intelligence—most likely GRU—but nothing else. Unless you want me to start putting on some pressure, I'm done with him."

I said, "No, let's try the guy who was shot. You said he was scared of something before. Maybe you can crack him."

She nodded and we switched them out, putting the bag back on the head of the boat guy and returning him to the car while we zip-tied the one I'd captured in his place. Knuckles and I left, letting her get back to work.

Shoshana approached him the same way she had the other man. Just letting him watch her, his body exposed with his arms cinched to the sides of the chair. He was older than the other they'd taken. Maybe fifty or fifty-five. And he was scared. She could see that. Not scared in a "I'm about to be tortured" way, but scared of something else. She saw it in his aurora. Read it in his soul. It was so hot, she was unsure of how to continue, the flame throwing off her planned attack.

She took the seat next to him and said, "What do you want to tell me? Before I start?"

He looked at her and said, "I want asylum in the United States. I want protection before I'll talk."

She showed no emotion, but the words were like a sledgehammer. It was not at all what she expected to hear.

She said, "I can't give you that, but the man outside might, if you'll tell me what you know. Who is the other man we captured? And who are you?"

"I'll tell you all of that, everything, but you need to stop the Ukrainians, because they're about to cause the annihilation of the entire planet. You're wasting time with me."

She laughed and said, "I'm sure they might cause the death of all that you hold dear, but that's not what we're going to talk about."

She traced her nail along his arm, and he broke, saying, "I'm a Horseman. I represent the end of the world. You *must* stop the Wolves. If they kill Putin, we're all dead."

And then he began talking.

I went to the office where Jennifer and Veep were ripping through the smartphones and said, "Get anything?"

Veep said, "Yeah, there are some call logs and things like that we can probably run back through the Taskforce for further exploitation, and they were sharing phone maps, so we have some geolocation data, but no secret plan hidden in them yet."

I nodded and turned to go when Jennifer said, "Wait, Pike, what is this thing? We can't get it to do anything with any tool we have."

She held up a device we'd found on the wounded man, something that looked like a cell phone but wasn't. I said, "I don't know. Let Shoshana get through with him, and when she comes out, I'll have her take it in and ask."

When I returned planeside, I saw Shoshana coming down the stairs, looking a little grim. I thought, *That was quick.*

I went to her and before I could speak she said, "Pike, did you find a strange device on that guy?"

I nodded, saying, "As a matter of fact, I was just talking to Jennifer about it."

"So it's real?"

"Yeah, why?"

"We have a significant problem. He cracked immediately, almost begging to talk. I know now why I saw an inferno."

CHAPTER 71

For the first time ever, George Wolffe arrived at the Oval Office before anyone else, but he understood why. There was a national security meeting happening in the Situation Room about the war in Ukraine, and every one of the Oversight Council principals were in it, including the president.

The president's secretary had graciously allowed him to wait outside on a bench, like the lobbyist his sign-in portrayed, saying, "The president is very busy today, I'm not sure you'll get an audience with him."

Wolffe had said, "I understand, but I think he'll see me."

She smiled and said, "I hope so. I've always liked you, even if I never understood what Blaisdell Consulting does."

He smiled back, thinking, *I'm not sure what that is now either.*

He waited for a few minutes, then saw a scrum coming to the Oval Office door. President Hannister saw him, and turned, talking to the people in the scrum, giving final instructions for whatever had happened in the Situation Room.

They drifted apart and he approached the office, the other principals behind him, saying, "George, I guess you have something important to say, since you called a Green alert."

The Taskforce had an ability to short-circuit all presidential communications to get an immediate audience, something that the unit had never used in its entire existence. It had been put in place in the early days after 9/11, precisely because the operations of the Taskforce were incredibly sensitive, but over time, they'd become routine, and nothing had risen to the level requiring initiation. Until now.

The code name in the communication Wolffe had used was Soylent Green, meaning if he didn't get an audience, they'd be eating themselves soon.

Wolffe said, "Yes, sir. We have some information from Finland, and it is—to say the least—not good."

"Come on in."

The president took his seat behind the Resolute Desk, the rest of the principals sliding into the couches left and right, and President Hannister said, "Okay, George, what do you have?"

"A serious issue. Can we go back down to the Situation Room without raising a spike?"

President Hannister said, "Yeah, I guess. Why? We just left there."

He held up a thumb drive and said, "Because I need to show you something, away from the crowds walking around."

The SECDEF, Mark Oglethorpe, said, "I have to get back to the Pentagon. Is this really necessary?"

"Yes, it is. Unless you feel that global thermonuclear war is the same as the press bitching about the new Army physical fitness test."

Nobody said anything for a second, and then President Hannister said, "Okay, let's go."

They marched down the hallway outside the Oval Office, took a short flight of stairs down, then entered the fabled Situation Room seen in pictures from the Cuban Missile Crisis to the death of Osama bin Laden. Wolffe went to the front of the room, booted up a laptop, then put in a thumb drive, saying, "You guys are up to speed on the mission in Finland, right?"

Amanda Croft, the SECSTATE, said, "Up to speed with the last meeting, where we told Pike to just collect. What happened?"

"Pike was attacked as soon as he tried to continue. He ended up killing one guy and chasing another one away. From there, it turned into a mess."

He proceeded to tell them the results of the mission, which caused everyone in the room to grow more and more concerned. When he was done, he said, "And now we have two Russian nationals in custody, inside Finland."

The room erupted, with shouting back and forth over his revelations. The president held up his hand, and everyone became quiet. He said, "Are you telling me that a Taskforce team now has two Russian nationals in custody? Right now? I'd say that's a Soylent Green alert. I can see why you used it."

"Yes, sir. Like I said—and absolutely like I warned about—the team was attacked and had to react to the situation." He looked at the SEC-STATE and said, "They could not 'remain on the sidelines' because someone was trying to kill them. When it was done, they held two Russians, but that's not why I called you here. That wasn't the Soylent Green alert."

Amanda Croft said, "Are you blaming me for *your* screwup? All they had to do was do nothing. If they got attacked, they were most definitely doing something that spiked Russian interests."

Oglethorpe, the SECDEF, said, "I agree. Are you saying you now have two Russian nationals that you believe are members of state-sanctioned organizations? This is a disaster. Every time Pike Logan is employed, something catastrophic happens. I think—"

President Hannister cut him off, saying, "Quiet."

The room fell silent, and Hannister continued, saying, "Capturing two Russian nationals who work for the Russian state is most definitely an act of war, but I'm apparently the only person in the room who heard your final sentence. Why did you call the Soylent Green alert, if not for this disaster?"

Wolffe said, "Because we interrogated them, and their answers scared the hell out of me. Can I continue, saving the first part about the capture for later?"

Amanda glanced at President Hannister and said, "Yes, I suppose, but we're going to get back to that, make no mistake."

Wolffe said, "I'm pretty sure you won't give a shit about the captures in five minutes."

He flipped a slide, showing a graphic of a system labeled Perimeter, saying, "This is a Cold War protocol in the old Soviet Union, but it's still alive today. Does anyone remember it?"

The SECDEF said, "Yeah, it was their answer to Reagan's Strategic Defense Initiative. What about it?"

Wolffe said, "That's correct. We purported to develop a 'Star Wars' structure that could knock out any missile sent by the USSR, and the Soviet Union realized that we could conduct a first strike without repercussions. They couldn't compete with SDI—regardless of the fact that it never came to fruition—but still needed something for deterrence. They came up with a procedure wholly different, called the Perimeter system—or as NATO calls it, the Dead Hand. Basically, they built an infrastructure that could launch a retaliatory strike from their missile silos in the absence of any commands from authorities. If we killed them, they'd still launch after the fact, meaning SDI didn't matter. And it still exists."

Amanda Croft said, "How does that work?"

"In a nutshell, they had a bunch of different systems meshed together inside the old USSR—still in place in the new Russia—from radars determining inbound missiles to seismic sensors registering blasts to wiretaps that were designed to determine a lack of communications between the high commands. If all those prerequisites were met— meaning the system determined that a first strike had happened, and then determined that nobody was left to command a counterstrike—it would launch, assuming that it was now in control."

President Hannister said, "I know all of this. I know about the Dead Hand. It's not that robust, and not that big a threat. There are multiple safeguards in place before that thing is initiated, not the least of which is that it requires an actual first-strike nuclear option, something we'll never do."

Wolffe said, "Yes, sir, but Putin has developed a new system, which he's calling the Dead Man's Hand—meaning his hand—and it's not tied into a system of control with multiple safeguards. Its sole criteria is if President Putin is killed. He developed the system not to deter the West, but to deter any palace coups. There have been a lot of rumblings inside Moscow, and Putin has decided the best way to protect himself is to simply let everyone know that if he goes, they will too. Basically, if he's eliminated, the Dead Man's Hand is initiated, and nuclear weapons are released. In his mind, such a system protects him from being removed."

Kerry Bostwick, the D/CIA, said, "Are you telling us he's developed a way to launch a nuclear war after he's dead? In order to prevent anyone inside his room of sycophants from trying to kill him?"

"Yes. And it's not tied into the old Perimeter system. It's something new that doesn't require any action from us. He's picked out four people—whom he calls his Four Horsemen—and told each of them that if he's killed, they are to initiate the Dead Man's Hand. All the men chosen are die-hard Putin lovers, and only one is needed to trigger. Nobody knows who the four are, but they're out in the wild right now, and if he's killed, we're going to reap the results."

CHAPTER 72

The room remained silent for a moment, taking in what Wolffe had said. Eventually, Amanda Croft said, "We've never heard about this before. Not even a whiff of intelligence on any 'Horsemen.' How do we know this is real? How do we know that the Horsemen actually exist?"

Wolffe said, "Because the man who Pike captured is one of them. Putin knew about the assassination attempt from the GRU and put him in charge of defeating it. His name is Victor Petrov, and he used to be the head of Putin's personal security. Now he's the commander of the entire Russian National Guard. He did his best to stop the Wolves' attempt and failed, and he knows what that means if they succeed. He's had a change of heart and gave it all up under interrogation, worried about his own family. He's telling us that if the Wolves accomplish their mission—if they kill Putin—we're going into a nuclear war."

The SECDEF said, "Wait, before we get all hot under the collar, you're holding a guy who failed to stop an assassination attempt against Putin. Maybe he's playing you. What threat vector is supposedly tied into this? It can't be the Perimeter system, because that's all legacy missiles, and we'd have probably found out about it. Did he say anything specific?"

"Yes, he did." Wolffe flipped a slide, showing a large intercontinental ballistic missile, the title below it reading "RS-28 SARMAT."

He said, "You recognize this, right?"

"Yeah, it's the Satan Two missile. The largest nuclear weapon on earth."

"That's correct. It holds fifteen MIRVs—Multiple Independently Targetable Reentry Vehicles—meaning each missile is literally fifteen nuclear weapons, and it's hypersonic. That's what is tied into the Dead Man's Hand. Putin controls them."

"But they're not functional. They've done some tests, but they haven't proven the system."

Wolffe put down his pointer and said, "All I know is that the man we hold—the previous head of President Putin's security detail, and the current commander of the entire Russian National Guard—has told us that Putin has five of them tied into this Dead Man's Hand, and if he's killed, they'll be launched. I find it hard to believe he'd be bluffing about that—especially since it hasn't been leaked to us for deterrence. Putin's using it to contain his own opposition, and I think it's real."

"How is it initiated?"

"Each Horseman holds a special device, but we don't yet know how it works. We have Victor's."

"You have the actual device that initiates?"

"We do, but we can't get anything out of it other than we know it works on cell, Wi-Fi, satellites, and probably other things like Bluetooth. It's robust, but we don't have the ability to exploit it in the field to determine how it's used."

President Hannister looked around the room and said, "Well, that tends to tamp down Victor just making this up. We need to get him and that device here immediately. Get it to the tech guys to learn how to defeat it."

Alexander Palmer, the national security advisor, asked, "How are the Wolves attacking Putin? Is it poison in the library or what?"

"They're using Shahed 136 drones. The same ones that Russia is flinging all over Ukraine."

President Hannister said, "How appropriate. Getting hit with Iran's gift. What's their threat envelope?"

Wolffe said, "Kerry, you want to take that?"

Kerry nodded and said, "They're basically slow-flying cruise missiles. They can't be controlled from a ground station like our Reapers or Predators. They're fire-and-forget. The good thing is they're fairly easy to shoot down—if you can find them. They fly low and slow, using an internal-combustion engine that would power a moped. The bad thing is they're extremely cheap, allowing Russia to launch about a hundred of them for the price of a single missile."

Palmer asked, "How much damage can they do?"

"Each one holds about a hundred pounds of explosives, so if it makes it to the designated target, it can do some damage. It navigates by GPS or the Russian version, GLONASS."

President Hannister asked, "How do you bring one down?"

"If you can find them, it's pretty easy. Even small arms can bring them down—and have in Ukraine. The problem is they're so small and fly so slowly it's hard to pick them up with radar. Usually, they get shot down because their sound alerts a ground station or from actual sightings of them overhead. The Ukrainians call them 'lawnmowers' because that's what they hear coming."

Amanda Croft said, "What's its range?"

"About a thousand kilometers. Remember when the Saudis' oil refineries were hit a few years ago? Those were early versions of the Shahed and they were launched from Yemen."

"So the Wolves don't need to get inside Russia to use them?"

"No, they don't. In fact, since the majority of Russia's air defenses are focused on Ukraine, if they were launched from one of the Baltic states, they'd have a good chance of slipping through."

President Hannister turned back to Wolffe. "Do we know the launch point?"

"We do not. The Russian GRU man we captured only knew the next meeting site, which is Estonia. It's a good bet they're going to launch from there, but we don't know a precise location."

"Do you think he's holding back on that?"

"No, I honestly don't. He refused to talk at first, but once Victor gave up the Dead Man's Hand, his mission focus changed. He gave us all the information he had, to include the Shahed drones and the linkup location for the final targeting information."

"So the Wolves don't know the target location either?"

"No, in fact, the GRU agent said they don't even have the instructions for assembling and launching the drones yet. They get that at the meeting as well."

Amanda Croft said, "Then why doesn't the GRU man just call his partner in Estonia and simply tell him not to show up? Wouldn't that end this whole thing? They'd have a truck with explosives, but nothing else."

"Pike's already tried that. The GRU team calls themselves the Valkyries, and since they've set this in motion, they've been attacked at every turn. Their leader was killed in that fight at the Tivoli amusement park, and since then, they've had several encounters with Victor's men. We don't know how Victor's team knew what they did, but assume it was a leak somewhere in the Valkyrie team. Because of it, they've firewalled themselves from each other. No one cell knows the entire plan, only their small part of it. Pike's man tried to get in touch with the other team, but that element has shut off their GRU cell phones for protection. He can't get through to them."

President Hannister looked around the room and said, "Okay, what are your thoughts?"

Mark Oglethorpe said, "Stop them. That's it. As much as I'd like to see Putin gone, we need to reassess because of the second-order effects."

Amanda Croft said, "I agree. Standing to the side is no longer an option. They need to be stopped."

Palmer simply nodded his head. Kerry said, "Agreed."

President Hannister said, "So, Pike gets what he wants. A mission. Prevent the Wolves from killing a direct enemy of the United States. I can't believe I just said that."

Wolffe smiled, then said, "Anyone still want to revisit the actions Pike took at the fortress?"

He saw President Hannister give him a glare and said, "Never mind."

CHAPTER 73

Wraith was awakened by a loudspeaker telling the passengers that they were approaching the dock. He rolled upright from the bench he'd been using for sleep, seeing the coastline of Tallinn, Estonia, gradually advancing. He hoped the Wolves' truck was still where he'd last mapped it.

He'd spent last night on the streets of Helsinki, going from one hotel lobby after another to stay out of the cold, using the business centers to log into his Gmail account and check on the location of his phone.

The truck had remained stationary in a parking lot called West Terminal 2. He'd googled it and found out it was another ferry terminal, different from the one where they'd originally located the Wolves on their way to the town of Porvoo. This one was for shorter-distance ferries, with most going to Tallinn, Estonia.

He'd thought about getting a ticket and just sleeping in the terminal, but he wanted to be absolutely sure where the truck was headed before committing.

Eventually, he'd found himself in the city center next to an ultramodern building, the architecture making the structure appear like a wave crashing over a beach. He was running out of hotels he could penetrate and didn't relish curling up on a park bench in the cold when he realized the building was a public library, open twenty-four hours. He went inside, looking for computers.

The interior was just as modern as the outer façade, full of glass and steel. He checked a map and saw that the lower level housed all manner of arts and crafts, from silk-screening of T-shirts to free 3-D printers, along with a bank of public computer terminals.

He'd taken an elevator down and found the bank against the far end. He'd settled in behind one and checked the location again. The vehicle was in the same place. He looked at his watch, seeing it was four in the morning. He leaned back, closing his eyes. Two hours later, he was awakened by a man saying he could use the computers, but he couldn't sleep in the library.

He'd nodded, shaking the cobwebs from his head, and pointed at the screen, apologizing. The man left, and he updated the phone location, seeing the vehicle had moved from its parking spot to sitting over the water.

They were on a ferry. But which one? He'd waited until 7 A.M., and the blip began to move out into the ocean. He'd remained, staring at the computer for the next two hours. He saw the blip approach Tallinn and realized that was the destination.

He'd pulled up the ferry schedule at Terminal West and saw the next one was leaving at 1030. He bought a ticket, retrieved it from the communal printer, then returned to the screen. He checked his watch, seeing he had about an hour before his ferry left, and decided to wait to see what the truck would do.

A little after 0930 it moved inland, then remained stuck. He hoped it was because of the line leaving the terminal and not that his phone had failed. Eventually, it began moving again, winding away from the Baltic Sea to the heart of Tallinn. It stopped at a small lot and didn't move again. Wraith zoomed in the Google Maps application and saw it was a parking area next to a hotel called Schlossle.

He went to the browser history, cleared it of everything he'd searched, then closed out the web browser itself. He'd jogged outside, flagged down a cab that took credit cards, and gave the terminal name, making it inside just as they were boarding.

This ferry wasn't nearly as fancy as the overnight one the Wolves had used from Copenhagen, but it was comfortable enough, with a few scattered coffee shops and plenty of seating. He'd found a bench, lay down, and went unconscious for the two-and-a-half-hour trip, only waking up at the announcement of their arrival. He glanced around, seeing everyone moving down to the lower level and the gangway. He followed, and soon enough was off the boat.

He went to a taxi stand, stood in line, and eventually loaded into a cab, giving the hotel he'd found. The cab had dropped him off in the front, but instead of moving inside, he'd gone to the left, tracing what he'd memorized from the Google Maps display.

He found a small lot hemmed in by buildings left and right, with only one row of parking lining both sides of the alley, making it easy to locate the truck. He withdrew his pistol, holding it low on his leg as he slowly eased down the side of the building, hoping the Wolves were sleeping inside. He found the cab empty.

He glanced around, saw no one, and thought about whether he needed the phone or whether he should leave it in place.

He decided he needed it, not the least of which was because it was most likely going to die soon anyway. He moved to the back, holstering his pistol inside his waistband, then loosened the straps on the canvas cover. He reached his hand inside, fishing left and right until it closed over his phone.

He brought it out, saw it only had about 15 percent, and went back to the road in front of the hotel, thinking about his next moves. The road was really just a cobblestone avenue barely wide enough for two vehicles to pass, built in a time when horses ruled as the method of transportation, with the ancient stone buildings sprouting right up to the edge of the lane.

He saw a coffee shop across from the hotel entrance and went inside, taking a seat, his eyes on the front of the small hotel. If it weren't for the various flags hanging over the entrance, he wouldn't have even known it was a place to stay, as it blended in seamlessly with the buildings up and down the lane. A nondescript door and a simple plaque outside were its only markers.

The Wolves were here, no doubt, but he didn't know what they had planned. Thinking about it logically, if they had their final instructions, they would have simply executed them—and they weren't doing that in Tallinn, unless Putin had a visit here he was unaware of.

It then dawned on him that the truck held the method of destruction, and he had no idea what it was. If he could disable that—whatever it ended up being—he could destroy the entire mission. It wouldn't give him the satisfaction of killing the Wolves, but it would accomplish the task.

He stood up, threw some euros on the table for his coffee, and saw the door to the hotel open, the leader of the Wolves stepping outside, followed by another one he recognized.

His lips curled into a smile. Only two left. *So we* did *kill some on that fortress island.*

He watched them walk down the street and his lust for vengeance overcame his ability to reason. The truck could wait.

CHAPTER 74

Perun exited a stairwell into the small lobby of the hotel, the roof arched with exposed bricks like he'd checked into something from a mashup of a medieval movie and a modern-day establishment. Behind him, Dishka said, "You have to admit, these Valkyrie guys don't skimp on the lodging."

Perun was pleased to hear the joke because it told him that Dishka had rebounded from the events the night before. Burying Javelin on an unnamed hill in Helsinki had been hard on both of them, but they'd managed to escape—and more importantly, the hotel reservation had worked.

They walked beneath the low-slung ceiling of the lobby, the brick archways and the subdued lighting making Perun think that a knight from the Middle Ages was going to pop out at any moment. The concierge smiled at them, and they exited out onto the cobblestone streets of Tallinn's old town.

Dishka looked at a tourist map he'd taken from the hotel and said, "According to the instructions Luka gave us, it's like a half a kilometer away, straight through the city center to a place called Freedom Square."

They started walking and reached an open area anchored by a church, seeing a crowd of people chanting and yelling at a building. Not wanting to get on any cameras involved with some labor dispute, Perun began looking for a way around them.

Dishka pulled his arm and said, "That's the Russian embassy. Those people are chanting for us."

And sure enough, it was a protest over Russia's invasion of Ukraine, right in an ancient square in Tallinn, Estonia. It gave him hope. He walked through the crowd, seeing the front of the embassy draped in Ukrainian flags and egg marks on the walls. He wanted to pat the crowd on the back, but did not, continuing onward.

They threaded through the small old town, getting lost once, but finding a narrow alley to put them on the right path, and eventually hit the ancient bastion walls that had protected the city in ancient times. They walked parallel to the wall until they finally ended up at a wide-open area, the space overshadowed by a large yellow church, with the granite courtyard interspersed with restaurants and cafés.

Dishka pointed at the map and said, "This is Freedom Square. The Carved Stone Museum is right here. We just have to find it."

Perun saw an obelisk with a cross at the top and said, "It's over there near that monument."

They moved toward it, the monument rising above them, an open area below with a concrete wall preventing them from crossing over. He saw a sign proclaiming the location of the stone museum. It was at the head of a stairwell leading down below ground level. Dishka said, "The instructions were to walk along the concrete barrier, and then jump over to a steel door."

Perun nodded, and they did just that, paralleling a modern concrete barricade, but looking over at the sunken brick wall built centuries ago. Dishka said, "There it is."

Perun leaned over and saw a steel door, covered in rust. He said, "That's it. Okay, we know the entrance."

He looked at his watch and said, "The meeting is in four hours. Let's just find a place to sit."

"For four hours? When we have a hotel room? Why?"

"I don't like the hotel. It was purchased by the Valkyries. It's a threat. If the meeting was tomorrow, I'd say yes. But it's close enough that we should stay in the crowds."

Dishka said, "Okay, if you say so. There's a courtyard café. We can go sit there for a while."

They walked that way, Perun saying, "Dishka, I know you think I'm being paranoid, but after what's happened to us on this trip, I think it's warranted."

Dishka said, "No, no, I agree."

"When we go in that door, be on the lookout. Those bastards have found us every step of the way, and I'm not sure I trust this contact."

We'd spent the night in the hangar, basically staring at each other and waiting on some response from the Oversight Council, when Blaine's cell finally went off. He answered it, waited for the encryption protocol to synch up, then said, "Sir? What's the story?"

He looked at me and nodded, saying, "Okay, sir, we'll get it done. Pike's got a plan to use Luka—the GRU guy who gave us the information—to contact the Valkyrie man meeting the Wolves."

He listened for a moment, then said, "Understood, sir. Hopefully it'll be no harm, no foul."

There was a pause again, and he looked at me, saying, "No, sir. I don't have any issues with leaving Pike alone."

I started turning in circles and he held up a hand to me, saying, "Yes, sir. I understand."

He hung up and I said, "What was that all about?"

Blaine said, "We've been given authority to prevent the Dead Man's Hand from initiating."

I waited, then said, "And?"

"And I'm taking the Rock Star bird home as soon as we get to Tallinn. You'll be on your own, which is not something the Oversight Council is happy about."

I said, "You can't take the bird. We need it."

He said, "Pike, we have a Russian national here under duress. He holds the key to a thermonuclear war. Yes, I'm taking the bird and flying home with him. You're going to do what you do to stop this."

I said, "Sir, not to go behind your back, but I'm going to call Wolffe."

He said, "Be my guest. Veep's coming as well."

I said, "What?"

"He's the guy that's worked the Dead Man's Hand device and the Taskforce eggheads want to talk to him."

I said, "This is getting ridiculous."

Blaine walked away and wound his hand in the air in a circle, telling the team we were leaving. They began scrambling, loading the bird, and the pilots began calling for a tow.

I called Wolffe, saying, "You're taking the Rock Star bird from me?"

I heard him sigh, then say, "Yes, Pike, I am. You get to Tallinn and stop this attack, but while you're doing it, the bird is flying home with Victor Petrov and his device."

I said, "Sir? I need the bird. It houses all our offensive capability, along with the ability to do electronic warfare. I can't send it home."

"Pike, that Dead Man's Hand is scaring the shit out of everyone. You have the man who knows what it is, along with his device. It needs to get here immediately."

"But what if I have to flex to a different location? What if these guys get on a bird and fly today? You're going to leave me out here in the wind. I can't stop this without assets."

"Pike, the thinking here is worst case. If you don't stop them, we want the ability to circumvent this device. You're holding it, and even you said you can't do anything with it over there. We need that back here."

"Let me put him on a commercial flight. I'll send Blaine home with him."

Even as I said it, I knew that was stupid. I'd never allow such a thing if I was in Wolffe's shoes.

Wolffe said, "Are you serious? The Rock Star bird can be back here in under fifteen hours. You put him on a commercial flight and we won't see him for a day, best case, and there's no way I'm putting a Russian national that you captured on a commercial flight. He's liable to scream kidnapping. Get to Tallinn and send him home."

I tried one more time, saying, "Sir, I'm going to need this bird. I can't leave myself without a means of follow. What if they leave Tallinn and go to some other Baltic state? Using assets from the GRU? I can't load my team up with weapons on a commercial airliner here."

Wolffe grew aggravated and said, "Then rent a damn aircraft."

I said, "Huh?"

"Get to Tallinn, send the Rock Star bird home, and rent another plane. You have carte blanche. I don't give a shit if you rent a 757. Just get that man and his device home."

Knuckles saw me turning in circles with the conversation, and he squinted his eyes. I said, "How about I rent a plane and send them home on it? Keeping the Rock Star bird? I won't get a 757, but I'll get something fast."

"Pike, I'm not flying home a captured Russian commander of their national guard in a rented plane flown by an Estonian pilot. That's not happening. The repercussions are already bad on this. Put them in the Rock Star bird and launch them back here."

I knew he was correct, but it still grated. I said, "Okay, sir. That's what we'll do, but you're really making this hard."

"Just stop the attack, Pike. That's all I want. Not an international incident."

I laughed and said, "You said it, not me. Gotta go."

I hung up and said, "Load up, we're out of here."

Knuckles said, "What was that conversation about?"

"We're sending the Rock Star bird home. We need to do an assessment of what we're going to use and get it out of the aircraft. It's only a forty-minute flight, so we don't have a lot of time. We hit the ground in Tallinn, and we lose the bird."

He nodded and said, "What about the Russians?"

"Victor and his device are going home with the bird. Blaine's going to escort him home, and Veep's been personally requested to go as well because of what he's done already with the device. I don't like that either, but it can't be helped."

"What are we doing?"

"Taking Luka to that meeting to short-circuit this whole thing, hopefully without any more bloodshed."

After thirty minutes of jockeying out of the hangar and getting in the queue for takeoff, we ended up in the air, flying to Tallinn. We rolled into the FBO and I told Knuckles to start picking out what we'd need from the aircraft, and told Jennifer to find us some rental cars. She left while the rest of the team started to help Knuckles, and Veep said, "What's the mission here? Knuckles said you had something for me?"

I said, "Yeah, I do, and you're not going to like it. The National Command Authority wants Victor and his device back home in a bad way, which means we're losing the Rock Star bird."

"What's that got to do with me?"

"Blaine's going to escort him, but you're going with them."

I saw his eyes flick to the ground, and then back to me, saying, "Why me?"

I said, "Because of your work on the device."

He said, "Send Jennifer home. She was right there with me. She can do it just as well as I can."

"Veep, don't fight me on this. It has nothing to do with your worth, and everything to do with your skill. You've spent the last ten hours trying to crack that device and got nowhere—but everything you did is something the Taskforce doesn't need to repeat. Your skill with electronic devices is why you're going home. I need you to tell them what you've done up until now and help them crack that thing."

He looked at me and said, "So it has nothing to do with what happened at the fortress?"

I said, "The fortress? What happened there?"

"I didn't call the gunfight soon enough. I saw them moving, but didn't call it until they started shooting. I thought you were pissed about that."

I honestly had no idea what he was talking about, but understood what was happening. At this level, you second-guessed every decision you made, convinced it was the wrong one.

I laughed and said, "No, it has nothing to do with the fortress. I never even thought that call was late."

He nodded, saying, "Okay. I'll take him home."

I said, "Get me the pilots."

He did, and the captain said, "Since you're ripping this plane apart, I take it we're flying home?"

I said, "Yeah, you are, but you're going to do something for me before then. I need you to rent me a plane—in Tallin."

"Rent a plane? What type?"

"I don't care, but I need something on standby when we get there. Whatever they have. Put it on the corporate card."

"You have to give me more than that. What range? When are you flying? How many passengers?"

I said, "I don't know the range, and I don't know when we're flying. The passengers will be the remaining team. Four of us, plus one including Luka, for a total of five."

He left and I went over to Luka and said, "You're sure about this meeting site?"

"Yes. It's all they know. They'll be there."

I looked at my watch and said, "We have about three hours. Have you tried his cell again?"

"Yes. It's still turned off, but he'll have to turn it on in the meeting. When he does, I'll give him a call."

"And you think that'll work?"

"They know me. They'll listen to me."

I nodded and said, "Okay, because I could just have the United States call the Estonian police and slam that place."

He slowly shook his head and said, "No, I would ask you didn't do that. It will end in bloodshed."

I grimaced and said, "I'm trusting you here."

He left and the pilot returned, saying, "We can't get a plane in Tallin. They're all already leased."

I said, "Well, shit. That stings."

He said, "They only had a helicopter, so I got that."

"Helicopter? Seriously? What kind?"

"An AgustaWestland AW109. It's like a Donald Trump helicopter from *The Apprentice*. Seats six, flies fast, and is very expensive."

I slowly nodded and said, "Okay, so it's on standby?"

"Yep. Waiting on you to board. With the cost, they'll wait twenty-four seven until you show. Or not."

CHAPTER 75

Wraith sat across the square until the sun dropped below the horizon, wrapping his coat around his body while keeping his eyes on the two remaining Wolves. He knew sooner or later they'd head back to the hotel, and if they took the path they had to get here there was one stretch of alley they'd use where he could kill them.

He knew from experience that people in foreign environments would choose the same path home that they'd used before, even if it wasn't the quickest route. Humans were creatures of habit, and he was sure that the Wolves would take that alley.

And he'd eliminate the threat to Russia because of it.

He stood up to stretch his legs and noticed that the Wolves' table was empty. In a panic, he surveyed the square under the harsh glow of the streetlights and saw them walking right at him. He pulled up the hood of his coat and wandered away, finally turning around to see what they were doing.

They slipped over the low wall he'd been sitting on, dropping to the ground in front of the old bastion next to a stairwell for the Carved Stone Museum. They disappeared from view and he was at a loss. He'd placed all of his efforts into killing them in the alley, not thinking that they had waited here for a reason.

Sooner or later, they'd have to come back out. He decided to simply sit and wait on them to return. Even if they were meeting someone, it wouldn't matter what they learned, because he'd kill them before they could use the instructions.

He wrapped his coat around himself to ward off the chill, and sat for close to twenty minutes, his eyes on the square. He was thinking about moving to a café with propane heaters when he saw three more people coming across the square, heading to the exact same spot. He recognized the first man. It was the one who'd given him his shame. The one who had made him run.

They went to the same wall and one of them dialed a cell phone, talking into it. The man hung up and nodded, and all three of them dropped over the wall. It was too much. He could no longer wait, the rage exploding from the depths of his soul.

He ran to the spot and saw an old steel door. He dropped over himself, went to the door, and listened for a moment. Hearing nothing, he opened it and saw a stairwell leading down.

Perun reached the bottom of the stairwell, seeing a dim glow from emergency lighting and a mannequin against the wall. He drew his pistol, saying, "What the hell is this?"

Dishka said, "Luka described it as the old underground tunnel that ran underneath the fortification walls, built to allow soldiers and ammunition to move securely while the city was under attack in the olden days. Apparently, this run of the tunnel is now a museum, with displays at each section describing how they were used over time."

Perun went down the tunnel holding his pistol close to his waist, his left hand out to keep from walking into a wall, saying, "This is creepy. Is this what he meant by going to exhibit nine?"

"Yeah. I guess that's a little humor. The Soviets kept their propaganda down here during USSR times, and that section explains it."

Perun said, "Great. Just perfect. How far away is that?"

Dishka stopped at a display of a man in a gas mask sitting on a bench, the image ghostly in the dim light. He leaned forward and flashed a penlight, saying, "This is fourteen, so if we're going lower, I guess five sections away."

They continued on, shuffling their feet and moving slowly, ducking their heads under the stone arches at each new section. Eventually, they reached section nine, complete with old USSR flags and posters of past Soviet premiers. They stopped, turned around in a circle, seeing only more mannequins standing like sentinels in the gloom, waiting to come alive.

And then one did, scaring the hell out of both of them.

A man separated from the wall, saying, "Perun, I assume?"

Perun caught his breath and regained his composure, saying, "What the fuck are you doing? You're lucky I didn't shoot you."

The man said, "You were given the location. I would assume you'd be professional enough not to do anything rash."

"This location is stupid. We're trapped down here. Why not meet aboveground, like normal assassins?"

The man laughed and said, "My name is Ivan, and it's for the protection of both of us. We've had some trouble on this mission, as you well know."

Perun said, "Just give me the information so I can get out of here."

Ivan said, "You know you're going to use suicide drones, correct? You've picked them up?"

Exasperated, Perun said, "Yes. What we don't know is how to launch them, where to set them up, and where they're going to hit. Basically, we know nothing."

"But you have them, correct?"

"Yes, I just said that." Perun glanced back down the tunnel and said, "You'd better start talking, or I'm leaving. This location does not give me confidence."

Ivan said, "Okay, here it is: Putin is at his estate on Lake Valdai, and he'll be there until tomorrow morning. We thought he would be there for a few more days, but he's leaving tomorrow."

Perun said, "His estate? The enormous one? Those drones don't have enough explosive power to destroy the entire estate. Is that the best you can do?"

Ivan said, "Wait, wait. Just hold your questions and let me finish. The drones are targeting a pinpoint area. One will do. We're using two as a backup, that's all."

Perun closed his mouth and Ivan continued, "As I was saying, he's going to leave that estate tomorrow morning to travel back to Moscow. He uses an armored train to go back and forth. It's a secret train station outside the village of Dolgie Borody. Before he leaves, he's going to hold a meeting with his generals about the war in Ukraine—but they aren't going to Moscow with him. The meeting is also secret, so he's going to have it on the train before it leaves the station. We don't know the exact time, but he takes a helicopter to go from the estate to the station. We have a man watching the helipad. When he takes off from the estate, we'll call you, and you launch the drones."

Dishka said, "How do you know this is accurate?"

"Trust me, it's accurate. Like I said, we thought the meeting was going to happen in two days, but it's happening tomorrow morning, before first light, so you don't have a lot of time. You need to leave here and get to Tartu."

Perun said, "Tartu? Why?"

"That's the launch point. We have the racks for the drones already in place. You just need to put them together, load them on the rack, and input the grid I'm going to give you. Then, you just wait for the phone call, and launch them. That's it."

Dishka said, "That's a lot."

Ivan ignored that, saying, "Did you bring a smartphone?"

Perun pulled out Daniel's phone and said, "Yes, I did."

Ivan withdrew his own cell and turned it on, saying, "Give me the number."

Perun did, and Ivan texted it to someone, then said, "Pull up the Bluetooth application and look for 'Valkyrie.' Attempt to connect to it."

Perun turned on Daniel's phone and did as he asked. As soon as it came up, Ivan's phone let out a ringtone. Perun thought that was supposed to happen, but Ivan's face showed confusion.

He pressed the button for an incoming call and put the phone to his ear, saying, "Ivan."

Perun saw him listen for a moment, then disconnect, saying, "There's been a change of mission. Luka is here. He's coming to talk about it."

"Luka? From Finland? That Luka? He ran and left us to die."

CHAPTER 76

Luka said, "The door is supposed to be just over that wall."

I said, "Want to try calling one more time? I'd rather he know we're coming than barge into a clandestine meeting full of men with guns."

Luka said, "I don't have my phone. You took it."

Which was true. I'd left Jennifer and Shoshana back at the general aviation terminal to continue working with Creed on the electronic devices from both Victor and Luka. He acted like he was on my side, but that didn't mean I wasn't going to exploit everything I could in case he was lying. I'd let him use the phone to try to call his partner several times already, without any luck.

I handed him my phone, watched him dial, then glanced at Knuckles. He said, "Maybe the fifth time is the charm."

I saw Luka's face light up and he nodded at me, speaking in rapid Russian on the cell. He hung up and said, "They're in the meeting right now, and my man finally answered. He's going to hold them there until we can get to them. Let's go."

He dropped over the wall and I followed, saying, "Why on earth did you guys pick an underground tunnel for a meeting?"

He opened the old iron door, shining a light on the stone steps leading down, and said, "It's the most secure spot we could find. Only one way in and one way out, and nobody else would be here at this time. It was a bona fides for the meeting. If someone showed up, it could only be the right person."

He started going down the steps and I said, "We call only one way in and out an ambush zone. We'll be trapped in here."

He didn't respond, but Knuckles did, saying, "You got that right."

We both pulled out our pistols, letting the mounted weapon lights shine the way, the tunnel looking like something out of *Close Encounters of the Third Kind* with the blades of light strobing back and forth. We moved rapidly through the darkness, passing by a mannequin in a uniform from the seventeenth century, then a guy sitting on a bunk wearing a gas mask, causing me to say, "What the hell is this all about?"

Luka turned to me and said, "It's a museum. Just keep coming. We're almost there."

And then an enormous crack split the air, the enclosed confines magnifying the noise. Luka was thrown against the bricks, his arm grabbing the mannequin with the mask and dragging it to the ground.

I whirled around and heard more gunfire, the air around my head snapping from the sound of bullets. I slammed against the wall to the left, Knuckles went right, and we both trained our weapons back the way we'd come, illuminating an apparition with a pistol.

The lights hit him in the eyes, blinding him, and Knuckles squeezed his trigger, shouting, "It's that thug motherfucker!"

I fired as well, and saw him take a hit, the strike causing him to roll backward through the last arch we'd passed. I stood up, shouting, "Moving!" and sprinted down the section of bricks. Knuckles kept up his fire, not hitting anything, but preventing the thug from firing back. I reached the arch, stopped on the near side, and said, "Go!"

Knuckles came forward while I kept my light aimed down the tunnel, not seeing my target.

He reached me on the other side of the arch, both of us protected by the bricks, and the thug came barreling through, shooting wildly down the black hole of the tunnel, not realizing we'd come forward.

I tripped his legs, throwing him face forward on the stones, and Knuckles leapt over him, putting his barrel next to the thug's head and pulling the trigger.

He looked at me and said, "How in the fuck do these guys keep finding us?"

I started to answer, then heard gunfire down the tunnel to our front.

Growing suspicious, Perun said, "What change of mission? And why is Luka bringing it?

Ivan said, "I don't know. He just said it was important and that he was coming down. It must be something radical, or he wouldn't have come here from Finland."

Perun withdrew his pistol and said, "Give me the information for the drones. Right now."

Ivan said, "Whoa, hold on, we're on the same team here."

"I'm no longer sure about that. Give it to me."

Ivan nodded his head rapidly, saying, "Okay, okay, but it might have changed. That may be why Luka's coming."

Dishka raised his own pistol and said, "Do it. Right now."

Ivan said, "Click on the Bluetooth for Valkyrie."

Perun did and Ivan started manipulating his phone. He looked up and said, "The information should be transferring. Do you see anything?"

"I've got a circle like a clock, with the hand moving down, shading the circle as it goes. Is that it?"

"Yes. It might take a minute. But we should really wait on Luka."

Perun said, "We will, but with our weapons out."

No sooner did he say that than a cacophony of gunfire erupted down the tunnel in the direction from which they'd come. Perun whipped his head toward the sound, then focused back on Ivan, snarling, "You fucking traitor."

Ivan held up his hands shouting, "No, no! That's not us!" and Perun pulled the trigger twice, hitting him in the chest.

Dishka shouted, "Let's go, let's go!"

Perun looked at his phone, saw the download was complete, and said, "We can't go back the way we came. There's no cover, and someone's shooting down there."

Dishka pointed the other way and said, "We'll find an exit on the far end."

They began shuffling as fast as they could in the gloom, eventually reaching a narrow stairwell winding upwards, the walls so close the bricks almost touched their shoulders.

They reached the top, finding a modern glass and steel door bolted into the ancient arch, an open space beyond it. Dishka tried the door and said, "It's locked."

"Break it."

Dishka rotated his pistol until he was holding the barrel and used it as a hammer on the glass next to the handle, shattering it. He reached through, fumbled for a minute, then flipped a bolt lock. He pushed the door open and they found themselves in a lobby for a museum. Perun saw light to his left and went toward it, saying over his shoulder, "I see the entrance."

He ran to a set of double doors with push bars across them. He pressed, and the door swung open, the crisp autumn wind hitting him in the face. He took one step outside, and an earsplitting alarm went off, shattering the quiet of the night.

He shouted, "Come on!" and took off running on a cobblestone street, not caring where it went as long as it was away from the alarm.

CHAPTER 77

I checked Luka while Knuckles searched the thug. He said, "Found a phone and passport, but that's it."

I said, "Luka's gone. Let's go see what the gunfire was about."

We started moving slowly down the tunnel, guns up, but weapon lights off. We'd gone an additional hundred meters when an alarm began clanging ahead of us. I said, "Whoever was there has fled. Let's go. White light."

We ran forward to the next section, the alarm sound growing, and found a body neither one of us recognized. I said, "That's not one of the Wolves. It must be the contact."

Knuckles searched him, finding a phone and a pistol, but nothing else of interest. He said, "We should go."

"Which way?"

"I say the way we came. Anybody coming here is going to be reacting to the alarm."

I nodded and we took off at a jog, passing Luka and the thug. I said, "That dumb-ass. He's running around here trying to stop the Wolves from assassinating Putin and by attacking us, he facilitated their mission."

We made it back into the square, a good five hundred meters away from the blaring of the alarm, and jogged to our rental, spending the twenty minutes back to the airport in silence.

We parked in the FBO lot and went inside the terminal, moving past the front desk to the business center in the back. We found Jennifer and Shoshana both working laptops, a stack of cell phones next to them.

Jennifer turned and said, "Where's Luka? How'd it go?"

"Not good. Luka's dead and the Wolves have their instructions. They're on the run again."

Shoshana said, "What happened?"

"The thug showed up. I have no idea how these guys are doing the tracking, but it's working."

I told them the story, then said, "Tell me you have something we can use."

Jennifer said, "Not yet. It's taking about two hours per phone, and so far all we have is past history—which we already know from experience. The phone numbers are all dead."

I handed her two more phones, saying, "One of these is thug's. The other is from the contact. Start working them. Somehow the thug knew to be here, so maybe there's a clue in his as to where the Wolves are going."

Jennifer plugged one into her computer and Shoshana took the other one. I turned to Knuckles and said, "Go to the front desk and find out the specifics on our Rock Star helicopter. If we need to leave in a hurry, I don't want to be messing around looking for a pilot."

He left the room and I began to pace, staring at my watch every five minutes. He came back and said, "Pilot's in a snooze room. Bird is gassed up and ready to go."

I nodded, and we spent the next four hours waiting on Creed to come up with something. I finally grew impatient and took the contact's phone, scrolling through the applications myself. I went to messages and saw the final text was a phone number.

One I recognized.

I didn't know why, but it looked familiar. I showed it to Knuckles and said, "Do you recognize this number?"

He looked at it, said, "Yeah. I've seen it before."

I said, "I think that's the number we tracked to Christiana originally. The one for the leader of that Russian hit team. I think I used it to locate him in the cemetery."

"Why would the GRU contact have his number?"

"I don't know, but it would explain why those guys kept showing up all over the place. The Valkyries had a traitor in their midst."

"Well, he paid for that mistake with his life."

I turned to Jennifer and said, "Pull up the old Growler logs with the numbers we tracked and run this through it. I think it's one of Victor's men."

She did, and her answer surprised me. "It's not one of Victor's men. It's not from the Christiana follow. It's Daniel's phone. The man who Shoshana met at the restaurant."

It was like an electric shock. "The one killed in Tivoli?"

"Yes."

Knuckles said, "So much for the mole in the machine."

I said, "Tell Creed to stop everything he's doing and get a geolocation to that number, right now."

She got on the chat and started typing, saying, "Why?"

"The Wolves have that phone. Remember I found it on the ferry when we were stealing a sock for the ticks, but it was dead?"

She nodded, now as excited as I was, and we waited for Creed to work his magic, leveraging NSA assets to penetrate the cell network worldwide, searching for the IMSI associated with that number. Thirty minutes later, he came back, giving us a grid, then my phone rang.

I answered, and Creed said, "That's it. That's the one. They're in Tartu, Estonia."

I turned to Jennifer, saying, "Pull up Tartu. Where is it?"

She did and said, "Second-biggest city, and very close to the Russian border. It's about two, maybe three hours away."

That's it.

I said, "Knuckles, go wake up the pilot." I turned to Jennifer and said, "Pack it up. We're leaving, right now."

CHAPTER 78

Dishka exited the main highway and entered the outskirts of Tartu, following the moving map on Daniel's phone, no longer able to drive as fast as he had before. He wound through a residential area, then entered a park, the trees rising on both sides of the road.

Perun said, "Your next left."

Dishka took it and Perun said, "We should see it soon."

They wound around a hill and he said, "There it is. Behind the tennis courts."

Dishka leaned forward and saw an ancient cathedral standing four stories tall, the front anchored by two towers on either side. He passed by it, then took another left, rolling into a gravel lot next to the ruins.

Illuminated by soft lights buried in the ground, Perun saw the center was walls only, the roof long gone. The southern end was connected to a modern structure built to look as old as the cathedral.

Perun said, "That must be the museum. It opens at eight A.M., so we need to be gone by then."

Adjacent to the southern tower was a small ticket booth and a wrought-iron grate covering an opening in the wall. Perun said, "Pull up next to that booth."

Dishka did and they exited, him saying, "Moment of truth here."

He shined a light on a combination lock holding the grate closed. Perun looked at the information on Daniel's phone, spun the numbers, then jerked. The lock sprang free.

Dishka turned the light into the building, seeing a stairwell. He said, "So far, so good."

They entered, climbing the steep steps until they reached a wooden walkway nailed to the inside wall, the cathedral space spilling out in front of it to the museum. The walkway spanned the length of the towers, with different stairways leading up to each one. Perun said, "It's supposed to be the south one," and led Dishka to that stairwell.

They climbed higher and higher, Dishka saying, "It's going to be hard carrying those crates up these narrow passageways."

Perun knew he was right, but said, "No way around it now."

They reached the top and found themselves on an open roof surrounded by four-foot brick walls with decorative wrought iron on top to prevent tourists from falling over, different plaques hung at intervals to inform the viewer what one could see in the distance. At the eastern edge of the platform were what looked like two tilted baking racks, the lower end about a foot off the ground, the higher one next to the wall about five feet in the air. They could easily have been mistaken for tools for some sort of renovation project.

Perun couldn't believe it. Everything the Valkyrie team had said had come true, making him regret killing the man in the tunnel, and wondering what the gunfight there meant.

He decided it wasn't worth the effort to decipher. Either the man watching Putin's estate called or he didn't. They needed to be ready if he did, though, and they were running out of darkness.

He said, "Come on," and they went back down to the truck. They spent the next two hours grunting up and down the stairs bringing the drone crates to the platform, the final trip carrying up the control box and a tool kit. Dishka used a small crowbar to crack open the crates while Perun opened up the detailed instructions for putting the drones together.

He saw a schematic with steps to follow like instructions for putting a bed together, complete with a list of tools. Dishka came over and looked at it and said, "Man, this isn't going to be tough at all. Put the fuselage on the rack, bolt on the wings, then the rocket, and we're done."

While the instructions were simple, it turned out the execution was hard, as the fuselage and wings weren't finely milled, causing them to expend enormous effort lining up the various holes with the bolts. Eventually, both drones were complete, sitting on their respective racks. Dishka pulled out the controller, a simple black box with a screen and numeric keypad, with a cable snaking out of one end.

He routed the cable to a connection on top of the first drone, turned on the controller, got a tone, and said, "It's ready."

Perun read him the coordinates for the attack point, and Dishka typed it into the controller. Dishka said, "Load it?"

"No, first read them back to me. I don't want any mistakes."

Dishka did, and Perun was satisfied. He said, "Load it." Dishka pushed a button and the controller beeped again. Dishka said, "It's in."

They repeated the steps with the second drone, and Dishka said, "Arm them now?"

Perun said, "Might as well."

Dishka reached underneath the fuselage and pulled out a pin with a piece of ribbon attached to it, then twisted a knob. He said, "Armed."

They took a seat next to the wall, their backs against the bricks. Perun put the phone next to his thigh and said, "Now I guess we wait."

CHAPTER 79

I had the gas pedal on the floor, trying like hell to get the tiny engine to go faster than thirty kilometers an hour, but it was having none of it. I hit a pothole and heard Knuckles shout from the bed in the rear.

I said, "I can't believe we're taking this stupid thing into battle."

We'd made it to the Tartu airport in record time, finding a single strip and one small terminal building, all of it closed. It turned out that sending the Rock Star bird home had been a good idea, as the runway wasn't long enough for it to land here.

Since it was the second-largest city in Estonia, I'd figured that the airport would be like most modern ones and operate late, with an ability to find a rental car. I was wrong. There were no commercial flights coming and going, and the terminal itself was closed, with a lone security guard sitting in a booth inside.

I'd explained my predicament and he'd told me to come back in the morning, when the terminal and FBO reopened. I'd told him I couldn't do that, then pointed to a small baggage truck with an open bed. He'd shaken his head no, and then I'd waved a wad of American hundred-dollar bills, asking to rent it for a few hours.

He'd seen the money, then said, "You'll bring it back before the terminal opens?"

"Yes, yes. I just need to meet someone in Tartu tonight. I can't wait until the morning. We'll be flying out of here before you open again."

He'd gone deeper into the terminal and come back with a set of keys, holding them back until I gave him the cash.

The small truck only had bucket seats, so Shoshana and Knuckles were forced to climb into the bed while Jennifer navigated, and I drove.

I said, "How much farther is it?"

"Looks like about two minutes, but I don't know why they're at an old cathedral. This place is really just a ruin with a museum on the end. It doesn't have anything special."

I wound past a grouping of tennis courts, the lights still burning but nobody on them, and the cathedral came into view. I saw the two intact towers and said, "That's why. They want the height to get the drones on the way."

I went past it, took the first left I could, and slowed as we approached through the trees. When I could make out the lights illuminating the walls, I cut my own headlights, driving the final hundred meters in darkness. We rolled into a gravel lot and Jennifer pointed to some type of covered booth, a vehicle parked next to it, saying, "There's the truck."

Which meant they were here. And if they'd already set up the drones, it meant the attack was tonight. I had no idea what the trigger was, but didn't want to wait around to find out.

I killed the engine, went to the bed, and said, "I think they're on one of those towers. Shoshana and Knuckles take the northern one. We'll take the southern one."

Everyone gave me a nod, and I raised my pistol, saying, "But first, we clear that truck. Jennifer and I will take the cab, you two take the bed. Nothing fancy, just get up there quickly and get a gun on it."

They nodded again, and I said, "Okay, let's go."

I raced across the open ground feeling completely exposed, hoping that if they were inside, they were sleeping and not drawing a bead as I approached.

I reached the cab with Jennifer on my left, both barrels trained on the cab. It was empty. I immediately rotated and went to the rear, finding Knuckles closing up the canvas and shaking his head.

I pointed at the open iron grate, then pointed up. He nodded, and took the lead, Shoshana behind him. I waited a minute, then followed, trying to remain quiet on the stone steps.

Jennifer and I reached a wooden walkway that had been bolted into the wall facing the ruins of the open cathedral, the starlight coming through where the roof used to be, a maintenance crane incongruously in the center of the space, apparently being used for renovations.

I saw Shoshana disappear up the stairs of the northern tower and went the other way, finding the southern tower stairwell.

Knuckles reached the top of the stairs and held up a second, listening. He heard nothing. He turned to Shoshana and motioned with his head, saying he was going to exit and for her to get ready.

She raised her weapon, keeping the barrel off Knuckles, and nodded.

He exited swiftly, working to remain silent, scanning the left side of the platform while Shoshana took the right. She saw someone stand up on the southern tower and she hissed, taking a knee behind the brick wall that surrounded the platform.

Knuckles saw him as well, but before he could get down, the man fired a pistol, then another man stood up, shooting wildly at them.

Knuckles and Shoshana returned fire, Knuckles saying on the net, "They're at the southern tower, I say again, southern tower. They're behind cover. I can't get a shot."

There was a lull in the fire, and he heard Pike shouting from the stairwell, trying to get the Wolves to surrender. Instead, one of the drones fired, the rocket assist blasting it off the cradle like giant Chinese fireworks, the drone shooting into the air with a trail of sparks behind it. The rocket assist fell off, and what sounded like a lawnmower took over the silence, the drone disappearing from view.

Knuckles said, "One drone's away. I say again, one drone's away."

Pike came back, saying, "Don't worry about the Wolves. Shoot that damn remaining drone. Make it inoperable."

Knuckles shifted his aim, starting to puncture the delta wings of the drone, hoping to stop it from being airworthy. He turned to Shoshana and said, "Hit the drone, hit the drone."

She did, peppering the fuselage. The rocket ignited and she shifted her aim, putting her sights on the nose cone and squeezing the trigger.

CHAPTER 80

Perun picked the phone up every few seconds, obsessively checking to see if it had a signal, then placing it back on the stone next to him. He checked his watch, seeing it was now five in the morning. With the coming of winter, it probably wouldn't be light enough to see until seven A.M., but he wanted to be off this tower long before then.

He said, "At six A.M., we're just going to launch these drones and hope for the best. If we haven't been called by then, the meeting is either off or the Valkyrie contact at the estate is dead."

Dishka thought about his words, then said, "We couldn't have come this far for the entire thing to fail now. We've lost too many men for that. He'll call."

Perun simply nodded, then cocked his head. He said, "Did you hear something?"

"No. What?"

"I thought I heard wood creaking."

"It's probably just the wind." He chuckled and said, "You killed the only man who knew where we were going."

Dishka leaned back into the wall and said, "Man, I wish I'd have taken a little more time to enjoy Europe before all this began. When the war's over, I'm going to go backpacking across Europe like an American college student. What about you?"

Perun didn't answer, and Dishka glanced his way, seeing him cocking his head. Dishka said, "What is it?"

Perun held up a finger, then slowly rose. Across the way, on the top of the northern tower, he saw a shape. Or thought he did. The shape disappeared. He raised his pistol, but didn't fire. Then he saw another shape, this one bigger. He fired at it, and immediately received return fire.

He slammed back down behind the wall while Dishka sprayed the northern tower, only ducking down when his fire, too, was returned.

Calm, resigned to his fate, Dishka said, "Guess I was wrong on that prediction. What do you want to do now?"

Perun aimed his pistol at the entrance to their tower, saying, "They aren't alone, I'm sure. Someone is coming up to this platform."

And then he heard a voice shouting in English, saying, "Wolves, Wolves, we don't want to harm you. Please stop shooting and let us come out and talk."

From his time at the unconventional warfare conference, he recognized the accent as American. But why? Why would the United States want to stop an attack on Putin?

The voice continued again, saying, "We are not your enemy. We're your friends. Let us come out."

He wanted to believe that. He closed his eyes, the weariness of the last week finally seeping in. He wanted to go home. To see the fields of his youth. To grow old with his wife.

And then he remembered his wife was dead. The phone at his side began to vibrate and he picked it up, hearing, "The vulture has flown. I say again, the vulture has flown."

He turned to Dishka and said, "That's it. Launch the first drone."

Dishka punched a button on the controller and the left drone sparked to life, the rocket building up energy until it launched off the cradle, rising into the sky. He heard the propeller motor kick on, and the little engine pushed it out of sight.

He heard a pinging and saw that the team on the northern tower had shifted aim, now shooting the remaining drone. He shouted, "The second one! Launch the second one!"

Dishka pressed the button, Perun saw the rocket ignite, and then his world disappeared in a blinding flash of heat and light.

CHAPTER 81

I raced up the stairs under the cover of the gunfire, hearing Knuckles give his situation report. I paused before taking the final flight of stone to the opening of the platform, knowing that was a funnel of death. There was a lull in the gunfire and I tried a different tactic—talking them off the ledge.

I shouted, "Wolves, Wolves, we don't want to harm you. Please stop shooting and let us come out and talk."

I paused, but nobody said anything back. I looked at Jennifer and she whispered, "Try again. They must be thinking about it, or they'd have screamed some obscenities at us."

I shouted, "We are not your enemy. We're your friends. Let us come out."

And waited again. Instead of a sign of surrender, I got a call from Knuckles, telling me the first drone had launched.

I came back, saying, "Don't worry about the Wolves. Shoot that damn remaining drone. Make it inoperable."

I heard a large volume of fire, then the unmistakable sound of the drone igniting, sounding like four hundred bottle rockets igniting at once. And then I was thrown against the stone walls of the stairwell by a gigantic explosion.

I picked myself off the steps, dust settling over me, then saw pieces of brick falling out of the walls. I said, "Avalanche, all elements, avalanche, get out of here."

I jerked Jennifer to her feet and pushed her down the stairs, wondering if we were going to be found tomorrow at the bottom of a pile of stone. We reached the wooden platform at the same time as Knuckles and Shoshana and I watched them race across it, the wood beams coming loose from the walls with every step.

The walkway bolts ripped out and the platform gave way. Jennifer and I fell back into the lower stairwell, watching Shoshana and Knuckles leaping forward. They slammed into the stone, their upper bodies inside the stairwell, their legs dangling into space.

We hauled them in and the falling pieces of brick began to grow like a devil's rain. We raced down the final staircase, spilling out into the courtyard. I looked up and saw the south tower viewing platform gone, a great cloud of dust above it. I had no idea if the rest of it was going to fall, but didn't want to find out like a fireman at the World Trade Center.

I ran to the cab of our truck, Jennifer sliding into the passenger seat next to me. I fired it up just as Knuckles and Shoshana spilled into the bed, and we raced out of the area, headed back to the airport.

I said, "That wasn't how I wanted this to end."

Breathing hard, Jennifer said, "I know, me neither."

She saw I was taking it hard and said, "You gave them the chance to surrender. You did what you could do."

I was kicking myself for giving the order to fire on a machine that was solely designed to explode. Those two men on the tower were doing what was right, defending their homeland. They hadn't asked for this war and had shown skill and cunning to get as far as they had. They'd defeated the Russians chasing them only to have me come in to destroy their mission. In a more just world, I would have been in Ukraine training them how to fight our common enemy. We would have been comrades in arms. Instead, after all of their sacrifices at home, after all of their patriotic dedication, I'd killed them.

I said, "I shouldn't have told them to shoot the drone. Bad call."

"If you hadn't, it would be flying to a destination just like the first one."

Which was a double kick to the gut, because it reminded me we'd failed. The drone was on the way to somewhere. I called the Taskforce, surprised to find Wolffe still in the building. I looked at my watch, did some quick math, and realized it was closing in on 11 p.m. there.

He came on the line and said, "Give me some good news."

"Unfortunately, no."

I told him what had happened, ending with, "One of those drones is on the way, and we don't know where."

Jennifer's phone went off, and she answered it, mouthing "Creed" to me. I nodded, hearing Wolffe say, "Are you sure it launched correctly? It didn't sputter for a bit and then crash?"

I said, "It might have, but if so, it didn't crash anywhere close to us. We'd have heard the explosion. Can't their air defenses pick it up?"

"They can if they know where to look, but according to Kerry, if it's flying in from an area that's not a threat vector and they aren't looking for small, low-flying, slow things, it'll get through."

"I know we don't want to do this, but don't we have some sort of hotline with Russia? Can't we call them and tell them to be on the lookout for a drone and to quit looking for inbound ICBMs or F-35s?"

"One, that drone will probably hit before we can get through all the red tape, two, we don't even know where to tell them to look, and three, they'll probably think it's a trick precisely so we can launch ICBMs or penetrate their airspace with F-35s."

I said nothing, and he continued, "I guess the best we can hope for at this stage is that it misses or crashes. They aren't the most reliable targeting systems."

I reached the airport and said, "That's not a recipe for success. I'm assuming everyone there is now puckered up for a nuclear strike?"

"Yeah, the president is ahead of the game on that. He's most definitely got *our* air defenses on high alert."

I said, "There has got to be a way to shoot that thing out of the air."

"Well, short of flying a NATO airplane into Russian airspace to knock it out, there's not a whole lot else."

"Maybe that's worth the risk on this."

"Pike, all that would do would be to focus the air defenses against that plane, causing a fight with NATO in addition to the Dead Man's Hand."

I said, "So we're just going to suck up a nuclear strike here?"

I heard resignation tinged with a little fear in his voice. He said, "I wish I could say no, but I can't. You did your best, Pike. Nobody's blaming you for this."

I said, "That's the least of my worries. Look, I've got to go. We need to get out of the blast radius here in Tartu, no pun intended."

I hung up and exited the vehicle, leaving Jennifer talking to Creed, knowing that none of that mattered now. I went back to the bed of the truck, saying, "Okay, who's the death dealer here?"

Shoshana raised her hand, looking contrite. She said, "I wanted to knock out the GPS guidance system. I guess I hit the explosives. I'm sorry. I didn't mean to kill all of them."

I shook my head, saying, "Well, you owe me one for that. But I don't fault you."

Knuckles climbed to the ground and said, "This is a little disgusting, like putting down a black bear because it killed a human. The bear is just being a bear, doing nothing inherently evil, and we take it out."

I thought about it and said, "Yeah, it does seem like that, doesn't it? Those Ukrainians were doing what they thought was right, not what they thought was evil. Doesn't make me feel any better. I just wish there was some way to cause that drone to self-destruct. I mean, we might literally be on the edge of thermonuclear war here."

Jennifer came out of the truck, saying, "Creed cracked that final contact's phone. He found the launch point location and instructions on how to build the drones."

I said, "Let me guess, it's at a place called the Tartu Cathedral?"

She said, "Yeah, it's not a whole lot of help, but it also has the attack point. We know where the drone is headed now. Some town called Dolgie Borody, near Putin's lake villa."

"Is Putin there right now?"

"No idea. That's not in the instructions."

"How long will it take that drone to get there?"

"A little over two hours."

I looked at Knuckles and said, "How long's it been in the air?"

"Maybe twenty-five or thirty minutes."

I remembered what Wolffe had said about getting the Russian air defenses to focus on a threat, and had an idea. A crazy idea.

I turned to Shoshana and said, "You remember that time a few years ago when you flew an aircraft out over the ocean with a suitcase nuke in it? And we parachuted out? That suicide mission?"

When Shoshana had conscripted for her initial Israel Defense Forces mandatory service, she'd become a helicopter pilot. It wasn't until later that the Mossad learned of her unique ability to kill up close, and I'd used that earlier skill on a mission that saved a lot of lives. Much like this one potentially could.

Warily, she said, "Yes. Why?"

CHAPTER 82

I said, "Knuckles, go get the pilot of our helicopter. Bring him over here, to the truck, out of sight of the building."

He left, and I said, "Russian air defenses won't be able to find that drone because it's flying low and slow. They have to actively be looking for a threat to see it."

"Yeah?"

"Well, that helicopter will most definitely show up, and it most definitely will be viewed as a threat."

Jennifer said, "What are you suggesting? Get the helicopter shot out of the sky? For what? I don't think the pilot's going to agree to that."

Shoshana said, "He's not talking about the pilot. He's talking about me."

I said, "Look, here's what I'm saying: That drone is flying very slowly. We can catch it in the helicopter, and when we do, we'll trigger Russian air defense systems. We get in, fly over that drone, and get out. From there, they'll be tracking it and destroy it."

Jennifer said, "Pike, that's insane. What if they shoot you down five minutes after crossing the border?"

"They won't. First, they're going to have to ascertain that we're bad. They're not going to shoot down a helicopter just because we appear. That'll take time. Second, when they do find us, they'll call and tell us to leave before shooting, which gives us more time, and third, none of that is going to matter because Shoshana here is going to do her IDF military thing and get under their radar, like she's flying the mission for bin Laden. Once we find the drone, we'll pop up, exposing ourselves, then fly straight back here."

I looked at her and said, "What do you think?"

"I'm going alone?"

"No. I'll be your navigator, just like I was in Brazil."

She said, "We don't have parachutes this time."

"We won't need them if you're flying."

Knuckles brought the pilot over and I said, "Hey, look, I'm sorry to tell you this, but we're stealing your helicopter."

He stiffened, and Knuckles put a barrel against his head. I said, "I wish I could explain, but we'll be right back. Forty minutes, an hour tops."

We jogged to the helicopter. I took a seat, put on my headset, looked at Shoshana, and said, "Let's go."

She put on her own headset, then spent a few minutes searching for something among all the switches and dials.

I said, "Can we go? We're losing time here."

"Pike, I need to find the transponder and turn it off, unless you want to squawk our position and altitude to the entire universe."

I remained quiet while she shut it down, then she began getting acquainted with the multitude of dials and readouts, putting her hand on the collective stick, moving it about, then doing the same with the joystick between her legs, her feet on the rudder pedals.

Exasperated, I said, "Seriously?"

She said, "It's been a few years since I've flown a helicopter, and I've never been in this one."

"How hard can it be? I mean, I learned how to drive in an old pickup truck. After that, I could drive a Mercedes no problem."

She cranked the engine, saying, "But you still adjusted the mirrors, played with the radio, and figured out where the gearshift was, right?"

I said, "Yeah, I guess so."

She applied power, taking us off the ground, saying, "Then shut up."

She rose above the city of Tartu and applied maximum power, the helicopter screaming to the east. I found the navigation system and began plugging in numbers, hitting "navigate" after I was done. The arrow on the screen rotated. Shoshana looked at it, and adjusted.

We left the city behind and she lowered down to treetop level, flying so low that I thought for sure our belly was going to scrape the tops. I watched the map, and, much sooner than I anticipated, saw the line between Estonia and Russia. I said, "Border. We're crossing the border."

She only nodded, applying more power until our nose was facing down, allowing me to see the trees rushing by, as if she thought that would be soothing.

She kept on her trajectory, saying, "Keep an eye out. We'll overtake that thing without even knowing it."

My ears squawked with someone speaking Russian. I looked at Shoshana and she replied in the same language. She went to internal and said, "So much for my vaunted IDF skills. They know we've crossed the border."

"What are they doing?"

"They told me to turn back, or risk getting shot down."

Great.

We continued on with me scanning the black sky looking for the MiG to come barreling in at us. I saw nothing but the edge of dawn on the horizon. It was getting light now, which only made our survival harder.

Shoshana shouted, "There! There it is. Three o'clock."

I looked that way and sure enough, there was the delta-winged Shahed drone, puttering along mindlessly.

Another Russian voice came on the net, and Shoshana again replied. This time the voice demanded something, and I saw an arc of tracers lazily coming up at us, looking like someone had released balloons from the ground. I knew that was an illusion, and that each piece of light represented at least five rounds in between.

Warning shots.

They went over the top of us, and I said, "Get near the drone and pop up, then get the hell out of here."

She did so, getting right over the little push plane. When she'd matched its speed, she jerked the stick and we violently rose in the air, the G forces pushing me into the seat. The gun, now behind us, fired again, and this time it found its mark, the bullets sounding like someone was using a ballpeen hammer on the skin of our aircraft.

I shouted, "Get out! Get out!" and she jerked the stick, sending us spiraling back to the ground, then righted the ship, rotating around back the way we'd come. We were buffeted by an explosion, the shock wave rocking the aircraft and causing Shoshana to fight for control. At first I thought we'd been hit. I looked to the rear and saw a fireball in the air.

The drone.

I said, "They got it! They got it! Get the fuck out of here."

She made a beeline for the border and our headsets came alive again with a different voice. She answered, then looked at me, saying, "That's a MiG fighter. He's coming in hot."

I said, "How far is the border?"

"Too far for a race against a MiG."

I felt the helicopter slow down and said, "What are you doing?"

"He can't match the velocity of a slow-moving aircraft. He'll fly by, and I'll speed up again."

Sure enough, the MiG came right over the top of us, flying so close

I could see the pilot. In seconds, he was lost from sight, and Shoshana slammed the throttle, racing to the border. I saw a speck in the distance and said, "He's coming back, he's coming back."

She said, "Almost there."

The speck grew larger impossibly fast, until I could once again see the pilot in the cockpit coming right at us. I flinched, and he pulled off, going straight up like a ballistic missile.

She said, "We're across."

She slowed down and I took in great gulps of air, incredibly thankful that the MiG pilot had actually followed his rules of engagement. Attacking an aircraft in a NATO member state would have been a shit storm, to say the least. If it had been me, I'd have splashed us on the Estonian side, border be damned.

We landed back at the airport with smoke coming out of the engine, the rear shredded by the antiaircraft fire. The pilot saw it and his mouth dropped open.

I said, "Sorry about that. It looks like we'll be taking a rental back to Tallinn. Is the terminal open yet?"

CHAPTER 83

Our plane landed at Dulles International Airport, and I couldn't wait to get off, my neck stiff and my legs feeling like they'd been cramped for hours. Which, of course, they had been. Knuckles was even more eager than me, since he was in the middle seat and I had snagged a window. He stood up, looked at the front of the plane, and saw Jennifer standing up and stretching in the rarefied air of business class.

He said, "Why in the fuck do we always sit in the back and she always gets a business class seat?"

I said, "She has our Grolier Recovery Services account. She racks up the points, and I'm too nice to not let her use them."

He said, "You're a better man than me."

I saw Jennifer look back and smile at me, and said, "Well, it pays off in other ways."

We'd fled Tartu as soon as we could, calling an Uber to take us into town, where we'd rented a van and driven back to Tallinn. I'd given Wolffe a debrief, and he was incredulous, although I could hear a little admiration leaking out. Right up until I'd told him about the damage to the helicopter. Thank God it had been rented by the pilot through Blaisdell Consulting and not Grolier Recovery Services, or I'd have been in deep shit. As it was, it was up to him to figure out.

We'd caught a Lufthansa flight out of Tallinn to Frankfurt, and we'd split ways with Shoshana there, which was bittersweet.

She had a flight to Tel Aviv, and we had one to the United States. I wish we'd had more time together, not the least to give her my appreciation, but her flight was leaving in twenty minutes and ours had an hour and a half.

All I'd been allowed was a brief hug. She'd kissed me on the cheek and said, "Do you believe now?"

I'd said, "Believe what?"

"You know what. The next time we meet, I don't want to hear about how I'm crazy."

I'd laughed and said, "But you *are* crazy. In a good way. Tell Aaron hello."

She smiled and said, "I will," then turned to Jennifer. She hugged her as well and whispered in her ear, causing Jennifer to laugh, then marched down the terminal hall headed to her gate, raising her hand in a wave.

We'd gone to our gate, found a bar near it, and I'd had my first beer in weeks, savoring the sweet nectar, even if it was some weird-ass European ale.

Knuckles said, "You ever think about the things we've done?"

"Of course I do. What do you mean?"

"Well, this mission was so fucked-up it's beyond belief. We're told to track a team out to assassinate Putin, and we do, but we want to help them do it."

I started to say something, and he cut me off, saying, "I'm not judging, but don't tell me you didn't want to do that. There's a punctured tire that would beg to differ."

I closed my mouth and he said, "Meanwhile, there's a bunch of Russian assassins from a national guard SOBR special operations unit that's trying to stop them. Midway through, *we're* told to stop them, and the last SOBR guy standing—that thug—ends up preventing us from doing that, almost guaranteeing Putin's death. The whole thing is just weird."

Jennifer said, "I'm surprised to hear that from you. I was thinking the exact same thing."

He clinked her glass and said, "Great minds and all that."

I said, "Don't look too deep into the abyss. It just is what it is."

Jennifer said, "You don't believe that. I saw you after the drone explosion at the cathedral."

I pursed my lips, thinking about the leader of the Wolves again, regretting his death at my hand and not wanting to talk about it. She put her hand over mine and said, "I didn't mean that in a bad way. I meant it in a good way. If you ever lose your ability for remorse, we're lost for good."

Knuckles said, "At least they figured out the Dead Man's Hand. If anything else, that was worth the mission."

Blaine and Veep had arrived home with Victor, turning him over to the Taskforce. They'd immediately set about trying to ascertain how the Dead Man's Hand device worked. In short order they'd discovered that it had a SIM card and an IMSI to transmit data over the cell network, as well as a dedicated MAC address for Wi-Fi, and the four devices that had been given out actually talked to each other, along with a mainframe computer located somewhere in Moscow.

Once they'd identified the devices, it was a simple operation to implant them with malware leveraging Victor's device, basically infecting it and having it infect the others when they came calling.

The end result was that Putin had what he thought was a failsafe to launch missiles, but in reality all of the Horsemen were now carrying dead weight. If they initiated, it would launch a Trojan horse that would destroy all four devices.

None of that was let out, of course, letting both Putin and the men he'd protected himself against by employing the system think it was still active.

I said, "I wonder what will happen to Victor."

Knuckles said, "No idea. He claimed he wanted asylum, but what he really needs is witness protection. If Putin finds out what he did, regardless of what we do for asylum, he's going to take a short walk out of a long window."

My phone flashed with an airline alert and I pulled it up, saying, "Looks like we're boarding."

Knuckles scoffed and said, "We? Or her?"

Jennifer stood up and facetiously said, "If one of you wants my seat you can have it. I'm not hogging business class."

Knuckles said, "Okay, I'll take it. I'm an employee of GRS just like you."

She said, "Should have told the desk when we checked in. You can't swap out boarding passes. After 9/11 they frown on that."

And then she sauntered away. I laughed and said, "Cattle car for us."

We'd boarded the aircraft and I'd zonked out for the entire flight, the lack of sleep from the past week seeping into my bones. I'd had weird dreams of the Wolves' leader chastising me for my decisions, so much so that by the time we'd landed, I was disoriented and sweating.

Jennifer had waited on us politely, not taking the ridiculous "mobile lounges" that Dulles uses on international flights. We caught the next one, taking us to customs and immigration, and I said, "Offer's still open if you want to come down to Charleston for a little R&R."

Knuckles smiled and said, "I might take you up on it next week, but this week, I'm just sleeping."

We exited the bus and followed the crowd down to immigration. I sighed when I saw the gigantic line to get to a passport control officer, and then was approached by a CPB agent who said, "Pike Logan?"

I said, "Yeah?"

He looked at Jennifer and Knuckles, saying, "Are they with you?"

I sighed and said, "Yes, they are."

"Come with me, please."

We followed him through the crowd to a back interrogation room, me wondering what had spiked and how I would call Wolffe to get us out of this. I needn't have worried. He opened the door, and both Blaine Alexander and George Wolffe were inside.

I said, "What the hell. You know we have a flight to Charleston in less than an hour, right?"

"Sorry, Pike. You guys need to come to the White House tomorrow for a debrief. No way around it."

I said, "You got the SITREP."

Blaine said, "That's not going to cut it. The Oversight Council wants to hear from you directly."

I said "Do we at least get a good hotel room?"

Blaine tapped on the door behind him, the one opposite we'd used to come in, and said, "Of course."

The door opened and Jennifer said, "Why do you need Knuckles and me? Seems like you've got Pike and that should be good enough."

Blaine said, "Well, it's either this, or you can finally do that night O_2 combat equipment jump from thirty K. I hear you missed that certification because of this mission."

Jennifer looked at me and said, "I think a debrief will be just fine."

ACKNOWLEDGMENTS

I always like a sense of history in my novels, because I'm sort of a closet history nerd, and when Russia invaded Ukraine (I mean overtly, with a blitzkrieg reminiscent of the Nazi invasion into France—although I'm fully aware of the "Hybrid Warfare" invasion in 2014, and give it its due), I started looking at it. Truthfully, I try to study the horizon in a novel, not a current iteration, because that's just too easy, but as I studied the war—not as a novelist, but a student of warfare—I saw something that just jumped out at me: the Perimeter Nuclear System, known in the west as the "Dead Hand." I had no idea such a thing existed even as I lived through the Cold War, and the thought that it was still in service was unnerving. I really didn't want to write a story about Ukraine because such a setting is a recipe for disaster. The problem with writing about current events is that they are *current*. One wrong move in the real world, and my novel could end up irrelevant. But that system was just too juicy to ignore. And so, I set out to alter it, deciding that Putin would leverage a different system to protect himself. This was obviously way before Wagner decided to launch a coup—but man, when that happened I literally thought to myself, *I hope Putin hasn't done what I've created in my novel.*

I'd told my publisher what I intended to write about, providing three caveats of risk: 1. The Ukraine war could be over by the time the novel came to publication, either through Ukrainian or Russian victory. I didn't think that was much of a risk, but it was there. 2. Sweden would probably get into NATO before my manuscript was published. I knew the intricacies of Turkey vis-à-vis Sweden and NATO, but didn't believe they were insurmountable, and the odds were that Turkey would acquiesce to Sweden's bid. I figured that wasn't a big deal, as I was going to set the novel on a specific date—before such an action occurred, and it wasn't a major part of the novel. Number 3, however, was significant. If Putin fell out of power through ill health, voluntary resignation, or other nefarious means, the book was dead in the water. On this count, I didn't think it would happen. Putin is a survivor and an expert player in the world of lethal politics, so I reassured my publisher that this was a small risk.

Then Wagner launched a coup, and the entire premise of my novel was coming to fruition in real time. Talk about mixed emotions. On the one hand, I thought it was just rewards for the invasion of Ukraine. On the other, it was disastrous for the manuscript, as I was just about to type, "The End."

Such are the vagaries of trying to predict the future when writing about events occurring in real time.

One element that worked out: while I needed a Russian agency as the antagonist, I'd resolved early on not to use Wagner. I'd already explored that organization years ago—before they became a household name—in both *Daughter of War* and *Hunter Killer*, so I didn't want to use them again. Then they made worldwide news going *against* Putin. That choice worked out well, as I dodged a bullet with the whole Wagner meltdown that occurred.

I always like to get my boots on the ground for actual research—but there was no way I was going to traipse around Russia or dodge bullets in Ukraine for this one. So I decided to go a little north, to the Scandinavian region. As usual, there were a plethora of discoveries and locations I wanted to cram into the novel from the research, but it just didn't work out. For instance, there's a church inside an actual cave in Finland that was perfect, and there are more than a few bars in Gamla Stan that I wanted to include. Maybe at a later date. Copenhagen's Christiana peace and love commune was perfect for the book, but definitely took Elaine out of her comfort zone.

I'm indebted to our tour guide of Sweden's runestones for showing me just how much I didn't really care. I'm like Pike on that one, but the "tribal council" area worked out for a scene, because it was right next to a large lake. I'm still convinced the entire area is a Swedish version of a boy scout camp that was created in the 1980s.

As for the fortress outside the Helsinki harbor, this once again proves my point about getting on the ground. We walked around that area for two hours in a light rain—just like Perun and Pike—and I was getting nothing but atmospherics and hypothermia. And then the tour guide pointed at a map and said, "This is where the secret tunnel comes in."

I immediately thought, *Oh, yeah, that's making the book . . .*

The tunnels surrounding Tallinn, Estonia, were the same way, and the tour guide there probably thought I wanted to smuggle in drugs because of the nature of my questions.

The fate of the good ship *Vasa* made me smile, but the museum itself was a rat-maze of killing areas that played perfectly in the book—to include the old cemetery just outside the grounds.

There is always a point during book research trips, when traveling to country after country, that things go wrong, and getting to Stockholm from Copenhagen was the first of those. Have you ever sat in a train station and waited for your train location to be flipped on a board, but it never does? Then you get more and more worried? Yeah, that happened. We found out the train from Stockholm wasn't going to travel all the way to Copenhagen, but if we took ANOTHER train to a small town in Sweden, we could transfer to the original train. I said, "What the hell? How many people have tickets on that train and have no idea it's not arriving? How does that happen? Who's running this goat show?"

We ran to the new train, made it to the town, found our original train while losing our original seats in the process, and then continued on. That wasn't the only time something unexpected happened. The DCOE says we should do the Amazing Race with our experiences, but I'll tell you, we'd end up killing each other—as we almost did on the morning we were trying to get on a train from Tallinn to Tartu, Estonia. It was morning, about six A.M., raining in forty-degree weather, and we were trying to find the train, but the track listed was not the one to Tartu. In a panic, we went to the nearest coffee shop only to find nobody spoke English, and then began to frantically search the tracks, the DCOE sure we'd gone to the wrong train station. But there was only ONE train station in Tallinn, so I knew I was right. From there, it was a comedy of errors, but we eventually made it.

I really wanted to use that experience in the manuscript, but it was just easier to fly the Taskforce to Tartu, given the time constraints of the threat I'd created. In Tartu, once again, getting on the ground proved the correct choice. There's a KGB museum near the old town I wanted to see, the entire place chilling. The building houses the original cells where they tortured dissidents during the Soviet days, and I wanted to include it in the manuscript, but in this case, I found something better. While walking around with a map and phone trying to locate the museum, the DCOE telling me we were going the wrong way, we found the Tartu cathedral—and that's what ended up in the book.

I try to stay on top of the relentless march of technology—which is a hell of a lot harder than staying abreast of current events—and I'm often asked if the devices I use in my books are real. Ninety-nine percent of the time, they are, but sometimes I push things a little bit. No, the Tick nano-drone isn't real—yet. I'd read about ongoing research trying to duplicate a dog's sense of smell for search and rescue purposes and saw a demonstration for a nano-drone swarm that fed off each individual device for geolocation and decided to fuse that technology together. The LANIUS attack drone, however, is very much real. Based on racing drones and designed to work in teams, with or without a man in the middle, it's a loitering munition that can zip around buildings or tunnels up to 45 miles an hour, then detonate multiple different ways, from command detonation, to an "ambush mode," to turning into a land mine, all powered by its own AI engine. Scary stuff indeed.

Even with all my research, I'm usually helped out by my daughters at least once a manuscript. I needed a way for Wraith to track the truck to Estonia but knew he wouldn't have any high-speed devices on hand, and I was racking my brain. My daughter was returning from college at the same time. I texted, "Where are you?" and she sent me a link from her phone. I opened it on my computer, and it turned into a moving map that tracked her progress all the way home. I said, "Show me how you did that...," and came up with the means Wraith would use.

As I said in the previous novel, my editor, David Highfill, decided to retire from publishing, and I was given a new editor, who also ended up leaving before this manuscript was done. In truth, she'd been offered a job opportunity in the publishing world that nobody would turn down, and I didn't blame her, but it left me with nobody to shepherd the book. David agreed to come out of retirement to edit this manuscript, and for that, I'm eternally grateful. His rules were, "Just the edits. Not all the other stuff."

The "Other Stuff" in this case is literally what an editor does—jacket copy, cover design, sales approaches, marketing focus, and everything else that goes into ensuring a book's success. To that end, I met Danielle Dieterich, and she has been laser focused on everything this manuscript requires. Thank you both!

As usual, I'm also indebted to my publicist, Danielle Bartlett, who tries to kill me with interviews, podcasts, and other publicity; to Tavia Kowalchuck, marketing guru extraordinaire, who also punishes me with social media posts, video requests, and anything else she can think of; and, of course, John Talbot, my agent, who has been with me from the start and continues to work on my behalf in the ever-changing world of publishing.

The final acknowledgment is to my wife, Elaine—otherwise known as the DCOE, which stands for Deputy Commander of Everything. She plans the research trips, is the first reader on my manuscripts, and conspires with both Danielle and Tavia to make my life a living hell, but in the end, if it weren't for her, none of this would be possible.